THE QUALITY
OF MERCY

———◆———

Siphiwe Gloria Ndlovu

AUTHOR OF
THE THEORY OF FLIGHT (2021)
THE HISTORY OF MAN (2022)

CATALYST PRESS
ANTHONY, TEXAS

For further information, write Catalyst Press at
info@catalystpress.org

In North America, this book is distributed by
Consortium Book Sales & Distribution, a division of Ingram.
Phone: 612/746-2600
cbsdinfo@ingramcontent.com
www.cbsd.com

Originally published by Penguin Books,
an imprint of Penguin Random House South Africa,
in South Africa in 2022.

FIRST EDITION
10 9 8 7 6 5 4 3 2 1

Library of Congress Control Number: 2023932124

Cover design by Karen Vermeulen, Cape Town, South Africa

In loving memory of my grandparents,
Sibabi Charles Ndlovu and
Kearabiloe Mokoena Ndlovu.
Thank you both for the love given
and the promises kept.

———◆———

Advance Praise for
QUALITY OF MERCY

———————•———————

"A wondrous performance – Ndlovu has succeeded yet again in telling a vast array of stories with intricate elegance... [and] proves that we do not yet know how the liberation struggle ends."
—TSITSI JAJI,
    Associate Professor of English and
    African Studies, Duke University

"In a crowded field of superb reads, *The Quality of Mercy* by Siphiwe Gloria Ndlovu is our Book of the Year. It's the final novel in her award-winning *City of Kings* trilogy, weaving together elements of social comedy and cozy crime while examining the history of a country transitioning from a colonial to a postcolonial state."
—*DAILY MAVERICK* (South Africa)

"Ndlovu's most recent novel, perhaps her best yet, reveals the history of a country transitioning from colonialism to independence. With compassion and an unflinching eye to important detail, Ndlovu explores the rough side of life in the *City of Kings*. This epic crime novel also builds up a quirky cast of Dickensian characters at every turn. [...] [P]erhaps the most monumental trilogy to come out of Southern Africa. Only time will tell. What is clear now is that Ndlovu's professorial knowledge is evident in her masterly storytelling. *The Quality of Mercy* is indeed a novel about mercy and forgiveness. It is also about kinship and unbroken bonds, and how love can be a balm to human

trauma. It is a story that deserves to endure into posterity."
— *AFROCRITIK*,
"Top 25 African Novels of 2022"

"Through characters whose stories are complex, layered, connected, and twisted by the aftermath of war, this timely book illuminates the possibility of light shining in humanity, despite systematic and pervasive inhumanity. In this, Ndlovu offers readers a walk with the spirit, prayers, grace and power that people of African descent have historically walked with…the audacity to dream, to make way, to Love anyway."
— SHARON BRIDGFORTH,
2022 Windham-Campbell Prize Winner in Drama

"In its epic and yet intimate portrait of Zimbabwe's colonial past, *The Quality of Mercy* finds tenderness where few writers dare to look. Ndlovu meets the gaze of white supremacy's henchmen full on, while embracing the complex pleasures of peering beyond social shorthand. Her loving account of Bulawayo and its surrounds across the twentieth century does something rare and breathtakingly hard: it enchants even as it unveils."
— JEANNE-MARIE JACKSON,
Associate Professor of English Literature
at Johns Hopkins University, author of
*The African Novel of Ideas: Philosophy and
Individualism in the Age of Global Writing*

"With the launch of the third in [her] trilogy, author Siphiwe Gloria Ndlovu has firmly established herself as a writer not to be ignored. […] She will sweep you off your feet all over again."
— DIANE DE BEER,
arts critic

"Siphiwe Gloria Ndlovu's trilogy of novels reimagine the history of a country much like modern Zimbabwe. Through her multiracial cast of characters (with weighty inheritances) and their

fantastical comings and goings, she realizes unpromised futures. *The Quality of Mercy*, set on the eve of that unnamed country's independence, and organized around a murder mystery, continues that quest."
—SEAN JACOBS,
faculty at The New School and
Founder-Editor of *Africa Is a Country*

"Read *The Quality of Mercy* [and] savor the extraordinary literary gifts of Ndlovu, her matchless cool and humor as she channels Zora Neale Hurston; revel in her dizzying, insistent eloquence as she lays bare the bloodcurdling crimes... Come face to face with the suffering and bravery of the displaced rural folk... Learn the meaning of survival, of the various types of love and the mercy which is their yield."
—BARBARA MASEKELA,
poet and former Ambassador to France,
UNESCO, and the United States

"The dazzling, heartbreaking, humane and heroic finale to a trilogy of extraordinary literary fiction."
—HELEN MOFFETT,
author of *Charlotte*

"Her most remarkable [novel] yet. Clever, compassionate and minutely detailed..."
—*BUSINESS DAY* (South Africa),
"Best Novels of 2022"

"[W]ritten in glorious prose and with a witty and ironic style [...] a powerful novel by a writer of considerable talent."
—*SUNDAY TIMES LIVE* (South Africa)

"*The City of Kings* trilogy is a deep ocean with many tides that carry you away. Ndlovu manages to hold a host of complex characters and painful histories with compassion, insight and tenderness.

Her writing is never strained, even when telling of devastating horror and pain that cuts to the quick. [...] This trilogy is beyond words in its scope and depth. It is essential reading for anyone who wants to better understand history, humanity, redemption, or be swept away by magical and utterly compelling storytelling."

    —BRIDGET PITT,
        author of *Eye Brother Horn*

THE QUALITY OF MERCY

Siphiwe Gloria Ndlovu

PROLOGUE

———◆———

Based on a story my grandmother told me.

Spokes M. Moloi, recently returned from the war, stood at the corner of Lobengula Street and Selborne Avenue and waited on a promise. In 1941, the British had pledged that if he went to fight against the Germans, they would give him many acres of farming land that he could call his own. What man did not want a piece of viable land that belonged to him? And so Spokes had eagerly signed the papers they put in front of him, immediately joined the ranks of the newly formed African Rifles, and gladly collected the issued uniform— feeling, all the while, certain that this was a step in the right direction for him.

Even when they refused to give him—a soldier in the African Rifles—a rifle, Spokes chose to overlook the irony of the situation and chose, instead, to believe that he was walking toward something truly glorious. So strong was his belief in this glorious something that when they made his unit carry things here and there and everywhere, Spokes steadfastly refused to call himself a porter. He had joined the war a soldier, and as he carried weapons, ammunition, sundry supplies and wares in all kinds of weather and across desert and tundra, he saw this as his necessary contribution to the war effort.

When others of his ilk began to criticize the British for what they perceived to be unfair and unequal treatment, Spokes valiantly refused to be drawn into their malaise. His only complaint, and it was a small one, was that the greens and slouch hats that constituted their uniform did not seem to have taken into consideration all the various climates through which they would have to travel.

As he walked alongside men whose boots had been filled with sand or caked in mud or frozen hard by snow, men bent double by the things they carried, men who wished they had been assigned to Burma where the real fighting—with rifles—was, or to Durban, where they could at least escort Italian prisoners of war, Spokes knew he had to tread lightly. This was because he was the only man in the entire history of his country, perhaps in the entire history of the world, whose grandfather and father had both been hanged by the neck until they were dead. This rather weighty inheritance not only made him a rare and unique man; it also made him realize that he needed to cultivate a tenable relationship with the British.

By joining the war, Spokes felt certain that the promised land would make him something that his grandfather and his father had never had the chance to become: a man with a future. So, as men around him were struck by bullets against which they could not adequately defend themselves, or were blown apart by landmines that they had previously carried on their backs, this is what Spokes held on to: a future.

Spokes, and others who had survived the war, had returned home in 1946, to much fanfare and a victory parade as their regimental song, "Sweet Banana," blasted from the army band on the stand, and confetti and ticker tape filled the air. There were many sensations to feel—pride was one of them. There were many things to believe—that they were heroes was one of them. There were many things to hope for—equality was one of them. A year after the parade, Spokes found himself standing in the long-anticipated future, waiting.

It was while he was waiting in that future that he saw something that he never thought he would see on Lobengula Street: a book. Not a scrolled-up newspaper placed in the pit of an arm, not a neatly folded pamphlet placed in a pocket, but a book—leather-bound and surprisingly new—held in a pair of brown hands with long, tapered fingers and delicate wrists. Books belonged in libraries where one could only touch them once one had donned a pair of white gloves, so what was this particular book doing in such beautiful brown hands, and on Lobengula Street of all places?

Spokes moved closer to the book and its owner until he could easily make out its title: *Pride and Prejudice*. Once he read the title, he became fully aware of his surroundings, and was shocked to find himself sitting in a bus. Somehow, as he followed those beautiful brown hands carrying the leather-bound book, he had managed to board a bus, pay the conductor and choose a seat, without his being aware of doing any of these things. The reason he could see the book's title so clearly was because he was now sitting adjacent to the beautiful brown hands.

The bus pulled out of the terminus rank, and, for the first time in his life, Spokes had no idea where he was headed. He should have been terrified, but, upon deeper contemplation, he found that he did not mind not knowing, because this seemed to him to be a beginning.

He hazarded a quick glance at the owner of the beautiful brown hands. She was so much loveliness that he quickly had to look away... until he felt bold enough to look again. In order not to be too overwhelmed by her comeliness, he could only look at her in parts. The neat overlap of her ankles as she sat with her silk-stockinged legs slightly stretched out in front of her. The gentle arch of her calves. The softness of the soft places, which he made sure not to look at for a moment longer than was necessary. The long, regal neck, like a column at a temple he had seen. The face—the pretty, pretty face—slightly upturned as though always waiting for a kiss. She smiled at a passage she was reading, and a dimple appeared. It was the appearance of that dimple that allowed Spokes to discover what he was about—that he meant to make this woman, who was loveliness itself, his wife.

He should never have acknowledged this to himself because all of a sudden, uncertainty plagued him. Where was he going? What would he do once he got there? The sun was making its way toward setting; where would he spend the night? He would have to put himself in a precarious situation and rely on the kindness of strangers—and strangers were not always kind. He became hopeful that she was heading to a mission station. He could pretend (not lie, mind you, he did not like to lie) that he had traveled all this way because he had heard that there was a post recently made available for a teacher. An English teacher. And then what? He looked at the beautiful brown hands holding the leather-bound book and knew that there was no easy way out.

By the time she alighted at her bus stop, there were a few stars in a sky that was languidly giving itself over to darkness. Spokes followed her off the bus, as did other passengers. Once outside in alien land, Spokes was evidently the only foreigner, as most passengers had people waiting ready to greet them and receive whatever luggage or parcels they had brought with them. Those who were not performing this particular act were congregated around the caravan of a travelling salesman, who kept taunting them about closing down for the night. His customers seemed to enjoy this, and taunted him back about how difficult it was for them to remove money from their pockets at this time of day. There was much merriment as they tried to hold off the night a little longer.

Upon seeing *her*, the travelling salesman left his caravan

and rushed to help her with her trunk. This was something that Spokes would have thought to do had he not been overawed by the newness of it all.

There were more stars in the twilight sky when Spokes eventually and hesitantly made his way to the salesman's caravan. The passengers who had been met by people had cleared away and left him standing there, a spectator of things he could not be part of.

Spokes found it rather surprising that no one had come to collect *her* as yet. Who would leave something so very precious unattended for so long? As if to answer his question, he heard her say to the salesman, "He always does this. Always keeps me waiting." To which the salesman replied, "He is a very important man; he keeps everyone waiting."

A very important man… Spokes understood then that he had no chance at whatever he was trying to have a chance at.

"May I help you?" the salesman asked, and all attention—even hers—turned to Spokes.

What had he planned to say when asked why he had journeyed so far? Spokes struggled to remember as he removed his fedora from his head. "A school," was all he could think to say at first before hastily adding, "I hear there is a mission school in these parts. I am looking for a job as a teacher." He could feel all eyes—even hers—looking him over, assessing his clothing and appearance, judging and determining whether or not he was teacher material. He dared not look at any of them—especially her—for fear that they were finding him wanting in some way. Where was the perfect exchange that he had imagined?

"I'm afraid you've been somewhat misinformed, but only slightly," the salesman said. "The nearest school is just over five miles away. Nearest bus station is Krum's Place. Spelled K-R-U-M, but not pronounced as crumb. It is pronounced as

K-R-O-O-M. You got off two stops too soon."

"When does the next bus come this way?" Spokes asked, crushing his hat in his hands, feeling the desperation that comes with futility.

"Very bus you alighted from. Early tomorrow morning. Heading back to the City of Kings," the salesman said.

Spokes's plight must have been palpable because most of the remaining customers, not wanting to be co-opted into his predicament, noted the lateness of the evening and made their various ways home.

"I travel to Krum's Place first thing in the morning," the salesman said. "If you are here bright and early, I could take you."

"That would be very kind of you, sir," Spokes said. He would have to go to Krum's Place and continue his job-seeking charade before returning to the corner of Lobengula Street and Selborne Avenue and waiting on a promise. Serve him right for not thinking things through.

"It is indeed a kindness on my part," the salesman said. "But not an altogether fortunate one. I cannot put you up for the night. Only room for one in my caravan."

Before Spokes had a chance to process any of this, she spoke directly to him for the first time, and it was like music.

"I suppose we could put you up for the night," she volunteered.

There were words he should say at a moment like this, words said by many before him, words that he himself had said innumerable times, words that would not come to him now. The words that came to him rather readily were these: "It is a truth universally acknowledged that a single man in possession of a good fortune must be in want of a wife."

Now, of all things, why would he go and say *that*?

She looked at him blankly as though she had not recently

read those very words herself. Spokes was desperately trying to formulate a single sentence in which he both explained that he had seen her reading the book and that it was his intention to be an English teacher when the salesman seemingly saved him by saying, "What an interesting thing to say in place of a simple thank you." There was obvious mirth in his voice as he continued: "So are you a man in possession of a good fortune?"

"No, no... not at all," Spokes stuttered honestly. Things were going splendidly indeed.

"And yet you are in want of a wife?" the salesman said, not allowing Spokes to suffer his mortification in peace.

"No... " Spokes began to say, but then realized that he would be lying outright. He made the mistake of looking at her. Was he imagining it, or was that a dimple in her cheek? The hurricane lamp provided poor light, but he was almost certain he could see a dimple. She was laughing at him and his blundering ways, and why wouldn't she?

Luckily for him, luckily for all of them, for God only knew what fresh calamity would befall them if he was allowed to open his mouth again, she pointed into the distance and said, "Finally!"

Spokes turned around to see two lights suspended in darkness, travelling toward them. It was only after they got closer that he heard the hooves of horses. So "He" was not only a very important man, "He" was a very important man who owned a carriage, like a European man.

The carriage came to a stop in a cloud of dust that in time settled to reveal "He"—a man with snow-white hair and the wisest eyes that Spokes had ever seen. The man seemed much younger than his white hair denoted.

"Loveness!" the man shouted as he alighted from the carriage.

Loveness—what a fitting name for such a lovely woman. What other name could she have possibly been given?

"You should have named me Dojiwe," Loveness said. "You certainly treat me like something you picked up along the way."

Father and daughter, Spokes happily deduced, feeling an undue hope.

"Sobantu seems to have been friendly with Mthembu's wife," the man with the wise eyes said as he and the salesman loaded her trunk into the carriage.

"Again," the lovely Loveness said.

"Again," the man with the wise eyes said. "And as you know, those cases tend to be rather lengthy affairs." He helped his daughter into the carriage.

Spokes and his dilemma seemed to have been forgotten as the man with the wise eyes offered the salesman a more comfortable place for the night, which the salesman graciously declined.

"This man came with me on the bus from the City of Kings," the lovely Loveness said, showing Spokes that he was anything but forgotten. "He was supposed to get off at Krum's Place, but got off here instead."

The man with the wise eyes looked at Spokes for the first time. It was rather evident from the arched eyebrow that slowly rose on the man's face that he did not believe the story about Krum's Place.

"I have offered to take him first thing in the morning," the salesman said. "But I've also explained that I cannot put him up for the night."

"I have told him that he can come with us," the lovely Loveness said.

"You have, have you?" the man with the wise eyes said.

"I have," she said, a definite note of finality in her voice.

THE QUALITY OF MERCY

"Splendid," said the salesman. "In that case, I will pick him up on my way to Krum's Place."

The man with wise eyes walked toward Spokes and offered him his hand, "I'm Msimanga. The village headman. But, as you can see, I am not the one with the power here."

"I am Spokes Moloi," he said, shaking Msimanga's hand. Spokes could not very well tell a man who was a chief that he was a man who was simply waiting on a promise, and so he said, "I recently returned from the war."

"Fighting for the British?" Msimanga said. "My father fought *against* the British."

"As did my grandfather," Spokes said.

"Then we have that in common, which means you are no longer a stranger, and are therefore more than welcome in my homestead. Acquaintances have begun on much less, I'm sure."

Without much warning, Spokes found himself sitting across from the lovely Loveness in the plush and swish surroundings of the carriage. For a long time, it seemed that their entire trip would be made in silence, but not even this could dampen Spokes's very high spirits. He was getting comfortable in the silence when she unexpectedly said, as the carriage came to a stop, "However little known the feelings or views of such a man may be on his first entering a neighborhood, this truth is so well fixed in the minds of the surrounding families that he is considered as the rightful property of some one or other of their daughters."

Spokes felt such a sheer, unadulterated happiness that he did not know whether to laugh or cry.

The sky was filled with so many stars it shone when Spokes and the lovely Loveness alighted at Msimanga's homestead. There was an entire group of people all waiting to receive her and welcome her back home. Their enthusiasm was tempered only by their open curiosity to know who the stranger unexpectedly thrust upon them was.

"This young fellow followed our Loveness here all the way from the City of Kings," Msimanga said. Spokes thought he was joking and expected the people gathered around him to laugh, but they did not; instead, they all slowly arched one eyebrow—a family trait.

"At least they are now coming from closer to home," a woman said matter-of-factly as she helped another woman to lift the trunk from the carriage.

"Remember the young man who followed her all the way from Pietermaritzburg?" another woman said.

"That one was studying to become a lawyer. An African lawyer. Imagine that? What does this one intend to be?" another woman said, looking Spokes up and down as she stood with her arms akimbo.

"What do you know of studying?" challenged a male voice from somewhere at the back. "You've never set foot inside a school."

"Is it any secret that I don't have an education? It is because you are too content to do and say the obvious thing that your wife has once again become friendly with Sobantu," the woman with arms akimbo challenged back.

There were some scattered chuckles at this exchange even as a few voices told the woman she did not have to make things so personal.

"Remember the man who followed our Loveness all the way from Johannesburg?" another voice said, hastily changing the subject.

"A poor mineworker, unfortunately."

"Much better than the one who followed her from Mafeking—a simple porter at the railway station, carrying things here and there and everywhere for the Europeans."

"I rather liked that one. He looked good in that uniform. Tall. The kind of tall that gives you confidence. This one is tall, too."

"Who cares for tall? Who cares for uniforms?" the woman who was standing arms akimbo asked. "Our Loveness is educated. She deserves only the best of men."

Spokes was confused. Were they having fun at his expense?

Msimanga looked at him and smiled. "You are not the first chap to come here wanting to marry our Loveness," he explained. "But you very well may be the last."

Spokes was even more confounded.

"Most of the time I am the one who has to invite the poor fellow—regardless of how flimsy his reason for finding himself amongst us is—to the homestead, but today our Loveness did that all on her own. So I would say that you, Spokes Moloi, stand a better chance than your predecessors."

What was this? What exactly had he got himself into?

"Now, although I am the headman in these parts, I am not very particular about the man that my daughter marries. I know that a young man—even one who has fought for the British in a war that was none of his business—can always build himself up. More importantly, I know that my daughter can choose wisely for herself, and if she chooses you, then so be it."

Spokes did not know what to feel. All he knew was that when something seemed too good to be true... it usually was.

"I will tell you a story," Msimanga continued. "After the story, I will ask you one question. Just one question. Then, I will let you sleep. First thing in the morning, I will ask you to answer the question, and if you answer it correctly, you can marry my daughter. It is that simple."

There it was. The catch.

"If you answer the question incorrectly, Raftopoulos, the

Greek travelling salesman, will be here to fetch you first thing in the morning to take you to Krum's Place, and we will ask you never to come back here under any pretext or pretense. Now, while all those who have come before you have failed, you should not take that to mean you will fail too—even if you did fight for the British in a war that was none of your business," Msimanga concluded.

After a hearty repast, everyone in the homestead, both young and old, gathered around the fire to listen to Msimanga's story, even though it was obvious that they had heard it many times before.

The story went as follows. At around the time that the British were building the nearby dam, which was some twenty-odd years earlier, since it was also the time that Mazibuko, Msimanga's wife, was expecting the child that would be Loveness, Msimanga's best friend, Zwakele Mkhize, went to a beer drink one night and was never seen again—alive or dead. The best trackers were employed to look for him, and none of them found a trace that led to anything substantial. Expert help was needed and Msimanga himself sought the services of the best San tracker, but not even he could find any trace of Zwakele Mkhize.

To give context to the story, it had to be known that the Mkhize lineage had been given the chieftaincy by King Mzilikazi himself, but that because of Zwakele's father's enthusiastic prohibition of all things British in his village, the British were now looking to change the lineage from the Mkhizes to the Msimangas. It was true that Msimanga's father had participated in the uprising against the British, but he had been charged with insurrection and had spent five years in prison, which had not only changed him, but converted him to Christianity and all things British. He had even gone so far as to have all his children, boys and girls, educated at the mission school that had been built near Krum's Place.

The British liked how very… amenable Msimanga's father had become, and when Chief Mkhize died, they took steps to change the lineage of the chieftaincy. Msimanga's father, although not altogether averse to the proposal, felt himself too old a man to start learning how to rule a people, and put forward his son's name in his stead. The British quickly corrected him, reminding him that it was the king in England who ruled the people, and that the headman's function was merely to guide his people toward being better subjects of the king. Having said that, the British did not mind having Msimanga's son as headman as long as he proved himself to be very like his father.

The British were pleased, the villagers less so. Their own king had, after consulting the ancestors, created the chieftaincy and chosen its lineage; as such, it was a sacred thing not meant for mere man to rend asunder. As much as they liked the Msimangas, the villagers wanted the Mkhizes to continue as headmen, and they made this very clear to the British.

This was exactly the kind of dogmatic traditional thinking that the British were trying to eradicate. They decided that instead of trying to reason with the villagers through verbal persuasion, which would probably prove pointless, they would build a dam instead—using labor from the village, of course—and show the villagers what the British could do for them.

Now, one would have thought that all this would have created a rift between the young Msimanga and Zwakele Mkhize, but their friendship—which had begun as most boys' friendships did, when they were herdboys together—had proved to be made of sterner stuff. The young Msimanga made it very clear that it was not his intention to be headman, and the villagers appreciated his not wanting to change the status quo. But then Zwakele Mkhize had disappeared, and the villagers had had no choice but to allow the British (whose hand the villagers suspected in the disappearance) to have their way and instate the young Msimanga as headman.

Since the British did not seem eager to have the British South Africa Police (BSAP) investigate the case, Msimanga had done so instead, continuing to do everything in his power to find out what had happened to his best friend.

Here Msimanga's story ended, and it was time for the one question to be asked: "What happened to Zwakele Mkhize?"

They all left iguma and retired for the night. Spokes was given his own indlu to sleep in, but even though he was lying on a well-made icansi and covered by a very warm ingubo, he had no other choice but to have a sleepless night as he tried to decipher the mystery. He had little hope that he could arrive at an answer that many before him, including a man training to become a lawyer, had failed to find.

But then the most amazing thing happened. His mind started sorting through all the information it had received—the beer drink, the dam, the friendship, the trackers, the chieftaincy, the British—retaining what was important and discarding what was unimportant. How did his mind know how to do this?

It was only when he started rearranging the key elements into a connected and cohesive whole that he realized what he was doing. He was reconstructing the plot of a story, which was something he had done many times, with both oral and written stories. The only difference now was that the story that Msimanga had just told him was not made up.

His mind worked for most of the night until what had happened to Zwakele Mkhize was very clear to Spokes. The truth left him cold, so cold that even though he was covered by a warm and heavy blanket, he shivered his way through the early morning hours.

It was Msimanga himself who came to fetch him as the day broke. Spokes found most of the homestead, including the lovely Loveness, waiting for him to either succeed or fail. Msimanga stationed himself and Spokes in the middle of the clearing, and everyone else formed a circle around them.

"What happened to Zwakele Mkhize?" Msimanga asked.

"If you don't mind, sir… is it possible, before answering, for me to ask one or two questions of my own?" Spokes asked in return.

Those in the circle made noises, none of them particularly encouraging.

Msimanga looked at Spokes with his wise eyes, and smiled his acquiescence.

"You mentioned something about a dam being built around that time."

"Yes."

"At what stage was the dam?"

"Completed, but yet to be filled with water. In fact, it was filled with water soon after," Msimanga said.

"It began to be filled the very next day," a male voice volunteered.

"Thank you. That is all I need to know," Spokes said before pronouncing, "Zwakele Mkhize is in the dam."

Even though it had been obvious from his questions where Spokes was going, his declaration was met with a shocked silence.

"You think someone pushed Zwakele into the dam?" Msimanga asked.

"I know so," Spokes said, before slowly adding, "and so do you, sir."

The shocked silence was scandalized.

Finally an elderly voice from the circle asked, "What is this young man saying?"

"He is saying that I pushed Zwakele into the dam," Msimanga replied, a smile on his face.

The silence became angry. Who did this young man think he was? What right did he have to say such things? The silence wanted him and his very dangerous ways gone, back to wherever he had come from... hopefully somewhere very far away.

But the silence did not belong to Msimanga, who simply asked, "How did you know?"

"You said if I answered the question correctly, I could marry your daughter. But how—"

"How could I possibly know what the correct answer was if I was not the one who had committed the crime?" Msimanga concluded, impressed.

The silence decided to turn into a murmur so that it could have something to do, and would probably have carried on thus, perhaps infinitely, had someone—a woman—not had the presence of mind to inquire: "Why would Msimanga have all these people look for Zwakele if he knew that he... " She lost her courage and would not finish her thought.

As it turned out, Msimanga had courage enough for all of them. His wise eyes looked very weary when he said, "At first I did it to ward off suspicion from myself... and then I did it because I grew tired of having got away with it. Another man's death is a very heavy burden to bear. I thought that what I desired more than anything was the power that came with being your headman. It was only after Zwakele was gone that I realized that what I needed even more was a true friend."

The silence wanted to be anywhere else but where it was.

Although Spokes had not spoken for quite some time, a man's voice said, "This young man should shut his mouth! Shut up and leave our village this very instant."

"No. This young fellow has done the right and honorable thing," Msimanga said. "Imagine the bravery it has taken him to tell the truth with so much to lose. Imagine the integrity. Imagine the intelligence… I doubt our Loveness could find a man more worthy in whatever corner of the world she looks."

The silence was not as convinced about Spokes's virtues and attributes as Msimanga was. Spokes was lost in that silence until the gunshot rang out and alerted him to the fact that Msimanga had left the clearing and returned to his hut. After the gunshot, the silence turned into chaos that could not contain Spokes within it. In fact, the chaos made it very clear that it wanted him gone. So when Raftopoulos arrived to collect Spokes, the chaos unceremoniously ushered Spokes into the caravan. The last thing that Spokes saw as he was driven away was the lovely Loveness crying as she sat forlornly in the middle of the clearing. He knew then that bravery, integrity, and intelligence could certainly be costly possessions.

Once he was inside it, Spokes realized why Raftopoulos's caravan could only accommodate one person. It was not so much that he had too many wares—bales of mostly second-hand clothing, stacks of threadbare blankets, mounds of blue and green soap, gallons of multicolored oils, packets of cheap toffees and caramels, boxes of that greatest creation of all: condensed milk; it was that alongside all this and his own bedding, he had impressively crammed in the complete works of Charles Dickens. The leather-bound volumes were neatly piled on top of each other in an area so clean it could pass for an altar.

Spokes reached for the book at the top of the pile, *A Tale of Two Cities*, opened it and was shocked by what he saw— such a quantity of marginalia that he, who had never been permitted to make a mark of any kind in a book, felt it was a desecration. He looked at some of the notes, and they all were about how to properly pronounce words. So this was how Raftopoulos had taught himself to speak English, Spokes deduced, as he looked at the scribblings with a much kinder eye.

Once in Krum's Place, Spokes was both surprised and pleased to discover that it was beautiful country with a river running through it—a river he could fish in the way his father had taught him. He saw himself happily settled there, and became convinced that, for him, Krum's Place was the promised land. He would only fish again in that river; it would make the realization of his dream that much sweeter.

Having found the land, Spokes made his way back to the place where the promise had been made: the corner of Lobengula Street and Selborne Avenue. The War Office where he had signed his name and joined the African Rifles had expanded over the years and now contained many offices, the smallest of which was set aside for returning native soldiers. It was in this office that he was told that Great Britain thanked him for his service but regretted to inform him that viable, commercial farmland had been set aside for returning British and European (but not German) soldiers and any British people who wanted to settle in the colony as they were the ones with the modern farming practices that would make the country a post-war agricultural giant. There was a proposed scheme to do the same for returning Coloured soldiers, only on a smaller scale, of course: where Europeans would receive hectares of land, quite naturally, Coloureds would receive acres of land. Perhaps a similar scheme, on a much smaller scale, could be proposed for the returned African soldier.

By the time Spokes left the office, he had talked the officer into holding out the possibility that in a few years, when the British had taken their fair share of the land, the returned African soldier would be able to occupy a few of the few remaining acres. He had even made the officer put his name—Spokes M. Moloi—on a list, and was comforted and gratified by the fact that his name was at the top of the list, and that next to it were two words: Krum's Place.

Disappointed but hopeful, Spokes left the minuscule office refusing to feel anger at the fact that the long-waited on promise had not been kept. Anger at the British was what had made his grandfather not only fight in the First Matabele War in 1893 but also join the umvukela in 1896, which in turn was what had made the British hang him by the neck until he was dead.

The unpromised future that now stretched before Spokes presented few possibilities, the most practicable of these being training to become a teacher at the mission school that had educated him—an English teacher. This was his mother's desire. She did not like the idea of her only child, a son at that, working in the City of Kings. All an educated African man could be in the City of Kings was a boy—a delivery boy, a messenger boy, a teaboy, a houseboy, a garden boy, a cook, a factory worker who was expected to do what the baas said and was never allowed to think for himself. She wanted greater things for her only child, a son at that. She wanted Spokes to be a man.

She did not say it, she did not have to—they both knew that the primary reason she did not want him working in the City of Kings was because of what had happened to his father. A delivery boy, Spokes's father had been very proud of his job and very happy in it. A naturally friendly man who struck up conversations easily, Spokes's father had one day been sent by a florist to deliver a bouquet of roses, and had, as was his wont, conversed with the European woman receiving the flowers. Her husband had returned just then and found his wife in too close a proximity to a native. It was only after the delivery boy had left, after the European woman and her husband had discussed the matter at great length, and after the husband—talking to the woman all the while about the proper and right thing to do—had soundly beaten her with the bouquet of roses that had not been sent by him—it was only after all this that the truth of the matter finally presented itself.

Immediately after beating his wife, the husband went and reported the great atrocity that he had witnessed to the BSAP. The BSAP were predictably outraged and went in search of Spokes's father. The woman, after she had healed from the wounds of the physical assault perpetrated on her person by her husband, swore under oath that Spokes's father had accosted her and attempted to touch her in a place that she, for propriety's sake, refused to mention.

The year was 1933, Black Peril was yet again feared to be on the rise, and so Spokes's father found himself a most wanted man. When questioned, he remembered the woman, he remembered her loneliness and sadness, he remembered wanting to make her happy, he remembered carrying the bouquet of roses into her home, he remembered her husband entering just as he put the flowers on the center table, he remembered leaving soon after without having received a gratuity.

But it did not matter what Spokes's father remembered or how he remembered it, because the woman in question had said otherwise and her husband, Erasmus C. Rutherford, was the owner of several prosperous factories, an upstanding citizen of the City of Kings, and a well-regarded member of a masonic lodge. In the end, it was Erasmus C. Rutherford's unimpeachable words that had made the British hang Spokes's father by the neck until he was dead.

As Spokes walked away from the corner of Lobengula

THE QUALITY OF MERCY

Street and Selborne Avenue with a promise unfulfilled, seriously contemplating joining the teaching profession and thus steering clear of the unpredictable European women of the City of Kings, he thought of his grandfather and his father and began to understand something about them that he had never done before. In living and dying the way that they had, they had given him an invaluable lesson that he could use at this very moment in his life: a place changes its character many times within its lifetime, and with each metamorphosis it asks those within it to change along with it. This was a choice, although those who held power never presented or treated it as such. A man could choose to let go and follow the tide of change, and a man could also choose to hold on to himself.

Before this realization, Spokes had never been able to do anything with the legacy of what had happened to his grandfather and father except accept and carry it with him here and there and everywhere. But now he knew that he need not just carry things; he could also help lighten the loads of Africans who had experienced wrongs that needed to be righted. Africans, like Zwakele Mkhize, whose deaths had left their stories only half told.

This realization gave Spokes a new purpose, and he found himself walking in a particular and definite direction that led him to the BSAP Drill Hall. He would use the qualities that Msimanga had highlighted—bravery, integrity and intelligence—to get a job as a constable in the BSAP. He would become a man who ensured that justice prevailed. This seemed to him to be the best way to do right by the memories of his grandfather and father.

There was no way that Spokes could have known in 1947 that it was these very qualities that would in the distant future —five months spanning 1979 and 1980 to be exact—make him the true inheritor of his grandfather's and father's legacy, and lead him down a path that would make him the kind of man that the government would hang by the neck until he was dead.

And just to think, all of this happened because Spokes had once stood at the corner of Lobengula Street and Selborne Avenue, waiting on a promise.

PART ONE

———◆———

CLEAVE

DECEMBER 1979

SPOKES

———◆———

Rumors were very rare occurrences at the Western Commonage Police Station, or, rather, credible rumors were. The station prided itself on being a place where reason and logic reigned, but it was really a place like any other and conjecture had long traveled its halls with ease. The latest rumor had been started by someone who had received the news (from an excellent source) that on the very next day, at Lancaster House in London, the peace agreement would finally be signed and the ceasefire would be announced.

Since then the station had not known a moment's peace, especially after the crates of Castle and Lion lagers had been smuggled in by a group of extremely enthusiastic young constables. By the time the rumor had reached every ear in the station, Lovemore Majaivana and the Jobs Combination's *Istimela* album was playing on a loop in the canteen, the tantalising smell of braaing meat was filling the air, and the sound of dancing and stomping feet had mingled with voices, not altogether sober, to create a mixture of cacophony and commotion.

The enthusiasm had proved irresistible for most officers, even the more senior ones, in the station. Amidst all this uncustomary chaos sat Chief Inspector Spokes Moloi in the Sergeants' Office which until too recently had been called the Native Senior Officers' Station. Although no longer a sergeant himself, Spokes shared the office with two senior sergeants and one sergeant major, and was extremely glad that they were all otherwise engaged because his aloneness allowed him to do what he needed to do without prying eyes looking on.

Even though he did not partake in it, Spokes understood his fellow officers' need for celebration. A ceasefire meant that there would no longer be any stints with the Police Anti-Terrorist Unit, and that, therefore, the chances of having the letters KIA attached to their names for an eternity had diminished greatly. With the future potentially this discernible and more certain thing, the station had decided that 20 December was as good a time as any for the holiday season to begin.

For his part, however, Spokes, chose to remain cautious. They had been here quite a few times in the past three years: talks that took place in other parts of the world, talks meant to broker peace, talks that had given much-needed hope—talks that had only amounted to continued disappointment and protracted war.

Spokes shrugged off his chariness as best he could, reached for two A4, station-issued, manila envelopes and placed them neatly in front of him, parallel to each other, on top of his desk. He was buying time, he knew, and found that he could not, as yet, bring himself to confront what lay within the envelopes. Instead, he turned his attention to his in tray.

There it was, where it always was at the end of every working day—the thin, light-blue manila folder, faded with age and dog-eared from too much handling. Spokes no longer had to open it to see the bulging burlap sack, the dead eyes, the severed limbs, the Y-dissection running down the torso, the brand-new dress. Yet he did open the folder, he did look at the dismembered body, he did feel the guilt of not having solved the case after so many years, he did deeply regret not being able to allow Daisy to rest in peace. He ran his hands over the contents of the folder in a gesture made more tender because his hands were trembling. Daisy: her unsolved murder made what he needed to do now very difficult—near impossible—but still he managed to close the folder carefully.

As Spokes looked at the two manila envelopes lying side by side on his desk, he reminded himself that he had successfully solved 113 cases in his twenty years at the Western Commonage, and 38 cases before the move to the City of Kings. Justice had prevailed 151 times. The good fight had been good to him, and he had no right to ask more than it was willing to give. It was time.

He deliberately opened the envelope on his left first, removed the single sheet of paper that it contained, and then placed it on top of the manila envelope before repeating the same actions with the other envelope. Two forms lay before him: the one on the left was an application to the 33rd Annual City of Kings' Township Ballroom-Dancing Competition, and the one on the right was a BSAP Application for Retirement. Because he wanted his intentions to be clearly understood, Spokes took from his desk a new sheet of blue carbon paper and two pristine white sheets of bond paper. He placed the blue carbon paper under the ballroom-dancing competition's application form first and then placed one sheet of white bond paper underneath it. In this way, he went about the business of filling in both forms.

Both documents required almost the same information:
Prefix—*Mr.*;
Surname—*Moloi*;
Christian Name—*Spokes*; Middle Initial—*M.*;
Date of Birth—*30 August 1923*;
Current Date—*20 December 1979*; and
Signature—*his two initials and his surname written in a dignified and controlled cursive that was both decipherable and decorative, and which the missionaries*

who had educated him had taken great pains to inculcate, believing as they did that good penmanship was an outward sign of good character.

The difference between the two forms was that the one on the left wanted information pertaining to his ballroom dancing experience:

Number of Previous Competitions—*10*;

Number of Placements—*5*;

Year of Competition and Position held:

1969—Honorable Mention; 1971—4th Place; 1973—3rd Place; 1977—2nd Place; 1978—2nd Place;

Professional or Amateur Category—*Amateur*.

The form on the left wanted information pertaining to his career as a police officer:

Division—*CID*;

Current Rank—*Chief Inspector*;

Years in Position—*1*;

Years in BSAP—*32*;

Other Ranks Previously Held—*Constable, Sergeant, Senior Sergeant, Sergeant Major, Sub Inspector*.

Now that both forms had been completed in duplicate, Spokes was rather amazed at the ease with which it had all been done. Even though he and his wife had promised each other that after their twenty-fifth anniversary they would retire to the ten acres in Krum's Place that they had painstakingly saved for and only been allowed to purchase legally in 1976, Spokes had found it difficult to actually act on the promise and had procrastinated in applying for his retirement for the past year.

His wife had been understanding while the prospect of his becoming the first black chief inspector loomed—so understanding that she had allowed them to forfeit the year's Annual

City of Kings' Township Ballroom-Dancing Competition—even though it was strongly felt that 1979 was their year to win the title. But now that Spokes had achieved the particular distinction of his promotion, she felt that they should happily retire, as agreed, and had recently filed her application for retirement from the Midwifery Unit at Mpilo Hospital.

Spokes knew exactly what he needed to do in order to reciprocate in full. He needed to let go of Daisy... finally.

To this end, he placed the two original forms in their respective manila envelopes, sealed and addressed them in the cursive that had made the missionaries not only proud of him but also have faith in him. Next, he placed the two duplicates in a white envelope and wrote his wife's name on it. Last, he placed the blue carbon paper in his top drawer and locked it—barely-used blue carbon paper was a much-prized commodity in these parts. When left unguarded, carbon paper had been known to either grow legs and walk out of the station, or develop magical abilities that allowed it to disappear into thin air.

It was long past the time that he should have left for home, he thought as he reached for his fedora, which hung on the hook behind the door. He opened the door carefully and looked down the corridor at the movement and noise coming from the canteen at the other end. The corridor itself was empty, and the Desk Sergeant seemed to be intently examining the backs of his eyelids. For all of this, Spokes was truly grateful. He confidently went to place one manila envelope in the Chief Superintendent's pigeonhole, and the other in the receptacle for outgoing mail. Before making an unobserved escape, he stopped at the Desk Sergeant's station and quietly placed a few coins on the desk. Next, he wrote on a piece of paper, "For Petty Cash. Took two envelopes—one manila, one white—for personal use," and then wrote his initials, S.

M. M. He placed the note under the coins, thankful that the Desk Sergeant was such a heavy sleeper.

He put the white envelope under his arm on his way out of the building and was just reaching for the handle of the door that would lead him into the cool evening air when he heard something fall over and the Desk Sergeant curse and then say, seemingly without missing a beat, "I've got it, sir!"

Spokes could have pretended not to have heard him above the din, but he chose to turn around instead. "Got what?" Spokes said, playing along, knowing full well what the sergeant was talking about.

"What your middle initial stands for," he said.

"What?"

"Marvelous!" he shouted.

Spokes looked at him and then said, "Couple of chaps came up with the same name on the second Sunday of June 1973, I believe."

"And?"

Spokes let him hang in suspense for a minute and then said, "Not it, I'm afraid."

The Desk Sergeant made a loud disappointed sound.

"Is it an English name?" the Desk Sergeant called after him as Spokes placed his hand once more on the door handle.

Spokes nodded.

"A proper English name or an African English name?"

"Both," Spokes mischievously announced over his shoulder.

An African English name was understood to mean an English word that expectant African parents had taken a particular shine to, regardless of what it actually meant, and which they would give as a name to their unsuspecting child. For instance, Spokes's first name was an African English name. When Reverend Michael of the London Missionary Society had ridden his bicycle to check on the health of one of his flock, the woman had been greatly enamored and fascinated by his bicycle, especially its wheels, especially the metal wires that ran in its wheels, especially the fact that the metal wires kept on rotating after the bicycle had come to a stop and the good reverend had lain the bicycle on its side in her front yard. She admired the metal wires' ability to carry on even after the journey had ended. The woman, who was not ill at all but expecting a baby, pointed at the metal wires and asked the good Reverend, "What is that?"

"A bicycle," Reverend Michael said, happy, as always, to be the bearer of not only salvation but knowledge as well.

The woman knew from received information that the bicycle was the entire thing; she did not mean the bicycle, and so she said, "No. Not that... but that," making sure to point where the round parts were.

"Oh, you mean the wheels?" a still happy Reverend Michael asked.

She had seen a few carriages and automobiles. The village owned quite a number of donkey carts. She knew what wheels were. She did not mean the wheels, and so she said, "No. Not that... but that."

As far as Reverend Michael could see, she was still pointing at the round parts, the wheels, so he was momentarily no longer happy; he was confounded. He looked at the bicycle trying to see what it was that she was pointing at. "Do you mean the spokes?" he asked presently. "The silver wires?"

"The spokes," she said, and it was her turn to be happy. The word was as beautiful as the thing it named. "Spokes," she repeated.

Now, as Spokes opened the station door, stepped into the cool evening air, and placed his fedora on his head, he was just grateful that his mother's fancy had not been caught by the handlebars or the tail light. Some others, he knew, had not been so fortunate as to have a mother name them for something that carried on after the journey had ended.

Spokes carefully placed the white envelope in the messenger bag that had once belonged to his father and which he kept in his bicycle's carriage, pegged the bottoms of his trousers, and then mounted the rusty but trusty Raleigh that his wife had bought him for his forty-fifth birthday to replace the ancient Raleigh that he had also inherited from his father. As he rode home through the townships, he followed the Milky Way with its constellation of many stars. The beauty of the moment made him feel better about the ending of things.

The scent of chicken and dumplings, his favorite meal, greeted Spokes even before he entered the red-bricked, five-roomed house with a tiny veranda that he and his wife had called home for twenty years. Spokes found himself salivating and smiling as he chained the bicycle to the laundry line and then locked it to his father's bicycle, removed the messenger bag from the carriage, walked onto the stoep, walked over the shiny surface of the veranda, and opened the door to his home—each step making him stand up straighter... taller... prouder.

It is quite possible that on 20 December 1979, many men in Mpopoma Township loved their wives, but it is not possible that any of them loved their wives as much as Spokes loved the lovely Loveness when he stepped over the threshold into his home, and was surrounded by the warm and inviting smell of the perfect welcome home.

"Is that you?" Loveness called to him from the kitchen.

"Yes, it's me," Spokes replied as he removed his fedora and placed it on the hat and coat rack behind the front door. He bent down and removed the pegs from the bottoms of his trousers and placed them, along with his home and office keys, in a basket that the lovely Loveness had made at the Women's Institute. He placed his father's messenger bag next to the basket and retrieved the white envelope.

"It is finally here," Loveness said when he entered the kitchen. She motioned with her head toward the kitchen table where a book, Elizabeth Gaskell's *Wives and Daughters*, was lying next to a vase of colorful flowers that Loveness had made out of silk stockings. She had, a few weeks earlier, placed her name on a list so as to borrow the title from their local library.

It took Spokes some time to look at the book because he was still taking in all the loveliness that was his wife as she stood there with a pink apron tied over her magenta, georgette A-line dress. What case could possibly be so important that it would make him put off spending each and every minute in her presence? Even though he did not want it to, the answer to that question came in the form of one word: Daisy.

Spokes sat by the kitchen table, placed the white envelope on it, and picked up the book.

"I thought we could start reading it tonight," the lovely Loveness said as she placed a small bowl containing a dumpling in chicken broth in front of him, thus allowing him to sample what he would soon have in abundance. He put a spoonful of dumpling and broth in his mouth and actually had to close his eyes so as best to savor it. It was the perfect union. "Is that what I think it is?" she asked, looking at the envelope. Spokes nodded, and she smiled.

"Nineteen-eighty is going to be good to us, you'll see," Loveness said as she sat on his lap.

"Aren't you going to open it?" he asked.

"No need to. I know you, Spokes Moloi. You always do the right thing."

"Word around the station is that the ceasefire will officially be announced tomorrow," Spokes said.

Loveness smiled and her cheeks dimpled as she gently placed the palms of her hands on either side of his face. "Have I not been saying all along that 1980 will be our golden year?"

"You have," he said as he watched a certain kind of fire enter her eyes.

"But I don't see why its goldenness cannot start... now," she said, slowly raising one eyebrow.

"Maybe *Wives and Daughters* can wait till tomorrow night," Spokes said.

"Maybe," Loveness whispered as she kissed her husband.

———◆———

Later, as Loveness snored softly in the gentle crook of his arm, Spokes looked at the slice of the silver moon that shone through the lace of their bedroom curtains and thought, as he often did before drifting off to sleep, of how he had come to be the luckiest of men.

The year was 1953. Although Constable Spokes Moloi had been stationed at the BSAP outpost six miles north of Krum's Place for the past two years, nothing had necessitated his having to visit Chief Mkhize's village in an official capacity, and so he had never gone there, even though it was so very close and he had something of a personal reason.... He never finished that particular thought because his mother wanted him to marry the shy and retiring Bodecia, and that was what he would do. He had already disappointed his mother by joining the BSAP, and so he was determined to make it up to her by marrying Bodecia and learning to be happy with the choice that his mother had made for him.

That is the choice that his life would have carried within it had not Sergeant Michael Meredith received, over the BSAP newly issued two-way radio, a call from one Emil Coetzee located at the Ashtonbury Farm and Estate saying that he had come across human remains in a burlap sack, and that he suspected that the body had drifted from upriver, perhaps Krum's Place, but most likely, Chief Mkhize's village.

Spokes, who was there when Sergeant Meredith received the call, was happy finally to have an official reason to go to Chief Mkhize's village, but, of course, he did not further investigate this happiness. *She* was probably married by now… had probably moved away… had probably long forgotten the specifics of the man who had brought about her father's suicide.

"You know what to do," Sergeant Meredith had told Spokes as soon as they had arrived at the many hectares of the Ashtonbury Farm and Estate and greeted Emil Coetzee who stood in the middle of all that land, wearing a brown Stetson that made him look like a cowboy in one of those westerns at the bioscope. As Spokes walked toward the burlap sack, he heard Sergeant Meredith say to Emil Coetzee, "He's our best man. Although you will never catch me saying that to his face, you understand. It never helps to have Africans hear praise of themselves. Always gives them ideas above their station."

Spokes chose not to think about what Sergeant Meredith had said, and to think, instead, of the fact that the sergeant had recently put his name up for both promotion—to Sergeant— and transferral—to the Criminal Investigation Department (CID). He knew that Sergeant Meredith was as good a man as he could be under the circumstances.

Spokes peered into the burlap sack and saw a woman's body hacked at the limbs—probably to ease her body into the sack. *The death could be either premeditated or accidental,* Spokes surmised as he leaned down for a closer look to ensure that he was seeing correctly. Yes, there was without a doubt a Y-dissection cut into her chest and abdomen. Now that was most interesting… as interesting as the quality of the brand-new dress that had been draped over her body.

As Spokes stood back up, he deduced the order of things: someone had killed her; then disrobed her; then dissected her chest and abdomen; then hacked at her limbs; then neatly draped the dress she had been wearing over her body. Why make an attempt to cover the nakedness of the person you have so brutally killed? There had been anger, passion and... *respect* in her death. The respect was so very out of place. Could it be that two different people were involved in the killing—one responsible for the anger and the passion, and the other for the respect?

It was only when Spokes had asked himself what he felt was the most important question that he started taking pictures. This was always how he preferred to begin things—with a particular question in mind.

"What do you think, Moloi?" Sergeant Meredith asked as all three of them carefully carried the burlap sack and loaded it onto the back of the BSAP bakkie. "Appears to be jealous husband to me."

Every time a woman was murdered, it appeared to be jealous husband to Sergeant Meredith. "I suppose it could be," Spokes said with a shrug.

"What else could it be but jealous husband?" Sergeant Meredith asked.

"There is no ring on her finger," Spokes said.

"Africans usually don't have rings on their fingers."

"Ones dressed like she is usually do. Mission-educated. Middle-class."

"Dress could have been bought by her lover, given as a present, hence the jealous husband."

Now that was something. If the dress was at the heart of it, that would explain the anger and the passion—but still, the respect remained. "Given as a present," was all Spokes said in response.

"Where to next?" Sergeant Meredith asked Spokes as they drove off.

"The mission clinic, and then Chief Mkhize's village," Spokes said.

"My thoughts exactly," Sergeant Meredith said.

———•———

Spokes found things greatly changed at Chief Mkhize's village. Raftopoulos, the Greek travelling salesman and his caravan were still situated at the bus-stop, but next to them was a newly built two-roomed store, the Idlazonke General Goods and Bottle Store. Although modest in size, the building looked hulking next to the caravan.

As was his habit whenever he came across another European, Sergeant Meredith struck up a conversation with Raftopoulos, who did not seem to remember Spokes. From the little Spokes could overhear at the respectful distance he stood, it was clear that Raftopoulos was not happy with the location of the Idlazonke General Goods and Bottle Store, or with its proprietor, Silas Mthimkhulu. Silas Mthimkhulu—Raftopoulos mentioned this more than once—was a man who did not know his rightful place.

Having heard enough, Spokes decided to enter the store and see what it had to offer. As he made his way inside, he heard Raftopoulos say, "One white... the other black... too dark to make out much, but I made out that."

"Don't be too long, Moloi," Sergeant Meredith said as Spokes entered the store. "Let's not lose sight of what we came here for."

Spokes had no idea how long he had been standing there looking at it—the same pretty dress as the one on the body in the burlap sack, hanging on display in the store—or how long the man beside him had been saying, "Hello. My name is Jasper Mlangeni. I'm the shopkeeper here. How may I help you?" Spokes only snapped out of it because he heard a voice outside that caught his attention. He walked out of the store and made his way toward the voice. Sure enough, there *she* was: Loveness, as lovely as ever, and standing right beside her was a girl of about five. Spokes would always remember but never be able to fully capture the true radiance of that moment.

When Spokes had returned the next day to ask Jasper Mlangeni about the dress, he found the Idlazonke General Goods and Bottle Store closed until further notice. Apparently, Jasper Mlangeni had left the night before, at the behest of his boss, Silas Mthimkhulu, to go and open another Idlazonke store in a country up north. All this seemed too coincidental and Spokes felt certain that in Jasper Mlangeni he had found his man and that, perhaps, in Silas Mthimkhulu, he had found Jasper Mlangeni's accomplice. He confidently felt this until all evidence pointed to the fact that Jasper Mlangeni had been in the City of Kings on the night in question. Spokes reluctantly let go of what had become the center of his case and watched things fall apart.

Spokes had still not found the proper place to store Daisy's unsolved case within himself when he came across the harbinger. Years later, during the war, while Spokes was helping his mother resettle in a Tribal Trust Land village, a boy had arrived in the dead of night. A stranger in the dead of night was something never to be welcomed, but Spokes had made sure that the villagers welcomed him because even though the stranger was weighed down by his army boots and AK-47, he was just a boy. The boy had screamed and smashed things, broken precious windows, shattered the quiet of the night— and still Spokes had made the villagers let him be, because it was evident that the boy was wrestling with something bigger than all of them.

It was only when the boy told them about severed limbs and torsos with Y-dissections cut into them floating in the Zambezi River that Spokes fully understood why the boy had come. He had been sent, by forces that they would never see and never fully know, to show Spokes that his inability to solve Daisy's murder had led to other deaths perpetrated by Jasper Mlangeni.

The boy left before sunrise and, within a year, Spokes's very healthy and strong mother died peacefully in her sleep. After the funeral, the villagers recalled the boy with the heavy army boots and AK-47, they remembered how welcoming Spokes had been, and it was then that they called the boy a harbinger. But Spokes knew the true purpose of the boy's visit.

After he had laid his mother to rest, Spokes lay in bed for weeks, his body debilitated by a painful stiffness along his spine. He would have lain there for a lot longer had not the lovely Loveness, in her infinite wisdom, suggested that they start taking ballroom dancing lessons at Stanley Hall.

At first, Spokes was more than reluctant. He was not the sort of man who danced. He had managed to live through the township jazz craze without moving to its rhythm. He liked the music, loved it, in fact—often whistled a favorite tune while he went about the business of the day; he just did not feel the need to dance to it. That said, once he found himself in Stanley Hall with the lovely Loveness in his arms, in front of a group of friends, neighbors and strangers, he realized that while he would never be a truly accomplished dancer, he liked having the opportunity and the occasion to hold his wife close in public, which was something, hitherto, that he and propriety had only allowed in the comfort of his own home. Let him trip over his two left feet if he must as long as the world got to look at the perfection that was Loveness. After a few lessons, the painful stiffness in his back disappeared.

Loveness had found the perfect remedy; she always did.

As he, the luckiest of men, drifted off to sleep, Spokes was happy that he had applied for his retirement—it was the least he could do to thank the lovely Loveness for all that she had done for him. Yes, he regretted not being able to solve Daisy's case, but he was also very grateful that Emil Coetzee's sighting of the burlap sack had brought Loveness back into his life.

SASKIA

---•---

Although Saskia Hargrave was making a point of not looking at any of her co-workers, she knew that they were all looking at her. She could feel their gazes crawling over her skin and there was nothing she could do about it. She most certainly could not turn back now. Of the many things that made her, cowardice was not one. As much as she would have liked to, she could not just walk to her desk and set to work because it was obvious that the features editor had prepared a party to celebrate her return. There were some lackluster balloons and a bakery-bought Black Forest cake at the tea station. And so here she was feeling awkward (a foreign feeling for her) and standing close to the editor, even though she did not want to be doing either.

Instead of acting, the editor stood beside her on tenter-hooks, and Saskia realized that none of this was going according to his plan. What had he thought would happen? Had he thought her colleagues would rush forward and welcome her back? Had he thought they would express feelings they had never felt toward her simply because the occasion called for it? It was not for nothing that she was called the Vulture (among other things she was sure she would never hear said to her face) within her circle of fellow reporters. She was determined and sometimes even ruthless when going after a story; or, for that matter, anything else she cared about. She was so relentless that she often was accused of muckraking, which was water off a duck's back to her. She liked these particular qualities about herself, was aware that they did not make her many friends, and had long reconciled herself to her fate.

"Here she is, folks!" the editor said. "Come and get her while she's hot."

The joke landed badly. No one laughed. Someone coughed. A chair scraped the floor as someone stood up to make themself a cup of tea. The editor blushed as he comprehended many things at once, none of them good.

"It's great to be back," Saskia said, rescuing the situation.

"And it is great to have you back after your... after your," the editor blundered.

"My visit to the funny farm," Saskia said matter-of-factly.

There were a few laughs in response to that, and Saskia decided it was best not to examine what lay behind them too closely.

"I think I'll head over to The Organization and see if I can get a start on that story that I was telling you about," Saskia said to the editor.

"So soon?" the editor said, not quite able to hide his alarm. "I thought you would want to take a week at least. Settle in. Find your feet."

"It was not my feet that I lost," Saskia said, smiling to assure him that all was well. "No time like the present. I'll settle in later."

"I had really thought... hoped this would go a lot better," the editor whispered apologetically.

"I know," Saskia said, gesturing toward the cake and balloons. "Share a slice when I get back?"

"That would be nice," the editor said with a grateful smile.

———◆———

Once out in the City of Kings, Saskia felt invigorated by her brisk walk to The Tower, The Organization of Domestic Affairs' headquarters. At the front desk she showed her press credentials, and lied, claiming she was going to visit the archives. Instead of going to the eighth floor, she got off the lift on the sixth floor. Emil Coetzee's office was at the end of the hall. She stopped by the WC facilities, which, given their state, were evidently only used by men, and looked at her reflection in the mirror. She was wearing an army jacket, khaki shorts, a white tank top and hiking boots. At thirty-six she could easily pass for twenty-six. Her beauty was not something that ever went unnoticed, but for added measure she removed her bra and threw it into her rucksack. She made a point of carelessly throwing her rucksack over her right shoulder to give the false impression that she did not take herself or her job too seriously. Undetected, she walked out of the WC, down the hallway, and knocked softly on Emil Coetzee's office door. She entered before he told her to do so because she wanted to catch him off guard.

Saskia had definitely taken Emil Coetzee by surprise; she could tell from the way his hands fidgeted with the things on his desk when he saw her enter his office. Even though he was doing an admirable job of feigning disinterest, she saw him give her body a full appraisal, and took a secret delight in it. Men were so predictable, and Emil Coetzee was perhaps the most predictable man of them all.

She smiled at him and offered her hand for him to shake. One of her front teeth was discolored, and she noticed Emil Coetzee trying not to stare at its gray dullness as he shook her hand. It was her one imperfection, and so she broadened her smile and experienced a perverse pleasure in making him have to be made uncomfortable by her tooth.

"My name is Saskia Hargrave. I am a journalist with *The Chronicle*," she said, sitting herself down opposite Emil Coetzee despite the fact that he had not asked her to. "I would like to write your story—a feature in *The Sunday News*."

"My story? I don't have a story," he replied.

"You're Emil Coetzee, The Head of the Organization," she retorted. "Of course you have a story. You're one of the country's heroes."

"The country must be in a truly bad state if it has a man like me for a hero," he said, sounding genuine.

Humble was not one of the many things Saskia had expected Emil Coetzee to be, and so what he said confused her until she realized that he was just saying what he felt a man so honored as to have a story written about him ought to say. "Oh... I see. Humility. A nice touch," she said. With practiced alacrity, she reached for her rucksack and retrieved her notebook and pen. She hurriedly wrote three words—"hero," "humility" and "honorable"—and then looked at him with an expectant smile. She made sure that he saw the words that she had written down.

"Miss Hargrave," Emil Coetzee said after stealing a glance at her scribbled words. "I really do not have a story for you."

Saskia knew that he had deliberately referred to her as "Miss" so that she could correct him, and so she equally deliberately did not correct him.

"But you're the man of the hour," she said.

Unable to hide his obvious pride at this statement, Emil Coetzee excused himself and went to open a bay window and stand by it for a moment. She watched him as he breathed in the polluted air of the City of Kings. As he looked down at the city, his chest puffed out, and it was very obvious that he loved this city. Of course he loved it. How could he not? He had stood over it like a colossus, reigned over it like a king, master of all he surveyed.

"Emil?" Saskia said tentatively, "I was actually contemplating doing more than a feature. I would like to write your biography. Your life has just been so full, rich and exciting.

Your story has to be told." She had decided that it was best to flatter him while his head was still full of the idea of his own grandeur. She saw him carefully weigh the impact of her words, and took that opportunity, while he was absorbed with himself, to look at the items on his desk top. You could tell a lot about a man from the contents of his desk.

Placed meticulously on his desk were five notes written in a left-leaning cursive on azure-colored paper. The notes were like beacons, and Saskia could not help but be drawn to them. She felt her right hand, as though of its own volition, stretch out to touch them. She had to use every reserve of self-control to reach out slowly and surreptitiously, so as not to bring attention to herself. From where she was sitting, she was able to make out three words: *Zora Neale Hurston*.

Saskia picked up the note and, before she could stop herself, found herself secreting it into her notebook. Emil Coeztee's wife was Kuki Coetzee and his long-term mistress was Marion Hartley; so who was Zora Neale Hurston, and why hadn't the never-tiring rumor mill of the City of Kings ever heard of her? As she mused over this, she scribbled in her notebook: "Who is Zora Neale Hurston? Find her!"

In the interests of time, Saskia reluctantly let go of this tantalising train of thought, and looked for something else that would catch her interest on Emil Coetzee's desk. Under a black orb that acted as a paperweight was a fragile-looking and gently folded paper that could not help but attract her attention: she knew instinctively it was the kind of paper that held secrets within it. As her fingers deftly pulled out and unfolded it, Saskia's breath caught, and as she read what turned out to be a letter, her hands began to tremble with the anticipation of discovery. The letter was not addressed or signed, so there was no way of initially knowing who had written it:

We arrived at the village just before dawn. We fired our rifles into the air so as to wake up the villagers. We had them all gather in the middle of the kraal. We asked them why they were aiding the terrorists. We asked them this as though we thought they had a choice in the matter.

Saskia knew that time was fast running out—any moment now Emil Coetzee would turn away from the window—and so she skipped to the end and read:

You finally got your wish. You have always wanted me to kill something and now I have. I hope you are finally proud of me. I have become the son you have always wanted.

Saskia realized that the letter was from Everleigh: Emil Coetzee's son, who had died in the recent war. She let the letter fall from her hands as though it had suddenly become too weighty for her to hold. It landed on the desk with a sound that seemed to belong to a much heavier object.

As she sat there, struggling to arrange her thoughts and emotions, she heard rather than saw Emil Coetzee turn from the window. She was happy to discover that her voice sounded normal when she said, "Emil, things are changing in this country... rapidly. Men like you may very well be forgotten in a year or two. You want to be remembered, don't you?"

Of course, he wanted to be remembered? What man did not?

"You want to be remembered, don't you?" she repeated.

"Not particularly. At least not for the things that people know me for—the big events of my life. If I am to be remembered, I want to be remembered for the quieter, truer moments of my life. I don't need a story for those. I need someone."

Saskia smiled at him, playing along with his performance of humility and modesty.

"Luckily for me, I already have someone who retains those moments," Emil Coetzee said, walking back from the window.

"Your wife?" Saskia asked, thinking, all the while of Zora Neale Hurston.

As soon as Emil Coetzee sat down at his desk, he noticed that one of the azure-colored notes was missing and that the folded letter was now half-open. Saskia saw him notice these things, and instantly regretted not having put back the azure-colored note.

"Did you take one of the notes on my desk?" Emil Coetzee asked, obviously fighting for civility. "Miss Hargrave?" he said when she did not immediately respond. There was a hint of severe reprimand in his voice and Saskia felt like a child caught in the middle of some mischief. She felt chastened, not by the man she had been flirting with and flattering, but by Emil Coetzee, The Head of The Organization of Domestic Affairs and one of the most powerful men in the country.

She had no choice but to retrieve the azure-colored note from her notebook and hand it to him. "It is such a pretty color... I was just admiring it... forgot it was there. I was so absorbed by our conversation," she tried to explain. As she was speaking, Emil Coetzee stared at her discolored tooth, and as he did so, she felt the sting of his withering look. To him, she was obviously nothing more than someone nonsensical who had wasted his most precious time—a nuisance. He wanted her to feel small. He wanted her out of his life now. As he, with a look of complete contempt, watched her walk out of his office, he almost succeeded in making her feel inconsequential.

Almost.

———•———

Saskia would get the better of him yet: she knew she would, which was why she was now, many hours later, cramped in her lime-green Renault 5, parked discreetly some distance away from Marion Hartley's front gate, just in front of the road's intersection with 3rd Street. She was parked there lying in wait for Emil Coetzee in the pitch-black darkness that existed just before the dawn because of his best kept secret—Zora Neale Hurston, the woman Emil Coetzee loved so much that he treasured the handwritten notes she had given him.

Saskia felt that she simply had to see the woman who had captured the erstwhile untouchable heart of Emil Coetzee. Instead of attending a ceasefire party at her editor's home, she had followed Emil Coetzee to what she had hoped would be Zora Neale Hurston's house, but had instead turned out to be Marion Hartley's. Marion Hartley was no discovery because the entire City of Kings had long known that Emil Coetzee was having an affair with his best friend's widow. Saskia sat patiently in her car waiting for Emil Coetzee to drive out the gate and take her to Zora Neale Hurston.

As she spent the night in her car, Saskia tried to imagine Zora Neale Hurston, and in her imaginings, she wondered many things. *For instance, what color hair did she have? Were the eyes that looked at Emil Coetzee blue, gray, brown, green or hazel? Was she a short or tall woman?* In the case of another man, Saskia might have been able to guess, because that man would have had a type, but Emil Coetzee was not the kind of man who had a type. Any white woman who was attractive seemed to him to be fair game. Over the years he had made eyes of every color blue, and he had left bruises and scars, Saskia was sure, on complexions of every hue. And yet through his frankly appalling treatment of women he had held on to Zora Neale Hurston. Why? Who exactly was she, and what was it about her that Emil Coetzee found worthy enough to hold on to?

The discovery that Emil Coetzee carried handwritten notes

from Zora Neale Hurston in his wallet had made Saskia understand that there was more to him than she knew—and she did not like this realization because she had made it the work of the past several months to know every minute detail about his life. She knew that he was a rabid workaholic and a rapacious womanizer. She knew that he was recently separated from his wife, Kuki Coetzee. She knew that he had lost his son, Everleigh, in the war… Was there a name for such a person? Saskia reached for her rucksack, pulled out her notebook and used the weak light of the breaking morning to jot down: "Look up the word for a father who loses his child. Oxford English Dictionary. Will be a nice touch to the piece. Less pedestrian." She frowned down at what she had written, and then she shivered. She finally admitted to herself that the khaki bomber jacket she was curled up under was no match for the early morning air, and had definitely not been a match for the evening air with its particular bite.

———•———

Sassie could smell the tobacco on her father's stale breath as he clamped a grimy and greasy palm over her mouth, stifling her scream while his other hand pawed the hem of her nightdress. She felt the heavy weight of his body push her into the mattress, which became water beneath her. She fought him off with all her might, but his body kept on pushing her further and deeper into the cold and dark water, drowning them both. She could not breathe. She could not breathe. The water was ice-cold and she could not breathe. She desperately needed to breathe. Suddenly she found purchase—a finger lodged itself in an eye socket and gouged. He had no other choice but to let her go. She used all her remaining strength to swim blindly through the frigid water. Still not able to breathe, she swam and swam, eventually surfaced, opened her mouth to gulp in much-needed air, and instead let out a primal sound.

Saskia woke up screaming as she opened her eyes to early morning light washing over a serene and subdued suburban street. Just as she was re-familiarizing herself with her sur-roundings, she saw Marion Hartley's gate swing open and Emil Coetzee's beige bakkie drive out. Saskia was a little surprised when he did not get out of his car to close the gate behind him, but was very grateful when the car turned not toward 3rd Street but toward Selborne Avenue, because she had not even had the presence of mind to hide from him. Given the direction he was taking, he was probably on his way back to The Tower where he would do horrible things to people... or had he stopped doing those things now that the ceasefire had been called? What would a man like him do now that the war was over? What *could* a man like him do now that the war was over?

As though she was the answer to these questions, Marion Hartley appeared at the gate. She was dressed in a lacy, light and flowing nightdress with matching gown, her hair tied back with a scarf—and even in the morning light she looked not altogether real, as ethereal as an apparition. But Marion was no vision; she was a woman, just as she, Saskia, was also a woman.

That said, there were some women, as far as Saskia was concerned, who were just too content with the hand that fate had dealt them. These women needed to learn some hard truths about life and its cruel nature. Marion Hartley was one such woman, Saskia decided, as she watched her standing in the light of morning, looking like a fragile flower, hugging herself to keep warm in the still cold air.

For a long moment after the beige bakkie had disappeared around the corner of Selborne Avenue, Marion Hartley stood there immobile as though hoping that the car would reappear. Saskia had relaxed into watching this scene when, without warning, Marion Hartley turned and looked straight at the lime-green Renault 5, which, Saskia knew, was made even more conspicuous by the army-green horizontal elongated Z that ran along its sides.

Marion Hartley hesitated and then started making her way toward the car, craning her neck, trying to see who the driver was. Saskia clutched the steering wheel with one hand while the other fitted the key into the ignition. Adrenaline made her shake so uncontrollably that she almost dropped the keys before the car, after a few false starts, revved to life and drove her away from Marion Hartley and her curiosity.

Saskia was sure that Marion Hartley had no idea that Zora Neale Hurston existed. She was sure that Marion Hartley imagined, as most of the City of Kings imagined, that she had tamed Emil Coetzee and made a ne'er-do-well suddenly do well. Saskia smiled to herself when she thought of the hurt that Marion Hartley would feel upon discovering that she was not the love of Emil Coetzee's life. She would be crushed by the knowledge of Zora Neale Hurston. She would join good company, of course; Kuki Coetzee and countless other women had all loved Emil Coetzee to their own detriment.

Saskia counted herself lucky for not seeking or wanting Emil Coetzee's love. She had no intention of becoming like the countless others. After the way he had looked at her, she was determined to do much more than simply matter in his life the way Marion Hartley and Kuki Coetzee did. She was determined to supersede them both in the space they took up in his life. Once she had done so, she would tear to shreds the love he felt for Zora Neale Hurston until she, Saskia Hargrave, was the only one left standing. Yes, when she was through with Emil Coetzee, there would be nothing left for anybody else: of this she was sure.

THE BEIGE BAKKIE

———— ◆ ————

Yesterday, when Vida de Villiers had been demobilized, he had found waiting for him at the Llewellin Barracks a letter written in a once beautiful but now spidery-with-age hand-writing that had informed him on pink paper with roses at the margins that it was sorry that his parents had died, and that he would be most welcome to stay at Flat 2A and call it home until such time as he felt ready to move on.

Now Vida, still in his military fatigues, stood at the corner of Selborne Avenue and Borrow Street and looked at the Prince's Mansions and at the street-facing windows of Flat 2A. As he did, he remembered the too brief but happy time that he had spent there with an old couple who had loved each other so much that they had invented their own sign language in order to make the world contain their particular kind of silence.

He knew that even now, after the war, Johan and Gemma Coetzee were in Flat 2A, living a very quiet existence, absolutely enjoying the peace all around them. He wished he too could have such a particular kind of love, one that would continue even after the bombs had fallen from the sky, the sound of gunfire had traveled through the air and hidden landmines had ripped the earth apart with loud blasts, but his love had not been so fated. The boy, Everleigh Coetzee, whom he had been allowed to love in Flat 2A, had decided to step on a landmine instead of coming back to him unscathed by the war.

The letter had been a very generous and attractive offer, and Vida knew that if he knocked on the door of the flat, the quiet would welcome him like a long-lost friend. Unfortunately, Vida could not help but feel that he would contaminate the silence somehow because within him there was a roaring and roaming rage.

He had taken his rage with him to war, hoping that it would make him reckless enough to die in the war. His rage had done no such thing; instead, it had put him in the path of Golide Gumede, who could have killed him, but had chosen not to. "You will remember me," Golide Gumede had said, and Vida had held on to those words as though they were a promise. A promise of what? He was not altogether sure. All he knew was that those words had made him see the war through to its end. He supposed they had given him purpose, something to live for. Memory needs survival to exist and, therefore, Vida had had not only to survive the war; he had to keep on surviving after the war had ended, so as to keep on remembering a man who wanted to be remembered.

So here he was safely deposited back into a country that was no longer at war with itself. They called it a ceasefire as if that was an easy enough thing to do: cease… fire. Stop hostilities. Quiet the raging.

As he ran his fingers through hair that was slightly too long, he felt so tired of the world that he was sure he had lived a lifetime much longer than his eighteen years. He should have been making his way home, like every other surviving member of the security forces, but he did not know where home was.

Vida could not bring himself to walk through the heart of the City of Kings, cross Lobengula Street, make his way to Thorngrove, the Coloured section of the city, and enter his parents' house that was missing not only their presence but their unconditional love. And, for now, he could not bring himself to cross Borrow Street and disturb the peace of Flat 2A.

He looked down the stubborn straightness of Selborne Avenue as though it would make up his mind for him. Of course the road did no such thing. What it did do, however, was present Vida with the beige bakkie that belonged to Emil Coetzee. As he watched the vehicle approach the intersection of Selborne Avenue and Borrow Street, Vida decided then, on the spur of the moment, that he would cross the road toward the Prince's Mansions only if Emil Coetzee looked up at the windows of Flat 2A.

Emil Coetzee drove through the intersection looking straight ahead.

Vida wondered how Emil Coetzee could drive by without looking, no matter how briefly, at the windows of the flat where his son had lived before going off to war. As he watched the beige bakkie travel into the distance, the rage within sounded in his ears and drowned out the stridency of the city around him. Vida knew then that he would never make a home for himself in the silence of Flat 2A. He turned his back on the intersection of Selborne Avenue and Borrow Street and walked aimlessly through the City of Kings—a man with no direction home.

———•———

As Lukha Hlotshwayo made his way to The Tower, he saw Emil Coetzee's beige bakkie approach up Selborne Avenue, and he allowed himself to feel something that he had not allowed himself to feel in such a very long time that he no longer remembered ever having felt it: relief.

Now he knew that his journey would not be in vain. He would go to The Tower, confess what he had done, and Emil Coetzee would punish him for it. Lukha felt certain that with every blow to his body, the weight of the world that he had been carrying on his shoulders for most of his years as an adult would fall away, leaving him as light as spirit.

It was not that he no longer wanted the responsibility for what he had done; he just wanted to lay his burden down. He had killed people; nothing could ever really take that away from him. The die had been cast a long time ago, and Lukha was as assured as he could ever be about anything that if he walked into The Tower and told them what he had done, Emil Coetzee would personally see to it that Lukha's feeling of relief was not particularly long-lived. Lukha almost smiled as he imagined the sweet release of being that would come with his final breath.

The thing that stopped him from smiling was not just that his mouth no longer remembered how to smile—which it did not—but also the knowledge that he was choosing his own death when the people that he had killed had had no such luxury. One minute they had been happy and alive and the next minute, without any warning or a sign from the vast universe, they had been killed; and not only killed, but killed rather effortlessly—as though their lives, dreams, hopes and joys had never mattered at all.

But of course, they had mattered and each one of those lives, dreams, hopes and joys had, over the years, come to accumulate and accrue on Lukha's shoulders until he stooped under their weight. So now, when the guerrillas he had fought with felt that they had won the war and were the heroes and conquerors, Lukha knew that he had been left so vanquished by his past deeds that he would never feel the victor.

Taking his own life would have been too easy a way out. He had committed the crime, tried the case, and found himself guilty. Now all he needed was the punishment, and since the punishment had to fit the crime he was making his way to The Tower. He had heard stories of how creative the operatives at The Organization of Domestic Affairs were in their methods. He had heard tell of how, in the basement of The Tower, in a dark, concrete and cold room that had the omnipresent sound of water dripping, a light would unexpectedly flicker and an open flame would singe the skin; of how sleep could be taken from you in a breath; of how you could be drowned with only a cup of water; of how electricity could be made to travel through your body, all in a matter of seconds, with the act complete before you could even register or scream the searing pain.

Lukha, filled with hope, crossed Selborne Avenue and watched the beige bakkie driving up the street, expecting it to turn right on Fife Street—but it did not. It carried on straight toward Main Street. It was not making its way to The Tower as Lukha had anticipated. The weight on his shoulders buckled his knees and crumbled him to the pavement like a man begging.

He would have to wait another day for his appointment with death. No longer able to stand, Lukha found himself crawling on all fours on the dusty pavement that was overcrowded with moving and milling feet. Perhaps it was telling that none of the denizens sharing the pavement with Lukha looked at him as though what he was doing were strange, if they looked at him at all. As far as they were concerned, the war had finally ended and so anything was now possible in the City of Kings.

———•———

Some guys have all the luck, Tom Fortenoy thought as he stood outside the Main Post Office War Memorial Courtyard, where he had spent the night, and watched Emil Coetzee's beige bakkie make its way through the roundabout surrounding the statue of Cecil John Rhodes.

In many ways Tom was very grateful to Emil Coetzee because it was the fact that they had a passing resemblance to one another that had kept Tom out of the poorhouse for a substantial portion of his adult life. Tom made an admirable amount of money impersonating Emil Coetzee at the various bars and clubs that the City of Kings had to offer. Unfortunately for him, at this point in his life, his only other talent was successfully managing to drink and gamble most of the money away.

Tom Fortenoy and Emil Coetzee had been born the same year, 1927, and when they grew up, they both were tall and handsome with blond hair and movie-star good looks. One would have been justified in thinking that, with these similarities, their lives would travel along parallel paths: but they had not, and a somewhat simple twist of fate had seen to it that as one man ascended the social ladder, the other descended it.

It had not always been obvious which man would come out on top and which man would find himself at the bottom. In fact, if anyone was a betting man, as Tom was, they would have stacked the odds squarely in Tom's favor: he had been born into a relatively well-to-do family that owned a bakery and a haberdashery and lived in a beautiful white bungalow situated on an acre of land in the placid suburb of Suburbs. Emil Coetzee had, on the other hand, been born into a family that had to stretch his father's civil service salary every month, and lived in a five-roomed flat, Flat 2A, in the Prince's Mansions.

It is true that Emil Coetzee had gone, on scholarship, to the best school in the country—the Selous School for Boys— while Tom had gone to both Milton Junior School and Milton High School, but from what Tom could gather, Emil Coetzee had been, at best, a middling student, whereas Tom himself had been a stellar student. So although Emil Coetzee had received a superior education, he had not made much of this advantage. As a matter of fact, he had been so unremarkable as a student that although their paths had crossed, briefly, at Milton Junior School, Tom did not remember him.

After school, Emil Coetzee had bumbled around for some years before finding work in the Department of Native Affairs. Tom, for his part, had gone to hone his craft at the Royal Academy of Dramatic Art. Full of the sure-fire politics of youth, he had returned to the City of Kings in the mid-1950s to act in some highly acclaimed and intelligently interpreted Shakespearean productions that had been directed by the incomparable Courteney Smythe-Sinclair. He had played a white Othello opposite a Coloured Desdemona and black Iago; a Macbeth whose desire for the throne makes him sabotage a Lady Macbeth poised to be the first queen; and an openly homosexual Coriolanus.

On the surface of things, it seemed that Tom still had the odds stacked high in his favor. However, it was at this time that both men began to experience a reversal of fortune. Tom married for love, fathered four children in quick succession, and, as the years progressed, developed a taste for gambling and drink, especially after the country's politics took a turn to the right in the 1960s and Courteney Smythe-Sinclair's inimitable productions were banned outright by the government for being too unpatriotic. Tom found the plays that he acted in during the latter years of the 1960s particularly unimaginative, uninspired and undemanding, and, as a result, unrewarding. The entire world was going through a seismic shift, and his country seemed a little too content to keep its head buried in the sand.

It was during a mind-numbingly faithful production of *The Boyfriend* that Tom, performing while he was three sheets to the wind (which was the only way he could go through with the performance) had abruptly turned to the audience and told them that they were emotionally, morally, spiritually and intellectually bankrupt. Then he vomited all the gin and tonic that he had consumed that day down the front of the leading lady's pastel-colored drop-waist dress.

Needless to say, Tom was banned from acting in any production in the City of Kings after *The Boyfriend* incident. Luckily for him, by this time Emil Coetzee's fortunes had changed for the better. He had conveniently married Kuki Sedgwick, the descendant of wealthy pioneer stock; he had fathered only one child, a son; and most ingeniously of all, he had somehow managed to turn his entry-level job at the Department of Native Affairs into the creation of an entirely new government department called The Organization of Domestic Affairs. In a surprisingly short space of time, Emil Coetzee had become a man so well known and influential that Tom could make a living by impersonating him.

A recent performance at the Palace Hotel had proved so lucrative that Tom had felt Fortune smile on him once more. Feeling the full warmth of that smile, he had gone to Ascot and bet all the money on a horse called Lucky Strike. The horse had not lived up to its name. With his pockets empty, Tom had not even bothered to go home because he knew that Doreen, his wife, who had informed him that she was at the end of her tether, was now beyond grace.

What a simple but cruel twist of fate, Tom thought as he watched the beige bakkie continue its journey along Main Street. Tom's stomach growled and he imagined that Emil Coetzee was going to have a wonderfully warm and scrumptious breakfast at the home of a woman who was still full of grace… a woman who did not even know that she had a tether to reach the end of.

Some guys have all the luck.

As Beatrice Beit-Beauford and Kuki Coetzee sat in the court-yard of the Pear Tree Inn, having their breakfast, Beatrice was pleased that Kuki was sitting with her back to the road because that way she did not see Emil driving by in his beige bakkie. *Probably on his way to another woman,* Beatrice thought as she slathered butter onto two still-hot halves of a scone, and, with satisfaction, watched it melt before plopping on dollops of strawberry jam.

In Beatrice's decided opinion, Emil Coetzee was as pre-dictable as the sunrise and the sunset, but his presence did not soothe the way those two moments of the day did. Emil was the very opposite of a balm; he was the sharp thing that cuts deep and leaves indelible, ever-festering wounds. Beatrice was sitting opposite one such wound, her best friend, Kuki, whose eyes were now, after her separation from Emil, usually either damp with ready tears or veined red by fallen tears. It was obvious from the way he had driven past that Emil had not seen Kuki sitting in the courtyard, which was no surprise to Beatrice. He had not seen Kuki throughout their long mar-riage, so why would he see her now that they were finally divorced?

Kuki made excuses, of course; well, not excuses as such, but she said she cried not because of Emil but because her golden-haired boy, Everleigh, had not returned from the war. However, that was just the surface of things: Beatrice was cer-tain that had Emil, the father, been kinder and more under-standing, Everleigh, the son, would not have chosen to step on a landmine and make visible for all the eyes that fell upon him the raw and gaping wound that he had always been because of his father.

History would say that Everleigh Coetzee was a casualty of war because he had been killed during the war, but Beatrice knew otherwise. She knew that Everleigh Coetzee had not been a casualty of war the way Beatrice's own two sons had been; she knew that Everleigh Coetzee had been a casualty of Emil Coetzee.

"Here's to your divorce finally coming through. Here's to your independence. Here's to your being a free woman," Beatrice said, offering Kuki half of the scone.

Kuki took the offered scone and placed it on her plate, where Beatrice knew it would remain uneaten. "I miss him so much," she said and pushed the plate away, as though rejecting all the possible sweetness in her life.

Beatrice leaned over and squeezed Kuki's hand in commiseration, wondering, all the while, if the festering wound always missed the sharp thing that had created it. She hoped not, for Kuki's sake.

————•————

Mrs. Louisa Alcott was beginning to despair at the hero's reluctance to see past his blind arrogance and notice that the pretty wallflower who was taming his most rebellious horse in the stables was really the woman that he loved, and not the entitled heiress who had been his childhood sweetheart. How could the hero not have noticed by page ninety-nine that the wallflower was, like him, wild at heart?

As Mrs. Louisa Alcott lay languidly on a white wrought-iron bench situated on an island of green lawn on her front garden, she turned to the cover of the Mills & Boon and looked at the ruggedness of the hero etched on it in relief, while the Australian outback stood hazily in the background. She had to remind herself of the reasons why she had reached for this particular Mills & Boon and not the dozens of others that the mobile library had brought within her easy reach the week before.

The artist who had painted the hero's face had not only

made it rugged and handsome but had also made it tanned to the point of being almost brown, but not so dark as to create confusion. His jaw was made of sharp lines, his chin was divided by a cleft, his cheek had the hint of a dimple, his nose was aristocratic and strong with nostrils flared slightly for the occasion, his mouth was made up of a curled upper lip and a slightly plump lower lip and gave the impression that he had just whispered something to the heroine, whom he held in his arms the way Clark Gable had held Vivien Leigh as Tara burnt. His hair was dark, full and thick with a slight wave to it that invited one's fingers to run through it. All these qualities made for a very attractive face, but it was the eyes—they had a smoky amber color and were nestled underneath beautifully arched brows—that had made Mrs. Louisa Alcott reach for the book and choose it from the multitude. There was undeniable passion in those eyes. A man who looked at you with those eyes could make you do anything and make you feel everything that he did to you.

But the hero who had held so much promise was disappointing her; she was now halfway through the book and he still had not even kissed the wild-at-heart wallflower. As Mrs. Louisa Alcott sighed and took in a deep breath, she noticed the freshness of the morning air for the first time. She knew that her husband, Mr. Louis Alcott, would not be happy to return from overseeing the running of the farm to find her sitting in the front garden.

Perhaps it was not altogether wise to sit outside, actively courting potential danger, but the radio had announced that there was a ceasefire, and Mrs. Louisa Alcott had had enough years of being cooped up in the house for her own safety. During the war, she had spent every morning of the working day barricaded inside the house, armed with both a rifle and a pistol, in case the terrs came traipsing along. As a girl, she had been taken hunting with a rifle by her grandfather; as a teenager, she had been taken to target practice by her father; and, as a wife, she had been taken to national security classes by her husband. So Mrs. Louisa Alcott was more than prepared to deal with the terrs and more than capable of giving them what they deserved.

The terrs had never come to the Alcott Farm, probably because it was too close to the main road that led to the City of Kings, and so she had spent a good portion of those armed days in much the same way she did now, reading Mills & Boon novels and sucking on koeksisters—only back then, she had done so in a barricaded kitchen.

She breathed in deeply again, and in that breath forgave the hero for not realizing that he was falling in love with the heroine and for not kissing her, although it was obvious that her waiting lips were ready to be kissed. She turned to page one hundred, sure that all would come right over the next hundred pages: it always did. The only place where happy endings were guaranteed was within the pages of a romantic novel.

She continued reading the love story that was playing itself out in the Australian outback, which was where Mrs. Louisa Alcott liked her heroes to reside because she could easily imagine the terrain to be very much like the farmland and veld that made up her world, and could, therefore, easily believe that it was possible for a hero to appear unexpectedly in her life.

Just then there was a loud bang, and Mrs. Louisa Alcott jumped off the bench, threw away the Mills & Boon, and upset the plate of koeksisters that had been comfortable on her lap. As she ran toward the house, she supposed that it would have been too much to ask to expect everyone to honor the ceasefire. She was halfway to the front door when she turned and saw a beige bakkie drive up the tarred road that led to the city. The car had curls of smoke unfurling from under its bonnet as it came to a controlled standstill at the side of the road just opposite the Alcotts' gate.

Mrs. Louisa Alcott stopped running and relaxed somewhat as she watched a man whom she swiftly recognized as Emil Coetzee step out of the bakkie. She was well aware that romance novels often begin in a similar fashion, throwing the hero and heroine together in surprising and seemingly improbable ways, so she began to entertain the possibility that this could be the beginning of something wonderful for her.

Emil Coetzee, with his blond hair, was not as dark as she liked her heroes to be, but he—in his denim shirt, khaki trousers, veldskoene and well-worn cowboy hat—was definitely dressed like her heroes. And there was never any denying that he was an exceptionally handsome man, even in the middle of his life. Mrs. Louisa Alcott watched him open and latch his bonnet in place before he became engulfed by the plumes of smoke that billowed from the car. Aware that he would probably need her help, she took a few steps toward him, and then remembered that she still had her pink, blue and yellow rollers in her hair, and was wearing a very comfortable but not very becoming or flattering yellow-and-white shift dress patterned with pink roses.

She watched Emil Coetzee open the tailgate of his car looking for things that could help him in his situation, and calculated that she had just enough time for a metamorphosis. She rushed into her house and made very quick work of changing into a navy-blue A-line dress with a white sailor's collar. The dress pronounced her breasts, cinched her waist and outlined her hips. She removed the curlers from her hair, brushed and teased it into Farrah Fawcett playfulness, put on a good and sensible pair of navy-blue shoes, applied enough makeup to make her glow appropriate for that time of day. Just as she was applying her lipstick to a pouted and kiss-ready mouth, she heard the engine of the bakkie start up again. Surely Emil Coetzee, a man of many obvious talents, could not have fixed his smoking engine so quickly?

When Mrs. Louisa Alcott emerged from the cocoon that was her home, she was a very beautiful butterfly, and when she looked at the road where the bakkie had been parked, all she saw was the trail of dust that the vehicle had left in its wake. Looking as pretty as a picture that had no one to admire it, she decided to make the best of a bad situation. She went to sit on her white bench, picked up the overturned Mills & Boon novel, and traced the gold, amber and brown lines that ran along its spine and under its title. Her hero had come and gone, but the war was over and there was still hope. Perhaps there would even be a happy ending for her.

———•———

Nothing truly surprising—something that she could not handle—ever happened in the small village nestled in one of the many almost-forgotten corners of the world that Dikeledi Moyana, the postman, called home, and she preferred it that way. She prized the equilibrium of her life above all else and was forever vigilant against anything that sought to disturb it.

Now that the war was over, it was a particular pride of hers that she had managed to defeat it and its determined disturbances by continuing to deliver the post throughout a countryside regularly traversed by both the guerrillas and the security forces. Dikeledi thought herself so much the unvanquished victor that when she heard and then saw a beige bakkie coming down the dusty road she was travelling on, she did not pay it much attention.

When the beige bakkie, driven by a white man, drove past, covering her in dust, she did not think much of it. When no sign of apology came her way, she did not think much of it. When the beige bakkie suddenly came to a stop… she did not know what to think. When the driver did not make any other move, Dikeledi decided to stop cycling toward the car and came to a halt at the side of the road.

For a long moment, as the dust settled, the bakkie and the bicycle were engaged in a standoff before the driver's window slowly rolled down. For probably the first time in her life something truly surprising—something that Dikeledi potentially could not handle—happened. Out of the window peeked a face that was familiar: Emil Coetzee, the Head of The Organization of Domestic Affairs. Was he going to do the unexpected and apologize for covering her with dust? And if he did speak to her, what was she supposed to say in response?

Thankfully, Emil Coetzee did not say anything. He just looked at her and looked at her and looked at her, as though seeing something that had him disbelieving. Not one to retreat, Dikeledi looked back at him and was very surprised by how very sad his eyes were. What business did such a powerful man have having sad eyes?

The thought belatedly came to her that perhaps he was looking at her and seeing not a postman in uniform, but the softness and gentleness of womanhood—the softness and gentleness that her mother, Daisy, had *leaned* toward men so readily and so casually. Was that what Emil Coetzee was waiting for her to do? To *lean* readily and casually toward him? Well, she, Dikeledi Moyana, would never *lean*.

Emil Coetzee opened his mouth as if to speak, and she was terrified of what he might say. But he shook his head, chuckled mirthlessly to himself, and then, as abruptly as he had started it all, ended it all by driving away and leaving her engulfed in a cloud of dust, for which he did not apologize.

Not knowing what else to do, Dikeledi shook her head, chuckled mirthlessly to herself, and then continued on a journey that had already begun.

———◆———

It had separately occurred to the two mujibhas—as one was perched on the gnarly branches of a tree and the other was balanced on the smooth surface of a kopje—that now that there was a ceasefire, they were without what the boys from the bush had called a *raison d'etre*. During the war, they had acted as spies for the villagers, and had alerted them when the boys from the bush and the security forces were approaching. They had also acted as the eyes and ears of both the boys from the bush and the security forces, as that was the nature of war. Although their lives had not been filled with many opportunities, they had been filled with purpose.

Before they had become mujibhas, they had herded cattle until the security forces had confiscated all the livestock from the village because it had been reported that the villagers always fed the boys from the bush when they passed by. Before that, they had attended the local school until the boys from the bush had destroyed it, saying that a colonial education did nothing but colonize the mind and prepare people for a life of subservience and servitude. Refusing to be rendered useless, the two industrious and enterprising boys had put together the knowledge that they had acquired from the lessons taught by the bush and the lessons taught at the school, and used them to become mujibhas and act as spies for the village.

They were both fifteen years old and had both been hoping, before the ceasefire had been announced, that in a few years they could join the boys in the bush and fight for their country. Therefore, the declaration of a ceasefire had taken away not only their reason for being, but their hopes and dreams for the future as well.

Naturally, when the mujibhas met, a few minutes later, to debrief each other on their separate reconnaissance missions, what they talked about was the seemingly unsustainable situation that the ceasefire had created for them. Having lived through a war, they had long reconciled themselves to the fact that the future for them could very well hold death; but at least death was something compared to the empty nothingness that now stretched before them and called itself their future. They were certain that the future, if it could not hold something, should hold the *promise* of something. With the ceasefire and the peace that accompanied it, their future could not even hold the promise of death.

Needless to say, they were very disappointed with the state of affairs that the ceasefire had created. With no other option presenting itself, they decided that they would have to go to the City of Kings and lose themselves in it the way everyone who lived there did. In sad consolation, together they climbed the modest hill that was the highest object in their environment so that they would have the best vantage point.

As they looked at the bleak horizon of a morning that was beginning to gather gray clouds, they saw a beige bakkie drive into view on a long and winding dusty dirt road. As it approached, their bush-smart eyes picked up that the driver was a white man. As the car neared and they saw the brown Stetson, they recognized the white man to be Emil Coetzee. They knew that Emil Coetzee was a very powerful man because his picture was often printed in *The Chronicle* newspaper. He seemed to be something of a hero for the white people.

From their position on the modest hill, the two mujibhas watched Emil Coetzee park his beige bakkie, climb out, and walk into the bush, toward the gathering gray clouds. They watched him walk on and on until he completely disappeared into the lush and green-gold elephant grass that heralded the arrival of the rainy season. It occurred to the two mujibhas, as they watched the elephant grass dance as it contained him, that Emil Coetzee was a man who knew exactly what to do with uncertain futures—he knew how to make them welcome him.

RUTHERFORD & JOSETH

———— ♦ ————

The bush telegraph let it be known that a white man, suspect-ed of being Emil Coetzee, had, the day before, walked into the veld and had, as yet, not walked out of it. The bush telegraph also stated with due delicacy that two leopards and a lion had been spotted in the vicinity. The worst was feared.

When the news reached Clement E. Rutherford, known to all as Rutherford, he was sitting in the glass enclosure that was his office in the Secret Intelligence Unit (SIU) section of the Central Intelligence building, and as he pondered what had been communicated to him, he began enthusiastically and spectacularly chewing down an HB pencil.

Rutherford doubted very much that the man who had walked into the veld was his lifelong friend, Emil Coetzee. He could not count the number of times, during the war, that the bush telegraph had claimed to have sighted Emil Coetzee doing something or other, usually truly Herculean, like sin-gle-handedly defeating a group of terrorists that had attacked a convoy he was in. Rutherford had always accommodated such stories because he understood that during times of war, people needed heroes wherever they could find them. But the war was over now, and Rutherford found that he could not be as good-humored and good-natured about this latest sighting as he had been about the earlier ones.

He attributed the multiple sightings of Emil Coetzee to two sources: mujibhas and housewives. The mujibha, having lived in the village all his life, and therefore having rarely seen a white man, naturally allowed his fancy to believe that whatever white man he saw must be Emil Coetzee. Emil Coetzee was, after all, the most famous white man in the City of Kings. Being rather photogenic, his picture often accompanied reports about the things that he had said, and during the war he had said plenty as The Head of The Organization. The mujibha, who spent many solitary hours in the bush, spying on everything and nothing, fearing for his own life, could be forgiven for seeing Emil Coetzee in almost every white man he came across, because otherwise every white man would have had to be the Prime Minister, who was the most famous white man in the country, and not even the mujibha could allow his imagination to run *that* wild.

The second source was just as innocent as the mujibha, and perhaps as easy to understand, but definitely not as easy for Rutherford to forgive. The savannah grasslands where most of these sightings allegedly took place were dotted with vast farms on hectares of land. On these vast farms there were homesteads. On these homesteads lived farm wives—harried, lonely, disappointed, sun-stricken—who were waiting for something exciting to happen in their lives. Emil Coetzee had a reputation with the ladies that had found its way to all the corners of the country, so if farm wives wanted to dream of having seen Emil Coetzee, they could and often did. Rutherford, believing that they should be contented with the husbands that they had, just chose not to forgive them for their dreaming.

The sound of something breaking interrupted Rutherford's thoughts, and he realized that the HB pencil in his hand had broken in half. He looked at the chewed-up pencil in disgust before throwing it in his waste-paper basket, where it joined another pencil that had had a similar fate befall it. Had the ceasefire made him tense, or had the production standards of

HB pencils dropped drastically over the war years? Rutherford suspected the latter. He shrugged as he accepted that there was nothing to be done for it. It was either this or he could and would go back to smoking a packet of Everests a day and die prematurely of the lung cancer his doctor had predicted. He had only stopped smoking because he did not want to give his doctor the satisfaction of being correct.

The pencils-for-cigarettes scheme had begun innocuously enough, but Rutherford knew it had long since got out of hand. He went through anything between seven and ten pencils per week, and no one in the office ever complained about it, let alone mentioned it—probably because they were all his subordinates. The only one who seemed to have something to say about his chomping ways was the stern Mrs. Belfry who "manned" the stores and supplies room. While she never said anything to him directly, she frowned very deeply at his weekly requisition slips for a box of twelve HB pencils. He agreed with her frown. Two pencils a week seemed perfectly reasonable. Perhaps three… maybe four? A gradual letting go always worked best, so he'd been told.

Had the pencil-chomping habit belonged to someone else in the office, of course Rutherford would not have been so kind as to offer silent observation. He would have found a lot to be mercilessly mirthful about, and he genuinely regretted that he did not have the opportunity to make jokes about this at someone else's expense. He had once thought of making the pencil-chomper someone else in the office, and sharing his jokes with Emil Coetzee in order to gauge how they landed. But he had remembered the rumors about Emil Coetzee's son, Everleigh, just in time to realize that the jokes would have been in very bad taste. Normally this would not have deterred Rutherford, but Everleigh had recently died fighting for his country, and even Rutherford knew there were some places that a man should never go.

Truth be told, even without the dead son, Emil Coetzee probably would not have laughed at the joke. Emil Coetzee had not laughed at one of Rutherford's jokes in a very long while. There had been a time when Emil Coetzee, then known simply as Coetzee, would have laughed at *all* of Rutherford's jokes. That had been at the Selous School for Boys when Coetzee, a scholarship student, had been struggling to fit in, and Rutherford had been his entry point into the upper echelons of the school's society. Given that Rutherford came from connected wealth, while Coetzee came from nothing more than a rented flat at the corner of Selborne Avenue and Borrow Street, there had been an imbalance in their friendship that had lasted throughout their school years and into adulthood. It had only ended after Coetzee married Kuki Sedgwick and became Emil Coetzee, the Head of The Organization of Domestic Affairs. Emil Coetzee—a man so important that everyone called him by his full name.

Over the past twenty-five years, Rutherford oftentimes found himself keenly missing that initial friendship and its great imbalance. It was with this missing feeling that he picked up his phone's handset and dialed Emil Coetzee's number at The Organization. He would make a joke about this latest sighting, and Emil Coetzee would surely find something funny in being reported missing when in fact he was sitting in his office, as happy as every man in the savannah had a right to be.

On the other end of the line, a voice with a slight tremor informed Rutherford that Emil Coetzee had resigned from work on the day of the ceasefire and had not returned. The reticence of the voice proved to Rutherford that there was more to the story than was being disclosed, and so he informed the voice that he was with the SIU, and that he wanted to know everything about Emil Coetzee's resignation that the voice knew.

"The girl who does the cleaning found a note under his desk just this morning. The note read, 'Will not be back. Find new head.' It was dated 21 December and initialled E.C. The note was definitely written in his hand," the voice informed Rutherford.

As he listened, Rutherford absent-mindedly placed the handset in the crook of his neck and sharpened an HB pencil in the rotary sharpener mounted on his desk. He was of the strongly held opinion that only a savage would start chomping away at an unsharpened pencil. "So when the man did not show up for work yesterday, where the bloody hell did you all think he was?" he demanded.

"Well since the boy... his son, Everleigh... there have been quite a few days missed," the tremulous voice informed him.

Rutherford hung up the phone without a thank-you or a goodbye because he felt that The Organization did not deserve any gratitude for obviously mishandling the whole Emil Coetzee affair—whatever it was. As soon as Emil Coetzee had not arrived at work as expected, they should have looked for him; and after not finding him, they should have immediately notified the SIU. That was the protocol for dealing with the absences of high-level officials. But, of course, The Organization, always the renegade, always imagining itself to be a law unto itself and not just another branch of the government, had seen it fit to do things its own way.

Rutherford turned in his chair and looked through the glass enclosure of his office at the twenty men under his direct command. All of them were keeping themselves busy with various tasks, but none of them were sitting comfortably at their desks because they were always prepared for something to happen. Rutherford was proud of what he saw. There were many signs of being ill at ease: legs pumping up and down, chairs swiveling in comforting arcs, fingers periodically running through hair. He had done this. He had created this atmosphere.

It was how the SIU liked its operatives—agitated, on edge, and more than a little uncertain. This was a brilliant tactic because it made every intelligence operative eager to demonstrate his allegiance and commitment. Anyone who entertained the thought of going against the grain of the unit did not entertain it for too long, because they were never allowed to feel as if they could get away with anything.

Rutherford's perusal of his surroundings stopped when his eyes landed on the only man who did not seem agitated or uncertain *enough*—Joseth Maraire. Joseth was not busying himself the way the other men in the office were, nor did he look ill at ease as he pivoted in too comfortable an arc in his chair. It was obvious to anyone looking at him that he was not doing any work. Rutherford was both irritated and intrigued.

Joseth had not always espoused this attitude. For many years, he had been as nervous as the rest of them and just as eager to please. Even after many jokes had been made about his misspelt first name, he had insisted that everyone call him Joseth and not Maraire. But he had definitely been more at ease and less eager to please after the country had elected its first black president. Now, when Rutherford's eyes met Joseth's, Joseth returned his gaze and held it, daring Rutherford to be the one to look away first.

Joseth was a very ambitious man and, even in his agitated days, had never bothered to hide this. It was not in Rutherford's disposition to quash such ambition; it was best to watch closely and see what actions and compromises such ambition would lead to. As the saying went, keep your friends close—and your enemies up your arse. It was Rutherford's sudden plan to keep Joseth closer than he had ever kept a black man. With a motion of his sharpened pencil, Rutherford beckoned for Joseth to join him.

Joseth stood up immediately but sauntered over to Rutherford's office with his hands in his pockets. Everything that Joseth did seemed premeditated. He had stood up immediately so that Rutherford could not reprimand him for insubordination. He walked leisurely to show that while he respected authority, he was still his own man; and, more specifically, to show that although he understood and appreciated that Rutherford was his superior, he was by no means, in turn, Rutherford's inferior. There was absolutely nothing that could be faulted in Joseth's actions, except perhaps that he seemed to be too much at ease.

Joseth entered Rutherford's office and removed his hands from his pockets and folded his arms, waiting. He would not speak until he had been addressed. This, too, was calculated on Joseth's part. Most African intelligence operatives more often than not became tongue-tied, obsequious caricatures as they shuffled, stammered and shifted before a white superior—growing agitated to the point of becoming almost incomprehensible. Joseth set himself apart from these men by being deferential without fawning.

Rutherford motioned for Joseth to close the door behind him and Joseth did so. All the busy eyes in the office surreptitiously stole glances at the glass enclosure, one eye on the tasks at hand and another eye on whatever fate was about to visit itself upon Joseth.

"Just got a call," Rutherford said. "Apparently a man thought to be Emil Coetzee walked into the veld and has not, as yet, walked out of it."

"What does that make, the fourth sighting of Emil Coetzee in as many weeks?" Joseth said, not attempting to make it a joke. He continued to stand because Rutherford had not offered him a seat.

"Yes. But I called The Organization, and they informed me that Emil Coetzee has not been to work since the ceasefire was announced. That he, in fact, seems to have resigned from his position."

"I see," Joseth said, his eyes not giving away exactly what it was that he saw.

"I don't need to tell you how delicate this matter is."

"Of course."

"I have called you in because I need to work with someone I can trust on this."

"Of course."

Rutherford stood up and placed the pencil back in the box. Surely he could handle whatever came next without finding comfort in a sharpened pencil. He motioned for Joseth to leave the office, and followed him out. He was all but out of the door when he went back to his desk and picked up the sharpened HB pencil and placed it carefully in his breast pocket. Just in case.

Rutherford and Joseth followed the directions contained within the bush telegraph until they found themselves parking their government-issued bakkie outside the first homestead of a middle-of-nowhere village that lay on the outskirts of the Matopos National Park. Without being summoned, two mujibhas materialized, seemingly out of nowhere, and led Rutherford and Joseth to the beige bakkie that was parked at the edge of far-reaching bush. The two mujibhas then vanished into the veld surrounding them before they could be asked any questions. It was moments like these that reminded Rutherford that the wild savannah was home to more than just wildlife.

The beige bakkie looked very much like Emil Coetzee's,

but to be sure, Rutherford opened the glove compartment of the vehicle, which had not been locked by whoever had parked it there. Before he opened the glove compartment, Rutherford patted his breast pocket: one, to make sure that the sharpened pencil was still there; and two, to steady a hand he strongly suspected was trembling. In the glove compartment was a driver's license belonging to Emil Coetzee. Happy to see that his hand was stable, Rutherford handed the carefully folded piece of paper to Joseth, who unfolded it, read it, and handed it back to Rutherford without saying anything. Rutherford placed the driver's license back in the glove compartment, straightened out of the bakkie, and closed the door. Both men looked at the veld surrounding them. Besides the village behind them, all there was, as far as the eye could see, was lush and green-gold elephant grass, dotted here and there with stunted trees that were reaching out to each other.

Although it was well after three o'clock in the afternoon, the sun in the sky was still punishing, and probably in its most unfriendly position. There was not the slightest hint that within the hour, everything would start cooling down as the day thankfully welcomed dusk. This type of unforgiving heat probably meant that the meager rainfall the region had enjoyed thus far would constitute the entire rainy season. The lush and green-gold elephant grass would soon succumb to a drought that would render it dry, blond and brittle.

When Joseth opened their government-issued bakkie and handed Rutherford a rifle and a bottle of water, Rutherford immediately checked that the rifle was loaded with ammunition. There had, after all, been two leopards and a lion sighted in this very stretch of bush. He took off his boonie hat and then poured a bit of water over his head to wet his hair and shoulders. This precaution would make his journeying under the scorching sun less insufferable. Joseth had no such ritual before venturing forth, and so he merely waited and watched Rutherford. He did not even take a few sips of water from his water bottle.

Rutherford and Joseth surprised each other when they collectively sighed before heading into the veld, which at their point of entry welcomed them with scrubs of clumped grass and thorn bushes. Nothing grew beyond knee-level here, and that was how the bush encouraged people to venture forth. Rutherford and Joseth stayed close together as their ears listened for every sound, and their eyes scanned the horizon for any movement. The thorn bushes happily and eagerly nipped and pricked their calves through their pulled-up khaki socks. When the savannah grass began to reach their waists, their movements changed and they slowly started to rotate a full 360 degrees of ever-widening circumference.

It was in mid-rotation, when they were about five meters apart, that Joseth saw it—a brown, well-worn Stetson, lying on the ground not far away. Joseth understood many things: he understood that Rutherford and Emil Coetzee were friends, and that if any discoveries were to be made here, Rutherford would like to be the one making them.

It had been almost imperceptible, and would have been to the untrained eye, but earlier Joseth had noticed the slight tremor in Rutherford's hand when he had handed him the driver's license. Joseth understood that although it had occurred to Rutherford that his friend had met a very sticky end, he had not, as yet, fully comprehended this possibility; which was why, in order to calm and reassure himself, his hand kept patting his breast pocket. Understanding all this and much more, Joseth allowed them to make another rotation so that it would be Rutherford who would discover the Stetson. But Rutherford did not, and therefore, after three more rotations, Joseth was forced to say, "I think I have found something," before going to retrieve the Stetson.

As Joseth handed Rutherford the Stetson, Rutherford had to stop himself from saying, "Took you bloody long enough." Rutherford had long seen the Stetson, but had decided to give Joseth an impromptu test, which he had almost failed. Rutherford decided not to say anything because he knew his voice would betray the anger he felt, and Joseth, not knowing the true source of the anger, would attribute it either to his having found the hat first, or to his having left the word "sir" out of the sentence "I think I have found something." What was the point of anger if the person it was directed at did not understand where it was coming from?

A few months, a few weeks ago even, such considerations would not have crossed Rutherford's mind. He would have vented his anger without giving a damn as to how comprehensible it was, as long as it made his subordinate know and feel how subordinate he was. However, a few days ago, there had been a ceasefire; and, in preparation for the ceasefire and eventual independence, the government had, some months earlier, started putting together meetings, seminars and conferences, all designed to teach government officials and civil servants a new language and ethos that would ensure that the different races got along well together and would be able to build and realize a peaceable future country. In these meetings, seminars and conferences, Rutherford was informed that things were changing and that his attitudes to, his relations with, and his expectations of Africans would have to change as well.

An expert—who over the years, like Emil Coetzee, had garnered a reputation as a man who "knows the African"— had been a guest-speaker at one such conference a few weeks prior, and he had stressed that words such as *kaffir*, *boy*, *madala*, and *bafana* no longer had a place in the lexicon of the workplace. That conference had been what... two, three weeks ago, and Emil Coetzee had definitely been very much alive then. And now here was Rutherford, holding his Stetson in his hands. Under the severe savannah sun, it did not take long for a man divested of his hat to start singing songs his mother had taught him.

Without warning, Rutherford doubled over and emptied the contests of his stomach in one far-spraying spew. Damn it all, he had just contaminated the scene, and spectacularly so, in front of a subordinate, Joseth Maraire, the man who wanted to take his place. When Rutherford stood upright, the air suddenly felt cooler and the sun actually felt like a salve on the skin.

Rutherford was just about to apologize, which was something he would have never thought of doing before the meetings, seminars and conferences. However, a young man with a Jewish last name, horn-rimmed glasses and the title "Dr." before his name had, just the day before, given a lecture on the importance of apologies. He had stated that apologies were necessary to the sustenance of any relationship, and that being able to apologize was a sign not of weakness but of strength. Real men—real leaders—knew the power of an apology and how to use it effectively. Perhaps, knowing full well that many in his audience would not believe him, the young man had presented a collection of examples of leaders apologising at crucial moments in history. Rutherford suspected that the collection was not very robust, and that the two examples that had actually been shared were probably all that there were. He did not want to apologize because he felt that it would be a sign of strength; he wanted to apologize because he knew that this move would take Joseth by surprise and perhaps make him think less of Rutherford, which would then make Joseth reveal more of his exact intentions.

Before Rutherford could utter a word, Joseth said, not looking at him, "It is getting cool. It will be dusk soon. It is probably best to head back."

Rutherford realized that he had not needed to apologize in order for Joseth to think less of him. Joseth, in suggesting that they return to the bakkie, had shifted the balance of power between them. He had spoken carefully and calmly, thinking he was giving nothing away, but Rutherford knew that not all power struggles had to be violent.

Rutherford was certain that a few months, a few weeks ago even, Joseth would have said "sir" at the end of every statement or question. He wondered, as he followed him back to the government-issued bakkie, if Joseth was attending meetings, seminars and conferences run by people who believed that they "knew the European" and encouraged men like Joseth to remove words like *sir, baas, picaninny baas* and *madam* from their vocabulary because such words no longer had a place in their workplace lexicon.

When Rutherford and Joseth arrived at their bakkie, they found the village headman, the two mujibhas and several other villagers waiting for them.

"Emil Coetzee go into the bush without weapon, sir... These two boys, they are seeing it." The headman addressed Rutherford directly and all but ignored Joseth. As he spoke, the two mujibhas and the gathered villagers nodded in solemn acquiescence. "He go into the bush like one... like so... like this," the headman said, putting up his index finger to stress the aloneness and the vulnerability of the man who had walked into the bush. "He is not having any weapon to protect himself. He just go like one... like so... like this. These boys they are seeing him... and we are waiting a long time for him to come back. We are waiting and waiting and waiting and he is not coming back and he is not coming back and he is not coming back... He is not coming back, sir. He go like one... like so... like this. These boys, they are seeing him do this thing."

Rutherford and Joseth left, having promised the villagers that they would return early the next morning with a larger contingent of men. They would come to investigate in full what had happened to the white man who had walked into the bush without a weapon. The villagers were ordered not to tell anyone else that they suspected that the white man was Emil Coetzee. They were strictly forbidden to go into the bush until the investigation was over. They were reminded, as though they were not the ones who had made the discovery in the first place, that there were at least two leopards and a lion in that bush.

For good measure, Rutherford told the villagers to beware. He pointed particularly at the two mujibhas and said, "Basopa, you hear me, you two—" He had been just about to say "bobbejane," but even though this particular word had not been brought up in the meetings, seminars and conferences, Rutherford strongly suspected that with the country gearing up for majority rule, it would not do to call black boys baboons. But what else did one call them? Not knowing what else to say, Rutherford let his warning hang in uncertainty.

———•———

If they had found any other type of hat, the ever-popular boonie hat, for example, there might have been some hope that the man who had walked into the veld had not been Emil Coetzee. But there was only one man in the City of Kings who wore a Stetson. Even when they had been boys together at the Selous School for Boys, Coetzee had worn a Stetson. However, that was the only familiar detail in this whole affair. It was not like Emil Coetzee to walk into the bush unprepared. In Rutherford and Coetzee's hunting heyday, their glorious twenties, before the arrival of Kuki Sedgwick and the creation of Emil Coetzee, before every hunt Coetzee would drape an ammunition belt like a sash over his shoulders, grab his rifle and then carefully place his Stetson on top of his head. The Stetson on top of his head was what let it be known that Coetzee was ready for the world and whatever it threw at him.

As he looked at the Stetson that Joseth had placed on his lap, Rutherford tried to reconcile the Emil Coetzee he knew well with this man who had gone into the bush unprepared for its obvious dangers... like one... like so... like this. Who was this man who had walked into the savannah unarmed, this man who had let go of the one thing that defined him—his Stetson?

Rutherford waited for the right moment to turn to Joseth and say, "It seems rather likely that the white man who walked into the bush and did not walk out of it is indeed Emil Coetzee." Joseth gave a slight nod from the passenger seat.

Rutherford looked at him before saying, cautiously, "What do you think happened?"

"I think Emil Coetzee walked into the bush," Joseth said.

For a long few minutes, Rutherford thought that that was all that Joseth had to say on the subject. Was he being facetious? Insubordinate? Downright rude? All three? Rutherford was on the verge of fury. But then Joseth added the word that changed everything: "I think Emil Coetzee walked into the bush *deliberately*."

Now that someone else had confirmed his own suspicions that Emil Coetzee had walked into the bush intentionally unarmed, knowing... wanting... willing something terrible to happen to him, Rutherford could not help but reach into his breast pocket and retrieve the sharpened HB pencil. This whole Emil Coetzee business was such a delicate matter, Rutherford acknowledged as he chomped down on the pencil and felt himself gradually relax and focus. He could never adequately explain to anyone else the satisfaction that he felt as his incisors broke through first the thin veneer of black and red paint, and then the resisting hardness of the wood.

Rutherford supposed he could understand his friend's actions, supposed he could understand why a man like Emil Coetzee would not want to live under the majority rule that would most definitely come with independence. But there was more to it than that. It was also Rutherford's job to understand what his friend's actions meant for more than just Emil Coetzee; he had to understand what the loss of Emil Coetzee would mean for those he had left behind—not just his family and friends, but even more so, the people who had turned him into a hero and a symbol, the people who saw him everywhere. Rutherford knew that Emil Coetzee had not been thinking of these people—nor, come to that, of his family and friends—when he decided to walk into the bush.

Rutherford knew this because he knew that his friend had never been one to see or fully appreciate the bigger picture. He just would not have seen how vital his presence would be in the next few months, years even, when people would need a sense of stability and continuity. Emil Coetzee could be an incredibly selfish man, and by choosing to walk into the bush... like one... like so... like this instead of choosing to walk into the future with the rest of the country, he had committed what was probably his most selfish act.

Rutherford chewed on the pencil a few times more before he said to Joseth, "Nature does not like a vacuum."

There was a very long silence, which made Rutherford doubt if Joseth understood the significance of what he had said. Did he even know what the expression meant? Rutherford tried a different approach. "We cannot have Emil Coetzee walking into the bush deliberately. Suicide by misadventure—

we cannot have that. Emil Coetzee was a hero to many; he is a hero to many. We are in the middle of a ceasefire that not everyone has adhered to."

Rutherford spoke with a confidence that a recent editorial in *The Sunday News* had given him. The editorial had cautioned, *"Of course they will not cease immediately, even assuming that the Patriotic Front leaders put all their efforts into the ceasefire exercise. Hatred, psychopathy and greed cannot be removed by the stroke of a pen; there are bound to be those who will be reluctant to lay down their arms. Additionally, there are too many renegades at large to whom banditry has become a way of life; they are likely to be responsible for incidents for some time."* The newspaper had already primed the people for the story that Rutherford was preparing to feed them. All he needed was Joseth's collaboration.

From the corner of his eye, Rutherford watched how Joseth was taking this. There was no discernible response. Perhaps he had not been clear enough, and so Rutherford said, "Emil Coetzee walked into the bush and unfortunately came up against one of these men who has not adhered to the ceasefire. A trained bandit… a terrorist." This time Rutherford looked at Joseth directly, trying to force him to respond in some visible way.

Again, his companion gave nothing away, and continued looking resolutely through the windshield. After a long moment, Joseth said, "Emil Coetzee was *lured* into the bush by a terrorist who still has not adhered to the ceasefire." Having made this pronouncement, Joseth rolled down the window, put out his arm and nonchalantly tapped his fingers against the door to the tune of "The Grand Old Duke of York".

Lured: that single word changed so much. Rutherford was deeply impressed in spite of himself. However, Joseth proved that he could do even better—by offering up a name for the terrorist. "Emil Coetzee was lured into the bush by Golide Gumede," Joseth said, his fingers still tap-tap-tapping the tune on the door.

The fiction was so perfect that it astounded Rutherford. He looked at Joseth as though seeing him for the first time. Yes, he was ambitious and did not hide the fact that he wanted to take Rutherford's place, but perhaps he was also a very intelligent intelligence man.

Golide Gumede was the best choice… a brilliant choice. A terrorist who had for years operated successfully under the radar of the security forces and become a general menace to society, Golide Gumede had eventually shot down a Vickers Viscount passenger plane nicknamed Hunyani. That single act had resulted in his becoming the most sought-after enemy of the state.

Wartime was not the time for subtleties of expression or nuanced rhetoric. Emil Coetzee, using the hyperbolic language that had become the order of the day, had demanded that the head of Golide Gumede be brought to him on a silver platter. The security forces, certain men in The Organization and some SIU operatives had heeded Emil Coetzee's call. Whether they had taken his words literally or metaphorically, only the successful capture of Golide Gumede would tell.

However, for over a year, Golide Gumede had proved elusive. Now he would play into Rutherford and Joseth's fiction perfectly because he had not, as yet, obeyed the ceasefire. He was still at large, roaming the countryside with an AK-47 and a sure-footed idea of himself always at the ready.

"Golide Gumede lures Emil Coetzee into the bush." Not only did the sentence have a nice ring to it—the kind of catchy sentence that could become a newspaper headline—but it encompassed so much. It was also, and this was the best part, incredibly credible. Of course Golide Gumede would want to take revenge on the man who had ordered that he be hunted and slaughtered like an animal. It made perfect sense that Golide Gumede would lure Emil Coetzee into the bush. It also made perfect sense that Emil Coetzee would go into the bush to meet with Golide Gumede, because Emil Coetzee had notoriously always courted danger—and because he must have felt some humiliation at not being able to capture the man who had become his nemesis. The more Rutherford thought of the story, the more it acquired the ring of truth.

"Golide Gumede lures Emil Coetzee into the bush." That was just the sort of headline that would stop white people in their tracks. A lot of whites, not wanting to witness the advent of majority rule and the independence of the country, were emigrating; and Rutherford believed that a headline such as this would make them see what he saw—that there was still so much to stay and fight for.

Looking straight at the winding road ahead, still tapping "The Grand Old Duke of York", and as though having read his thoughts, Joseth informed Rutherford, "Some people would like to see Golide Gumede as the Prime Minister of the new independent country."

Rutherford looked at Joseth incredulously and almost laughed. The very idea was ludicrous, but there was absolutely no mirth on Joseth's face; and that was when Joseth told him of another Golide Gumede—the Golide Gumede whose great escapes had become legendary and turned him into a mythological hero for many villagers in the country. This Golide Gumede could shape-shift, disappear into nothingness, hide in plain sight. This Golide Gumede was a story that they told around the fire at night. This Golide Gumede was a dream in their hearts and minds. This Golide Gumede was the promise of the much-awaited and anticipated future.

Rutherford sobered up as he realized that if one man's

hero could be another man's villain, then the converse was also true: one man's villain could be another man's hero.

Rutherford found himself wondering who Joseth's heroes were. *Did they share the same heroes? Were their reasons for setting up Golide Gumede the same? Did it matter?*

THE VILLAGERS

As soon as the two men left, the villagers congregated at Chief Cele Mkhize's homestead for an impromptu meeting. Those two cannot be trusted, they said. Did you see how the black one never looked anyone in the eye? A man like that has too much to hide. And what was going on with the white one? Why was his hand always fluttering over his chest like that? Some kind of nervous tic, probably. Nervous men were not to be trusted. And what business did a white man have being nervous? Besides, they were not policemen, they were intelligence boys. You could tell this not only by the fact that they did not wear uniforms, but also by the fact that they did not introduce themselves or provide their names at any point. They always demanded everything and gave nothing, those intelligence boys.

The wireless said, every hour of every day, that there had been an end to hostilities; that there was currently a ceasefire after an agreement had been reached at Lancaster House in London; and that there would most likely be majority rule and independence in the very near future. The voices on the wireless sounded optimistic and almost certain about the future, but they would, wouldn't they, given that radio stations were owned by the government?

The battle-battered and war-weary villagers found it difficult to share in the hope for a better future. They had heard it all before. How many talks and agreements had there been over the years? Earlier in the year, those of them deemed eligible had been corralled and forced to vote for the country's first black president. He would, they had been informed, by his mere presence, bring an end to the war. He would work well with the whites and ensure that, for the first time in the country's history, things would run fairly and smoothly between the races. The villagers had obediently voted for the man they had been told to vote for, and he had indeed been elected as the country's first-ever black president. But then the boys in the bush had refused to recognize him as such and had chosen instead to call him a puppet of the white minority regime. The international community, in seeming agreement with the boys in the bush, had refused to recognize the legitimacy of the new president, and the war had raged on.

When the boys from the bush arrived after the elections, they punished the villagers for having been so gullible as to vote for an obvious buffoon. They made all the men who had voted lower their trousers, lie on their bellies and place their hands above their heads. They made the rest of the villagers form a circle around the men. The boys from the bush then whipped the naked buttocks of the men as they lay there in front of their wives and children. They whipped them with sjamboks until their behinds were not only patterned with welts but also raw with broken skin and oozing with blood. The boys from the bush had punished every man who had voted, including Chief Cele Mkhize. And they wanted to be the ones to inherit the earth, these boys who had no respect for authority… or their elders… or their traditions… or their own people? Afterwards, without a hint of irony, these very same boys who had beaten the men had asked the women to show their support for the liberation struggle by cooking for them, which the women had done. After eating, the boys from the bush had built a huge fire and forced the hurt men, the harassed women, and the hungry children to dance around it and sing songs of liberation—songs of freedom.

The boys from the bush, of necessity, conducted most of their dealings with the villagers clandestinely, under the cover of darkness. When the day broke, the boys from the bush would be long gone, but the day would almost inevitably bring with it a visit from the security forces who, through the bush telegraph, had heard that the villagers had entertained the boys from the bush. The villagers would be reminded, as though they could ever forget, that the boys from the bush were terrorists, and that to support them in any way was to break many of the many laws of the country. Those who broke the laws of the country had to be punished. The security forces' punishments ranged from humiliating to deadly, and the villagers never knew what to expect from their government—humiliation or death.

So when the ceasefire was announced, and the future spoken of with such enthusiasm, the villagers, having long been treated as fools, could be excused for choosing to be angels instead.

And now, of all things, they had to figure out how best to deal with the intelligence boys. If we are not careful, they will lay whatever has happened to Emil Coetzee at our feet, the villagers said. Did you notice how they were surprised when we called Emil Coetzee by his name? Do they honestly think that we do not know what Emil Coetzee looks like? Everyone in the country knows exactly what Emil Coetzee looks like; he is like the Prime Minister—his picture is in the newspaper almost every day.

Why do you think they left the beige bakkie behind? They did not even take the driver's license in the glove compartment. They took the hat they found in the bush, though. What does one do with another man's hat once it is off his head?

You know these intelligence boys have more tricks up

their sleeves than sense. Emil Coetzee walked into the bush and did not walk out of it. Two intelligence boys walked into the bush and came out holding a hat and the promise that they would return the following day with a larger crew. We need to act fast, the villagers decided. We need to tell Chief Inspector Spokes Moloi what has happened.

Chief Inspector Spokes Moloi was the only lawman that the villagers trusted completely. Spokes Moloi was one of them—well, not "one of them" in the truest meaning of that phrase, but one of them in the sense that he had married into the village. The villagers' chests puffed with pride whenever they thought (and they had this thought often) of how Spokes Moloi had gloriously risen through the ranks of the BSAP to become the country's first black chief inspector. He would have risen higher, they were certain, been Chief Superintendent, Commissioner even, had his skin color permitted.

They had every reason to be proud of him because Spokes Moloi had begun his illustrious career in this very village by successfully solving The Case of the Missing Would-Be Headman. From the moment the case had been solved, he had become a hero in their eyes and proven himself to be a man of bravery, integrity and intelligence. At least, that was how the villagers chose to remember it.

By the time they had finished singing Spokes Moloi's praises and basking in the perpetual glow of his grace, they realized that it was almost five o'clock in the evening. If they rushed, they could find the shopkeeper of the Idlazonke General Goods and Bottle Store still open for business. They all turned to Joli Msimanga, who not only had the most reliable car in the village but was also Spokes Moloi's brother- in-law, and, as such, deserved to play a prominent role in whatever unfolded. Chief Cele Mkhize, Joli Msimanga and the two mujibhas piled into Msimanga's Ford Mustang, which had traveled better days. Lurching here and there and raising a lot of dust in its wake, the car arrived at the shop just as the shopkeeper was pulling down the iron grille that protected the goods from potential theft. The two mujibhas, ignoring the shopkeeper who held his arms outstretched and waved the palms of his hands in the universal gesture of refusal, rolled under the safety grille, entered the shop and started ordering all manner of sweets they had absolutely no intention of paying for: apricots, fudge, everlastings, liquorice, jelly babies, Red Mouth sherbet, double-deckers and more. When Chief Cele Mkhize and Joli Msimanga approached the store, the shopkeeper verbalized what he had long been gesturing: "The shop is closed. I cannot serve you. I have already locked the cash register."

"There is no problem then, because it is your phone that we are wanting to use," Chief Cele Mkhize informed him.

"The shop is closed. The phone is in the shop; therefore, you cannot use the phone."

"Don't talk to the headman as though you are talking to just any man," Joli Msimanga warned the shopkeeper.

"I do not work for the headman. I work for Silas Mthimkhulu. I follow his rules. If he says that I should lock up the shop at five o'clock sharp and not allow anyone entry after that time, then that is exactly what I will do."

"This is an emergency, man!" Chief Cele Mkhize said, trying another tactic.

"An emergency? What has happened?" the shopkeeper said, betraying himself by being too eager for information. The villagers had long suspected him of being the spy among them—the sell-out—the one who called the security forces and told them that the boys from the bush had been in the village and politicized the people, while forgetting to mention that he too had danced around the fire and sung the liberation songs the loudest. The villagers did not have any real evidence that the shopkeeper actually communicated with the security forces. What they knew was that the shopkeeper owned a walkie-talkie and no one else in their community did, so it stood to reason that he was using it to communicate with the security forces. He probably was the one who had informed the intelligence boys that Emil Coetzee had walked into the bush and not walked out of it.

While they would never trust the shopkeeper further than they could spit, the villagers had long reconciled themselves to the fact that they needed his presence amongst them. He was not without his uses. Now Chief Cele Mkhize and Joli Msimanga both regretted not having had the foresight to bring a woman with them. The shopkeeper, it was a well-known secret, was very susceptible to the flutter of a skirt and the buxom curve of an ample bosom. He liked nothing more than to have the loneliness of his days alleviated by the entry into his store of a shy giggle and the scent of Lux soap mingled with cocoa butter.

Having no one soft and supple with whom to bribe the shopkeeper, they realized there was nothing else to be done but drive all the way to the City of Kings and talk to Spokes Moloi in person. Chief Cele Mkhize, Joli Msimanga and the two mujibhas left the shop and the rather self-satisfied shopkeeper behind. They all looked at the road-weary Ford Mustang and hoped and prayed that it would see them through to their journey's end.

Luckily, at that very moment, a near-miracle occurred. Dikeledi Moyana, resplendent in her postman's uniform, was peddling up a dust storm on her way to deliver what they all needed most. The cuffs of her trousers were pegged, the sleeves of her shirt were rolled up, and the brim of her cap was set low, shielding her eyes from the setting sun... and sitting on the bicycle's carrier, like a queen on a throne, was Noma, her face freshly cold-creamed, her skin freshly cocoa-buttered, her afro freshly glycerined. Both women squinted through the dust raised by the bicycle on the road as they came closer to accomplishing their mission.

When Noma alighted with a shy giggle, the flutter of her A-line skirt in the cool evening breeze brought forward the shopkeeper, who no longer had a care about closing the shop and doing what Silas Mthimkhulu had told him to do. All he wanted to do now was to speak his insupportable loneliness to the twin curves of Noma's bosom.

As the sun began its final journey toward setting, Chief Cele Mkhize and Joli Msimanga triumphantly lifted the iron grille, freely entered the shop and telephoned Spokes Moloi. The two mujibhas went on the lookout for any unwanted visitors. And, for its part, the Ford Mustang was more than happy not to have its roadworthiness further tested.

Dikeledi knew that it was the wont of men not to thank women for saving the day, and so she thanked herself by entering the shop and helping herself to an ice-cold Castle Lager, a family-size packet of beef-and-tomato crisps and a Swiss-army knife that she had long been wanting to buy. As she stood in the shop's doorway, downed her beer and watched the sun become a great ball of furious fire in an amber and purple sky, she knew that all would be right with the world because she had made it so.

SPOKES

———————•———————

Internal mail was notoriously slow at the Western Commonage Police Station, and that was because the mail passed through two or three hands on its journey from the pigeonhole to its recipient. First someone had to check that there were no letter bombs, and then someone had to check that there were no coded messages, and then someone had to deliver the mail. Now while most officers understood taking such precautions with external mail, very few understood why internal mail had to be treated the same way. The official word—from the highest office in the land—was that since the country was at war, enemies were everywhere and vigilance was key. The country was no longer at war, but vigilance was apparently still key.

Knowing all this, Spokes had given his application for retirement enough time to go through the necessary protocols before finding its way to its final destination. So, when he entered the station for the twelve to six shift on 23 December, he knew that a visit to the Chief Superintendent's office was imminent.

The day began as expected. The Desk Sergeant greeted him with, "Is it Memorandum?"

"Not even close," Spokes responded, making his way to the Sergeants' Office.

Just then Chief Superintendent Griffiths intercepted Spokes's progress and steered him in the opposite direction. "Ah, there you are, Moloi… just the man. Just the man. Follow me, if you please." Spokes followed the Chief Superintendent to his more spacious office at the other end of the corridor. There they found the Assistant Commissioner and the Deputy Commissioner, sipping tea and evidently waiting for Spokes.

Spokes knew what this was about, of course, and the letter on the Chief Superintendent's desk confirmed it.

"The boys have been razzing Spokes about his middle name again," the Chief Superintendent told the Assistant Commissioner and the Deputy Commissioner as he prepared two cups of piping-hot, good, strong Taganda tea. The Assistant Commissioner and the Deputy Commissioner both smiled at Spokes genially as the Chief Superintendent poured a dash of milk into both cups, added two lumps of sugar to one cup and one lump to the other, stirred the contents with the same teaspoon, placed the teacups on two saucers and then nestled three lemon creams on one saucer and one lemon cream on the other. Handing Spokes the saucer with the single lemon cream, the Chief Superintendent said, "After all these years, I think I know how you like it."

"You do, sir," Spokes said accepting the cup of tea.

"Have any of them ever guessed Moustache?" the Assistant Commissioner asked, mirth all over his face.

Spokes did not say anything, but he twirled one end of his waxed moustache before taking a bite of the lemon cream. His three superiors laughed a little too heartily, and that was when Spokes began to suspect that the day would not contain any of what he had expected.

"I could put the boys out of their misery, tell them what that M stands for once and for all," the Chief Superintendent said, taking a seat and gesturing for Spokes to take his.

"Please don't, sir," Spokes said as he sat down. "I was rather thinking I would tell them on my last day, as I walked out the door—make a grand gesture out of it."

As Spokes spoke, the three men exchanged glances and

the atmosphere in the room changed a little.

The Chief Superintendent harrumphed before saying to Spokes, "The boys and I are going to Kariba for the holidays. A spot of fishing before the New Year. We would have invited you, of course, but we were thinking that you should act as Chief Superintendent in my absence."

So that was what they had been up to. Spokes contemplated the three men, and they all looked like Cheshire cats that had got the cream.

"I see, sir," Spokes said.

"I am glad you do, Moloi. I am glad you do," the Chief Superintendent said.

His three superiors, looking very pleased with themselves, smiled at Spokes and then got up to leave. On their way out, they all made sure to shake his hand as though in congratulation.

And that had been very much that.

Spokes, his life suddenly trapped in novelty, paced around the Chief Superintendent's office. He looked at the opened envelope on the desk—the envelope that contained his application for retirement. He understood, of course, that as soon as he had agreed to sit in the Chief Superintendent's office during his absence, he had tacitly agreed to rethink his retirement and consider a promotion instead. He also understood that by entering into this unspoken agreement with the Chief Superintendent, he was on the verge of disappointing the lovely Loveness for the first time in their twenty-seven, long-loving years of wedded bliss.

And so, for much of the afternoon, Spokes had busied himself by moving the contents of his desk to the Chief Superintendent's office and by responding to every variation of the question "Do you really think you will become the country's first black Chief Superintendent?" that the sergeants and several officers asked. Finally, having done all he could do to put off doing what he must, Spokes started pacing as he tried to think of ways to break the news to Loveness.

His pacing soon found its rhythm. Man leads with right. Forward. Side. Close. Back. Side. Close. Forward. Side. Close. Back. Side. Close. One. Two. Three. One. Two. Three.

It was as his pacing turned to dancing that the solution to his problem presented itself. The only thing that could compensate for Loveness's disappointment was for him to have them win the 33rd Annual City of Kings' Township Ballroom-Dancing Competition, which was only a few months away.

The Molois had come second in the competition two years in a row; the Sigaukes, fifteen years junior and more extravagant, energetic and effusive on the dance floor, had happily seen to that. The secret to success lay in making the dance your own—Spokes knew that. One. Two. Three. One. Two. Three. The fault lay not with the lovely Loveness. One. Two. Three. One. Two. Three. She did all things well and was perfection itself. One. Two. Three. One. Two. Three. The fault lay squarely with Spokes—he was no Nathaniel Sigauke. One. Two. Three. One. Two. Three. Forward. Side. Close. Back. Side. Close. Forward. Side. Close. Back. Side. Close. One. Two. Three. One. Two. Three.

Man leads with right...

Just as Spokes was beginning to think he was on to something, the phone rang. The Chief Superintendent's phone had a different ring to it—a shrill trill—another newness to which he had to accustom himself.

Chief Cele Mkhize was on the other end of the line, and he informed Spokes that a man... a white man... had walked into the bush and not walked out of it. The man's beige bakkie was still parked where he had left it. There was a long pause before Chief Cele Mkhize informed Spokes that the two mujibhas who had seen the white man said that it was the same man who had found Daisy's body all those many years ago. The fact that Chief Cele Mkhize chose to give him a clue and not a name let Spokes know that there was more to the story than was being communicated.

It took Spokes quite a while to realize that the silence that existed was waiting for him to speak. "I will be there as soon as possible," he said. He looked out of the Chief Superintendent's office window and noticed for the first time that the sun was setting. "I will be there first thing tomorrow morning," he corrected himself.

Spokes held the handset to his ear long after Chief Cele Mkhize had hung up. He listened to the busy signal and found its incessant sound oddly comforting. The man who had found Daisy's body all those years ago: Emil Coetzee. The man who had been so disturbed by what had happened to Daisy that he had established The Organization of Domestic Affairs: Emil Coetzee. The man who had brought the lovely Loveness back into Spokes's life and who, for that reason, would always be the man to whom he owed more than a debt of gratitude: Emil Coetzee.

"Is someone on the line?" a white woman's clipped and officious voice inquired, startling Spokes. "Whoever you are, please get off the line at once! I would like to place a rather urgent trunk call," the voice said before the line was filled with clicking sounds as the woman on the other end pressed on the plungers of her phone. "Party line, you see. You need to get off the phone now," the voice said before adding, "Good grief! Some people."

Spokes slowly hung up the phone and continued with what had become a most unexpected day. The twenty-third of December was usually an unremarkable day. Understanding as it did that it came right before the two most important days in the country's calendar, it was a day that tended to behave itself as it allowed people to do their last-minute Christmas shopping and make their long-yearned-for journeys home. However, this particular 23 December, 1979, perhaps understanding that it needed to be different since it came just two days after the ceasefire had been announced—or perhaps sensing that, in the next decade, 22 December would become Unity Day and, therefore, that it, 23 December would be forever squashed between three very important days—had decided to have its first and last hoorah.

As Spokes walked out of the Chief Superintendent's office, he did not know what the future held for 23 December; what he did know was that 23 December, 1979 would be a remarkable day for him, not least because for the first time in his long career, he was headed to the Eastern suburbs to investigate a potential case, and not to the townships or the villages.

———•———

Even in the evening, the yard was magnificent with large jacaranda trees, not in bloom, and flame trees, in bloom; evergreen grass; an impressively ebullient rose garden; a tournament-sized tennis court; and a sparkling swimming pool. All of this splendor was bathed in the yellow glow of innumerable floodlights. The driveway wound its way up a steep gradient toward a house that was so majestic as to be almost palatial. *How the other half lives,* Spokes thought as he got out of the BSAP bakkie and looked at his surroundings.

"Please, sir. Are you knowing where my baas is, sir?" the man (probably the gardener) who had opened the gate for Spokes asked, without even enquiring who Spokes was.

"I am Chief Inspector Spokes Moloi," Spokes said, offering the man his right hand to shake while showing him his badge with his left hand. "I am with the BSAP."

"Something is happening to baas, sir?" the man asked,

worry furrowing his brow as they shook hands.

"I am sorry, I cannot say as yet," Spokes said, genuinely apologetic. "When was the last time you saw him?"

"On the day that they are announcing the ceasefire. He is going early to work, and he is telling me at the gate there that he is bringing food for us to be taking to our homes in the village for holidays, but then he is not coming back. Up to now he is not coming back... When you are hooting at the gate, I am thinking you are him. But you are not him, you are you, sir. It is being like last time."

"Last time?"

"Yes, last time. When he is falling on steps at work, and he is being in the hospital many many many days. And those who are working with him, they are not telling us that he is in hospital. And we are waiting and waiting. One day... two days... three days... we are worrying. And then Miss Marion, she is coming, and she is explaining to us not to be worrying."

"Miss Marion?"

The man had a brief look of guilt and then assuaged it, "Yes. Miss Marion," he said with a slightly raised chin. "She is being a very nice lady. We are liking her very much. She is not coming all the time, she is coming only some of the time. And Madam... she is no longer living here."

Spokes was beginning to get the measure of things.

The man removed his hat from his head and started turning it around and wringing it in his hands. "Please, sir... I am having to be going home. My wife, she is having a baby. The other boys are going to their homes already. The baas, he is not coming, Miss Marion, she is not coming... you are coming. Please, sir, I am having to go home. The last train, it is leaving at eight o' clock, sir. I know baas will be very angry with me, leaving the house alone... I am head boy. But I am having to go home. You are understanding, sir?"

Spokes looked at his watch. It was just gone past seven o' clock; the man would not make it to the train station on time if he did not leave soon. Spokes was more than understanding, "I will give you a lift to the train station," he said.

"No, sir. No. That is not what I am asking. My brother-in-law, he is coming soon," the man said, pointing at something on the lit veranda. It was a battered and almost-bursting suitcase. "Please do not be worrying yourself about me, sir. It is just that I am having to leave the house with no one... you are understanding?"

Just then the hoot of a car sounded at the bottom of the driveway, and the man became even more visibly agitated.

"It is all right," Spokes said. "I will see to it that someone comes to guard the premises during the holidays."

"Ah, thank you. Thank you, sir. You are coming just in time to be saving me. God bless. God bless," he said, pumping Spokes's hands in his, and placing in them a bunch of keys that he had retrieved from the pockets of his overalls. Once the keys had passed from his hands to Spokes's, the man looked very relieved. "You are saving me," he repeated as he ran to get his suitcase.

"I'm afraid, I did not get your name."

"Sorry, sir. It is Machipisa," Machipisa said, offering his hand for one last handshake. "I am being the garden boy here."

Spokes shook Machipisa's hand and, looking him straight in the eye, said, "You are not a boy, Machipisa."

Machipisa stood up a little straighter. "Thank you, sir." He put his hand over his heart and then ran down the driveway, lugging his heavy suitcase.

It took Spokes three tries to find the right key to open the front door.

After being so awe-inspiring from the outside, the house

proved to be anti-climactic on the inside. Expectedly, the interior was beautifully furnished in opulence. There were many things within the house, most of them elegant. If one were prone to envy, one would envy the man who had such possessions. But there was an... emptiness to it all that one could not envy and it was this emptiness—this lack of a some-thing—and not the material possessions of the house, or how it had been furnished, that one found disappointing. Such a house deserved to be filled to the brim with the very things that made a life: love, laughter and long Sunday afternoons spent together. And you could tell just by looking at it that although the house may once have had those things, it no longer had them. Spokes stood in the living room and looked out at the rose garden. Entire lives had been lived here, and together they had managed to leave behind only emptiness. That was a sadness in itself.

So lost was Spokes in his thoughts that he was not aware of her presence until he breathed in something overwhelmingly sweet. He turned from the rose garden, and there she was standing self-assuredly in the doorway.

"I'm Saskia Hargrave," she said marching over to him without being prompted. "You're with the BSAP. Saw the bakkie outside." She offered him her hand to shake and flashed a smile that had a discolored tooth in it.

She casually wore an army-green jacket over a white dress. The dress was so sheer that you could see her undergarments through it. Perhaps because of the army-green jacket, she felt the need to wear rugged hiking boots. To Spokes's eyes, the whole of her seemed to be confusion. She wanted men to look at her and appreciate her for what she thought was her beauty, hence the sheer dress; but she also wanted men to take her seriously for what she thought was her toughness, hence the jacket and boots.

Saskia Hargrave did not understand men, and the evidence in front of Spokes strongly suggested that she did not understand herself either. She seemed to be... searching. They did that, didn't they, white women? Lost a part of themselves somewhere along the way, and then went in search of it— sometimes at another person's expense. Spokes found himself wondering when exactly Saskia Hargrave had lost the part of herself that she was now in search of.

"I'm Spokes Moloi," he said, shaking her hand.

"What are you doing here?" *she* asked *him*.

Before Spokes could give any sort of answer, Saskia Hargrave put two and two together in her head and came up with the Lord-only-knew-what number. She looked both afraid and excited as she asked, "Has something happened to Emil?" Her eyes widened as the reality of what she had just asked began to sink in. That would have been the first thought of anyone who had entered a home with a policeman in it, but that had not been her first thought. Spokes wondered what exactly her first thought had been. "Nothing has happened to him, has it? It couldn't have—I am in the middle of writing his story," she said.

That explained everything for Spokes. Because Saskia Hargrave still needed Emil Coetzee, she did not want anything to have happened to him. With this realization, Spokes had a complete understanding of the kind of person she was. He always found it fascinating how much information about themselves people gave away without really knowing it, information that they were not always aware of themselves. It was this constant discovery of the inner workings of the lives of others that kept Spokes fascinated with his job.

"Are you a writer? A journalist?"

"Both. I write for *The Chronicle* and *The Sunday News*, but I am also working on Emil's biography."

"I see. Miss Hargrave, I am afraid you cannot be here. You will have to leave now. I am sure you understand."

"But I am in the middle of writing Emil's story."

"And I am in the middle of an investigation," Spokes said, leading her out without touching her. Even though black people were on the eve of achieving independence, Spokes was sure that a black man could still not touch a white woman without there being serious consequences. There was a nervous energy about Saskia Hargrave that made Spokes wary; she could turn a harmless act into a dangerous one.

Her face crumpled as she stammered, "I didn't want to have to divulge this, but Emil and I are… lovers."

It was too late; Spokes already had the measure of her. "Is that wise?" he asked her.

"Is what wise?"

"To be romantically linked to your subject. Does not good and objective writing require a distance? How will you be able to see him clearly if you are already so connected to him?"

Saskia Hargrave's mouth fell open and she blinked up at him. She was beginning to see him for the first time, and he was something completely unexpected. He was no longer the object through which she would obtain the information that she wanted; he was now the man who stood in the way of what she wanted. He was an intelligent man who could trip her up when she least expected it. A force to be reckoned with. Spokes almost smiled as he watched this realization sink in.

She recovered enough to say, "You will have to tell Zora, of course. Zora Neale Hurston."

Even though he understood that this was mere bait, Spokes almost bit. He wanted to know who Zora was, and he had to stop himself from betraying this fact in any way. He looked resolutely ahead until he felt her give up this round of their game.

He led her out of the front door, but she left behind a strong sweet scent. As he watched her drive off in a Renault 5 with an elongated "Z" on its side, Spokes realized that Saskia Hargrave was not the kind of woman who allowed herself to be easily forgotten.

When he was sure she was gone, Spokes picked up the phone, dialed the Hillside Police Station and asked for two constables to stand guard over Emil Coetzee's property over the holidays.

———•———

Never having been one to keep secrets from his wife, almost as soon as he got home Spokes told the lovely Loveness about the day he had spent in the Chief Superintendent's office. Never having been one to fight with her husband, Loveness listened to him carefully and gave nothing away. He only knew the depth of her disappointment in him when, later that night, as he watched her put on her nightdress, he suggested that he read her a few pages of *Wives and Daughters* before they went to sleep, and she responded, "Please go ahead and read whatever you want. I'm afraid I have a headache." Then she did something that she had never done in their long-loving marriage; she slept with her back to him.

Spokes experienced the coldest night he had ever had as a married man.

They both understood that the real threat was not a potential promotion, but Daisy's unsolved case. As long as it remained an open case, Spokes would find every reason to postpone his retirement, even though he knew that waiting for them in Krum's Place was the hard-earned promised land—ten acres of it—on which they had built an eight-roomed house that comfortably contained all their future dreams.

Not used to sleeping in an unwelcoming bed, Spokes woke up before sunrise the next morning. He went to the station and dragged six very reluctant and disgruntled officers to the village with him to go and investigate what had happened to Emil Coetzee. Besides the beige bakkie, Emil Coetzee had left absolutely no trace behind. No spoor suggested that anything untoward had happened to his person. The only thing they found of interest was a spray of vomit, but that seemed more consistent with the tracks that must have been made by the two boys from intelligence that the villagers said had come the day before to investigate. Another thing that the villagers told him that they had not hazarded to reveal to him over the party line was that the two boys from intelligence had come out the bush carrying a man's hat; and that the hat looked very much like the one Emil Coetzee had worn in all those photographs they had seen of him in *The Chronicle*— the hat that made him look like the Sundance Kid.

KUKI

———◆———

Kuki looked at the Chief Inspector with his closely cut salt-and-pepper hair and magnificent moustache, and he slightly frowned and studied her as though she were speaking a foreign language. Of course he did not understand. How could he possibly? African lives were so much simpler. "I do not want them," she repeated. "They are no longer mine." The Chief Inspector looked at the bunch of keys in his hands, obviously not knowing what else to do with them. Kuki envied him because he was blissfully oblivious, in a way that she could not be, that the little key at the end was for the treasure chest that Emil had bought Everleigh for his eleventh birthday.

And then she was crying again.

The Chief Inspector, not knowing what else to do, tentatively offered Kuki his handkerchief, and she gratefully accepted it, which surprised them both.

"My son died last year... the war," Kuki explained as she wiped the tears from her eyes.

The Chief Inspector's brow uncreased itself.

"He was a beautiful, golden-haired boy," Kuki hiccupped. She saw the Chief Inspector reach out to touch her and then hesitate. Instead, he looked at the images of the boy that graced every surface of the living room. "The war... it took so much," he said as his eyes came to rest on her.

Kuki looked at the Chief Inspector, and it occurred to her that the war was paradoxically the one thing that had united the country. She remembered all those situation reports, all those thousands of dead black bodies—the bodies that had given her so much confidence that her side was winning the war. It hit her with the force of a true revelation that all those black bodies had had people grieving them all the while. Before they had been bodies, they had been people. They had belonged to families: they had been wives, husbands, daughters, sons, sisters, brothers, aunts, uncles, nieces, nephews, cousins—even grandmothers and grandfathers. Kuki knew, from years of having to grant leave to servants whose relatives were ill, dying or dead, that African families were an intricate and vast network. The loss of a great-aunt was as deeply felt as the loss of a sister. There was no remove for them—just family. All those dead black bodies had been connected, part of an imbricated and intimate web. Where Kuki had simply seen a dead terrorist, another woman might have seen a dead son, and wondered at the callous cruelty that allowed his body to be photographed and the image disseminated for the whole world to see. Kuki could not even imagine seeing the image of the blown-apart dead body of her beautiful, golden-haired boy on the television screen. Some things were meant to be sacred.

"I'm so sorry," Kuki apologized, "I cannot seem to stop crying. Having a really bad time of it, I'm afraid."

The Chief Inspector nodded his understanding.

"It is somber, isn't it? The mood and atmosphere after the ceasefire," Kuki said. "You cannot even tell that today is Christmas Eve."

The Chief Inspector nodded again.

Kuki stood up and went to retrieve something that she handed to the Chief Inspector. It was a photo album filled with the Coetzee's holiday pictures—an archive of the family's happy moments throughout the years. The Chief Inspector paged through the album and watched the boy, Everleigh, grow up and Emil and Kuki grow older on various different kinds of film stock.

"It was our time, you see," Kuki said, wiping her eyes and nose. "The three of us. From the 15th of December to the 2nd of January. The holidays were ours. The boy loved to travel, especially by road, and so that is what we did mostly. And you have no idea how we… came together in those two weeks. How we were a family… how happy we were and could be. My husband, I'm sure you know, is The Head of The Organization of Domestic Affairs. My ex-husband, I should say rather. It is a very demanding job and does not leave room for much else. But from 15 December to 2 January, he was not Emil Coetzee, Head of the Organization. He was just simply ours, and it was lovely, absolutely lovely." Kuki sighed deeply before adding, "And now it is no more. And so I cry."

The Chief Inspector nodded yet again, and Kuki was more than certain that he did understand.

They sat together in the long silence that followed.

"I know the person you can give the keys to," Kuki said at last, standing up.

The Chief Inspector's forehead creased.

SPOKES

—————◆—————

The woman opened the door expectantly, and Spokes immediately thought of those scenes he had seen at the bioscope in which the heroine, newly in love, opens the door to the hero, but does so only after standing in front of a mirror and making sure that she looks immaculate. As she gazes up at the hero with as much nonchalance as she can muster, the camera obligingly softens the look of her face so that it does not seem to have ever been affected by the ordinariness of everyday life.

The woman, Marion Hartley, stood before them looking both cool and warm, and managing, somehow, to make it not seem a contradiction. She wore a lemon-colored dress, and there were ready tears in her astonishingly azure eyes. Before she could stop her half-smiling mouth, she said one word: "Emil."

Beguiling. Spokes had always loved that word, and now he had found someone—besides the lovely Loveness, of course—to attach it to. He watched as Marion Hartley's hopeful look began to actually register the incongruous scene in front of her. Instead of the hero standing before her, there was a white woman she knew and a black man she did not. Her eyes went from one to the other, and then widened as she comprehended what Spoke's presence there probably meant.

She fixed her eyes on Kuki Coetzee and said, almost in a whisper, "Emil… something has happened to him." It was not a question, so Kuki Coetzee could be excused for not responding.

An awful breaking sound escaped from Marion Hartley, and in a pathetic show of strength, she squared her shoulders and lifted her chin. Her eyes left Kuki Coetzee and traveled to Spokes. "Please. Tell me," she said.

Spokes could tell that Marion Hartley was normally a proud and strong woman; therefore, he understood that what he said next and how he said it mattered most. He told her what he had told Kuki Coetzee earlier that day, in what he hoped was the same measured tone, one that gave nothing away. "Mr. Coetzee seems to have driven to the Matopos area a few days ago; and I somehow find myself the bearer of his keys."

Marion Hartley's lips formed an "O" but the sound never came out. She seemed to relax into the news somewhat, and Spokes watched as several different emotions played over her facial features: relief, anger, disappointment, overwhelming love, and something else that he could not quite read. It was that something else that let him know that he could not fully believe whatever Marion Hartley said and did next.

"He has up and disappeared, it seems," Kuki Coetzee said. "But I apparently have more experience with him doing so than you do. He was always disappearing on me. Once disappeared on me for more than a week. Turned out he had been with you the entire time," Kuki Coetzee said.

Spokes was caught between the proverbial rock and a hard place. For many reasons, he could not, as yet, tell them that Emil Coetzee had entered the bush completely unarmed, that his Stetson had been found, and that no one seemed to have seen him since. One, Emil Coetzee had only entered the bush two days ago, so it was early days yet. Two, there was no evidence to suggest that something unfortunate or untoward had happened to him. Three, his walking into the bush had been a deliberate act. If, as Kuki Coetzee was saying, he often "disappeared," then chances were high that he would reappear. There was no need to tell the women things that might make them worry unnecessarily. But, even so, Spokes had to admit that the business of returning the keys that Machipisa had left in his care was getting a little out of hand.

"You wouldn't know where he is, would you?" Kuki Coetzee asked Marion Hartley. "It would save us all a heap of trouble."

Gone was the Kuki Coetzee who had cried into his handkerchief; standing next to Spokes was a woman who was more hurt and angry than broken.

"I think we may want to continue this discussion inside," Spokes said delicately.

Marion Hartley's left hand came up to hit her forehead in a rather theatrical manner that was not performance at all. "Where are my manners? Please do come in," she said, as she opened the door and stretched her mouth in a smile of warm welcome.

Spokes gestured with his hand for Kuki Coetzee to go in before him, which she did with great reluctance.

The house was as beautiful on the inside as it was on the outside. The cozy atmosphere created by the English rose garden and the maroon wrap-around veranda, with its hordes of potted succulents, creepers and elephant ears, was continued in the house, which was filled with overflowing bookshelves, overstuffed sofas, and overused throws and rugs. This was a house that had been made into a home because every room was lived in and loved. It was difficult to believe that Marion Hartley, after having been widowed, had lived here alone. There was a comfortable and almost well-worn quality to everything. And then Spokes realized that perhaps the home's easy embrace was the result of Marion Hartley having kept the house exactly as it was when her husband died.

"I cannot cook a thing to save my life," Marion Hartley said. "Have actually been known to burn a salad on occasion, and the workers have gone home for the holidays, but I believe I can just about manage a cup of tea or coffee. On the other hand, I *am* rather good at pouring a drink if you would prefer something stronger." The last offering was suggested with a glance at Kuki Coetzee.

"Nothing for me, thank you," Kuki Coetzee said in a clipped way as she took a seat on the sofa that was farthest from where Marion Hartley stood. Spokes watched as Kuki Coetzee valiantly fought off the plush and pliant sofa's attempts to engulf her.

Marion Hartley's eyes turned to Spokes. "Nothing for me either, thank you," he said, taking a seat in an armchair that immediately encouraged him to sit back and relax in its luxurious lushness.

"Are you sure I cannot tempt you?" Marion Hartley said, and it was obvious from the easy way the words tripped off her tongue that she had said them often, that she was used to being the accommodating hostess.

"Unlike my husband, I'm afraid you'll find me not so easily tempted," Kuki Coetzee said, as she sat upright on the sofa and continued to rebuff its inclination to draw her in. She reddened, probably angered less by the words themselves than by the emotion they betrayed.

In response, Marion Hartley's eyes merely smiled as she turned them to look at Spokes. She was a woman who absolutely refused to be ashamed of the choices that she had made in her life.

"Not while on duty," Spokes said, with a shake of his head.

"Then, if you both don't mind, I'll go ahead and pour myself something stiff and probably a little sinful," Marion

Hartley said, with a full smile.

Spokes could easily understand how and why a man would fall in love with Marion Hartley. She had an alluring fluid quality about her and an endearing playfulness that he could see Emil Coetzee tripping over; and then, thereafter, having lost his footing, never being able to quite right himself again. It was not just her looks that were beguiling; it was her entire person. A woman like that could be extremely dangerous.

While Marion Hartley was preparing her drink, Spokes marveled at her transformation within a matter of minutes. By the time they sat themselves down in her living room, she seemed to have convinced herself that she really did not have to fear the worst where Emil Coetzee was concerned; and Spokes wondered what it was she knew that made her almost certain that all was well. Kuki Coetzee had her "disappearances" to rely on: what did Marion Hartley have?

She re-entered the living room in that fluid way of hers, carrying a glass of something that looked tropical and indeed sinful.

"It does not feel like Christmas Eve, does it?" Marion Hartley asked as she took a seat on the same sofa as Kuki Coetzee. She seemed to do so because she understood that Kuki Coetzee and she, in loving the same man, had to be there for each other at this time. She also understood that Kuki Coetzee did not have the same assurance that all was probably well that she had.

Spokes watched as Marion Hartley placed her glass on a coaster on the side table that was closest to her end of the sofa before reaching out a hand to Kuki Coetzee. She managed to give Kuki Coetzee's hands a gentle squeeze before Kuki Coetzee removed her clasped hands from Marion Hartley's touch, and not knowing what else to do with them, sat on them as though she were a punished schoolgirl.

"I'm sure it will all be all right," Marion Hartley said, reaching for her drink and taking a long sip. "He probably just needs to clear his head."

"So you don't think you've just been supplanted? That he's chosen someone else to spend his nights with?" Kuki Coetzee asked, her words slings and arrows.

Marion Hartley smiled softly and sympathetically at her. No, she definitely did not believe she had been supplanted.

"Why would he need to clear his head?" Spokes asked. "Do you have some idea as to why he went into the bush?"

Spokes could tell by the way Marion Hartley scratched the back of her head and then smoothed over the uncreased skirt of her dress that these questions had taken her by surprise, and that she was, for the moment, wrong-footed. "Why? Why? Well, because of the ceasefire, surely," she eventually said before taking another generous sip of her drink.

It was obvious to Spokes that she was lying. She knew something that she desperately wanted to keep secret. He could tell from the intelligence held in her eyes that she was a woman long accustomed to knowing what others did not. She was a woman used to secrets: to having them, keeping them and storing them safely away.

"When did you last see Mr. Coetzee?" Spokes asked.

"On the day the ceasefire was announced," she replied without hesitation. "Well, actually, the morning after," she went on, looking at Kuki Coetzee before continuing. "He came in the afternoon, spent the evening… and the night. He left just after dawn the following morning."

"When he left, did he say where he was going?" Spokes asked.

"He did not say," Marion Hartley said, and chose that moment to look at her polished fingernails instead of him. She was not lying this time, but she was definitely hiding something.

"Did the two of you have a fight… quarrel?" Spokes asked.

Marion Hartley's eyes flew up at him. There was a truth in his words that she could not deny, and then she said, almost in a whisper, "No, not quite. But it would have been better, I think, if we had."

"Better? How? Why?"

She looked at him for a long time as though trying to gauge something before she replied, "I'm sorry, I cannot seem to remember your name—did you tell it to me?"

He had not, he realized, introduced himself, and so he said with some embarrassment, "I'm Spokes Moloi. I'm with the BSAP." He intentionally omitted his rank, division, and station.

"I see," Marion Hartley said. "It is wonderful to meet you," she added before taking another sip of her drink. She was playing for time, contemplating her next move.

"What is it that you probably should have fought about?" Spokes pressed.

Her eyes flew up at him again, and then she said, rather too quickly, "He had resigned from The Organization." Again, she was not lying, but she was not telling the whole truth either.

"Had he? Really?" Kuki Coetzee asked, curious in spite of herself.

"Yes. He had. As soon as he could after he heard about the ceasefire."

"I cannot imagine him not working for The Organization," Kuki Coetzee said.

"Neither could he, I think," Marion Hartley said. The way her lower lip trembled as she said these words let Spokes know that she was lying outright. "Which was why," she continued, "when I suggested that he become a game ranger, he did not take kindly to it." She said all this without looking at

Spokes; she was definitely lying, and definitely hiding something now. "He thought I was making light of who he was and what he did, you see. I was not, of course. I never would… we should have argued about it, but instead, he just left. I should have stopped him. I should not have let him leave. Not the way he did."

She seemed to be saying the last three sentences to herself, and the way she said them revealed to Spokes that the truth of the entire matter lay there: in the thing that had made Emil Coetzee leave, in the thing that had made Marion Hartley let him leave without a fight.

At last Spokes knew something really worth knowing about the case. Emil Coetzee and Marion Hartley had had a discussion that had made him walk away from her. The conversation had definitely not been about his becoming a game ranger; it had been about something that mattered more to the both of them than what he did for a living. Whatever it was, it had made Emil Coetzee walk into the bush unprotected and unarmed, Spokes was sure of it.

"When he left you," Spokes said purposefully, and watched Marion Hartley flinch at the phrase, "When he left you, where did you think he was going?"

"Home," she replied. She looked at him then, her eyes a little wounded.

"Did you try to contact him there?"

"Yes. Several times. I telephoned. Last night and this morning. I was thinking of going to the house. I was getting ready to leave when you arrived." All that she was saying now was true.

"And when you could not find him, what did you think had happened?"

"I don't know. Like I said, I knew he needed to clear his head. I knew he needed time away from me to think things through."

"Because you suggested that he become a game ranger?"

Marion Hartley ignored his question and asked her own: "Since you have the keys, I gather you have been to the house."

"Yes. I was there yesterday evening."

"And?"

"He was not there. There was a worker waiting for him. The gardener—"

"Machipisa," Marion Hartley said.

"Yes, that's the one. Gave me the keys to the house."

"So you think Emil has been in the bush this entire time?" Marion Hartley said, following her own train of thought. "He grew up there, you know, on the outskirts of the Matopos National Park." She sat up more confidently. "He is more than familiar with the territory."

"We are aware of that," Spokes said, choosing not to mention all the other evidence which indicated that Emil Coetzee had entered the bush without a weapon or any means of sustaining himself.

"Is there something you are not telling me? Something that I should know?" Marion Hartley shot at him. "Something that we should know?" she corrected, her hand reaching for Kuki Coetzee's again. Kuki Coetzee was still sitting on her hands, but her eyes were now searching Spokes's eyes for the something that he might be hiding.

"It is early days yet, and to be honest, we don't really know what we know. You have both been very helpful and co-operative, and we thank you. It is probably as you say; he is just giving himself a few days to clear his head, and then he will resurface. If he contacts you, please let us know immediately," Spokes said, and then he stood and offered both women his card.

"I will definitely contact you as soon as I hear from him," Marion Hartley said as she took his card. "Chief Inspector," she added.

As Marion Hartley led him and Kuki Coetzee out of her living room, it struck Spokes that she seemed certain that she would be hearing from Emil Coetzee again. Whatever she was hiding, she fully expected him to return to her. Spokes remembered the relieved and excited way she had opened the door to them when she thought they were Emil Coetzee; he remembered the flawless perfection of the bioscope heroine she must have mastered just before opening the door. She had let Emil Coetzee go without really letting him go; she had, even in that moment of letting him go, wanted him back again.

Spokes hoped, for her sake, for Kuki Coetzee's sake, and even for Saskia Hargrave's sake, that Emil Coetzee would return.

As Marion Hartley opened her front door and let the sun shine in, Spokes said, as though only now remembering to ask a question that he had meant to ask all along: "Do either of you know anyone by the name of Zora?"

Marion Hartley frowned, and Kuki Coetzee looked at him blankly. Oh well, it had been worth a try. Saskia Hargrave had dropped the name tantalisingly, as though it were a delicious morsel, and Spokes had thought that maybe Zora was somehow tied to all of this. But most probably, Saskia Hargrave, who definitely was hiding something and not doing a very good job of it, had deliberately tried to send him down the wrong path.

Marion Hartley suddenly laughed, a deep, throaty laugh, and Spokes knew that this was something else that Emil Coetzee had tripped over. "Unless, of course, you mean Zora Neale Hurston," she said. It was Spokes turn to frown and look at her blankly. "I will go and fetch her. Please wait a moment," Marion Hartley said, the laughter still in her voice.

Spokes and Kuki Coetzee stood awkwardly under the archway, not quite knowing what to do next.

Marion Hartley presently returned carrying a magazine—*The World Tomorrow*. She opened the well-thumbed magazine at a particular page and carefully placed it into Spokes's hands. Spokes gingerly held it and saw an essay by Zora Neale Hurston titled "How It Feels To Be Colored Me."

Her expression guarded, Marion Hartley waited for Spokes to read through the essay before she said, "Zora is such a unique name. Who mentioned it?"

"The name was written on a piece of paper that was found on Emil Coetzee's desk, I believe," Spokes lied, rather easily.

Marion Hartley's stance softened somewhat. "Over the years I sent him passages from her book, *Their Eyes Were Watching God*. Perhaps he used her name as a code or password."

"Perhaps," Spokes said noncommittally as he handed back her obviously much-cherished magazine.

After they said their goodbyes, Spokes opened the door of the BSAP bakkie for Kuki Coetzee, and as she settled into the passenger's seat, she said: "She is rather good at what she does, is she not?"

"And what is that?" Spokes said, realizing he still had Emil Coetzee's keys in his possession.

"Getting men to fall in love with her.'

SASKIA

———◆———

The two men—one white, the other black—in Emil Coetzee's disarrayed office looked like they had been caught with their proverbial trousers around their ankles. What showed Saskia that they were not supposed to be doing whatever it was that they were doing was that they were too busy thinking of a plausible excuse that would explain why they were in an office that had obviously been tampered with to ask her why she was there.

"My name is Saskia Hargrave. I am a journalist for *The Chronicle*. I am working on Emil Coetzee's biography, but I cannot seem to get hold of him," she said by way of introduction.

"He has gone walkabout," the white one said, coming forward, almost stumbling in his eagerness to get close to her. Saskia read the situation clearly: these two men, whoever they were, had taken advantage of Emil Coetzee's absence to look for something. She was naturally curious as to what that something was, and saw no reason not to ensure that they both divulged this information to her at a later date. The white one offered his hand and said, "Clement Rutherford. Everyone calls me Rutherford."

Saskia could tell that Clement Rutherford was one of those middle-aged men who had had quite a bit of luck with women in the past, but who had recently gone to seed and was desperate to reclaim something of his former glory.

"Clement—my pleasure," Saskia said with a smile. She

shook his hand and judged its size and the firmness of its grip. "And you are?" Saskia asked, turning her attention to the black one. She let go of Rutherford's hand and noted with satisfaction that he was disappointed by the briefness of the contact between them.

"That is Joseth Maraire... my associate," Rutherford hastened to say before Joseth could speak for himself.

From the way he looked at her, Saskia concluded that Joseth Maraire was one of those African men who desperately wanted to know what it was like to be with a white woman, and, after having fantasized about it for most of his adult life, felt that (now that majority rule was around the corner) this was what independence should mean for him.

"Joseth Mara... " Saskia made sure to prettily struggle with his last name as she offered him her hand.

"Maraire," Joseth said, as he shook her hand. "But please call me Joseth."

Saskia shook his hand and judged its size and the firmness of its grip. Both were more impressive than Rutherford's. "Joseth?" she said.

"Yes. Illiterate parents, I'm afraid."

"More like a not-so-literate records officer," Saskia said with a smile.

Joseth smiled appreciatively back at her.

Saskia slowly pivoted around the ransacked room, letting both men appreciate the movement of her body. She caught both of them looking at her breasts more than once.

"What to do, what to do," Saskia said with a slight pout. "Emil gave me some information when we met, but not nearly enough. I have to find him." She placed a hand casually on Joseth's arm, which predictably drew Rutherford closer. Men... "I thought I could whet the readers' appetite with a feature in this week's *Sunday News*."

"And you still can," Rutherford said, expertly leading her away from Joseth. "I'd be happy to help whichever way I can. I have known Emil Coetzee most all of my life."

"Most all your life?"

"Yes. We were boys together at the Selous School for Boys."

Saskia stopped in her tracks—this was unexpectedly brilliant news. "You attended the Selous School for Boys?"

"Yes. I did," Rutherford said, his chest puffing out with pride. "Best school in the damn country."

"It turns boys into the men of history," Saskia said, making sure to look Rutherford in the eyes.

"That it does," Rutherford said smugly.

"Are you a man of history?"

"I am a man for all seasons."

The smugness on Rutherford's face did not last long because from somewhere close in the room, Joseth's voice said, "You're very taken with him, aren't you?"

"With him?" Saskia asked, confused as she looked at Rutherford.

"Emil Coetzee," Joseth said in a way that made it clear that he was not referring to Rutherford.

Saskia could tell from the look in Joseth's eyes that it had occurred to him that she was loitering in order to communicate something—the easy transfer of her adoration, perhaps from Emil Coetzee to Clement Rutherford or, better still, Joseth Maraire. It suited her purposes for him to believe that she was so fickle in her affections, and so she said, "Taken with Emil Coetzee? I am rather, I suppose. He is a very powerful man."

"And it's the power that does it for you, isn't it?" Joseth asked, growing bolder.

"It very well may be power that does it for me," Saskia

said, shifting her weight from one foot to the other in a way she knew men found becoming.

"I wonder if you will write my biography someday," Joseth said.

Rutherford cleared his throat and Saskia ignored him.

"Well, that depends, doesn't it?"

"Depends? Depends on what?"

"On whether you have a life that is worth writing about?"

"I'll make sure I have that kind of life."

Saskia had the distinct impression that Joseth was not a particularly brave man, and yet here he was being fearless enough to stop pointing at the edges of a thing and delineate it clearly instead. She knew that what Joseth was doing had as much to do with her as it did with Rutherford. Joseth was letting Rutherford know their dynamic was shifting, that things between them were in flux, and that Joseth had every intention of coming out on top. For Saskia, this was a very interesting development—one she could see working to her advantage.

But there were other considerations. An affair with a black man? Could she do it? It would be scandalous—the sort of thing that would have the tongues of the City of Kings wagging for months to come. It would make the city afraid of this thing called independence, and that would be a prodigious triumph in itself.

"You go ahead and make sure of that," Saskia said, smiling encouragingly at Joseth, driving a wedge into the chink that had appeared in the relationship between Rutherford and Joseth, and ensuring that they would both be eager to win her over. "What do you think of the title *Emil Coetzee: A Son of the Soil*?"

Joseth grinned at her and took a step closer. His teeth were perfectly white and even, and were probably the most unimpeachable thing about him. She imagined those teeth playfully biting into the flesh of her skin, and the thought was not altogether unwelcome or unpleasant. "I prefer *Joseth Maraire: A Son of the Soil.*"

She looked away from those teeth into Rutherford's grim and angry face and sweetly said, "Clement, I am sure you also have a story worth telling." She placed a placating hand on his forearm before walking out of Emil Coetzee's office. When she closed the door behind her, Saskia knew that her mission had been accomplished.

———◆———

For a rather tall woman, Kuki Coetzee seemed small. There was a haunted expression in her eyes that had probably been placed there by the son whose image, in some shape or form, adorned many surfaces of the living room in which they sat. The other woman, the one sitting next to Kuki, was genuinely small, but seemed larger than life. Her personality created a reputation that always preceded her: Beatrice Beit-Beauford. Both women lived the kind of exciting lives whose episodes had periodically graced the pages of *The Chronicle*.

Saskia picked up one of the framed photos of the son, Everleigh, on the mantelpiece, and tried to find a resemblance. "He looked so much like his father," she said, turning to Kuki with the sad smile that she had practiced over the years whenever she visited the family of a fallen soldier.

"Yes. He was a precious and beautiful child," Kuki said as she stood up. "We did not deserve him."

"I wrote about Everleigh several times. His wins at eisteddfods. He really had the voice of an angel."

"Yes. He was a precious and beautiful child. We did not deserve him," Kuki repeated as she took the framed photo from Saskia's hands, wiped it with the cuff of her blouse, and placed it back in its rightful place on the mantelpiece.

"So many pictures of him and none of your husband—"

"Ex-husband," Beatrice corrected.

"There are no pictures of your ex-husband—or of you, for that matter."

Kuki looked around the room as though this realization was new to her.

"You are wonderfully observant. You have a journalist's eye for detail. Bravo for you. Now do you mind telling us why you are actually here?" Beatrice said.

Saskia was not surprised by the hostility. Women of a certain age tended to dislike her for obvious reasons.

"I am working on a piece on Emil for *The Sunday News*, but my bigger plan is to write his biography—*Emil Coetzee: A True Patriot*."

"A biography?" Kuki asked. "Is this... is this something he wants?"

"Yes. He is very excited about it. Unfortunately, he seems to have gone walkabout and—"

"The preening popinjay," Beatrice interrupted. "Are you sure you'll have enough material for a book—or even an article? All you need to know about Emil Coetzee can be summed up in three sentences. He came. He saw. He destroyed everything in his path."

"B!" Kuki protested.

"Don't 'B' me. Look at what he did to you, Kicks!"

"You don't like him very much, I take it," Saskia said to Beatrice.

"Definitely no love lost here," Beatrice said.

"I must say, I find that very interesting."

"Interesting? Why?"

"Well... " Saskia said, trying to sound like she was being sensitive as she looked at Kuki. "I got the impression that women... "

"Women cannot resist him?" Beatrice finished the sentence for her. "Women fall at his feet? Lie prostrate in front of him so that he can walk all over them? True, some women do. But no one man can be universally loved. I mean, he is an exceptionally handsome man, and there is a gravelly quality to his voice that is pleasing to the ear. But it is all style and no substance, you understand. He is really just a beautiful bag of hot air."

"B!"

"Don't 'B' me. If anyone needs to hear this, it is you, Kicks. Though I have been telling you this for long enough," Beatrice said, patting Kuki's hands, which had reached out to stop her from saying more. "He became her entire world, you see, and she got lost in him," she explained to Saskia.

"You make me sound so pathetic," Kuki said.

"Well, that's because you are, love."

"He was a good husband and a great father," Kuki said.

"Oh, Kicks! He was no such thing," Beatrice protested.

"That is what you will write about Emil Coetzee in your article," Kuki said, speaking directly to Saskia, and evincing a determination that was surprising. "He is not a perfect man by any means or measure, but he was a good husband and a great father."

"And where in that very diplomatic description is the man who left you to grieve the death of your son alone while he made sure to put it good to Marion Hartley? I found you, sixteen hours after you had received the news, still cradling the phone in your arms, still crying! Where is the good husband and great father in all of that?"

"B!"

"Don't 'B' me, Kicks, love. You want to re-write history, and I won't let you. You want to make Emil Coetzee the paragon of man. But he is not," Beatrice said before she took

Kuki's hands in hers and gave them a gentle squeeze. "I know you need him to be good… for your sake… for the boy's sake. But he is not, Kicks. He is not."

Kuki started crying, racking, tortured sobs that sounded ugly in Saskia's ears. Saskia did not believe in crying. Crying did not accomplish anything. Crying was what girls did when they thought the world gave a damn.

As she watched Kuki place her head on Beatrice's lap and Beatrice stroke Kuki's hair, Saskia felt not just disgust, but also a deep revulsion. Although she did not really know what she had been hoping for, Saskia was sure that what she was witnessing was not it. *Was this the healing power of sisterhood that feminists were always banging on about?* she wondered as she saw herself out the front door. Saskia did not need sisterhood. She had other ways of coping with the world.

Once back in the brightness of day, Saskia looked at the framed photograph of Everleigh that she had taken from the key table in the corridor on her way out. He was about fifteen years old in the photo, and he looked so very happy. It was hard to imagine that only four years later, he had died an awful and tragic death.

Saskia placed the photo more carefully than she had intended in her rucksack. She blamed her need for care on the gentleness she had just witnessed between Kuki Coetzee and Beatrice Beit-Beauford. Women…

——————•——————

In Flat 2A, at the corner of Selborne Avenue and Borrow Street, Johan and Gemma Coetzee were eager to tell Saskia all about Emil. It would be their pleasure. He had been a good boy who had become a great man of history. His was an amazing life so, quite naturally, someone wanted to write about him and, quite naturally, they were happy to oblige by sharing. They especially loved the title that she had come up with for the biography: *Emil Coetzee: A Real-Life Hero*—how very fitting.

Johan and Gemma Coetzee had a wealth of information about the one they called "Our Boy," even though he was now—wherever he was—a man of fifty-something. They brought for her to peruse and parse, photographs of him as a child, yearbooks of his adolescence at the Selous School for Boys, and newspaper and magazine clippings of him as an adult. As Saskia looked at the photograph of the toddler Emil Coetzee walking into the Indian Ocean holding his mother's and father's hands, she wondered why they had only one photograph of him as an adult. This photograph had been taken at his wedding. In the photograph, the bride was missing and Emil Coetzee, looking happy enough, was flanked by his obviously overjoyed parents. Behind them all there stood, rather ominously, a towering, tiered wedding cake.

Saskia could easily see how Emil Coetzee had had no choice but to be so handsome; his parents had been and still were very beautiful. There was something especially bygone era about them, like movie stars from the silent era. Perhaps knowing this about themselves, they had the tragic self-absorption and self-indulgence of former celebrities. In listening to them talk about "Our Boy," Saskia got the distinct impression that his story was merely an extension of their own story. They loved him as one would come to love a favorite accessory: not for the thing itself, but rather for the fact that it made its possessor look good and, perhaps, feel better.

"I thought one or both of you were deaf," Saskia said, once she felt comfortable enough to broach the subject. "People say you communicate with each other in sign language."

Johan and Gemma looked at each other as a sadness fell over them. "We did use a sign language of our own invention for a long time," Gemma said. "But then Our Boy lost his boy in the war, and he became this broken thing. A parent cannot see their child in so much pain and not say something... grief needs words."

"Tell the girl how we met, poppet," Johan said, after a pause, attempting to lighten the mood.

"Oh, you'll love *that* story. It is absolutely marvelous," Gemma said with the voice and cadence of a gifted story-teller. She took Saskia affectionately by the arm like they were old friends, and Saskia let her, surprising herself by not feeling too uncomfortable.

"It was a windy day in November and the year was 1920," Gemma said, leading Saskia to stand by the window overlooking the intersection of Borrow Street and Selborne Avenue. "I was a student at Eveline High School, straw hat and all, and he was a traffic conductor, white gloves and all... kismet. A match made in heaven. A gust of wind blew off my straw hat, I went in chase, and he stood there... gazing. Can you picture it?"

Saskia could picture it. She could see them. Both of them young, full of the vigor of life, and ready to fall in love. Very easily, Gemma had cocooned her not only in her voice and story, but in her life as well. Saskia felt something that she had not felt in a very long time—she felt safe. Suddenly discomforted, she, feigning a forgotten prior engagement, hastily left the company of Johan and Gemma Coetzee before they could finish their story. She dismayed herself by promising to visit again soon.

As she walked through the City Hall's courtyard on her way back to *The Chronicle's* offices, Saskia removed the Selous School for Boys 1942 yearbook that she had spirited away from Johan and Gemma's flat. As Saskia flipped through the pages of the yearbook while walking, she found many images of Emil Coetzee in class, team and club photographs. She was somewhat surprised to find that he looked exactly like every other fifteen-year-old boy. His smile, although rehearsed for such occasions, seemed uncertain. Whether his hands were clasped at the back or his arms folded at the front, his puffed-out chest looked as if it was imitating rather than feeling the bravado it depicted. His "feet apart" stance, calculated to make him look like he was ready to take charge of the world, seemed unsteady, and only succeeded in making him look stiff. In short, he was desperately trying to look the part of a self he was still unsure of. There was absolutely nothing remarkable about Emil Coetzee at fifteen. He was not mature or wise beyond his years; he was merely a boy of fifteen.

———◆———

Saskia entered the editor's office and easily lied: "The Emil Coetzee story is shaping up nicely."

"Is it really? When can I expect it?" the editor asked, giving Saskia a craven look.

"Soon."

She was just about out the door when he said, "A caregiver has called for you several times. Something to do with your mother." He hesitated before continuing, "Something to do with Christmas. Apparently your mother was expecting you. Has been agitated ever since."

Saskia had stopped cold. Her mother had no business interfering with her life. And what right did the caregiver have to divulge so much to someone she had never met?

"Do you want me to come with?" the editor offered.

"Why on God's green earth would you want to do that?" Saskia asked as she turned to him. As soon as she saw the expression on his face, she realized she had hurt him. Men... the problem with them was that once you had slept with them a few times, they thought they needed to start doing nice things for you. "My mother has always been untrust-worthy... prone to dramatics... an attention seeker," she explained as she headed out of his office.

Saskia arrived at the cottage on Ninth Avenue that her mother had lived in ever since she and her husband had separated, but not divorced. It had all been too little too late, Saskia determined as she opened the squeaky gate. The cottage looked like it had been torn out of the pages of a children's book of fairy tales. It had a verdant and overgrown garden with effusions of rose bushes and flower beds everywhere, and there were climbers and ivy plants creeping up the walls, almost choking the cottage—someone's green thumb obviously knew no bounds. Saskia walked up the crooked stone path that led to her mother's front door and used her key to let herself in.

She found her mother sitting by the window and painting a sunset. Her mother looked so peaceful, everything around her was so tranquil that Saskia knew immediately that she should not have come. It was yet another false alarm.

"This is what you called me for?" Saskia asked the caregiver standing beside her. "You called me here so that I could watch my mother be happy?"

"She was really bad a few hours ago. Very agitated… kept calling your name," the caregiver defended herself.

"I'm a very busy woman. I don't have time—"

"Sassie? Is that you, dear?" her mother said, turning away from the sunset to give her a look filled with hope. Her flowing, snow-white hair and black dress with a cape made her seem as though she were at once both benifecence and maleficence when all she really was was a mother.

Saskia took a deep breath. The caregiver escaped the room and closed the door behind her.

"Yes, Mother. It's me."

"Come here, dear," her mother said, motioning with her hand. "Come see the beautiful bounce in the sky."

Saskia maneuvered her way through the comfortable but overcrowded living room and went to stand by her mother, but made sure to stand just out of reach. Even so she could not help but sneeze, and she was pleased to note that she still reacted adversely to her mother's proximity.

"It was orange a moment ago," her mother said, sadly placing her untouched outstretched hand on her lap. "Now it is peach. If we are lucky, it will become a deep red... and then magenta... and then purple... and then darkness."

Her mother motioned toward her again, but Saskia did not move any closer. Giving her hands something else to do, her mother pointed at her canvas, at the painting of a sunset taking shape on it.

"Do you think I've got it right?" her mother asked, always seeking attention, appreciation and approval, like a little girl.

"Is that why you made such a fuss earlier?" Saskia asked. "So that I could come and tell you what I think of your painting?"

Her mother reached out to touch her again.

"Can't keep your hands to yourself, can you?" Saskia bit out. "So like your husband. Birds of a feather, I guess."

Her mother looked like she had been slapped in the face and cowered in her chair. Good.

"I am working on a feature—a biography of Emil Coetzee," Saskia removed the framed picture of Everleigh Coetzee and the Selous School for Boys 1942 yearbook from her rucksack and handed them to her mother. She watched closely as her mother frowned at the things she now held in her hands.

"Is this wise?" her mother asked. "Should you be working so soon after... " she let her voice trail off.

"So soon after what, mother?" Saskia taunted. "So soon after your husband's actions secured a place for me in the madhouse?"

The framed picture and yearbook slipped from her mother's hands and Saskia moved swiftly to catch them before they fell onto the floor. As she placed them in her rucksack, she wondered why she was still taking so much care.

Her mother folded into herself and began rocking back and forth. She flailed her arms in front of her as though chasing something away, and in so doing, upset the easel. The beautiful painting of the sunset came crashing down.

"Look Mother," Saskia said, pointing at the sudden black night beyond the window. "The darkness is already upon us."

As Saskia walked out the house, she heard her mother call out, "Sassie... Sassie... Sassie!"

Saskia did not turn around. Sassie was not her name. Sassie was the name of a girl. It had been a very long time since she had been a girl.

JOSETH

———◆———

Joseth looked at the madala who had just entered the Chief Superintendent's office, and could not believe that *this* was the man who had put a kibosh on the most brilliant plan that he had ever come up with. As he watched the madala respectfully remove his hat, Joseth felt grateful that his own life had presented him with opportunities beyond being an officer of the BSAP. CID be damned. As far as he was concerned, there was nothing as useless as the BSAP—any Tom, Dick and Harry who could run, jump and say, "Yes, sir, no, sir, three bags full, sir," could join the force. You did not need to have a brain to belong to the BSAP; in fact, having a brain seemed to be something that was strongly discouraged.

The madala standing in front of him had only very recently crawled—at a snail's pace—into his current rank of Chief Inspector, but Joseth could tell by the man's genial smile and content expression that he was very happy with his lot in life and had never had a higher ambition. That was what was most of the problem with the older generation; they lacked ambition and initiative, and were all too happy with the few crumbs that fell off the table. How a madala like this—with his old-fashioned hat (a fedora, for Christ's sake), waxed full moustache (as though a moustache trimmed to almost non-existence was too much to ask for), and still-pegged trousers (advertising to everyone that he rode a bicycle, as if that were a point of pride)—did not see or understand that he was a caricature, was beyond Joseth. The madala had obviously mimicked his sense of style on a character (the hero most probably) he had read about in a detective novel set in the 1940s. The man was out of time—stuck in one of the many cul-de-sacs of history. He was like a tributary that had veered away from the river and was fated one day to be cut off and eventually dry up. Just thinking of the man was a waste of time.

As Joseth watched the madala deferentially place his fedora in the middle of his chest, he had to use every ounce of self-control not to snort at the gesture.

"Back from your fishing trip, sir?" the madala asked Chief Superintendent Griffiths, after nodding briefly at Joseth and Rutherford.

"That I am, Moloi, that I am," Chief Superintendent Griffiths said with a beam. "Caught the biggest bream you have ever seen. Almost toppled the boat over. It was so big, bigger, even, than my '75 catch."

"Bigger than the '75? It couldn't be, sir."

"Photos are being processed as we speak. You will not believe your eyes," the Chief Superintendent said. "Brought you some rainbow trout. It is in the fridge in the canteen," he went on, as he patted his pockets until he retrieved a piece of paper. He continued, "My wife says that she recently found this recipe for a lemon sauce that goes very well with trout." He handed the folded piece of paper to Moloi, who received it with obvious gratitude. "Ah yes! I was to remember to tell you to tell Loveness that she needs to zest the lemon before she squeezes it. The sauce needs both the zest and the juice."

"As you know, sir, I am the one who cooks the fish at home," Moloi said, as he put the recipe in his overcoat pocket. "Please thank Mrs. Griffiths for me."

Joseth was sure that Moloi cooked the fish and more besides in his home. He was probably married to a woman who had long-hooked him through the nose and led him whichever way she wanted him to go. He seemed to be just the sort of man that a woman could and would take advantage of.

"And the Assistant Commissioner and the Deputy Commissioner: how did they fare, sir?" Moloi asked.

"Returned home green with envy, which is as it should be," the Chief Superintendent said with a hearty chuckle.

Joseth had had enough of this camaraderie and pleasantness and so he cleared his throat, loudly, reminding the Chief Superintendent of his presence.

"Ah yes!" Chief Superintendent Griffiths exclaimed. "Moloi, these gentlemen are with the SIU, and they would like a word with you."

Moloi did not move from the door, but simply nodded at Joseth and Rutherford. He looked at them expectantly, like an eager dog that had just performed a trick. He probably thought that they were here to praise him, and was completely unaware of the humiliation that they had in store for him. Moloi was about to learn that not all his superiors were like the Chief Superintendent, and Joseth was chomping at the bit to teach him this lesson.

"Please take a seat," Chief Superintendent Griffiths said, gesturing toward the only empty chair in the room.

As Moloi made his way to the seat, the Chief Superintendent explained to Joseth and Rutherford, "Moloi has been acting Chief Superintendent while I was away. Did a better job of running things than I have ever done, by all accounts."

Unimpressed, Rutherford said, as soon as Moloi sat down, "We understand that a few days ago you and your men went to the village that abuts the Matopos National Park."

"You understand correctly," Moloi replied.

"Why?" Rutherford said.

"Why what?"

"Why did you go to the village?"

"We received an anonymous call saying that a man believed to be Emil Coetzee had walked into the bush unarmed, and that he had not, as yet, walked out again. We thought it was best that we look into it, and so we went to the village to investigate."

Moloi's use of "we" really grated on Joseth's nerves because he could not tell if it was collective or royal.

"And what did you find?" Rutherford asked.

"A beige bakkie, belonging to Emil Coetzee, parked on the perimeter of the bush. And that is all, I believe." Rutherford was about to ask another question when Moloi said, "Actually, that is not altogether correct. There was evidence that someone had been sick. Vomit on the ground."

Out of the corner of his eye, Joseth thought he saw the Chief Superintendent chuckle into his handkerchief.

"And from this evidence, you believe what?" Joseth asked, speaking for the first time and covering for Rutherford, who was momentarily at a loss for words. "That Emil Coetzee walked into the bush and threw up?"

"No. Not at all. The vomit was too recent to have been Emil Coetzee's. Most probably it was one of the two men who vomited."

"The two men?" Joseth asked, trying to keep the surprise from his voice.

"Yes. The two men. One white. The other black. They entered the bush the day before we went there to investigate. They were luckier than we were; they came out carrying a brown Stetson."

This time the Chief Superintendent did not bother to conceal his laughter.

"Unfortunately, they contaminated the scene," Moloi said.

"Which is a pity, but I think we were able to gather enough evidence."

"Evidence?" Rutherford asked.

"Foot prints, animal tracks, spoor, broken grass, that sort of thing. Evidence." There was a silence that lasted long enough for Moloi to ask, "Will that be all?"

Chief Superintendent Griffiths nodded hesitantly, and looked at Joseth and Rutherford, awaiting their acquiescence.

"No. That will not be all," Rutherford said, removing a sharpened HB pencil from his breast pocket and twirling it between his fingers. "You did not follow procedure, did you Moloi?"

"Did I not?"

"No. You did not. And you bloody well know that you did not. What is the first thing that you are supposed to do once you receive a report of a crime involving a high-level official?"

"Call the SIU."

"Exactly! Call the SIU. And did you do that?"

"No."

"Exactly! No. And why did you not call the SIU?"

"Because they had already been to the scene. The two men I spoke of earlier. One white, the other black. They are with the SIU."

"And how could you possibly know that?"

"The number plates of their bakkie. 700L5. We checked the database. The vehicle is registered with the SIU," Moloi said.

Chief Superintendent Griffiths was openly enjoying himself by now.

Joseth had long understood that Moloi—who gave all his answers with a straight face that did not hold the slightest hint of humor in it—had decided to impress his superior at their expense. But again, not all superiors were made the same, and

Joseth wanted to teach Moloi this particular lesson.

"You are retiring, aren't you, Moloi?" Joseth said, revealing that he too knew things that he might, hitherto, have not been suspected of knowing. "After thirty odd years of service, the good Chief Superintendent here throws you a bone and lets you run the station, for what? A few days? Power is a very powerful thing. Intoxicating, even. And so you let it go straight to your head."

"Now, steady on there—" Chief Superintendent Griffiths interjected.

"Perhaps these young men coming up these days do not take you seriously," Joseth continued undeterred. "Make a joke out of you. Think you are old-fashioned. Call you 'madala' behind your back. You would like to show them, wouldn't you?"

"Everyone, and I mean *everyone*, in this station has the utmost respect for Moloi, I can assure you," the Chief Superintendent said.

"And so you receive a call," Joseth continued, ignoring the Chief Superintendent. "Not really anonymous as you say, because the village next to the National Park is the village that your wife is from, is it not? And so you most likely know the caller. He tells you that Emil Coetzee, The Head of the Organization of Domestic Affairs and one of the most powerful men in the city—in the country even—has walked into the bush. And you think to yourself, this is my chance. Thirty-something years is a long time to work at something and have very little to show for it. Perhaps all you want is to see your name associated with a white person. Little men tend to have little ambition."

Joseth noticed that Rutherford was nodding encouragingly, and continued: "And so you receive a call and decide not only to eschew procedure, but to overstep your bounds as well. The Matopos area is not under the jurisdiction of the Western Commonage. Neither are the Eastern suburbs. You are only supposed to look into cases that take place in the Western townships. You've only been at it for a few days, but your incompetence has all but erased the great work we had already done. You do realize, don't you, that you could lose your badge over this? You are obviously prepared to retire from the force; how would you feel if you were fired without benefits instead?"

"Now, gentlemen!" Chief Superintendent Griffiths barked. "You were caught with your trousers down and your hands where they should not have been, and Moloi rightly pointed this out. I should not have laughed—I admit that, and I apologize. But we are gentlemen all."

Moloi was removing his badge.

"Over my dead body, Moloi!" the Chief Superintendent exclaimed. "The gesture is, quite frankly, beneath you."

Moloi placed his badge on the Chief Superintendent's desk and stood.

"Moloi! Sit down, man."

Moloi made his way to the door.

"Apologize!" Chief Superintendent Griffiths commanded.

Joseth, satisfied, watched Moloi visibly stiffen before he turned around to look at the Chief Superintendent. Joseth allowed himself to smile slightly in triumph.

"You have made your point, Moloi. But you know that you did not follow procedure, and that you should not have been anywhere near that village. You were wrong, and you know it. So apologize," Chief Superintendent Griffiths said.

Moloi looked at his superior for quite some time, and then took a deep breath before saying, "I apologize."

Joseth was not surprised by Moloi's easy capitulation. What else could he expect from a man who had long become accustomed to following orders?

"Good man. I knew you would do the right thing," the Chief Superintendent said.

Joseth watched Moloi's eyes leave the Chief Superintendent's and travel to him, and that was how he knew that when the Chief Superintendent said, "Apologize," this time it was directed at him.

"I beg your pardon?" Joseth said.

"You can beg for it all you want, but I am not granting it," Chief Superintendent Griffiths said. "I don't know who you think you are, young man, but I will not have you coming into my station, my office, and humiliating my best officer. A man, who by the looks of it, is a far better human specimen than you could ever dream of being. You and your partner obviously confused your arses for your elbows, but that is not Moloi's fault or problem. It is yours. Deal with it like men and not like boys out pissing. You want him to drop the Emil Coetzee case? Tell him to do so. But before you do that, apologize."

Something very bitter filled Joseth's mouth before he bit out the words, "I apologize."

"Very well," said the Chief Superintendent. "Now we can put them back in and zip up our flies. I think we have established whose is the biggest." He smiled at them, showing that all was already forgotten. He picked up the badge that Moloi had deposited on his desk and handed it to him. "You know where that belongs."

Moloi took the badge and put in its place a bunch of keys.

"What are these?" the Chief Superintendent asked, looking at the keys that he found himself holding.

"The keys to the Coetzee house," Moloi said, before walking out the door.

Rutherford promptly took the keys from the Chief

Superintendent.

With Moloi gone, the Chief Superintendent said, "In case there is any doubt, gentlemen, mine is, quite naturally, the biggest. Never forget that. And the man who just walked out of this office is not only my best officer; he also has the best reasoning mind in the country. Never forget that either. I have always been wise enough to keep him out of all things political. And you have just dropped him right in the thick of it. All I can do now is wish you gentlemen good luck."

SPOKES

---·---

It was 28 December, and the station was still decorated in the tinsel and paper decorations that the officers' wives made every year. This year the lovely Loveness had not contributed to the decorations, and Spokes noticed, as he walked from Chief Superintendent Griffith's office to the Sergeants' Office, that the Christmas tree looked incomplete without Loveness's twinkling star affixed atop it; and the ceiling looked bereft without her intricately interlocked decorations and bunting. Spokes had had to reconcile himself to a festive season that had been anything but.

"Merry Christmas," one of the junior officers said to him as he walked along the corridor.

"A few days late, aren't you?" Spokes said with a weak smile.

"Your middle name, sir. Merry Christmas," the junior officer said with a much broader smile.

"Back in my day a superior would have had you running around the station yard until you could not remember how to smile," Spokes said, chuckling and shaking his head so that the junior officer knew that he was in jest. As he neared his office, he saw that the sergeants with whom he shared it were standing outside, and looking at him with open curiosity, as though they were expecting something to happen. Had they also noticed the missing twinkling star? Had they overheard the conversation with the two men from the SIU who had been ready to humiliate him, but not as ready to fail? Instead of the sergeants saying anything to him, they just grinned and opened the office door.

"Merry Christmas, Chief Inspector Moloi, albeit belated," Marion Hartley said as he entered the office. She was sitting by his desk on the chair opposite his, and she smiled and her eyes twinkled up at him.

Spokes now understood the look his fellow officers had given him. Not knowing what else to do, he responded with a "Merry Christmas" of his own, and then stood there awkwardly, as though he was a visitor in his own office.

Well aware that they had a captive audience in his fellow officers, who had seated themselves and their curiosity and expectation down at their desks, Marion Hartley said, "I have something that I would like to share with you. In private."

Spokes could feel the sergeants trying to read the situation.

"The courtyard," Spokes suggested. "We will have privacy there."

Marion Hartley nodded and stood up. She looked at the sergeants and said, "It was an absolute pleasure." The sergeants seemed to have been rendered mute, but somehow managed to respond with silly schoolboy grins as she picked up her handbag and followed Spokes out of the office. *Poor Emil Coetzee,* Spokes thought as he shut the door behind them. He had never stood a chance. Marion Hartley was a very powerful force.

"Would you like a cup of tea?" Spokes asked perfunctorily, over his shoulder, fully expecting her to decline the offer.

"That would be more than lovely," Marion Hartley said.

Spokes could hear her footsteps behind him as he changed direction and headed over to the canteen. She followed him there, and he knew that she knew that she was not supposed to be there. He knew that she liked knowing that she was trespassing, and that there was nothing that he could do about it.

"How do you take it?" he asked.

"With lots of lemon and no sugar," she replied, walking casually about the room, absent-mindedly examining the crockery and cutlery.

Spokes busied himself pouring hot tea from a large silver tea urn. Even above the noise that the machine made, he could hear Marion Hartley walking toward him. He placed her white cup on a white saucer, and she accepted them with both hands. As he prepared his own cup of tea, she watched him closely, so that he became self-conscious about the splash of hot milk and the lump of sugar he added to his cup. He opened a box of Lobels' Choice Assorted Biscuits and hesitated slightly before offering it to her. She picked out two shortbread biscuits. He picked a single lemon cream for himself, and then closed the box.

"You strike me as a very disciplined and principled man, Chief Inspector," Marion Hartley said. "One dash of milk. One lump of sugar. One lemon cream."

"I am just a simple man," Spokes said.

"You are many things, Chief Inspector. A simple man is definitely not one of them."

Again, Spokes stood before her, not knowing quite what to do. "Shall we head out to the courtyard?" he asked at last.

Her smile disappeared and the twinkle left her eyes, and Spokes was sorry for it—sorry for the history that could not and would not let them take the first steps toward friendship.

Marion Hartley nodded and followed him out.

In the courtyard, they shared a whitewashed bench that was situated underneath an acacia tree in bloom, and which provided wonderfully dappled shade that cast them both in light and shadow.

They drank their tea in silence for some time. She made rather fast work of her two shortbread biscuits, and then sipped at her tea. He took gulps of his tea and saved his lemon cream for last.

When she finished her tea, she placed the cup and saucer on the ground, then reached for her handbag, opened it, and retrieved a packet of Madison cigarettes. "Do you mind?" she asked. He shook his head. She hit the pack against her left palm, several times, and he got the impression that she was playing for time. She pulled out a cigarette, scooped a silver lighter from her handbag, lit the cigarette, and then, in near disgust, threw the pack of cigarettes and the lighter back into her handbag before clasping it shut. She put the cigarette to her lips, inhaled deeply, and exhaled a cloud of smoke.

"I had not smoked in over twenty years—and now look at me. And all because of him. When he comes back, he will have a lot to answer for." She tried to smile, failed, and then took another drag of her cigarette and exhaled the words, "Here it goes, Marion," without looking at Spokes. "You have to understand that I did not know. I grew up on a farm, the Hartley farm. It belonged to my grandfather and would one day belong to my father. All I knew was that while my father lived in the farm house, my mother, my grandmother, my cousins and I did not. We lived in a series of rough brick-and-mortar structures at the periphery of the farmstead. This arrangement of affairs did not seem at all odd to me. It was all I knew...

"I rarely saw my father, and when I did see him, he barely spoke to me. I did not mind. It never occurred to me to mind because I did not feel the need to be special to him in any way. He seemed to like my mother well enough, and she would sometimes be happy because of him and she would sometimes be sad because of him. Sometimes when he came to visit her, she would chase us children out of the house and tell us to go and play with the children in the neighboring village—and that, I suppose, was her way of loving him. When he did come and visit her, he told her she was the most beautiful woman that he had ever seen and brought her some very pretty things to prove it—and that, I suppose, was his way of loving her.

"My memories of that time are very happy. I remember days filled with nothing else but playing and playing and playing with my cousins. My grandmother had had four daughters, my mother being her youngest, and by the time I came along, my three aunts had had two children each. There was so much laughter and adventure that sometimes we would get into fights just to do something different. I suppose, now that I think back on it, we may very well have been poor, but my grandmother's pride would not let us feel it. She was the granddaughter of Frederick Courteney Selous, you see, and she never let us forget it."

Marion Hartley decided that it was time for another cigarette, and paused to crush the butt of the cigarette she held into the ground. She retrieved another cigarette from her handbag, lit it up, and continued.

"My grandmother was a beautiful and formidable woman, and we loved her and she loved us all fiercely in return. But her love had not been enough where her children were concerned. Her three older daughters lived rather wild and chaotic lives in the City of Kings, and my mother seemed to be content with a rather wild and chaotic life on the farm. My grandmother wanted more for us, her grandchildren. She saw the farm offering us very limited horizons and wanted us to escape it. I have used this to try to better understand why she did what she did… but I am getting ahead of myself and that is not the way to tell the story.

My father went to the City of Kings for work, and a year or so later word reached us that he had married a woman there. Afterwards, everyone said that my mother had died of a broken heart, but what she really did was go to the City of Kings and drink herself into an early grave. My father, upon hearing news of her death, shot himself. That was, I suppose, their way of loving each other till death. I was an orphan before I was nine years old, but I did not feel it because I had a grandmother and cousins and love all around me."

It was time for another cigarette. Marion Hartley trampled the one she had barely smoked underfoot before taking a fresh cigarette from her handbag and lighting it. This one she smoked for quite some time, and Spokes began to feel that perhaps that was the end of the story—or, at least, the part she was comfortable telling him.

"My father's spinster sister," Marion Hartley continued, "and his only surviving sibling returned from England to be with her parents who had lost two sons during the Great War and one during peace time. She felt sorry for me and one day decided to take me with her to the City of Kings. She bought me a new dress and new shoes and fussed over me until I was feeling like a little Miss Somebody, I can tell you. We went to La Grange Skating Rink, and I fell in love with the carousel, the cotton candy, the chaos—with everything about the place, and especially with the skating rink. The feeling I felt when I first wobbled on its surface was sheer freedom. It was like I had found a magical kingdom, and, quite naturally, I never wanted to leave it.

"But all good things, as they say. Eventually it was time to leave and I became difficult. All of a sudden, I understood what my grandmother meant about the limited horizons of the farm. I understood why my aunts had chosen to go wild in the city, why my mother had chosen to die in the city, my father too. I told my well-meaning aunt that I was never going back to the farm and that I would stay at La Grange Skating

Rink forever. I said all this rather loudly and my aunt, who had no experience with children, must have wondered what had happened to the little angel that she had been with all day. But I was throwing my first ever tantrum and making the most of it.

"A woman said, very kindly given the circumstances, 'Here, perhaps this will make your daughter feel better.' She handed me a blue-and-white scarf... so delicate... so light... so seemingly made of air and even more refined things. It was the most beautiful thing I had ever seen, and I loved it immediately. I guess I was my mother's daughter because the present of a pretty something had the desired effect: I stopped my crying and screaming and just gazed at the thing I held in my hands."

Marion Hartley stopped again and reached into her handbag. However, this time she did not retrieve the box of cigarettes. She removed a gorgeous and much-loved blue and white scarf and handed it to Spokes.

"I had hardly paid attention to the woman's words, but my aunt had, and those words were to change my entire life. On the farm, everyone had a different hue. There were different textures of hair, eyes of different colors. No one looked the same, but there were some similarities, family resemblances. I understood that the Hartleys on the farmstead were all white. I understood that the people who lived in the village were mostly black. I understood that my family was made up of members who were various shades of brown. I understood that I was the lightest, that I had the straightest hair, that I had the bluest eyes. But none of it had ever really meant anything to me, or to anyone else, for that matter, who lived in that series of brick-and-mortar structures on the periphery of the Hartley farmstead. Until my aunt asked my grandmother if I could be her daughter—and my grandmother, with very little hesitation, agreed."

"You have to understand that I was never anything else but a child who grew up in a family where everyone looked different... and then I was suddenly white. My grandmother had skin the color of your cold tea there, and she told me to never tell anyone that I belonged to her... and for the longest time I did not. She said that it was only by denying her and my mother that I could have a fulfilling life. I became the daughter of Cecilia Hartley, an eccentric, once-upon-a-time suffragette who made up a vague story about a boy loved who had come back after the war lost and broken, and who had died before he could marry her and see his daughter be born."

Marion Hartley sat up straighter and smiled defiantly, before she carried on. "Cecilia was a brilliant mother to me. She gave me many things: genuine love and affection, friendship, security, freedom, happiness... and whiteness. She fostered in me a love of reading and an intellectual curiosity that I will be forever grateful for. She treated me with respect and as her equal, even when I was a child. After she enrolled me at Coghlan Primary School, she encouraged me to think for myself. She also made me enjoy life. On holidays we took trips, mostly by train. I loved her immensely. She never tried to erase or have me forget who I was. She is the one who introduced me to Zora Neale Hurston. She arranged it so that my grandmother could see me without creating too much suspicion, by having her sell wares at a concession stand at La Grange Skating Rink, where I spent every weekend."

"Cecilia was my mother. She gave me the Marion Hartley you see before you today... and then again, she also gave me the Marion Hartley you see before you today. It is a dual inheritance. One I have had to live with for most of my life. I love both my mothers: the one who taught me how to love and the one who taught me how not to love. I love my grandmother, who gave me the courage to see beyond my limiting horizons. I love Marion Hartley, wherever I may find her."

She paused for some time, allowing Spokes to absorb and process all that he had heard.

"I have always told the truth to those who mattered. I told my husband, Courteney Smythe-Sinclair, when we first met. I am telling you now because when we met before, I could tell that you knew I was keeping something from you. Now you know what it is. I told Emil that morning. It is why he left and drove to the bush… it is why he still has not returned. I always knew that he would take the news rather badly, and he did. I suppose I should not be too hard on him for being a little pre-dictable. I hope you understand why I could not tell you any of this while Kuki was there."

"Yes. Yes, of course."

"Not because it is my secret, but because it is now his as well, you understand?"

"I understand," Spokes said as he handed her the blue-and-white scarf.

"I now only wear it when I need a certain kind of cour-age," Marion Hartley said as she took the scarf from him. She looked at him: "I notice that you never address me directly. You don't know what to call me, do you? Madam? Mrs? Miss? Well, I have never been a madam. I was married, but never was a Mrs. I am too old by far to be Miss anybody. So I think you have to call me Marion."

It took Spokes a long while, but in the end he said, "Marion…"

Marion Hartley's smile broadened and beamed. "Can you believe that we are only three days away from a brand-new year?" she said. "I tell you what, Emil better be back by New Year's, or he really will be unforgiven."

Spokes was happy to see the twinkle back in her eyes.

JANUARY 1980

TOM

—————◆—————

Tom Fortenoy had played the part of Emil Coetzee so many times that he found that he definitely did not need to be present for his own performance in order for his audience to enjoy it, and so he always spent quite a few hours at the bar before staggering onto the stage. Tom's pre-performance preparation seemed rather fitting because his Emil—clad in khaki safari suit, khaki knee-length socks, khaki veldskoene and khaki boonie hat—was a man of many words, most of them slurred, mumbled or mispronounced, and spoken while he was holding a bottle of Castle Lager, which he referred to as "my best girl," in one hand, and a handkerchief, khaki, of course, in the other.

During the very last hours of 1979, Tom's Emil found himself swaying slightly on the stage as he said, "Did you hear the one about the blonde?" and then immediately forgot the punchline because just then, Tom was pantomiming a woman passing by, and Emil, who loved a skirt almost as much as he loved "his best girl," followed her with his eyes, craning his neck until she was out of sight. Having been thus absorbed, Emil lost his train of thought, removed his boonie hat, ran his fingers through his blond hair, and asked the audience, "Now where was I?"

"Did you hear the one about the blonde?" they good-naturedly shouted back. "As a matter of fact I did," Emil said. But before he could get to the punchline, he was distracted again, this time by some exploit of Sixpence and Lobengula.

"Which reminds me of something that one of the boys said to me this morning," Emil said. As soon as he said "the boys" the crowd started laughing and applauding.

The "blonde bit" was Tom's favorite skit because he felt that it perfectly captured the essence of Emil Coetzee; and, for their part, the audience appreciated it well enough and were generous enough not to let the joke ever grow stale, but their favorite skits were the ones that contained Sixpence and Lobengula. The highly popular act, called "Emil and the Boys," played on Emil Coetzee's reputation as a man who "knows the African." In the performance, Emil would regale the audience with tales of his adventures with the two Africans in his employ: Sixpence, the garden boy, and Lobengula, the houseboy. Emil would tell the tale as an example of how he understood the African's state of mind, but what the tale would inevitably reveal was how much Sixpence and Lobengula played on the sympathy of their baas, and always got the better of him.

Sixpence and Lobengula were perennially lazy and would do anything to escape an honest day of hard work. Humorously believing themselves to be equal to their baas, they refused to speak to him in Chilapalapa, or "Kitchen Kaffir," as Tom made a point of calling it on stage, and opted instead to hybridize it with a broken English delivered in a plodding way that revealed how extremely slow their brains were at formulating thought. Chilapalapa consisted mainly of command words, accusatory phrases, and very few words that helped explain things. The language had borrowed in-sufficient words from English, Afrikaans and various local African languages, and although it was the *lingua franca* of baas-boy relations, beyond that context it was utter gibberish. Tom's audience ate up the act and loved every minute of it; it did not help matters that Sixpence and Lobengula spoke their irreparably broken English with the stage presence of great Shakespearean actors.

Now on stage, Emil had just caught Sixpence, for the umpteenth time, taking his afternoon nap. "Baas, mina, I'm making garden nice-nice for you, baas... I'm making everything nice and pretty like woman you are always looking at, baas. But this one, fanakalo, he is making kitchen pig sty, baas," Sixpence complained to Emil about Lobengula. "He is doing such bad job, baas, that mina, I'm having to do job kayena as well, baas. So I'm getting very tire, baas... no, no, not lazy, baas, mina never lazy! Mina working job of two boys, kamina and kayena. So not lazy, baas. No, not sleeping, baas, never sleeping. Just watching my eyelids, baas."

The audience joined Emil for the "just watching my eyelids, baas," punchline. "Just watching my eyelids, baas," was Sixpence's catchphrase, and had proved so popular that a line of T-shirts with the catchphrase printed on them seemingly could not be produced fast enough.

Tom was aware that he had resorted to stereotype in order to portray the two Africans, but he knew which side his bread was buttered on. He consoled himself with the fact that his "Emil"—a deluded fool who thought too highly of himself and believed too sincerely in his own intelligence—was also the worst kind of white man. Tom had hoped, however, that some members of his audience would pick up on the satire and realize that the joke ran both ways. They, forever beneath him and many steps behind him, never really picked up on the irony of the act. Never had and never would because they had not been reared to understand nuance, and more was the pity. He performed his act mostly in bars that had carpeted floors smelling strongly of spilled beer and stale tobacco and faintly of stewing piss, so what did he expect?

Tom would have given up the act years ago, but the

audience had kept on coming and growing, especially after the recording of his popular skit called "Emil in the back of the Bakkie" in which, at a braaivleis, Emil, who has a cold, recounts the story of how he came to have a cold. The story involves him driving Sixpence and Lobengula to the bush to do some hunting. On their way, they sit at the back of the bakkie and Emil and his Alsatian, Johnny Boy, sit in the front. In the bush, Sixpence and Lobengula find ways not to do any work. On the way back, after spotting a graying cloud, Sixpence tells Emil that he can drive better than Lobengula, and Lobengula says that he is the better driver. They decide that perhaps the best thing is for each of them to drive the bakkie at intervals, and let the baas decide. Emil agrees, and finds himself sitting at the back of the bakkie with his Alsatian, Johnny Boy, just as the rain cloud bursts open. The skit cannot end here, of course, because then the joke would be squarely on Emil. It ends with Sixpence and Lobengula coming up with the brilliant idea of jointly driving the car so as to get home faster, at which point they succeed in driving into a ditch.

Tom Fortenoy had long been a drunk, but he liked to think that he became a more devout one thanks to the increased popularity of his one-man show.

The instant success of the "Emil in the back of the Bakkie" recording had led to another recording and then another, and another, and another; and, in turn, these recordings found their way into enough homes on the eastern side of every city and town in the country that, as a result, the war years treated Tom rather well. The royalties that he received from the "Emil and the Boys" series, although no king's ransom in and of themselves, kept Doreen and the little Fortenoys out of the poor house—that is, when he did not drink or gamble them all away. The recordings also enabled him to get many free drinks at almost every bar with a white proprietor in the City of Kings. Realizing that he had sunk unforgivably low for one who had been classically trained and who had cut his teeth in Shakespearean productions, Tom allowed himself to drink himself to near oblivion every night, and gradually pickled his liver. Cirrhosis, his doctor had called it. That was what? Two years ago. Now he was calling it cancer.

Tonight was no different. It was New Year's Eve, and all the men at the bar were feeling more than a little generous and very willing to ply him with libations. When he received his payment for the gig, he determined that the first thing he would do as soon as he left the bar would be to go home and press the newly minted money into Doreen's hands. He remembered making a similar resolution around Christmas, but then something had happened that prevented him from going home. What was it? Something about a lucky strike. No worries. This time, this time he would keep his promise. And... he would ring in the New Year with his family.

Just then the men at the bar started counting down toward the New Year: ten... nine... eight... seven... so maybe he would not be able to ring in the New Year with Doreen and the little Fortenoys after all, but he would definitely spend the New Year, 1980, with them. Three... two... one: "Happy New Year!" He joined in the cheer, and then began singing the first chorus of "Auld Lang Syne."

Should auld acquaintance be forgot
And never brought to mind?
Should auld acquaintance be forgot
And days of auld lang syne?

By the time Tom left the Dilettante Club, in the early hours of New Year's Day, he was so drunk that he forgot Emil's khaki boonie hat, and left it on the back of his bar stool.

As Tom lurched and swerved and swayed his way home along Selborne Avenue, he heard footsteps approaching. The footsteps on the floorboards were the clickety-clack of a woman's heeled pair of shoes. Floorboards? A woman? Was he back on stage? Who was he playing in this moment? What was his role? Was he finally playing Lear? Was this Cordelia approaching? Was he about to tell Ophelia to get herself to a nunnery, or let Lady Macbeth persuade him to get blood on his hands? Tom tried to push through the fog of his mind so that he could remember what great role he was supposed to be playing. Shylock? Was this Portia come in the guise of Balthasar to teach him the difference between justice and vengeance? There was a clearing, and Tom remembered that gone were his glory days on the stage, and that he had been reduced to playing Emil Coetzee at bars. In that case, the woman was a lover. Emil Coetzee certainly had plenty of those. The knowledge that it was a woman following him allowed Tom to relax. There was never anything to fear from a woman except the end of her tether.

The heeled clickety-clack crept closer on the floorboards… no, Tom remembered, he was not on the stage now: the footsteps were on the concrete pavement of one of the streets in the City of Kings… Selborne Avenue. Clickety-clack. Clickety-clack. As the footsteps came nearer, the strong scent of a cheap woman's perfume grew stronger. No, not quite right— modifier in the wrong place—a woman's cheap perfume. *There was a world of difference between a cheap woman's perfume and a woman's cheap perfume,* Tom thought, just before the woman called out to him.

"Emil!" she said.

Tom turned around and heard three shots being fired from a gun. It was only when he began to sink to the cold concrete of the pavement that he realized that he had been shot. Had the woman who shot him given him a moment to pause and reflect, Tom would have been happy to know that his performance as Emil was so complete and so convincing that the woman thought that he was indeed Emil Coetzee.

As Tom struggled to turn his lolling head, he heard the clickety-clack of the heels come nearer still. The scent of a woman's cheap perfume... a cheap woman's perfume... tickled his nostrils and he would have sneezed, had his body not been in distress. He opened his eyes with great difficulty to see leaning above him a woman who was now so close that he could hear her shaky breath. Her back was to the streetlight and so her face was poorly lit, but Tom could tell that she was anywhere between the ages of thirty and sixty. Although he could not see her clearly, he was certain he had never seen the woman before.

The woman reached out a gloved hand and tenderly stroked his cheek.

"I did it to protect you... because I love you," she said before she leaned down and kissed him full on the lips. The kiss lingered, and then she straightened up and was gone.

VIDA

———◆———

Vida de Villiers was finding his way home when he heard gunshots—three in total. At first he thought the shots were just part of the noise in his head; the sounds that were always trying to return him to the bush… to the fight… the battle… the war. He had almost convinced himself that it was all in his head, and then he heard the sound of something that had no business being in the bush—a woman's shoes clickety-clacking along a concrete pavement. The brittle-sounding heels were moving toward him, and Vida had the presence of mind to duck into the nearest alleyway.

Had the woman seen him? Was she after him? He could not hear much above the frantic beating of his heart. He tried to quiet it, but there was too much adrenaline coursing through his veins for his heart to heed his desires. All he could think of was that he had survived the war, if only barely, just to be gunned down in the streets. He would die not a hero, but a victim of something that he did not even understand.

The alleyway smelled of all the things you expect an alleyway to smell of—old urine, beer, neglect, dankness and decay. Maybe the smell of beer came from him. But there was something else, something unexpected. Was that the smell of bread? Warm, oven-fresh bread? Where exactly was he? Soon another scent invaded the alleyway. A woman's cheap perfume? A cheap woman's perfume? The scent meant that the woman was near. Vida felt his nostrils tingle with the desire to sneeze, and had to use all his willpower to suppress the urge. He stopped breathing, and thought he heard the shoes clickety-clacking up the pavement and away from him.

Vida had no idea how long he stood in that alleyway with his back plastered against the wall. A few minutes? An hour? A lifetime? All he knew with certainty was that it seemed to take forever for fear to leave him and allow him to exit the shadows and venture onto the well-lit streets. It was not that he was no longer apprehensive and suddenly courageous; it was that the body and the mind can only hold onto fear for so long. His heart was still pounding as he left what he soon learnt was the alleyway next to Downing's Bakery. *What if she were lying in wait for him?* Even as he thought this thought, he crossed the street and headed toward where he had heard the three gunshots coming from. He wished that other people were out and about so that someone else could come across whatever crime had taken place. But there was no one else. There was just him alone on this lonely night. The moment had chosen him, of all people, to bear witness.

He thought he remembered seeing the silhouette of a man fall, but he could no longer be sure. He could not be sure of anything, to be honest. He had had six bottles of Castle Lager and a rather potent blunt—perfect way to end a bloody year. That he still remembered his name—Vida de Villiers— was the real mystery here. He probably had imagined, no, hallucinated it all.

Just as he was beginning to convince himself of the im-plausibility, there appeared before him the shape of some-thing under one of the in-bloom trees that surrounded the City Hall. Vida made his way to it. If the woman was still close by and still waiting to shoot him, she would have done so already, he reasoned as he finished crossing Selborne Avenue. He marvelled at how very quiet, almost peaceful, a street that was always bustling during the day could actually be.

When he looked down at the shape of something, it was a man looking up at him with dead eyes. Vida had seen men with dead eyes before, so that was not what caused the terrified sound which escaped his mouth. What made him scream was the fact that looking up at him with dead eyes was Emil Coetzee, Everleigh's father—the man who, not so long ago, had driven past Flat 2A without looking at it; and, in so doing, determined Vida's future. If only fear had not captured Vida's heart and rendered him immobile, perhaps he would have been able to get to Emil Coetzee in time to save him in some way. Even though Vida was not sure that the man who had refused to look up at Flat 2A was deserving of salvation, he knew that he would have tried to save him because he was Everleigh's father.

Now that the opportunity to save Emil Coetzee had passed, Vida did not know what else to do but look at his dead body. It was the missing Stetson that made Vida notice the khaki knee-length socks. Khaki knee-length socks worn with khaki shorts, while the style of many a farmer, were not really Emil Coetzee's style. The shirt, with its three bullet holes, was mostly covered in blood, but the right short sleeve looked khaki as well. No, not Emil Coetzee's style at all. And where was the hat? The Stetson? Emil Coetzee without his Stetson was no Emil Coetzee at all.

Vida took a closer look and realized that while the man who looked up at him with dead eyes looked very much like Emil Coetzee, he was not Emil Coetzee. He also realized that whoever the man was, something would have to be done about his being dead—and that something would have to be done by Vida himself. Vida looked at the man and decidedly did not like him. He did not like him because he was making Vida, who would have preferred to be responsible for no one—not even himself—responsible for him.

There was a choice—there always was. Vida could simply walk away. No one knew that he was there. No one knew what he had seen. He could let the dead man with the dead eyes be discovered by someone else—let him be someone else's problem. But even as this choice presented itself, Vida knew it was not a real choice. He was being forced by circumstance to make a decision that affected another person. He knew that he would do what he would have done had the dead man actually been Emil Coetzee; he would go to the Central Police Station, which was just two streets up the road, and report a murder.

———•———

The merriment in the police station reminded Vida that it was New Year's Eve—well, actually probably New Year's Day now, given the unforgivableness of the hour. Without any real warning, it was 1980. Another year. Same life.

The Desk Sergeant, who looked as if he would be happy to lock up Vida under any pretext—for simply being Vida, for coming into the station on New Year's Day, for coming into the station on New Year's Day to report a murder, or for all of the above—only seemed to pay attention to what Vida was saying when he said, "At first I thought it was Emil Coetzee." All of a sudden, the sergeant had a lot of questions and wanted to know every detail, until Vida even gave him what seemed to him to be the most useless detail of all: "She smelled of a woman's cheap perfume... or a cheap woman's perfume." Although he meticulously took down every piece of information, the Desk Sergeant did not commend Vida for reporting the crime. Instead, he charged him with loitering and locked him up in one of the holding cells, which only served to cement Vida's resolve to not intervene in the lives of others.

TOM

———— ♦ ————

Tom woke up to find himself naked and alone in a very cold room. What on God's green earth was going on? How drunk was he? What day was it? Was he in hospital? Had he made it home? He really hoped he had not gambled or drank away whatever money he had to his name. He had promised Doreen that he would be good this time, but while he remembered the promise, he did not remember the keeping of it.

His brain felt like cotton wool, his limbs were stiff and immobile and he seemed to have lost his voice. His tongue was thick and swollen and refused to move. This was all too familiar. He was trapped in one of his early morning stupors in which he was filled with a deep sense of foreboding, but could do nothing to escape it. But why was he naked?

Before he could find an answer, Tom heard voices, and as he listened to them, he relaxed. The voices spoke with authority: the people coming knew exactly what was going on and would explain it to him. The door opened and two men—one white, the other black—looked down at him. They looked at him for quite some time, and both smiled as though they had found a long-lost friend. They did not seem to make anything of his nudity. They did not seem to mind his silence. They seemed happy to take him as he was.

"It is almost uncanny," the white one said, as he slowly leaned closer.

Tom wished he had the voice to tell the man that something was either uncanny or not—nothing could be *almost* uncanny. Unfortunately, he still did not have enough saliva to lubricate his heavy tongue and set it in motion.

"Yes… yes. You will do quite nicely," the white one said before turning to the black one and saying, "I must say, great idea of yours, this. Great idea."

It was the black one's turn to lean closer. "Even I didn't know how great an idea it was until this very moment. He looks almost exactly like him."

There was that "almost" again.

"That madala… I mean, that man over at the Western Commonage stitched us up good and proper," the white one said. "Made it impossible for us to put our plan into motion, and what a beautiful plan it was. 'Golide Gumede lures Emil Coetzee into the bush.' I could already see the headline… the uproar."

"Yes, it was the perfect plan," the black one said.

"But now there is this," the white one said, looking at Tom. "And this is pure gold. Pure gold."

Tom had no idea what they were talking about, and began to despair that they would not and could not explain his situation to him. For his part, he felt so out of it that he could not be sure that any of it was really happening. Jesus! He must have drank as much as an elephant at a watering hole the night before.

"Where are our manners?" the white one said. "Introductions are necessary, I think." But before he could introduce himself, the man had a severe attack of the giggles.

Were they… drunk?

The black one started laughing too, if you could call a reluctant chuckle a laugh.

"My name is Clement Rutherford," the white one said. "But everyone calls me Rutherford, and so should you, because we are going to become really good friends. And this is my colleague—"

"Joseth Maraire," the black one said.

Did he just say… Joseth? Yes, they were definitely drunk. With dismay, Tom realized that the only authority that these two men possessed was the deepness of their voices.

"No need to introduce yourself," the white one, Rutherford, said. "We know who you are. You're the famous Tom Fortenoy." He made flattery seem like something that was used to grate the skin.

Rutherford and Joseph exchanged a look before Rutherford said, "Look here, Fortenoy, I am not a man who beats about the bush… except when it is nestled between a woman's thighs."

Apparently this was something that they both found highly amusing, and so nothing else was said for quite some time as one giggled and the other reluctantly chuckled. Dear God. He was in the presence of fools.

"How would you like to do this—be Emil Coetzee—for a while longer?" Rutherford eventually asked.

"Don't worry. Not too much longer," the black one—Joseph—said.

"About a day, maybe two—maybe a little more," Rutherford expounded, after exchanging another glance with Joseph.

Tom had many questions. But his voice still failed him.

"Ah, I see. You're wondering where Emil Coetzee is. Well, if we told you that, we'd unfortunately have to kill you," Rutherford said.

Tom expected him to giggle again, but he did not. Neither man even smiled. Was Rutherford being serious?

"We're with secret intelligence. We know how to do things," Rutherford said. Again, neither man laughed.

Tom had many jokes, good ones too, about the Secret

Intelligence Unit. He was glad that he had been struck dumb, because this was definitely not the audience for them.

Rutherford began giggling again. Joseph was still not laughing. "Relax, Tom. Of course, we are not going to kill you. Friends don't kill friends. And besides, what would be the point?"

————◆————

What a difference a day makes, Tom, no stranger to clichés and hackneyed expressions, thought as he rolled from one side of the king-sized bed to the other. Just to think, yesterday morning, he had woken up stiff and sore on the cold concrete of one of the Main Post Office's corridors, after shivering himself to sleep the night before. He had been Tom Fortenoy yesterday, he was Emil Coetzee today—and Emil Coetzee lived the kind of life that began each morning on the world's most magnificent mattress.

Tom lay on the bed feeling a now alien feeling: contentment. He allowed himself to enjoy it as he gloried in the warmth of the duvet a moment longer before he winked one eye at the midday sun. Looking at the gentle light that the cream-colored curtains filtered into the room, Tom knew that Emil Coetzee had never, not once, allowed himself to experience and enjoy the beauty that lay before him. Emil Coetzee was always up and out before the dawn, preferring to watch the sun rise over the City of Kings from the confines of his office at The Tower rather than from the comfort of his own bed.

Tom's stomach growled, and he became aware that he was hungry; no, not hungry, famished. Usually he ignored the grumblings of his stomach, but today he did not have to, because today he could actually do something about his hunger. He languorously yawned and stretched his way out of bed, and when he put his feet on the floor, he found a pair of navy-blue slippers patiently waiting for them. He put the slippers on and stood up, stretched and yawned again before making his way out of the room. Hooked behind the bedroom door was a morning gown with navy-blue and khaki stripes, because God forbid there could be a moment of the day in which Emil Coetzee was not somehow clad in something khaki.

When Rutherford and Joseph had dropped him off, Tom had been too happy to be coming in from the cold to notice much about the house. All he had noticed was its warmth. Now, as his practiced nose followed the faint smell of food to the kitchen, he noticed how very extravagantly furnished the house was—and how very, very silent. There was something remarkably lonely and definitely not new about the silence. As he walked through the stillness of Emil Coetzee's house, Tom wondered *if the lucky life that Emil Coetzee had had brought with it any regrets: regrets that could turn themselves into such a profound and established silence.* He did not preoccupy himself with this thought as he followed his nose to a spacious kitchen that was adorned with every modern appliance, and where the silver of stainless steel glittered from every surface. *A man who had built such a life for himself surely would have nothing to regret,* Tom thought as he looked around for a place to start putting together his feast.

He could not remember the last healthy meal he had had. His staple diet, ever since Doreen had come to the end of her tether, had consisted of alcohol of varying quality (he was not very particular) and the cream doughnuts from Downing's Bakery (he was very particular). He gleefully rubbed his hands together as he determined that he would have himself a proper English breakfast—bacon, sausages, eggs, grilled tomato, baked beans, buttered toast, and a cup of strong black coffee —the works—black pudding too, if it was there. He was already salivating when he eagerly opened the fridge. Because he could already see the meal in his mind's eye, it took him some time to grasp the fact that there were no eggs, no sausages, no bacon—no meat of any kind in the refrigerator. There was milk and cheese and butter and many tubs of plain yogurt and… no meat. In disbelieving desperation, Tom flung open the freezer compartment, but it was empty save for an icicled five-liter tub of Dairiboard Neapolitan ice cream. What was it that Emil Coetzee ate? Tom wondered as he slowly closed the fridge.

He laughed into the silence of the room as the thought occurred to him that perhaps Emil Coetzee was a vegetarian. What a preposterous notion! Of course Emil Coetzee was not a vegetarian, and, as though to prove this point, there were no vegetables or fruits in sight; not even one tomato that he could grill.

None of it made sense. Emil Coetzee was a red-blooded male who, in Tom's performance of him, attended braais every weekend and told bawdy jokes around the braaivleis stand while prodding at a coiled kilogram of boerewors with one hand and proudly holding "my best girl" in the other. "What happened when the blonde put her head on the pillow? Her legs flew open," his Emil had said countless times as he flipped over the boerewors. Tom could see his Emil chuckling at his own inanity as he popped a juicy chunk of meat into his mouth and then downed it with an ice-cold Castle Lager. Where was *that* Emil, *his* Emil, Tom wondered as he reached into the fridge, retrieved a block of mature cheddar cheese, and let his dreams of having a proper English breakfast for lunch turn to nothingness. He cut a healthy chunk of the cheddar into bite-sized pieces, put a piece in his mouth and savored its sharpness as he imitated Emil Coetzee chewing his boerewors with great relish.

With a few pieces of cheese in his hand, Tom decided to explore the rest of the house. The more he acquainted himself with Emil Coetzee's surroundings, the more he lost sight of *his* Emil. Besides the khaki stripes on the morning gown, there were a few pairs of khaki trousers in Emil Coetzee's wardrobe, which was otherwise filled with many shades of blue. There was no Clem Tholet record in Emil Coetzee's album collection, but there was every album that Kenny Rogers had ever recorded—*The Gambler* was on the record player. In addition, there were four LP records by The Carpenters, three records by Nana Mouskouri, two by Dionne Warwick, the same number by Dolly Parton, one by Demis Roussos, another by John Denver, and another by Don Williams—and so Tom had to let go of the Emil Coetzee who was so blindly patriotic that all he did was listen to Clem Tholet. Most surprising of all was the fact that while Emil Coetzee predictably had a den, in that den, instead of there being mountains of magazines with pin-up centerfolds, there were stacks upon stacks of *National Geographic*.

Who exactly was Emil Coetzee? Who was Tom supposed to be pretending to be? Who had he been pretending to be all these years?

As Tom put the last piece of cheddar in his mouth, he heard the sound of a car driving up the driveway. Soon voices approached, and as Tom listened to them, he relaxed and went to the corridor to meet them. Rutherford and Joseph entered the house with several other men. This time around, Rutherford and Joseph were very sober and very very serious. They barely acknowledged Tom as they walked past him, obviously men on a mission.

Tom followed them to the living room, where Rutherford immediately started ordering the other men around. Everyone received an order save Joseph who set off to do his own thing.

Tom watched with great perplexity as windows were broken, furniture overturned, and a door forced open. Within minutes, they had created a rather convincing scene of a break-in, complete with a point of entry, various signs of tampering, and evidence of struggle.

Their job done, the men seemed to be waiting only for praise. The Secret Intelligence Unit had spent decades perfecting the art of fabricating reality, and they had every reason to be proud of the job they were doing at the Coetzee home. Tom decided to go to the den to see what Joseph was up to. He found him writing something in red ink on the wall: G O L I D E G U M.

"Sweet Jesus!" one of the operatives screamed from another room in the house. His voice when they next heard it say, "Sir!" was more subdued, although it was still obvious from its tone that something had gone terribly wrong with their plan. "His arms won't move," the operative said.

"And for a relatively thin man, he's quite heavy," another operative said.

The two operatives entered the den carrying... Tom's body.

Now for quite some time Tom had been aware that things were not quite what they seemed—the men had not only ignored him, but treated him as though he were invisible. Many things had entered his mind suggesting themselves as reasons: perhaps he was still sleeping and this was but a dream; perhaps he was drunk and his mind was playing tricks on him; perhaps this was all a story that he was making up—it seemed fantastical enough. But none of the things that had suggested themselves to Tom had made him think that perhaps he was dead. And the reason that he did not think that he was dead was because he did not remember having died. Surely, if he had died, he would remember his own death. Surely...

TOM   153

He tried to feel something, but he could not feel anything. What was a man supposed to feel about his own death?

"Rigor mortis has set in," one of the operatives said. "We cannot make it look like a fall."

"Trust a ham actor to mess up an entirely perfect plot," Rutherford said, disgust and disappointment plain in his voice.

After a long moment of silence, Joseph, rubbing the red paint off his hands, said, "Let it be messy. That old madala over at the Western Commonage wants to get his picture in the paper so very badly; perhaps we should give him what he wants. A mess. Let him come here and try to make sense of it all."

Rutherford nodded his head slowly. "And let the delectable Saskia Hargrave come and find the story we give her to write," he said.

Tom felt something unexpectedly, and definitely not gently, pull at him, eager to drag him away. His life had been so shambolic that he firmly believed that he deserved a better death. As he listened to the cold-hearted men say words around his dead body that did nothing to reassure him that it was safe and wise to leave his body behind and in their care, he decided to do something that he had not done in a long time—fight for himself and for his dignity. And so he resisted the strong force pulling him into nothingness.

SPOKES

——————◆——————

It was not in his pigeonhole. It was not with the Desk Sergeant. If it was not on his personal desk, then he was in a world of trouble. 1980 was so far definitely not the golden year that Loveness had said it would be, and it was all his fault. His marital bed continued to be cold, and the copy of *Wives and Daughters* continued to be unread. Spokes had taken to sleeping on the sofa, but not even this had melted Loveness's heart. Chief Superintendent Griffiths had long returned from his fishing trip, and Spokes had gone back to being the Chief Inspector, but he knew that without the written approval of his retirement application, he would remain unforgiven for having entertained the idea of a promotion over the promise of Krum's Place.

So he was happy to note, as soon as he entered his office after his holiday break, that there was a BSAP envelope waiting for him on his desk. However, when he discovered, upon closer inspection, that the envelope was not sealed or addressed, his happiness waned. Still, he tried to hold on to as much of it as possible as he wished the three sergeants with whom he shared the office a "Happy New Year" and opened the contents of the envelope. Written on paper from one of the station's memo pads was the message: REPORTED. MAN SHOT DEAD. EMIL COETZEE? CENTRAL POLICE STATION. Although Spokes had wanted to receive something very different, he could not help but be excited by what he held in his hands.

"How long has this message been here?" Spokes inquired of his fellow officers. They all blankly stared back at him. "Does anyone know who put this here?"

"Must have already been on your desk when we came in this morning," one of the officers said.

Spokes unhooked his fedora from the back of the door and left the office.

On his way out of the station, Spokes asked the Desk Sergeant if he knew anything about the note that had appeared on his desk, but the sergeant, having just taken over from the Night-Duty Officer, found the note a mystery as well. Spokes signed out a set of keys for one of the police bakkies, and only noticed how anxious he was when his initials—S.M.M.—were written in a handwriting so shaky as to be almost illegible.

"Your middle name wouldn't by any chance be Miscellaneous?" the Desk Sergeant asked.

"A brand-new year, and that is the best that you can come up with," Spokes said with a smile as he walked out of the station.

Before he opened the door to the police bakkie, he removed the note from his pocket and read it again. REPORTED. MAN SHOT DEAD. EMIL COETZEE? CENTRAL POLICE STATION. Why the question mark after Emil Coetzee's name? A punctuation error? Or was there something more? Shot dead. Where? Reported by whom?

———•———

At the Central Police Station, everyone was busy. Officers were carrying files and boxes out of offices and up and down stairs.

"For the incinerators," the Central Police Station Desk Sergeant nonchalantly explained to Spokes's quizzical brow after he had seen the Chief Inspector's badge.

Spokes was at a loss as to what could be so disposable at a

police station. "Isn't that evidence?" he asked.

"Exactly," the Central Police Station Desk Sergeant said. "We don't want these guys that the new regime is going to bring in to know exactly what we've been up to, now do we? The *comrades* may not be as understanding and forgiving as we would like them to be." The Central Police Station Desk Sergeant looked at Spokes until he felt that he was understood. "I am sure you guys over at the Western Commonage are up to the same thing."

"Not to my knowledge," Spokes said.

"Of course," the Central Police Station Desk Sergeant said with a knowing wink.

As Spokes reached into his pocket to retrieve the note, another officer, junior in rank, came to whisper something in the Central Police Station Desk Sergeant's ear.

"Wanted upstairs, I'm afraid," the Central Police Station Desk Sergeant explained, before leaving his station.

The junior officer, a Section Officer, took over the Central Police Station Desk Sergeant's post so that Spokes had no choice but to show him the note.

"I received this today," Spokes said, holding out the note. "Could have been left on my desk last night or early this morning. Or any day over the past three days."

"Sorry, can't help you, sir," the Section Officer said after barely glancing at the note.

"Can't help me or won't help me?" Spokes asked.

The Section Officer had the effrontery to look offended. "Can't help you, sir, because no such report was made. At least not from this station."

"And how can you possibly know that?"

"Because I was on desk duty, sir."

"When?"

"I beg your pardon, sir?"

"When were you on duty?"

"Last night. This morning. Over the past three days."

"How very convenient."

"Probably someone just making a joke, sir. Some New Year's Day fun."

Spokes did not know what to do with his frustration. He looked at the officers busying themselves with getting rid of evidence, and realized that there was no use in even asking to see a superior. He walked away from the Section Officer. Perhaps this had indeed been meant as a joke. He could think of two people—Clement Rutherford and Joseth Maraire—who would think it was worth their time to waste his.

"You forgot your note," the Section Officer called after him.

Spokes was certain that the note was safely tucked away in his breast pocket. He turned, and the Section Officer was indeed holding up a note. He returned to the station's front desk, took the note from the Section Officer, put it in his pocket without reading it, and left the station.

Once Spokes was safely in the police bakkie, he retrieved the note the Section Officer had handed him. It simply read: PIONEER HOUSE. FIVE MINUTES. Spokes drove to Pioneer House and had just parked the car when the Section Officer opened the passenger door and entered the car.

"You don't remember me, sir. I don't expect you to," the Section Officer said. "But I remember you. You gave a lecture on ethics my first year in the force. I wasn't lying, sir, when I said I was on duty. Early hours of yesterday. A young man comes in and says someone's been shot. There's a body. A man. Looks very much like Emil Coetzee, but is almost certainly not Emil Coetzee. Body's on the Selborne Avenue pavement over at City Hall. Young man says a woman did it. Young man, Vida de Villiers is his name, smells strongly of beer and dagga, but he is in military fatigues and so I take him seriously… eventually. I take down his report and then put him in one of the cells, just in case. Two patrol officers go investigate, and sure enough, there is a dead body, and sure enough, it looks like Emil Coetzee. And so I call the Western Commonage because I have heard that Emil Coetzee is suspected missing and you are working on his disappearance. I go to the morgue, but as soon as I see the body, I know it is not Emil Coetzee: it is Tom Fortenoy. Mr. Fortenoy makes a living, or rather, made a living, impersonating Emil Coetzee."

"And this is why you denied the report earlier?" Spokes asked.

"No, sir," the Section Officer said. "Soon after I returned from the morgue two men from secret intelligence arrived—"

Spokes felt something within him sink like a stone. "Don't tell me. One was white and the other black. Real specimens."

"Yes, sir. But how did you know?"

"Let's just say that I have recently had the pleasure of making their acquaintance."

"I see. Well, they arrive and say there is no case. Nothing was reported. Make sure I understand that. Make sure the young man in the cell understands that… and just in case he does not, they use their fists to make sure he does, and then release him into the night. I didn't tell them about the call I had already made to your station. They took the report. From what I understand, they took the body from the morgue. What could they possibly want with a dead man's body, sir?"

"I don't know, but I am sure we will soon find out."

"I am just trying to do the right thing here, sir."

"You and me both."

The Section Officer smiled at Spokes, and then prepared to exit the bakkie.

"The young man said he saw a woman shoot Mr. Fortenoy?"

"He didn't see her. But he heard her."

"Heard her?"

"Heard her shoes running along the pavement and..."

"And?"

"He smelled a scent."

"A scent? What kind of scent?"

"A woman's cheap perfume or a cheap woman's perfume. He could not be sure which it was."

"A woman's cheap perfume or a cheap woman's perfume," Spokes said as he thought of the women who were connected to Emil Coetzee, and tried to decide which one of them fit that description.

"Yes."

"Have you ever considered joining the CID?" Spokes asked the officer.

"Not until this very moment," the Section Officer said with a smile.

"I think there will soon be a position available for someone who wants to do the right thing," Spokes said, with a smile of his own.

———◆———

It was the kind of crime scene that had not been created by a natural crime, but by someone who wanted it to appear as though there had been a crime. It was all just too... orchestrated. Why would anyone, having succeeded in breaking through the door then go through the trouble of smashing the windows as well? What was the purpose of overturning the furniture in the sitting room when the man you were supposed to be struggling with was in his den all the while? How had Emil Coetzee sat through the noise of the door breaking, the windows shattering, and the furniture falling over? Surely he would have gone to investigate and would have taken some kind of weapon with him. This poor chap in khakis—Tom

Fortenoy, no doubt—lying on the den floor with his arms obediently by his sides and no weapon in his hand had not been disturbed by anything, at least not in Emil Coetzee's house.

Spokes knew that he was looking at something more intriguing and elaborate than a simple cover-up or whatever it was that the Secret Intelligence Unit was up to, which is why he decided not to share with them that he was aware of what had happened to Tom Fortenoy. Clement Rutherford and Joseth Maraire had called him to come and investigate a crime, and he would investigate a crime.

"Was the body moved?" Spokes asked.

"No. We found him as you see him," Clement Rutherford said. "We decided to call you since you had already started investigating Emil Coetzee's disappearance."

"Very interesting that he was shot three times and did not bleed out," Spokes said, leaning over the body, but making sure not to touch it. "Blood on his clothes, but no blood stain on the carpet. No blood anywhere else as a matter of fact. Usually with gunshot wounds there is blood... blood spatter... a pool of blood. In all my years in this job, I don't think I have ever seen anything quite like this. Most interesting indeed."

Clement Rutherford and Joseth Maraire shared a look that became increasingly accusatory. *What a detail to overlook*, Spokes thought. They had probably been too intent on overturning the living-room furniture and writing Golide Gumede's name—G O L I D E G U M—on the den wall to pay attention to the most important detail of all. Spokes privately concluded that this was what happened when incompetence was continuously rewarded.

"We can see that you are not fooled," Clement Rutherford said.

"You are a very clever man... smart," Joseth Maraire said,

convincingly if begrudgingly.

They were trying to flatter him. To get him to go along with whatever it was that they were planning.

"We had to make the crime scene media-friendly. After the war, readers and viewers don't want a lot of gore," Clement Rutherford explained.

Spokes nodded his head, understanding more than what had been said.

"The death of a powerful man is inherently a political act," Clement Rutherford said.

"And the death of a man like Emil Coetzee—well, that death has to be the most political of all," Joseth Maraire said, used to elaborating on someone else's point.

"So Emil Coetzee cannot just commit suicide, say; someone has to kill him. And it is even better if that someone who kills him is someone whom the country has come to fear and loathe," Clement Rutherford said.

Spokes looked at the red letters spelling out G O L I D E G U M.

"Did he?"

"Did who what?" Clement Rutherford asked.

"Did Emil Coetzee commit suicide?"

"A man does not just walk into the bush and then not walk out of it," Joseth Maraire said.

"And besides, two lions and a leopard were spotted in the area," Clement Rutherford said.

"Two leopards and a lion," Joseth Maraire corrected.

The two men shared another look, this one more difficult to read.

"Emil Coetzee was probably the best friend I ever had," Clement Rutherford said. Spokes felt it was the most honest thing that he had said in the entire exchange. "So I definitely did not arrive at this decision lightly, you understand. It seems to us that his was definitely death by misadventure. But, of course, we cannot have that be publicly known."

"It would not be good for morale... for politics... for the country. As a nation, we need to congregate against a common enemy," Joseth Maraire said matter-of-factly. "We are just galvanizing the people toward that end."

Spokes looked at the writing on the wall: G O L I D E G U M. "I see," he said slowly, aware that he had to play his next several moves very carefully.

"We are glad that you do," Clement Rutherford said. "We have always found that it helps tremendously when the BSAP and CID see eye to eye with the SIU."

"What about the beige bakkie in the bush and the people who reported missing the man who was driving it, the man they were very sure was Emil Coetzee?"

"We have ways of making people unknow what they think they know," Joseth Maraire said with confidence and pride.

"If the war we have just been through has taught us anything, it is that the truth, Chief Inspector, is a very malleable thing," Clement Rutherford said, showing off how intelligent he thought he was.

Spokes understood that the men from the Secret Intelligence Unit had their job to do. He also understood that he had a job to do as well. His job was to find out the truth, the unmalleable truth, about what had happened to Emil Coetzee. The men from the Secret Intelligence Unit did not need to know this. Nor did they need to know that he and Emil Coetzee had been irrevocably connected by what had happened to Daisy. It was best for them to continue thinking in terms of malleable truths.

SASKIA

———— ◆ ————

Saskia had to admit that everything about the Selous School for Boys was impressive—the grandiose grounds, the beautiful buildings, the hallowed halls—there was nothing that did not mark it as the best school in the entire country.

"Not often that we see women in these parts," the headmaster, Mr. Stuardts, said as he opened one of the many trophy cases in the Great Hall. He did not have to say it; Saskia had known from the way his eyes had appreciatively traveled up and down her body when he had come to greet her in the parking berth earlier that it had been quite some time since he had seen a woman—and probably even longer since he had seen one that looked as good as she did.

"So you have no women on staff at all?" she asked as she perused the trophies looking for Emil Coetzee's name. His name appeared on many trophies between the years 1940 and 1945.

"No. No women on staff, unfortunately," Mr. Stuardts said.

"Interesting policy," Saskia said. "Does the Selous School for Boys not believe in the mental capacity of the fairer sex?"

"No. No, not at all. It is just that there once was an incident… years ago."

"An incident?" Saskia said, feigning mild interest.

"Yes," Mr. Stuardts said. "Very long time ago now." He seemed to have thought better of talking about the incident, for that was all he said.

"But surely male staff members are allowed to bring wives."

"No. No women. No wives allowed," Mr. Stuardts said with finality.

"That must make things rather hard," Saskia said as she watched him firmly shut the trophy case and lock it.

Just then two black women in maids' uniforms quietly passed by carrying buckets and mops.

"Oh, we—we… manage somehow," Mr. Stuardts stammered as he blushed profusely. "So you are writing on Coetzee's days here at Selous?" he asked, eager to change the subject.

"It's a biography that looks at his entire life."

"You know we were boys together, Coetzee and I," Mr. Stuardts said, with not a little pride, as he opened another case—this one containing yearbooks from the 1930s and 1940s. "He was my senior," he declared as he reverentially removed nine yearbooks—1937 to 1945—and placed them on a long table for her to peruse.

"My goodness, he is everywhere," Saskia said as she thumbed through the yearbooks, watching Emil Coetzee grow from a boy to a young man.

"There was nothing that he couldn't do," Mr. Stuardts said, the admiration plain in his voice. "It came as no surprise to any of us that he became who he became."

"May I take some pictures of the photos?" Saskia said, holding up her camera and flashing her most dazzling smile.

"Of course, of course," Mr. Stuardts said, happy to oblige.

As Saskia took photos of Emil Coetzee from the ages of ten to eighteen, she noticed that through the many changes he underwent, one thing remained constant—the uncertainty in his eyes.

"He loved his time here," Mr. Stuardts was saying. "We belong to the Selous Old Boys Club."

Saskia came across a photograph from 1941 that contained within it a Mrs. Findlay. "Mrs. Findlay—the lady involved in the incident you spoke of earlier, I presume?" Saskia said.

Mr. Stuardts blushed profusely again and did not know what to do, and so started closing all the yearbooks and putting them away. "I—I take it you've taken all the photos you—you need?"

"Yes. Yes, I have," Saskia said, delighting in his discomfort. "Let me guess, she made all the male teachers fall in love with her, and there was a duel at dawn that ended rather tragically."

"No. No such thing. It was… it was… really, Miss Hargrave, the imagination you have," Mr. Stuardts said, putting the yearbooks back and not in the correct order. "Mrs. Findlay was married to a member of staff—"

"A Mr. Findlay. Yes, I saw him in the photo. I assumed that he was the one who had met a rather unfortunate end."

"No. No such thing. Lived a long life. Went on to establish himself quite remarkably in business."

"You have a great institution here, Mr. Stuardts," Saskia said, putting him out of his misery.

"That we do, that we do," he said, very happy to change the subject. "One hopes, of course, that we will be able to hold on to that greatness."

"Oh?" Saskia said, placing a hand lightly on his upper arm.

"Our first intake of a multiracial cohort, you see. Adding fi—five Africans, t—two Coloureds and one Indian to the m—mix… a Mohamedan at that. Ch—ch—changing times and all that. But one worries, doesn't one? About standards. About the ability to uphold standards—to keep tradition as it were, you see."

Saskia did see, and so she said, "Surely standards have always been of great concern to the Selous School for Boys."

In response, Mr. Stuardts smiled a weak smile that was certain that Saskia did not see.

"Oh my!" Saskia said, bringing his attention to another

case. "You even have a 'Man of the Year' medal."

"Yes. Yes, we do," Mr. Stuardts said, opening the case. "Coetzee won it in 1942, I believe… yes. Yes, 1942." He delicately removed the 1942 medal from the case and handed it to Saskia, who also held it delicately.

"What makes one the 'Man of the Year' at the Selous School for Boys?" Saskia asked as she felt the weight of the medal in her hands.

"Popularity. It is entirely determined by the students via vote."

"And what, pray tell, made Emil Coetzee so popular in 1942?"

There came the distant ringing of the telephone, and Mr. Stuardts apologized before rushing off to answer it. He returned a few moments later with a message from her editor saying that Clement Rutherford wanted her to get to Emil Coetzee's home in Brookside as soon as possible. Saskia closed the medals case and began to hasten out of the building.

"Rutherford… another proud Old Boy, that," Mr. Stuardts said, but not with nearly as much pride and awe as when he had spoken of Coetzee. "You will, of course, give him my best regards," he said, rushing ahead in order to open the door for her.

"Rutherford?"

"No. No. Coetzee. I mean Coetzee."

"I will, and I will let him know how absolutely helpful you've been."

"Thank you. It has been my great pl—pleasure," Mr. Stuardts said.

"All mine, I assure you," Saskia said, placing a hand on his upper arm once more.

There was that profuse blush again as Mr. Stuardts's eyes managed to linger over her entire body before he shut the door.

Yet another mission accomplished. Once the door was firmly closed behind her, Saskia quickly removed the 1942 'Man of the Year' medal from her jacket pocket and dropped it in her rucksack before making her way to her car.

———— ◆ ————

The man lying on Emil Coetzee's den floor was obviously Tom Fortenoy. Norman, Saskia's unlamented erstwhile husband, was a huge Fortenoy fan, and had zealously collected all his appalling "Emil and the Boys" albums over the years. Much to her dismay, before Norman had decided to leave her, he had dragged her to a Fortenoy show, which had proved to be one show too many. All this was not to say anything about Norman, but to say that Saskia knew exactly what Tom Fortenoy looked like. So she therefore knew that the body on the floor did not belong to Emil Coetzee. She knew that Rutherford and Joseth wanted her to believe that it was Emil Coetzee on the floor dressed in khakis. She also knew that they wanted her to believe that Golide Gumede was responsible for whatever had happened to the body on the floor. What she did not know was how Tom Fortenoy had come to be lying there.

"So you will write the story?" Rutherford asked.

"The story of how Golide Gumede attacked Emil Coetzee in his home?" Saskia asked in turn.

"And killed him," Joseth provided.

Even as Saskia wondered what exactly these men were up to, she asked no further questions, and simply and compliantly said, "I guess instead of writing a biography, I'll be writing an obituary."

Rutherford and Joseth looked very pleased with themselves and with her.

Once outside and alone again, Saskia could not stop herself from reaching her right hand into her rucksack and touching the Selous School for Boys 1942 "Man of the Year" medal. The touch stopped her feeling sick to her stomach.

SPOKES

———◆———

Spokes placed *The Chronicle* on his desk and began reading Emil Coetzee's obituary as written by Saskia Hargrave:

Emil Coetzee: A True Patriot.
As the nation mourns the loss of one of its greatest sons, Emil Coetzee, it is important to remember the life that Golide Gumede has taken from us all.

Emil was born in Durban, South Africa on 18 April 1927. His parents, Johan Coetzee and Gemma Coetzee (née Roberts) had met seven years earlier at the intersection of Borrow Street and Selborne Avenue, right here in the very heart of the City of Kings, so Emil was very much one of our own.

Emil spent his early childhood at the Williams' Arms surrounded by a loving mother, a formidable great-grandmother, and the colorful lodgers of the board-ing house that his great-grandmother owned, which is probably where he developed his admirable ability to fully understand his fellow man.

In 1933, the Coetzees moved to a BSAP outpost located at the foot of the Matopos Hills on what is now the Ashtonbury Farm and Estate. It was here, with the veld all around him, that Emil's true character began to take shape. He was deeply attached to the land and, by extension, to his country, and this attachment was further fostered at the Selous School for Boys...

The rest of the obituary carried on in the same vein. Perhaps the heading and the biographical parts were true enough, but the story that placed Emil Coetzee's death in Golide Gumede's hands was a lie. And the fact that it was a lie was there for all the world to see if they knew how to look for such things. The first clue lay in the brevity of the obituary. Usually a man of Emil Coetzee's stature had pages written about his life and death, and yet Saskia Hargrave had devoted only ten paragraphs in total to the man she claimed to be writing a biography about. True, the paper was shifting gears, preparing its pages for inevitable majority rule by gradually devoting space to black lives in order to prove that it had always believed that they mattered; so although there was still the usual overwhelming coverage of white people and their exploits, there was now diminished space in which to do so. Even while knowing this, Spokes felt that Saskia Hargrave's reasons for not writing much on Emil Coetzee were more calculated. She was probably saving the story—the real story, the bigger story—for herself and her glory.

Given that Spokes' first impression of Saskia Hargrave had been that she was a vulture, it would have been easy to believe that she had simply done what the Secret Intelligence Unit wanted her to do because it gave her the opportunity to tell a great story that would hold the attention of the entire country for a long time to come. However, because she was holding out for a greater story, Saskia Hargrave knew that the story that she had written was a lie.

Spokes remembered their encounter, and the way her outfit had revealed too much. He remembered her dead tooth. He remembered the scent of decaying flowers that clung to her. He remembered her desperate need for something—attention, recognition, adoration—that was not altogether clear to him; and while this made her unpredictable and perhaps even volatile, he had to admit that for now, at least, they seemed to be on the same side—the side of truth.

Spokes picked up his phone's handset and dialed *The Chronicle's* phone number, and when his call was answered, he asked to speak to Saskia Hargrave.

She was soon on the other end of the line.

"Hello?"

"Saskia Hargrave?"

"Yes," she answered, sounding tired.

"I am Chief Inspector Spokes Moloi. We've met."

"Yes," she said, but Spokes could not tell from the tone of her response whether she remembered meeting him or not.

"At Emil Coetzee's house."

There was a long pause before she said, "Yes."

"Before Golide Gumede ransacked the house and wrote his name on the den wall."

This time there was no pause before she said, "Yes, yes—I remember you." She no longer sounded tired.

That's more like it, Spokes thought. "Do we understand each other?" he asked.

"Yes, I understand you perfectly."

"Good. I have information that I think will interest you greatly."

"Information? What kind of information?" she asked, sounding slightly hesitant.

"Information about a hat... Emil Coetzee's Stetson."

"Emil Coetzee's Stetson?"

"Yes. Found in the bush where he parked his bakkie the day after the ceasefire."

"Bush? Bakkie? Ceasefire? Found by whom?"

"Two gentlemen who work for Secret Intelligence."

"In the bush?"

"Yes."

"The day after the ceasefire?" Saskia Hargrave said, her voice little more than a whisper.

"Yes. I thought you would want to know," Spokes said.

"I do. Thank you for telling me."

As Spokes hung up the phone, he was certain that he had made the right decision. Saskia Hargrave with her desperate need to tell the true story herself was the perfect person to help him get to the bottom of what had happened to Emil Coetzee. She would do everything in her power to ensure that the truth about Emil Coetzee came to light.

Just then his phone rang.

"There is something that I just remembered," Marion Hartley said on the other end of the line, after they briefly exchanged their hellos. "It is probably not important, but when Emil drove off that morning, there was another car there. A Renault 5, light in color. It had a design on its side. An elongated 'Z.' I cannot be completely certain, but I think a woman was driving the car. She drove off before I could get a good look at her."

A Renault 5 with an elongated "Z." Spokes had also seen that car—the night he had met Saskia Hargrave at Emil Coetzee's home.

Spokes looked at the grainy black-and-white picture that accompanied the obituary piece. Many images could have been chosen—Emil Coetzee giving a speech, Emil Coetzee shaking the hand of the Prime Minister, Tom Fortenoy on the floor of Emil Coetzee's den, GOLIDEGUM—but none of those images had been chosen. Instead, Spokes found himself looking at an ordinary picture of a father and his son out fishing and holding a Kariba bream triumphantly between them, both of them smiling and happy. It seemed a rather odd choice, but Spokes understood instantly why it had been made. Both father, Emil Coetzee, and son, Everleigh Coetzee, had tragically and violently been taken too soon. It was the kind of picture that filled readers with many emotions, and, therefore, filled the paper's condolences section, which meant good business for the paper. Evidently, Saskia Hargrave was not above manipulating a situation in order to benefit from it.

Spokes decided that as soon as he got off the phone with Marion Hartley, he would have two plainclothes detectives follow Saskia Hargrave. What if he had misread her confusion? What if she was not after finding the truth, but burying it instead? And he had just shared a vital piece of evidence with her. Could he have been so very wrong about her?

"Did the Renault 5 follow his car?" Spokes asked with veiled unease.

"No. Drove off in the opposite direction. Like I said, it's probably nothing, but I thought I should let you know in case it is something."

"Every detail matters. Thank you, Marion."

There was a long but comfortable pause before Marion Hartley said, "It has been more than ten days, Chief Inspector. New Year's has come and gone, and he still has not returned. I know he is punishing me, but he doesn't have to be so bloody thorough about it, does he?" She sounded vulnerable for the first time since Spokes had met her. "I'm not going to lie to you, I'm worried—afraid. Clement Rutherford of the SIU came here and tried to sell me a tall tale. Something about morale and national security. The side sticking together. As though he and I could ever be on the same side. It is almost as if he doesn't know that the war is over. I didn't believe a word of his story. It's obvious he has no idea what has happened to Emil, and yet he speaks with so much authority. Never liked the man. Dastardly. Always seems up to something even though he is definitely two cents short of a tickey. And now there's this guff about Golide Gumede in the papers, which, if Emil comes back from the bush tomorrow, the SIU will deny any part of. They will hang this Hargrave woman out to dry, poor thing."

Spokes understood that Marion Hartley was speaking because for her silence was no longer a trusted thing—it held too many possibilities. And so he let her talk. "I suppose there is some brilliance in using Golide Gumede in this Emil affair," Marion Hartley continued. "There's still a lot of anger about the downing of the Vickers Viscount. People will eat it up even though it is untrue… even though it is misinformation. Stroke of genius, really. So definitely not Clement Rutherford's idea." There was another comfortable silence before she said, "The Clement Rutherfords of the world are used to winning. You don't seem to be the kind of man who will let them win. So I am choosing to take a lot of comfort in that, Chief Inspector."

SPOKES

————— ♦ —————

The sound of a gentle tap woke Spokes up. He opened his eyes and, through the window, saw a new day break. His body was stiff and, folded as he was in a confined space, he did not have room to stretch it. He felt trapped. A creaky cupboard door opened and closed. He made a mental note to fix it. Soon after, the oven door yawned open, and then snapped shut as the air filled with the scent of warm vanilla. Spokes looked in the direction of the kitchen, and there was the lovely Loveness as becoming as ever in her pink nightdress, gown and slippers. She looked like all the softest things, and Spokes was sure moments like these were created solely to remind him of how much he loved her.

"How many nights do you intend to spend like this?" she asked without looking at him.

"As many as are necessary to have me finally be forgiven," he said.

She watched him try to stretch his stiff and aching limbs again, and made a frustrated sound. "You cannot spend every night on the sofa." Her hands came to rest on her hips, and Spokes' hopes sank. A standing akimbo Loveness did not bode well for him.

"Well, when we married, I promised myself we would never go to bed angry with one another," he said.

"I'm not angry with you," she said.

"Your back turned toward me every night says otherwise," Spokes said as he got off the sofa and went to stand as close to her as he felt he could at this moment, which was not nearly close enough.

She looked at him for a long minute before dropping her arms to hang by her sides. "And look at this collar," she said, eventually reaching out to touch him. She tried and failed to smooth out his collar. "Have you been ironing it?"

"Yes," Spokes said, grateful and glad for her closeness and her touch, and no longer feeling trapped.

"With starch?"

"I cannot find the starch."

"You cannot find the starch that is exactly where it has always been for the past twenty years? You just don't know how to properly starch a collar."

"There may be a lot of truth to that," Spokes said. He reached out to take her hand in his, and she let him.

"Tell me one good thing," Loveness said.

"I can tell you many good things about this very moment," Spokes said.

"I see you woke up with sugar on your tongue," Loveness said, allowing herself to lean toward him. "I meant, one good thing about being the Acting Chief Superintendent."

"Griffiths came back. I am back to being Chief Inspector."

"And?"

"And... one good thing?"

"One good thing."

"For the first time in my long career, I had an office all to myself. But then I realized I was already the king of infinite space because of you."

"There is no end to the sugar on your tongue, I see," Loveness said with a smile as she relaxed into his touch.

Spokes gratefully smiled too, "I promised you that I would retire, and I will. My application is sitting on Griffiths' desk. Any day now it will start going through the process."

"Oh, I know you will do the right thing," Loveness said. "I have never doubted it." She allowed him to touch the soft folds of her gown and gently pull her closer still until their bodies touched.

"You know *Wives and Daughters* is still unread," Spokes said, not quite able to keep the hope from his voice. "Maybe we can read it together tonight."

"Maybe. But it seems to me that there is no better time than the present," Loveness said, slowly raising an eyebrow.

"So you think we can start reading the book now?" Spokes said.

She looked at him and smiled her dimpled smile. "I don't see why not," she said, leading him toward their bedroom.

Spokes leaned over and kissed the back of her neck in appreciation of all the softest and gentlest things.

———◆———

Much, much later, Spokes carried the His Master's Voice gramophone that he had inherited from his mother, and followed Loveness as she carried one of the kitchen chairs out of the house. She looked absolutely breathtaking in a turquoise chiffon dress, and Spokes would have followed her anywhere.

Together they walked toward the untarred road that was the street where they lived. She, in all her loveliness, put the chair on the ground and he put the gramophone gingerly on top of it. He put his hand on the crank handle and wound it several times. The record started rotating, and the needle lifted its head briefly before gently settling on the black vinyl. As the needle traveled along the grooves of the record, "Hamba Hamba Madala" by the Los Angeles Orchestra filled the air. When Spokes held out his hand and the lovely Loveness placed a beautiful brown hand in his, he could not help but marvel at how absolutely radiant she looked in the blush of dusk.

Man leads with right. Forward. Side. Close. Side. Back. Side. Close. Side. Slow... quick, quick... slow... slow, quick, quick... slow... slow...

As the Molois danced the quickstep in a promenade up and down the road, a light trail of dust following them like stardust, Loveness beamed her love up at Spokes, and he knew without a doubt that he was the luckiest of men.

In time, a small crowd gathered and watched the Molois dance into the twilight, and all was right again with Spokes' world as he gazed into the eyes of his one good thing... his best thing... his truest thing.

FEBRUARY 1980

SPOKES

———◆———

The white and otherwise nondescript Peugeot 504 was parked opposite the Main Public Library on Fort Street. Spokes opened the door to the back seat and entered the car. Two plainclothes detectives sat in the front—one completing the TARGET puzzle in *The Chronicle* newspaper, and the other reading a well-thumbed *Beano* comic book.

"Gentlemen," Spokes said, by way of greeting.

"Sir," both men replied.

"You're sure she has no idea you're following her."

"None whatsoever," the comic-reader responded, without looking up from his comic book.

"She is a reporter. Very vigilant," Spokes said.

"You trained us well," the puzzle-solver said.

Spokes let go of the nagging feeling that something was not quite right, and allowed himself to be somewhat at ease. "It's been several weeks. Your reports do not have much varying detail. Almost identical logs."

"That's because she is a woman of routine," the puzzle-solver said.

"More like a creature of habit," the comic-reader said.

The puzzle-solver ignored his partner and removed a writing pad from his breast pocket. "Which, of course, makes our job easier, even if a little predictable," he continued as he flipped through the pad. "At work every morning at seven forty-five. Leaves at five thirty every evening. Has lunch by herself at City Hall—by the courtyard—every afternoon at twelve."

"She may be unvarying, but this is where things get interesting," the comic-reader said.

"In what way?" Spokes asked.

"Reading material. Same thing all the time. The Selous School for Boys 1942 yearbook. Just flips through it, almost absent-mindedly, as she eats her lunch. Always leftovers," the comic-reader said. "Always drinks from a flask. Not so sure she is drinking coffee or tea."

"I suppose it makes sense for her to be so thorough as she is writing his biography," the puzzle-solver said, choosing to ignore the comment about the flask.

"But... " the comic-reader said.

"But?" Spokes prompted.

"But for someone whom we suspect of having had something to do with Emil Coetzee's disappearance, she seems to be carrying on as normal," the puzzle-solver said.

"Or maybe she wants to be seen carrying on as normal so as to throw off suspicion. She did spend time in a mental institution, so obviously something is not altogether all together with her... I mean, flipping through the same book day after day for weeks on end," the comic-reader said.

"She spent six months at Ingutsheni after her father committed suicide," the puzzle-solver said. "She was treated for severe exhaustion. I really don't think we should make too much of it."

"Then why is she still seeing a psychologist over at Galen House?" the comic-reader asked.

"Because her father recently committed suicide, and by all accounts she was the one who found him as he lay dying. She seems to be doing what any normal person would do under the circumstances," the puzzle-solver said.

"And her history of petty crime?" the comic-reader pressed,

undeterred.

"Shoplifting trinkets from stores is not the same thing as suspicion of murder," the puzzle-solver said.

"She's been doing it since adolescence. It establishes a pattern," the comic-reader said.

Spokes could see why their reports were so scant on detail; the two detectives could not agree on what mattered and what didn't where Saskia Hargrave was concerned. "So what are we thinking?" he asked.

"I think she is who she says she is—a journalist working on a story," the puzzle-solver said.

"I think she is somewhat obsessed with Emil Coetzee. Perhaps they were once lovers and he jilted her. He has a bit of a deserved reputation in this area," the comic-reader said.

"She visits her mother once a week, for Pete's sake," the puzzle-solver said.

"And what does that prove?" the comic-reader asked. "She never stays longer than an hour, and it's not like her life is full of other things."

"When was the last time you visited your mother?" the puzzle-solver shot back.

"Isn't there a husband? I thought there was a husband. A Norman Hargrave," Spokes said.

"Left her recently," the puzzle-solver said.

"Not that she misses him any," the comic-reader said. The two officers exchanged a look. "A few days ago when she got home, one of the boys from secret intelligence was waiting for her," the comic-reader continued.

"The white one?" Spokes asked.

"No. The black one," the comic-reader said.

"There was nothing to suggest that it was a social call," the puzzle-solver said.

"If it had been strictly business, then he would not have

stayed overnight," the comic-reader said.

"We have no evidence that he did," the puzzle-solver said.

The two officers shared yet another long look, and Spokes decided that he had seen and heard enough. "I'll leave you two to it," he said.

"It's been weeks, sir," the puzzle-solver said. "She more or less does nothing out of the ordinary. Do you want us to carry on with our surveillance? I'm not sure we will learn anything new."

"She's definitely hiding something," Spokes said as he stepped out the car. "We'll stop following her when we find out what it is."

———•———

It had not been Spokes' intention to do so, but once he crossed the street, he decided that he might as well go to the Main Public Library. If there was nothing, then there was nothing. If there was something… well, then that would be something.

"Good afternoon, Madam," Spokes said, removing his hat from his head.

Even though he had greeted her and she had heard him, the ancient head librarian did not respond, and simply looked at him from over the rims of her spectacles. Her pallid face had long since set itself into a permanent look of absolute displeasure, and even the rouge and powder she applied had given up on giving her a softer look.

"You wouldn't happen to have the Selous School for Boys yearbooks, would you?"

Her eyes gave him the once-over before she said in a rather stern voice, "Year?"

"1942," Spokes replied.

She stood up and Spokes was overwhelmed by the smell of talcum powder. She did not say anything else to him as she creaked away into the darker recesses of the library. She was gone for so long that when the assistant librarian appeared and asked him if he was being helped, Spokes did not know exactly how to respond. As he was deciding to repeat his request, the head librarian creaked her way back.

"Name?" she said, hugging the yearbook to her bosom.

Spokes showed her his badge. She took it from him. Looked at it skeptically, flipped it over to examine its back, and then looked him over more than once before she began very carefully and minutely to write down his details in her sign-out register. "Please handle it with care," she said as she pointed him toward the rows of readers' desks. "Maximum two hours."

Spokes sat down at a desk and turned the pages of the yearbook, not really knowing what he was looking for—until he found it. There it was. Printed in black and white. A resemblance. A striking resemblance, where he least expected it. He looked and looked, somehow hoping not to be seeing what he was seeing, but his trained eyes would not let him see otherwise. He slowly and carefully closed the yearbook as the disparate pieces of the case began to come together.

He was certain that he had it, but he was also hoping that for once in his career, he was wrong. He desperately wanted to be wrong. There was only one way to be sure either way. He picked up his fedora from the reading desk and began hurrying out of the library.

'Walk, don't run, for Christ's sake," the ancient head librarian called. "And where is the book you checked out? It needs to be returned and signed in," she shouted as he ran past the front desk. There would be time for that later, Spokes decided. At this moment there was only one important thing. "You lot!" the ancient head librarian screamed as Spokes ran out the door.

Spokes got there just in time to find the Peugeot 504

pulling out of its roadside parking bay. He got in front of it and placed his hands on the bonnet, alarming the two detectives in the vehicle. Their shock gave way to puzzled concern. There was chaos and pandemonium as other cars travelling up and down Fort Street hooted their objections to the interruption.

"Mother's name?" Spokes screamed, unsuccessfully trying to be heard above the din.

"Get off the road, you bloody munt," someone shouted from a car that was manoeuvring around him.

It was Spokes' job to restore order, and so he motioned for the two detectives to park again.

As he opened the back door of the car, he heard a pedestrian passing by say, "Good luck running the country."

"Is everything all right, sir?" the puzzle-solver asked once Spokes was settled in the back seat—even though it was obvious that everything was not all right.

"You said she visits her mother once a week. What is her mother's name?"

The puzzle-solver reached into his breast pocket and retrieved his notepad. Spokes felt every flip of the page.

"Mother's name? Mother's name? Here it is... Mrs. Prudence Findlay," the puzzle-solver said.

Spokes had held on to the hope that he was wrong until the very last.

"You've solved it, haven't you, sir?" the comic-reader said in absolute awe.

"I'm afraid I have," Spokes said.

SASKIA

———◆———

Ever since writing Emil Coetzee's obituary, Saskia had felt perpetually tired. It was the secrets… the secrets and their weight… the secrets and their weight, and her having to be the one to carry them. She found her mother sitting in her room looking quizzically at the painting of yet another sunset, as though genuinely surprised that she could have created something so exquisitely beautiful.

Feeling a fatigue that was beyond exhaustion, Saskia, instead of standing as far away from her mother as she could, sat down next to her. It was their first closeness in months. Her mother looked at her with a weak, but hopeful smile. When Saskia did not move away, her mother tentatively took her daughter's hands in hers. Saskia stifled a sneeze, affected, as always, by her mother's presence.

"Sassie dear… I am worried about you," her mother said. "I do so hope that all is forgiven?"

Her mother made it impossible to be forgiven. "You are worried about me *now*?" Saskia asked, as she disengaged her hands from her mother's. She tried to keep her voice calm, but could not as she stood up and went to stand by the wall. "It is definitely too late for that. You should have worried about me when I was fifteen. When your husband started climbing into your daughter's bed at nights."

"I didn't know… " her mother said, beginning to rock her body back and forth.

"Don't even start. You knew because I told you after the

very first time it happened, and you told me he would never do such a thing. You chose not to believe me."

"He was your father—"

"He was *not* my father. He explained that to me the first time he climbed into my bed. He told me that he was not my father, and that that was why he could do it."

"Please, Sassie… let us let the past be the past."

Her mother's scent pricked and tickled Saskia's nose so that she had no choice but to sneeze and sneeze and sneeze. The sneezing spree was in fact a godsend, because it stopped Saskia from physically harming her mother, which was what she really wanted to do. How did one let the past be the past when the past was always present?

Using all the strength she had to remain calm, Saskia said, "He waited to exact his revenge. He raised me; he seemed to love me; he called me 'Sassie'… but all the while he was waiting, biding his time, waiting for me to turn fifteen. Why would he wait until then, Mother?"

"He loved you, Sassie… he loved me—" her mother said, her arms beginning to flail, trying to push the truth away.

"Why did he wait for me to turn fifteen, Mother?"

"He loved us! He was a good father to you!"

"He made you think that all was forgiven for fifteen years. And then he punished you through me. Your husband made sure that what you had created would be broken, useless and unwanted—that his revenge would be complete and lasting."

"You were going to tell him, weren't you?" her mother said, suddenly and oddly composed.

"Tell him? Tell him what?"

"The truth," her mother said.

Saskia was afraid that she was losing her mother to a train of thought that she could not follow.

"The truth would have destroyed him."

"The truth? Him?"

"You were going to tell him. I could see it in your eyes that day you came here with the picture and the yearbook."

Saskia finally realized what her mother was so afraid of. "You're worried about Emil Coetzee. You are many years too late, don't you think?"

"I couldn't let him know the truth, you understand," her mother said. "I couldn't let you destroy him—such a beautiful thing—and so I saved him," her mother said, triumphantly.

It took some time for the words to sink in. "You saved him? How did you save him?" The floor felt uneven beneath Saskia's feet as her world tilted off its axis.

"I made sure to get to him before you did, dear," her mother said, an intelligent glint in her eye.

The import of what her mother had said dawned on Saskia and the full weight of it sunk her to the floor.

"Mother, what have you done?"

"I did what I had to do. You wanted to hurt him, and I could not let you. He was the most beautiful thing. The most beautiful thing. You should have seen him... wait, I'll show you," her mother said. She stood up and left the room. Saskia sat paralyzed. Her mother returned shortly carrying painted portraits of a young Emil Coetzee, which she now proudly arranged on her mantelpiece. "Your father is gone now, so I need no longer hide these," she said as she examined her handiwork with great satisfaction. "He was the only man I was able to truly capture as an artist. There was a way he would look at me, you see. That was what nobody understood... the very deep connection we had."

Saskia felt sick to her stomach. "Emil Coetzee was just a boy, Mother. You took from him something that you had no right to," she managed to say before she got up and rushed out of her mother's cottage. Once outside, she vomited and vomited and vomited the vodka and scrambled eggs that had been her only sustenance that day. She knew that she would only feel better once she was pain-free... when all of her was blissfully numb, and everything was a blur.

———•———

Saskia had no idea how she had come to be lying underneath the full weight of yet another man she did not like, but here she was. She had expected Rutherford to be a disappointment: most men were, but he had exceeded her expectations.

"That has never happened to me before," Rutherford said, not really apologizing as he made another impotent grope at a part of her body that she no longer felt connected to.

"I am sure it hasn't, Clement," Saskia said as she pushed him off of her.

"I swear. It is the first time."

"I swear. I believe you," Saskia said as she swung her legs off the bed. She reached for her lacy panties and felt disappointed in herself because she had evidently gone the extra mile to seduce him. Rutherford pulled her back onto the bed a little roughly and slovenly slavered over her left breast. "I am done, Clement," she said, roughly pushing him away—knowing full well that men like him did not take rejection well.

"What? You don't want me anymore? You've been practically begging for it since you set eyes on me. You've been gasping for it," Rutherford spat at her.

Saskia laughed in his face, knowing full well that what a man like Clement Rutherford feared most was being laughed at by a woman. So when he backhanded her across the face, she was ready for it and welcomed the pain. She found that she wanted the fight. She slapped him back.

Livid, Rutherford made for her throat, but she pulled away just in time and scrambled off the bed. He leapt out of the bed and knocked Saskia to the ground. There were stars in her eyes and there was blood in her mouth—she could both taste it and smell it. He placed his entire weight on her and pinned both her hands above her head. Saskia did not put up much of a struggle. Not yet. She had been in this position many times before. She knew how to bide her time.

Rutherford looked at her long and hard before spitting on her face. "You wanted Emil Coetzee, didn't you? You wanted him to have, not just to write about." It was Rutherford's turn to laugh. "I can see you now in his office, pirouetting in front of him the way you did in front of me—and Joseth. It takes a certain kind of white woman to do that in front of a black man. Coquettish to the core—like a whore. A born tease. You thought all he had to do was look at you, and he would want you. He would not be able to resist you. What man has ever been able to resist you?"

The mockery in his voice and in his eyes made Saskia turn her head away.

The truth was not too far off.

Rutherford was still laughing when he said, "What happened? He didn't want you, did he? He took one look at your puny, sagging breasts and your sad, spreading thighs—and he did not want you. This man who just lived to have his hand up a woman's skirt did not want *you*, Saskia Hargrave: the woman no man can resist."

Saskia had been wrong about Clement Rutherford. He was not just pathetic. He was the worst kind of man. He was both pathetic and cruel.

It was only when Saskia tasted the saltiness in her mouth that she realized that she was crying. Ugh! Crying like a little girl. Crying like Sassie.

"I, on the other hand, want you," Rutherford was saying. "You're not much to look at now that you're well past your sell-by date, but you do have such a pretty swan-like neck. I have always been partial to a swan-like neck."

It was her moment to strike. "Unlike you, Joseth was able to finish what he started. Every... single... time," Saskia said before pushing him off of her with great ease.

————•————

Her mother and Clement Rutherford were, unfortunately, not altogether wrong. Saskia had been dreaming of and scheming about her revenge ever since Mr. Findlay had told her who her biological father was. After years of her pleading for him to tell her, he had waited until he was certain he was about to die—just before he put a bullet through his brain—to whisper the name of her father—Emil Coetzee—in her ear.

The nearness of the vile and corrupting Cornelius Findlay had sickened her. The knowledge of who her biological father was—a man only sixteen years her senior—had sickened her. The realization of what her mother had done had sickened her.

Saskia, long at sea, had become completely unmoored by the truth, which turned her life into an emotional tailspin that had landed her in Ingutsheni. Through all the madness, however, she was sane enough to devise a plan—Cornelius Findlay was dead; her mother was too far gone; and so Emil Coetzee would have to pay the heaviest price for what had happened to her.

As Saskia struggled back into her clothes and stumbled away from a still shocked Clement Rutherford, she realized that she had become Cornelius Findlay's perfect creation—a person deformed and distorted by their need for revenge. She had meant to lure Emil Coetzee with the promise of writing a very flattering biography, had thought he would not be able to resist the idea of being immortalised and idolised by an attractive, sexually available woman. One father had violated her; why not another? Emil Coetzee was a man whose appetites and proclivities were well known. This, getting him to sleep with her, had been the surest way she knew how to destroy him. She had not just wanted to tell him the truth; she had wanted to make him complicit in every bad thing that had happened to her beyond her conception. Never having shared in each other's lives, she had wanted them to share in each other's hurt and pain and humiliation—to be bound together by something even stronger than biology: shame.

When, six months after her hospitalization, Saskia was deemed recuperated enough to reintegrate into society, she had found that her wimp of a husband, Norman Hargrave, had, in her absence, found the courage to ask her for a divorce, which he had done as soon as she returned home. Saskia did not love Norman. She never had. She had married him only because he had asked her to marry him. But she did not want him to leave her, either. She did not want her marriage to fail like the many others that had become the casualties of war. She did not want their thirteen years together to be reduced to a statistic. It was a matter of pride. It was a matter of survival. It was a matter of… normalcy. If their marriage failed, it would mean that she had failed at building a normal, adult life, and then what would have been the point of any of it—all that suffering?

Above all else what Saskia desired most was to be normal… to *feel* normal… to feel as though her utter brokenness had still left her with a kind of beauty that the world wanted and appreciated. Desperately needing to have done the right thing for herself and her life, Saskia had begged Norman to stay. This had been a mistake because then, when Norman walked away, he had done so with his head held high, thinking that he had something that she wanted and believing that that something was himself—when really what she wanted from him was her appreciated self.

Now, as Saskia parked the car outside her flat, she felt empty… devoid… culled. This was probably how she would have felt after she had told Emil Coetzee their truth. She would have felt: nothing. She would have felt like the truth did not matter. All there was—all there had ever been—all there ever would be for her was this emptiness.

Saskia wanted to believe that she was capable of being different, perhaps even better, but she could not be sure or convinced of this because everything that had made her had been wrong. She opened her rucksack and retrieved the Selous School for Boys 1942 yearbook in search of the man who was her father, but found in it what she always did—not a man but a boy, a boy of fifteen—a boy in need of love and protection. Emil Coetzee.

SASKIA

———— ♦ ————

Saskia's hand was just about to open the gate that led to her mother's cottage when she stopped. Had that little girl at the corner just called her a bitch? A group of young girls from Coghlan Primary School were standing a few meters from the cottage on Ninth Avenue. They would have looked like angels in their blue and white uniforms had their little faces not been contorted into confused hatred as they screamed, "Witch! Witch! Witch!"

Well, witch was better than bitch, if only marginally, Saskia thought as she opened a squashed packet of Everests that Norman had left behind. She never smoked—but then again, she never visited her mother more than twice in one week. Twice seemed to be going beyond the bounds and bonds of filial duty. Her mother—weak and self-absorbed—had, throughout her life, disappointed her at every turn. And now this. Saskia had absolutely no idea what to do with what she knew.

The two plainclothes detectives had not followed her for a few days, so at least she was probably no longer a suspect. She was rather relieved that she would not have to spend her days watching the detectives. If they were not following her anymore, then they would not find their way to her mother. But was that what she wanted—for her mother to get away with murder when she had already gotten away with so much?

"Witch! Witch! Witch!" the Coghlan girls shouted.

"Shoo-shoo!" Saskia said, her hands making a go-away

motion. *The girls' insistent interference was rather inconve-*
nient, she thought as she watched the cigarette ash from her
unsmoked Everest fall to the pavement, shatter and scatter.
She needed a smoke to help calm her nerves, and these little
devils were making sure she squandered her opportunity.

"A witch lives there," a little face under a big blue hat
informed Saskia.

"I should think not. I know the lady who lives here, and
she is many, many things, but a witch is not one of them."

"She is, too. We've seen her pointy hat and broomstick and
everything," the obvious leader of the girls said with authority.

Saskia wondered how this was a conversation that she was
actually having. There had been a time when children had
taken heed of what adults said, when they would have been
more manageable, even to their own detriment. Now, listening to these little monsters, Saskia was glad that she had been
so determined not to have a brat of her own. She definitely did
not regret the two abortions she had had.

"Maybe she's a witch too," another girl declared.

What made them believe so steadfastly in witches that
existed outside the pages of a book of fairy tales? Saskia
wondered as she stomped her cigarette underfoot. Had she
also believed in witches at their age or was this yet another
gift of war—the sincere belief that evil did exist and manifest
itself in the world? Should she have also started believing in
witches at some point? Was it too late to start believing in
them now?

"You're a witch! You're a witch! You're a witch!" the
Coghlan girls screamed at her with both fear and excitement.

They would have done well in Salem, Massachusetts,
Saskia thought as she placed another cigarette between her
lips, inhaled and mumbled, "You're right, Little Saints. You've
caught us out. The woman who lives here is my mother, and

we are both witches. Here, let me show you my pointy hat."
She theatrically reached into her rucksack. The girls, with a
mixture of terror and anticipation, prepared to run as soon as
they saw the pointy hat.

Just then the last person that Saskia wanted to see at her
mother's gate—Chief Inspector Spokes Moloi—joined her.
She was too shocked to do anything else but stare at him and
let the cigarette fall from her mouth. He couldn't possibly
know the truth, could he? The plainclothes detectives had not
followed her today, so how did he know to come here? It
was impossible that he could have known in advance that she
would be here now. And yet here he was.

"Whatever she is, she's also a kaffirboetie," the leader of
the pack said, interrupting Saskia's thoughts.

The Chief Inspector removed his wallet and showed the
girls his badge. "I'm with the BSAP and you, young ladies,
are disturbing the peace. Disturbing the peace is a punishable
offense."

His tone was somewhat jocular, but the girls looked up
at him with wide eyes that were confounded and scared. A
few months ago, a black policeman would not have talked
to them the way he just had—of this they were certain.
However, they knew enough to know that since the end of
the war, things had changed. Some of the girls had parents
packing up their belongings so that the Biddulphs van would
come and carry them to new homes in South Africa. Some
of the packed belongings would eventually make their way
to Australia, New Zealand, Canada, and the United States of
America—any English-speaking country that had a comfortable, predominantly white settler population that did not ask
itself too many uncomfortable questions.

All the girls had family and friends who had been part of
similar moves over the past five years, so they all understood

that things were changing. Even at their school, a few black girls had been admitted. What was not so clear to the girls was what all this change meant for them in this particular moment –that is, in their interaction with the black policeman who was not dressed like a black policeman, and who had just spoken to them with uncharacteristic authority. Perplexed, their eyes turned to the one who had called Saskia a kaffirboetie; the obvious ringleader. She blinked myopically, her world much smaller than it had previously been, and turned and slunk away. Deflated, the others followed suit.

"Why are you here?" Saskia asked at last, looking at the Chief Inspector in much the same way the girls had—with due suspicion.

"Because this is where your mother, Mrs. Findlay, lives," the Chief Inspector said matter-of-factly.

Saskia looked at him for a long time again before taking a deep breath and saying, "I see." Resigned, she slowly opened the squeaky gate and walked into the glorious overgrown garden. "It is like walking through a picture-book illustration," she said as she led the Chief Inspector up the crooked stone path that led to the front door. "Perhaps that is why those girls believe it is the home of a witch." She turned to him and attempted a smile before knocking on the cottage door instead of using her key. The cottage did not have the ceremony of a veranda, and so when Saskia knocked on the door, it seemed as though the cottage had been taken by surprise.

There was the movement of curtains by the window before the door was opened. Her mother definitely looked like a character from an illustrated fairy tale—flowing, snow-white hair and black dress with a cape. Her face was still very beautiful, and, although she had just turned sixty-two, the wrinkles on her face were not deep, but of a fine gossamer quality that made her seem almost perfect. She looked like a fairy godmother, but, of course, looks could be deceiving, and a pointy hat might have changed the whole effect.

"You had a run-in with the Coghlan girls, I gather," her mother said, as she motioned toward two chairs in her comfortable but overcrowded living room where years of her life had been deposited after Cornelius Findlay had eventually separated from her.

"Yes. Awful little things, aren't they?" Saskia said.

"Just confused by the changing world around them, I think," the Chief Inspector said, diplomatically.

Saskia looked at her mother intently, trying to telegraph the danger she was currently in, but her mother seemed to think nothing of the presence of a black man she had never seen before in her home. She offered him a cup of tea as though he were a family friend, and not the most dangerous man in their lives.

"This is Chief Inspector Spokes Moloi," Saskia said, hoping that her mother would get the hint and be on her guard.

"I didn't know the BSAP promoted Africans to such high ranks," Mrs. Findlay said as she poured tea into two cups.

"It is a recent occurrence," the Chief Inspector said good-naturedly. "And it might help that I am with the CID."

Mrs. Findlay brought the cups of tea and offered them to her visitors. Saskia took hers, wondering if her mother thought that she had brought the Chief Inspector. Was that why she was so calm? Saskia looked pointedly at her mother again, trying to communicate that she should not say anything to the Chief Inspector. Her mother smiled at her, and Saskia was not sure what the smile meant.

The cup and saucer were still in her mother's hands, and Saskia looked over at the Chief Inspector, wondering why he had not taken them from her mother. He did not even notice he was being offered a cup of tea. He did not even notice because at that very moment, something else had caught his eye—the array of paintings on her mother's mantelpiece of Emil Coetzee during his Selous School for Boys days. Even though it was already too late, Saskia's first instinct was to remove the paintings. She jumped up, forgetting about the cup of tea on her lap, and sending it sploshing to the floor.

"Oh Sassie, look at the mess you've made," her mother said.

"The mess *I've* made?" Saskia said, fear making her almost scream as she went down on her hands and knees and rubbed at the stain with the hem of her dress.

"Sassie!" her mother admonished. "What is wrong with you? Remember to blot, not wipe. I'll go fetch a cloth."

Her mother was obviously oblivious of the danger she was in. She smiled at the Chief Inspector, who had, at some point, taken the cup of tea from her hands. "Would either of you like some biscuits?" she asked, making her way to the kitchen.

"None for me," the Chief Inspector said. "I will not be staying long." He said this last sentence looking directly at Saskia. "This is purely a social visit," he added, again for her benefit.

Saskia wanted more than anything to believe him, but she felt all the anxiety and apprehension that her mother clearly did not feel.

"What do you think of the portraits, Chief Inspector?" her mother asked, handing a cloth to Saskia while pointing at the mantelpiece.

"Emil Coetzee?" the Chief Inspector asked.

"Yes. Done years ago, of course," her mother said. "I'm very proud of them. My best work, I think. Couldn't display them for years. My husband would not have it. Too jealous of a beauty he never possessed. But he is not here anymore, and I can do as I please."

"Can I speak with you outside," Saskia quickly said to the Chief Inspector, and before he could respond she got up, leaving the cloth on the unblotted stain.

"You'll have to excuse my daughter's manners, Chief Inspector," her mother said.

The Chief Inspector stood up obligingly and carefully placed his tea on the coffee table.

"It won't take long, I promise," Saskia said as she led the Chief Inspector out the front door. She walked onto the almost wild lawn of the garden, and wished she had had the foresight to bring Norman's packet of Everests. The Chief Inspector preferred to stand on the crooked path. They stood there in separate silences for what seemed like the longest time until Saskia eventually asked, "What do you know?"

"I know that Golide Gumede is reported to have killed Emil Coetzee," the Chief Inspector said.

Saskia looked at the Chief Inspector, confused. "Then why are you here?"

"Because I know that it was Tom Fortenoy who was found dead in Emil Coetzee's home," the Chief Inspector said.

None of this told Saskia how much the Chief Inspector actually knew.

"I am not sure I see the connection," Saskia said, taking a chance.

"I am sure not many people do," the Chief Inspector said.

Saskia was at a loss. How to proceed? "How did you know for sure?" she asked, giving up, but not giving in.

"Your mother wears a very memorable scent," the Chief Inspector said. "So as soon as she opened the door, I knew for certain."

Saskia was even more at a loss. What did that have to do with anything?

"What will you do?" she whispered.

"Nothing to be done. As I said, officially Golide Gumede killed Emil Coetzee. I just came here to make sure of things, and I have. Soon I will be on my way."

"It can't be that easy," Saskia said, not able to stop herself.

"It never is," the Chief Inspector said, before turning back toward the cottage.

Saskia found herself joining him on the crooked path and staying him with her hand. She had carried so much on her own for so long.

"He is my father," Saskia said, her voice stronger than she had expected it to be. "Emil Coetzee is my biological father." She was surprised by how utterly relieved she felt. Chief Inspector Spokes Moloi looked saddened, but not surprised. So he knew. "How did you know?"

"The Selous School for Boys 1942 yearbook."

"That would have shown you my resemblance to her. There isn't much, but the coloring is the same, and the long neck. But him...how?"

"You inherited his eyes... and the uncertainty they hold," the Chief Inspector explained.

"How did you know it was her and not me? Could have very easily been me."

"Whoever shot Tom Fortenoy obviously mistook him for Emil Coetzee... You never would have. But someone who perhaps hadn't seen him in years... "

"He was just a child and she was his teacher." For some time, Saskia was at a loss as to what to say next. "He had no idea about me," she continued. "I had no idea about him until the man who had raised me told me as he lay dying. My mother thought I was going to tell Emil Coetzee the truth. In her own way, she stopped me."

The Chief Inspector nodded slowly as the last piece of the puzzle fell into place for him.

"It is my fault," Saskia said.

"What is your fault?" the Chief Inspector said, frowning for the first time.

"All of it. Emil Coetzee… Tom Fortenoy… all of it."

"Mrs. Hargrave—"

"No. Don't you see? I paid Emil Coetzee a visit the day before he disappeared. I went to see him at The Tower, and… and he looked at me with such disdain—like I was nothing that mattered. He had no idea who I was. How could I fill him with such contempt when he had no idea who I was? But maybe… maybe he knew exactly who I was the second he saw me. Recognized some trait, some feature, some characteristic of hers, and knew. Just knew. And this knowledge is what made him drive to the bush and never walk out of it. It was the sort of thing she was afraid he would do once he knew, and he did it… and I made him do it."

"Mrs. Hargrave," the Chief Inspector said, reaching out to put a hesitant hand on her shoulder. "You cannot do this to yourself. I happen to know why Emil Coetzee drove to the bush. You can rest assured that you are not the reason why he did what he did."

The Chief Inspector was trying to let her off the hook, but Saskia did not want to be let off the hook. "Tom Fortenoy is definitely my fault. She wouldn't have killed him if she hadn't been afraid."

The Chief Inspector gave her shoulder a gentle squeeze. "In my long life I have learnt that it never helps to carry someone else's burden."

"Chief Inspector—"

"Decisions were made that affected you, but none of them were your decisions. You are not directly responsible for anything that has happened here."

"But surely you must see that if I hadn't paid that visit to

Emil Coetzee... if I hadn't wanted to tell him the truth, she wouldn't have... she has absolutely no idea that what she did was wrong—then and now. She's too far gone, you see. Has always been. And I... I have always been alone. And empty."

"Empty?" the Chief Inspector said.

"Chief Inspector... " Saskia said, wanting to be understood and not merely placated. "I know how I feel... what I am inside."

"You can only be what you choose to be."

For some reason, those words allowed Saskia to begin letting go of what she had long been holding on to. "You are really not going to arrest my mother for Tom Fortenoy's death?"

"Secret Intelligence has seen to your mother's continued freedom."

"She deserves some form of punishment," Saskia said, feeling guilty and defeated at the same time.

"And you?" the Chief Inspector asked in that restrained way of his. "What do you deserve?"

Saskia had no idea.

SPOKES

———◆———

Saskia's decision to place the photo of a happier time—a father and son out fishing together—next to Emil Coetzee's obituary had proved to be more than the right choice. For many people, all that Emil Coetzee had ever been was contained in that one photo. He was remembered as a devoted husband, a loving father, a hero when his country needed him most—and, above all, a true patriot. Saskia Hargrave might as well have written a hagiography. For many weeks, condolences poured in from all over the country, filling in pages upon pages of the newspaper. Even without a public funeral, no one seemed to doubt, not even for a moment, that Emil Coetzee was dead, or that he had been killed by Golide Gumede. There were no questions, just a lot of emotions—the way the secret intelligence boys liked things.

Emil Coetzee's untimely and tragic end allowed many to share not only their adoration, but to also vent their anger, frustration, and other baser emotions; so that as Emil Coetzee was glorified, Golide Gumede was vilified with equal measure and zeal. Whatever his war-time fortunes had been, Golide Gumede became something to fear in peace time: a coward who had ruthlessly killed a defenseless man; a terrorist who did not appreciate that the war was over; a sociopath who cared nothing for the lives of others; a continued threat to the state because he was still at large and suspected to be roaming the countryside. Politicians of all stripes weighed in on the issue; and because the future was not a certain thing, they seemed happy to come together to condemn Golide Gumede based on very little evidence. They basked in the freedom of the amnesty that had chosen to overlook their wartime activities, but refused Golide Gumede that same freedom—because it was more convenient to brand him a rogue agent.

Spokes had to accept that Clement Rutherford and Joseth Maraire had been right about malleable truths after all. It really was that disturbingly easy to shape people's reality. For years, he had been doggedly investigating crimes without realizing that the war was not only decimating the majority of the people, but also qualitatively changing who they were. Years of propaganda and heavy censorship, coupled with the constant fear of death and loss, had made them afraid to openly question anything, which was something that the secret intelligence boys had understood very well. Battered and wearied by the protracted war, the people's eyes were no longer for beauty to see, and here they were all marching toward independence together.

Every day Spokes read through the condolences section of the newspaper, he became afraid of a future where reality could be so easily manipulated, truth so easily distorted, and lies so easily believed. He knew there was only one way the future would be golden for him, and so he had made Chief Superintendent Griffiths promise—on the mounted trophy of his '79 bream—that Spokes' request for retirement would be granted soon after the elections in April.

But Spokes needed to be doing something in the meantime—he was not one to sit and wait—he needed to be saved from the futility that came with thinking too deeply about things over which one had no power. It took him a long moment to see his salvation. It was squeezed into the bottom right-hand corner of the page, along with the condolences; just as he was about to turn the page, he saw it—firmly standing its ground and refusing to be pushed off the page. The notice read:

> LOOKING FOR TOM FORTENOY. 50s. GRAYING BLOND HAIR. TALL. MEDIUM BUILD. LAST SEEN AT THE DILETTANTE CLUB. NEW YEAR'S EVE. IF YOU HAVE ANY INFORMATION, PLEASE CONTACT MRS. T. FORTENOY ON 53470.

There it was. Exactly what Spokes needed. A silver lining. Something unmalleable.

He stood up from his chair, folded the newspaper and placed it under his arm, removed his fedora from the hat hook, opened the door, and happily set forth to be himself— a man seeking truth and justice.

———•———

Spokes looked at the sight and could not believe his eyes. The man was contained in glass. He saw Clement Rutherford sitting in his office and wondered what the effect of the set-up was supposed to accomplish. Who was watching who? Was the arrangement meant to give one a sense of power, or was it supposed to instill insecurity? The atmosphere was tense, to say the least. Was that the point? To keep everyone on edge and constantly striving? But striving for what? All these questions accompanied Spokes on his journey toward Clement Rutherford's office. Before he got to it, someone had joined him. Joseth Maraire. Of course. Once in the office, both men looked at him with a deep displeasure that felt better to Spokes than any welcome could have.

"I won't take up too much of your time," Spokes said, placing the newspaper on Clement Rutherford's desk. "I just want to know what you intend to do for the widow."

"The widow? You mean Kuki—Mrs. Coetzee?" Clement Rutherford said, his eyes skimming over the condolences. "We had a nice chat with her. Explained the needs of the country at this time. She understood perfectly, as I knew she would. Made of stern stuff, that one. Pioneer stock. Blue-blooded."

"I meant Mrs. T. Fortenoy," Spokes said, pointing to the notice at the bottom right-hand corner of the page.

Clement Rutherford and Joseth Maraire exchanged one of their many looks.

"And she concerns us how?" Joseth Maraire asked.

"Her husband, Tom Fortenoy, apparently built himself something of a career impersonating Emil Coetzee. I am not surprised at your not knowing this; I only heard of him recently myself," Spokes said.

"Of course I know who Tom Fortenoy is," Joseth Maraire said.

"Then you understand how Mrs. Tom Fortenoy looking for her husband concerns you," Spokes said.

The two men exchanged yet another look before Clement Rutherford resignedly reached for an unsharpened HB pencil and bit into it.

"I thought we had an agreement, Chief Inspector," he said.

"Malleable truths?"

"Yes, exactly."

"I think Mrs. Fortenoy needs to know the actual truth about what happened to her husband. She needs to stop looking for and waiting for a man who is not coming back."

"Tom Fortenoy was a known drunk and all but a derelict. Anything could have happened to him. She knows that. In time she will come to accept it," Clement Rutherford said.

"Or we can make her accept the actual truth," Spokes said.

"We?" Joseth Maraire said.

"I am sure you wouldn't want me to visit her alone, now would you?" Spokes said.

The HB pencil in Clement Rutherford's hands broke into two.

There is a particular way that a person with something to hide opens a door. They crack the door just enough so that you can see their face, especially their eyes—the guilty ones look directly in your eyes, trying to gauge what it is that you already know. This person with something to hide usually places as much of their body as they can behind the door, and never removes their hand from the door handle. Mrs. Tom Fortenoy was not a person with something to hide. As soon as she saw the three men on her doorstep, she opened the door wider and let them look on her full glory—her slatternly appearance, her unkempt hair, her soiled and frayed apron, her dirty fingernails. None of these were recent occurrences. Mrs. Tom Fortenoy was poor, and had been living in reduced circumstances for quite some time; so long, in fact, that she had allowed herself to lose some of her pride.

"You're with the BSAP, I gather," she said, and Spokes nodded his head. "So that is how it is," she said as her right hand came to rest on her belly. "He spent more time on the street than he did at home, but the one thing he always did was spend New Year's Day with us. It did not matter what state he was in, he always appeared in time to mark the New Year. Only this year, he did not. I knew immediately that something was wrong. I could feel it here," she said as she gave her stomach a not-so-gentle squeeze. She turned around and the three men had no choice but to follow her into the room.

Spokes' first impression of Mrs. Tom Fortenoy had been correct; she was indeed poor, but she had not always been. He walked into a home made up of five rooms, all of them barely breathing. Scents from the kitchen, bathroom, and two bedrooms all mingled in the minuscule sitting room in which he found himself as soon as he stepped into the doorway. Five rooms in the townships where he lived were considered a luxury, and made a man like him appear to be a prince among paupers. But here, in the heart of the city, in the caretaker's quarters at the bottom of a block of flats, five rooms made a man seem down and out. The rooms seemed inadequate—unable to contain everything that they were expected to. True, the rooms were small, and did not seem to allow for much life to be lived in them, but Spokes was used to living in such rooms. The trick was to arrange the furniture in such a way that the rooms appeared to be larger than they really were—and therefore able to contain all the joys and disappointments of life. This was something that the lovely Loveness knew how to do perfectly. Every room in their five-roomed home was filled with sunshine and more happiness than any one man deserved.

Mrs. Tom Fortenoy had no such guiding principle in her home arrangements. She had taken all the many years of her life and stuffed them into the five rooms. Spokes could only see into the kitchen and the bathroom from where he was sitting, but he believed the bedrooms were equally crammed with bric-a-brac. There was evidence everywhere—in the wedding photos framed in sterling silver, in the leather-bound A-Z encyclopedia collection, in the many incomplete sets of the finest china placed on lace doilies in the glass display cabinet, in the Persian rug under the coffee table—that showed that the Fortenoys had not always been poor. They had had a rather comfortable life, a life that some might have even considered affluent, and Mrs. Tom Fortenoy (who could have used the money from the sale of some of these items) wanted this to be something that was remembered.

"He was not really a bad man, my husband," Mrs. Tom Fortenoy said. "He was not even a disappointment. He was a brilliant man in a country that only understands mediocrity. He played Othello... Macbeth... Coriolanus: all the great heroes. They wrote about him in the paper. Rave reviews. And then he fell from grace, and we moved here so that we could have a place to live in in exchange for his being a caretaker. But he cannot take care of anything anymore, and so I do. I take care." She ran her hands over her soiled apron, and Spokes noticed how chapped and calloused her hands were.

"Mum!" a voice called out from one of the bedrooms.

"My son," Mrs. Fortenoy said. 'Just returned home from the wars," she explained before she made her way to one of the bedrooms.

The three men looked at each other, not sure what to do next.

"It must be nice finally rubbing shoulders with the madams," Joseth Maraire said as Spokes made himself more comfortable on a maroon sofa showing lots of wear and tear. "You think you're no longer some 'boy' in their eyes. You think they now see you as a man. You think that they care about you— care that you are trying so hard to please them. But they don't care, and they never will."

Spokes smiled as he placed his fedora on his knee before saying, "If I cared for the opinions of others more than I cared for my own, I would be a very different man."

SASKIA

———— ◆ ————

As soon as Saskia saw the note on her desk, she knew that it was from the Chief Inspector, not so much because of what was written on it: Zora Neale Hurston—"How It Feels To Be Colored Me"—*The World Tomorrow*, but because of the dignified and controlled handwriting with which it was written. The elegant handwriting gave the reader confidence in the character of the writer.

It took eons for the ancient and powdery head librarian at the Main Public Library to retrieve a copy of the magazine, and Saskia used that time to get over, as best she could, her disappointment in learning that Zora Neale Hurston was no one exciting—just a writer.

After receiving the magazine, Saskia sat in the packed reading room, *The World Tomorrow* before her. She could not connect to the story about a young black woman's experience of growing up in the American South, and being transformed and transported by jazz music. Saskia could not think of a life that was more removed from her own than the life of Zora Neale Hurston; until she got to the very end and read the lines:

> But in the main, I feel like a brown bag of miscellany propped against a wall. Against a wall in company with other bags, white, red and yellow. Pour out the contents, and there is discovered a jumble of small things priceless and worthless. A first-water diamond, an empty spool, bits of broken glass, lengths of string, a key to a door long since crumbled away, a rusty knife-blade,

old shoes saved for a road that never was and never will be, a nail bent under the weight of things too heavy for any nail, a dried flower or two still a little fragrant. In your hand is the brown bag. On the ground before you is the jumble it held—so much like the jumble in the bags, could they be emptied, that all might be dumped in a single heap and the bags refilled without altering the content of any greatly. A bit of colored glass more or less would not matter. Perhaps that is how the Great Stuffer of Bags filled them in the first place—who knows?

Saskia found that she liked the idea of being a bag of miscellany so much that she copied the paragraph onto a piece of paper, and left the library with much more than she had entered with—a Zora Neale Hurston that she could carry with her everywhere she went and choose to treasure, if she so pleased.

Now, as she sat at her desk at *The Chronicle*, she thought of the "jumble of small things" that her particular bag carried. When the phone on her desk rang, it took her a long time to answer it.

"Is this Saskia Hargrave?" the female voice on the other end of the line inquired.

Saskia could not quite read the emotion held in the voice, and so she said a little hesitantly, "Yes."

"You the one who wrote that nonsense about Emil Coetzee?"

"Nonsense?"

"Yes—about his being killed or some such by Golide Gumede."

So it was one of those calls, Saskia thought with a sigh. She had been receiving at least three of these kinds of calls per week, ever since she had written the obituary. People, mostly with theories of their own about what had happened to Emil Coetzee, were eager to get in touch with her. Not everyone, despite the SIU's best efforts, seemed ready to embrace the fact that Emil Coetzee had been murdered by Golide Gumede, especially after the stately hero's funeral that everyone had been expecting had not come to pass. Why would Emil Coetzee be given a private burial attended only by his family? Suspicion soon led to conjecture, and Saskia started receiving the phone calls.

There were some rather imaginative and creative ideas out there, some even outlandish. The most inspired of these was one in which Emil Coetzee had been seized by a group of Amazonian feminists to go and start a new colony where no other men were allowed. Why the women had to be feminists in the theorist's imagination was anyone's guess. And what would happen to the boy children that would surely be born? Since no men, save Emil Coetzee, were allowed in the colony, would the boys be banished once they became men? The caller feared much worse—perhaps they would be ritually sacrificed or cannabalized.

Saskia's particular favorite was the man who not only firmly believed that Emil Coetzee had been abducted by aliens, but also claimed to have physical evidence of the UFO in question.

Saskia did not judge, she simply faithfully jotted down the strange stories many were willing to tell her. Until recently she had had no idea of how... inventive her people could be. Discovering this side of them made her appreciate them more. Or, perhaps, she appreciated them more because they had turned the disappearance of her father into a larger mystery than it already was; and in that way, they helped keep him very much alive for her.

Her father: Emil Coetzee. The man who, wherever he was,

might or might not know that he had a daughter.

"Miss Hargrave? Are you still there?" the voice on the other end of the line asked.

"Yes," Saskia said.

"Well, I have just seen Emil Coetzee drive past in his beige bakkie not looking dead at all! What have you got to say for yourself?"

"You saw him? You saw Emil Coetzee?"

"Yes."

"Are you sure it was him?"

"Yes. Of course I'm sure."

Saskia exhaled shakily before asking, "How can you be absolutely sure?"

"Well, because he waved at me and everything… and because it is not the first time that he has driven past, now is it?"

"You mean he has driven past before?"

"Yes. He drove past… let's see, when was that? The day after the ceasefire was announced," the voice on the other end said matter-of-factly. "Car trouble just beyond my gate. Drove off before I could provide him assistance. Today, just seen him driving, going the opposite direction, toward the City of Kings. Obviously heading back from wherever he's been all this time."

There was no mention of colonizing feminists or tinfoil crop-circling aliens. No theory was offered; it was just a good, old-fashioned sighting, with enough credibility to make Saskia reach for her notepad and ask for the woman's particulars.

"Louisa Alcott… Mrs."

Saskia jotted down the name as it had been given to her, then asked: "Where are you located?"

"On the Alcott Farm on the Old King's Road. About thirty kilometers from the city center. Huge, sprawling place… you can't miss it."

"I would like to come and interview you, if that is all right."

"You mean, you will put my name in the paper and everything?"

"And everything."

"Best to start getting ready, then. How do you feel about koeksisters?"

"I rather like them, and the feeling seems to be mutual, especially over the past five years, and definitely over the hip area."

Louisa Alcott, Mrs., laughed so hard at this mediocre joke that she actually snorted into the phone, and then apologized profusely.

When Saskia arrived at the Alcott Farm about an hour and a half later, she found Louisa Alcott, Mrs., waiting for her on her veranda. She was a pretty woman, not quite middle-aged, but definitely wearied by the war. She had prepared a wonderful tea spread. On the table, there was a beautiful tea set of the finest china, decorated with pink periwinkles. On this china, there was a mountain of scones slathered with butter and strawberry jam, a pyramid of koeksisters doused and dripping with syrup, a tray of Choice Assorted biscuits, and an arrangement of sad-looking cucumber sandwiches that seemed like an afterthought. There was also a half-read Mills & Boon romance novel, lying open and facedown on the table.

When Saskia got back to *The Chronicle's* offices, she, perhaps because of the sweetness of the day, could not help but sour it a little by adding salt to a wound that she was sure had not yet healed. She used her index finger to search for and locate one of the many telephone numbers jotted down on her desk calendar. The person on the other end answered after the second ring, and Saskia told this person about her meeting with Louisa Alcott, Mrs., and stressed how well the meeting had gone—how credible Louisa Alcott, Mrs., was. So credible, in fact, that she was planning on publishing the interview in the paper.

The person on the other end of the line was silent for a long time, and Saskia took pleasure in that until the person said, "I would strongly advise against you doing that, Mrs. Hargrave."

The "Mrs." was stressed as though it was meant to sting, but Saskia did not allow herself to feel that sting as she, having expected discouragement, asked, "Why?"

"Well… because Mrs. Louisa Alcott is no stranger to us," the voice replied, a little too smugly for Saskia's liking. "Rather sad story, really," the voice continued. "During the war, she accidentally shot her husband and killed him. He, instead of going on a recce, had gone on a weekend bender and returned home unexpectedly in the middle of the night. She thought he was an intruder. Apparently, after that she lost the plot entirely and disappeared into her own make-believe world. Judge could not even send her to prison. She spent about a year or two in the same place you did, Ingutsheni. Must have been there around the same time. I am not surprised the two of you got along, or that she seemed credible to you. I am surprised you didn't recognize her, but then again, you were in the special ward, weren't you? They were afraid you were going to harm yourself or those around you, weren't they?"

Saskia did not know what to say or do in response. The voice on the other end took advantage of the situation and asked: "Were you telling the truth about Joseth?"

"Yes," Saskia said, before hanging up the phone. She was glad he had asked the question about Joseth Maraire because that made her realize that Clement Rutherford was also just a jumble of small things.

Louisa Alcott, Mrs., had called Saskia because she had news to share and Saskia worked for a newspaper. Louisa

Alcott, Mrs., had made herself pretty and had been the perfect hostess. Saskia had taken pictures and promised to have them printed in the paper, along with the story. Saskia would keep her promise. She would tell the story of how Louisa Alcott, Mrs., had seen Emil Coetzee, alleged by the SIU to have been murdered by Golide Gumede, driving his beige bakkie toward the City of Kings.

"Do I have your permission?" Saskia asked the editor as she stood in his doorway. She had told him everything that Louisa Alcott, Mrs., had told her and none of what Clement Rutherford had said.

"Of course," the editor said enthusiastically.

"We could get into some real trouble with the authorities," Saskia half-heartedly cautioned.

"Authorities are in the process of changing. And besides, we've toed the party line long enough," the editor said.

The story, or at least its first three paragraphs, appeared on the front page of *The Sunday News* and was continued, accompanied by the pictures, on the third page.

When Saskia's phone rang on Monday morning, and a woman's voice on the other end asked to speak to her, she thought that it was Louisa Alcott, Mrs., and was therefore very surprised when the voice said, "My name is Marion Hartley and I am calling to inquire about this piece you have written about someone sighting Emil Coetzee." Saskia waited for the emotions she thought she felt toward Marion Hartley to surface—resentment, jealousy, anger—but none of them did.

She decided to tell Marion Hartley the entire truth about the story.

"He would like that, I think. Like to have people see him driving around... roaming the veld. He was very much at home there," Marion Hartley said. "Thank you."

As Saskia hung up the phone, she thought to herself, *why*

not? Why not also print the stories of the Amazonian feminists and UFO abductions? Why not have Emil Coetzee exist wherever people wanted him to? It was so much better than the alternative.

In the months and years to come, Saskia found herself writing articles on every theory about Emil Coetzee and every sighting of him that came her way in a series she titled, "Where's Emil Coetzee?" It became so very popular that it even had the full support of the editor-in-chief.

The "Where's Emil Coetzee" story that became the most widespread over time was the one Saskia received and reported with characteristic fidelity from Machipisa, a man who identified himself as Emil Coetzee's gardener. Machipisa said that his baas's ghost came down every morning for breakfast wearing a navy-blue and khaki morning gown with navy-blue slippers, opened the fridge, and helped himself to the mature cheddar cheese. Although bad enough, this was not the worst of it; the ghost, according to Machipisa, had three bullet holes in his chest—all oozing blood.

SPOKES

———◆———

It was the kind of day in which a man chooses to walk his bicycle instead of ride it, and so Spokes walked his Raleigh all the way to the Mpopoma Public Library. Once outside the library, he carefully removed *Wives and Daughters* from his messenger bag, and then entered the building.

As always, the library was filled with people, young and old, all eagerly reading books, magazines and newspapers. Most of the people—young and old—greeted him and asked after the health of Mrs. Moloi as soon as he walked into the library. Spokes removed his fedora, greeted them back, and asked after the health of their loved ones. He allowed the exchange to be the lengthy process that it always was before taking his place at the back of the queue. As always when he stood at the back of the line, people protested, and as always he firmly stood his ground—both these things (the customary recognition of hierarchy and the refusal to take advantage of it) were expected and necessary to the equilibrium that existed within the Mpopoma Public Library.

"Did you get your man?" the head librarian asked Spokes by way of greeting as he—with impressive alacrity—took the novel from his hands, removed the sign-out card from the adhered sleeve, stamped the return date, and then filed the sign-out card away.

"Not a man this time," Spokes said in response.

"Women! Can't trust them," the head librarian said as he placed the book on the neat pile of returned books. "That's why I sleep with one eye open."

"You certainly have to choose them carefully."

"Yes, but none of us could have been as fortunate as you."

"That is so true."

"How did that wonderful wife of yours enjoy this one? Renewed it twice. Very rare for her."

"We enjoyed it quite a lot. Until we read the ending."

"Why? What happens in the end?"

"Nothing. The author died before she could write the ending."

"Ah, I see. So no happy ending. And that wonderful wife of yours likes her happy endings."

"That she does. Consequently we preferred *North & South* to this one."

"*We?* What is this *we* business?" the head librarian said with a chuckle. "Still trying to convince me you're an avid reader, Chief Inspector?"

"I simply am what I am."

"That you are, Chief Inspector. That you are. And what you are is a brilliant detective. I have been waiting for you to stop by so that I could ask you what *really* happened to Emil Coetzee. If anyone would know, it's the Chief Inspector, I said to myself."

"Emil Coetzee walked into the bush and did not walk out of it," Spokes said.

The head librarian looked at him for a moment, and then burst out laughing. "I think I prefer the one with the Amazonian feminists," he said. "Now what would that wonderful wife of yours like to read next?"

"You wouldn't happen to have a copy of Zora Neale Hurston's *Their Eyes Were Watching God*, would you?"

The head librarian—with impressive alacrity—opened a series of roll-out drawers and checked and cross-checked files and index cards. "It's in Special Collections," he declared triumphantly. He always took it rather personally if the library did not hold a particular title.

"Ah. So it can't be checked out," Spokes said.

"You're the Chief Inspector and you're married to that wonderful wife of yours and so—"

"Rules are rules. I don't expect—"

"Those rules were made by the same people who used to make us wear white gloves before we could even touch a book. Remember those days? To think they actually thought our blackness would rub off on everything. And you'd be amazed at how many books written by black people are held in Special Collections. These people! They definitely knew what they were doing." The head librarian said all this as he—with impressive alacrity—prepared a new sign-out card and adhesive sleeve. He left to go and fetch the book in question, and Spokes did not stop him.

In no time at all, the head librarian was back. "Some things have to change and they are changing… finally," he said as he—with impressive alacrity—affixed the new adhesive sleeve in the book and placed the new sign-out card, the date already stamped, in the sleeve. He proudly handed the book to Spokes and added, "We cannot take this thing called independence lightly."

"No, we cannot," Spokes agreed.

As Spokes left the library with *Their Eyes Were Watching God* held firmly in his hands, most of the people—young and old—waited for him to put his fedora on his head and then asked him to "see" Mrs. Moloi. He in turn asked them to "see" their loved ones. He allowed the exchange to be the lengthy process that it always was before walking out of the library.

Once outside, Spokes opened the book out of curiosity, wanting to know who had donated it. He found written on the title page, in a left-leaning cursive, the words "This book donated to the Mpopoma Public Library by Marion Hartley." *Of course,* Spokes thought with a smile, as he closed the book and placed it in his messenger bag.

It did not take long for Spokes, who was once again walking his Raleigh, to notice that two men were following him, and had been ever since he left the library. They had taken every turn he had taken, even when he had gone around the same block of houses twice.

There was an Idlazonke General Goods and Bottle Store up ahead (where wasn't there an Idlazonke store nowadays?). Spokes decided to park his Raleigh and enter the store and see if the men followed him in or continued on their merry way. He did not much relish the idea of entering an Idlazonke store and purchasing something. Ever since Daisy's murder, he had made sure never to patronize an Idlazonke store. Besides, Silas Mthimkhulu had over the years seemed to become more interested in monopolizing the market than in providing quality goods to the people—his entire business model spoke of a greed that Spokes found disturbing.

The inside of the store was rather dark and dank, and smelled overwhelmingly of green soap and paraffin. A Lovemore Majaivana song blared from the tinny speakers. There were all manner of goods on display—from sweets to cheap perfumes and colognes. From the shopkeeper's shifty eyes, which chose not to look at anything else but him as soon as he entered the store, Spokes suspected that there was more on sale in this establishment than met the eye. The fact that half the loitering youths that seemed to be the store's regular customers left the premises as soon as the shopkeeper, in an oily voice, greeted Spokes with, "Chief Inspector Moloi, to what do we owe the pleasure?" cemented this fact.

Spokes removed his fedora and walked up to the counter.

"Please may I have a bottle of Stoney Ginger Beer," he said.

"Of course you may, Chief Inspector. Anything for you," the shopkeeper's slick voice said as he retrieved an ice-cold drink from the fridge behind him. He opened the drink with a bottle-opener that he kept attached to his belt along with a Swiss Army knife. "On the house!" he declared.

"Thank you. But I can't accept it, I'm afraid."

"A gift is a gift, Chief Inspector."

"When you're a policeman, a gift can be a bribe."

"Now why would I bribe you, Chief Inspector?"

"I didn't say you were," Spokes said as he placed the exact amount for the drink on the counter.

"I just wanted to thank you for finally gracing our little establishment here with your presence, Chief Inspector," the shopkeeper said as he put the money in the till. "I have seen you—and that beautiful wife of yours, Loveness—walk by many times over the years... but neither of you ever enters. She is also like you—often walks alone. But now here you are. Today must be a special day indeed."

"We prefer the hypermarket," Spokes said, before taking a few gulps of the ginger beer.

"Ah, I see, Chief Inspector. You prefer to give your hard-earned money to the white man instead of Silas Mthimkhulu."

"If that is how you choose to see it."

"I meant no disrespect, Chief Inspector."

"And none was perceived."

"I am genuinely happy to see you in the store, Chief Inspector."

"I am sure you are," Spokes said as he finished off his drink and placed the empty bottle on the counter.

"I don't see why we can't be friends, Chief Inspector."

"Neither can I," Spokes said before leaning over the counter and saying, "As long as next time you find my wife's name in your mouth, you spit it out before I hear you say it. Understood?"

"Yes, Chief Inspector," the shopkeeper said, his oiliness having suddenly dried up.

"Good," Spokes said as he put on his fedora and left the store.

As expected, the two men had not walked past the store—or rather, one of them had not—he stood under an in-bloom acacia tree, opposite the store. Where was the other one—up ahead lying in wait? Spokes stepped off the dusty Idlazonke stoep and headed straight to the man under the tree. As Spokes approached him, the man looked trapped. He moved this way and that, and then stood very still, as though waiting for something truly terrible to befall him. The closer Spokes got to the man, the more he felt certain that he knew him… but not as a man… as nothing more than a boy: a boy in big muddy boots carrying an AK-47 that seemed heavier than him; a boy smashing windows and screaming into the night; a boy already haunted by a war that was going to get much worse: the harbinger.

"You're the one who was screaming about limbs and torsos in the Zambezi," Spokes said to the man.

The man who was a boy no longer looked at Spokes blankly, "Limbs? Torsos? Zambezi?" he managed to say at last.

He had probably seen much worse since then. "Yes. Torsos with Y-dissections cut into them, floating in the Zambezi."

"Yes… " the man said slowly, as though wanting to remember and not remember at the same time.

"You came to the Tribal Trust Land that my mother lived on. Broke windows… "

"Yes," the man said in that slow way of his. "Broke so much more." He picked up the interestingly shaped bottle of a Canada Dry Ginger Ale that lay at his feet. The action held no threat or malice. "So... you remember me?" the man said, evidently full of hope.

"Yes."

The man looked relieved. "I remember you too," he said, twirling the bottle in his hands.

"Is that why you and your partner have been following me? Because you remember me?"

"Partner," the man said, confused. Something clicked. "That is not my partner. That is my commander." The man seemed genuinely concerned that Spokes could make such a mistake.

"My apologies. Your commander: where is he? Up ahead?"

The man nodded slowly.

"Shall we go to him, then?" Spokes said before going to collect his Raleigh from where it leaned against the Idlazonke store.

"One of the boys who came out of the store soon after you went in—he tried to take that messenger bag. I stopped him by showing him this bottle."

Spokes knew that he had done more than show the boy the bottle. "I would like to thank you," Spokes said, "but I need to know your name first. Last time we met, it wasn't something that you could freely give."

"Lukha... Lukhayezi Mzingeli Hlotshwayo."

"Thank you, Lukhayezi Mzingeli Hlotshwayo," Spokes said, offering his hand for Lukha to shake.

"You are Chief Inspector Spokes Moloi of the CID. You're the man that *The Chronicle* says is investigating what happened to Emil Coetzee," Lukha said, shaking his hand.

"I am that man, yes."

Lukha did not say anything else, and Spokes, although intrigued, let the matter rest there—at least for the time being.

They walked silently together some distance, and then

Lukha whistled loud and sharp. A clear whistle responded from up ahead, but even with his trained eyes and ears, Spokes could not pinpoint its exact location.

Now all his life Spokes had only ever been in complete awe of one man, and one man only—the incomparable Pele—and he had thought that there would never be any need for him to be in awe of another man ever again—until he saw the impossibly tall man with gleaming white skin walking toward him. And then there was only one possible emotion that he could feel.

"My father named me Livingstone Stanley Tikiti," the man said, offering Spokes his hand. "But my name is Golide Gumede."

For the first time in a long time, Spokes did not know what to think, feel or say, and so he just shook Golide Gumede's hand.

"I had absolutely nothing to do with whatever happened to Emil Coetzee," Golide Gumede said.

"I know," Spokes managed to say, still shaking his hand.

"The war is over, Chief Inspector. I am just a man like any other. All I want to do is make my way to my family. I have a little girl… beautiful and golden… born while I was fighting. I would like more than anything to see her."

Spokes nodded, trying to see the daughter that Golide Gumede spoke of instead of the amateurish G O L I D E G U M that the secret intelligence boys had left painted on Emil Coetzee's den wall. "I think you are the only man who can help me. Lukha here says that he met you before, and you struck him as a man who would do the right thing. I trust Lukha with my life. He served us well as a medic. Saved my life more than once."

Lukha was embarrassed by the praise, and, not knowing what else to do, threw the empty bottle of Canada Dry in a perfect arc through the air.

Spokes finally knew what to think, say and do. "It is Saturday afternoon and my wife is making her famous scones," he said as he let go of Golide Gumede's hand.

The two men looked at him and each other, confused.

"I take it you are hungry? I am inviting you to my home for tea, gentlemen," Spokes said before he continued walking his Raleigh.

It was during this journey homeward that Spokes made a promise to Golide Gumede: a promise he would keep.

PART TWO

———•———

CLEAVE

MARCH 1980

THE LOVELY LOVENESS

In all the twenty-seven years of her long-loving marriage, nothing had threatened the privileged position Loveness had in Spokes' heart and life. Well, that was not entirely true. There had been one adversary: Pele. Pele who could butt a header from midfield; Pele who could somersault through the air and kick a ball straight into the back of the net; Pele who could dribble a ball from one end of the field to the other—and, of course, score a goal; Pele who was too quick, too clever, too creative for any other man on the soccer field. Pele! Pele! Pele! What was it that Pele could not do? There had been periods of their marriage that coincided with the years that Pele had won the World Cup for Brazil—1958, 1962 and 1970 to be precise—that Loveness had been almost certain that if she asked her husband, as he sat in their sitting room with his ear only an alarming inch away from the wire-less, who made the best chicken and dumplings, the answer would too readily and easily have been: Pele.

Pele, her old nemesis, had thankfully and, in her decided opinion, belatedly retired in 1977, leaving her husband in peace. But now, just as Loveness was beginning once again to feel completely unrivaled, and just as the promise of retiring to Krum's Place was becoming a reality, here was Daisy not allowing Spokes to see things clearly. Loveness would have none of it.

For Loveness, Golide Gumede's visit had presented a challenge. There needed to be additional movement—a third person—one who was extremely trustworthy... and she knew exactly where to find such a person. The way forward was clear, but she was sure Spokes could not see it because of Daisy. Well, there was much that she, Loveness, would have to do about that.

Loveness remembered Daisy as a pretty woman who laughed easily and thoroughly appreciated the attention of men—the kind of woman that a man went after with great zeal, the kind of woman who made a man believe he had received a prize in obtaining her, the kind of woman whose effortlessly obtained affections eventually made a man worry about the prize in his possession. Spokes, however, remembered Daisy as a grotesquely chopped-up body stuffed in a burlap sack and dumped in a river.

Loveness had liked Daisy and her easy ways well enough when S'jumba had brought her, already pregnant, to the village from the City of Kings. He had obviously meant for her to be far out of the reach of men who could lure her away from him, and had hoped that the ever-watchful eye of the people he was part of, the people he had grown up amongst, would make sure that no other man took his chances with her.

At first, there really was nothing for the villagers to see. Daisy was expecting after all, and it was taboo for any man to approach a pregnant woman with amorous or more nefarious intentions. And so the villagers had relaxed. But then only three months after Loveness had helped Daisy deliver a daughter into the world, the shopkeeper at the newly built Idlazonke General Goods and Bottle Store, Jasper Mlangeni, had gifted Daisy with a brand-new dress. He had excused his gift to a woman who was obviously attached to another man by stating the rather embarrassingly noticeable fact that Daisy only owned maternity clothes. Since Daisy accepted the dress without the qualms that the villagers had expected, there was very little that they could do about it. They felt the same when Raftopoulos, the Greek travelling salesman, and the arithmetic teacher over at the mission school near Krum's Place, started to give Daisy assorted knick-knacks here and there. Daisy (who would never divulge where she came from) accepted her gifts with grace, and since she was a foreigner in these parts, the villagers felt that they could not force her to conform to their ways and customs.

If Loveness' conjecture—after Daisy named her daughter Dikeledi—that Daisy was from Bechuanaland was correct, then the villagers' hands were truly tied, because who knew what was contained within the customs and traditions of the Tswana people? Perhaps all this gift-giving and receiving was part and parcel of their gender relations. The union (which was not a marriage) between S'jumba and Daisy was the perfect example of why elders always warned against going to look for a log for your home fire in faraway places.

To be fair, the villagers thought and felt these things only during the beginning of their co-existence with Daisy. They tried to keep her at bay, but she was so pleasant and helpful to everybody that in time, it became difficult for the villagers to build a solid wall of spite and malice against her. When village men made advances toward her in not-so clandestine ways, and she, in that easy laughing way of hers, spurned them, no one, especially the men's wives, could take offense because she made it clear that she was not interested in any of their husbands. The men in turn were let down so gently that they were not allowed to feel the rejection. What really won over anyone who still had reservations about Daisy was how she devoutly and painstakingly went around the village salving the bent and cracked backs of the truly ancient villagers with her own secret concoction.

In time, Daisy was, if not universally loved, then definitely highly esteemed. So when S'jumba came home for the one month in the year that his factory baas allowed, the villagers decided not to tell him about Jasper Mlangeni, the Idlazonke shopkeeper, Raftopoulos, the Greek travelling salesman and the arithmetic teacher over at Krum's Place—after all, all they had witnessed was the receiving of goods and nothing else.

And then just as everyone had gotten used to her and her easy ways, Daisy was dead.

When Constable Spokes Moloi came and told them that her remains had been found by a bend in the river in what had once been Qhubeka Village and was now the Ashtonbury Farm and Estate, the villagers were surprised to discover how very little they knew about Daisy. They wished they had not let her charm them into leaving her a thing unknown amongst them. Eager to prove to the constable that they knew more than they did, the villagers began to dispute everything that they had hitherto known.

When Loveness said she clearly remembered that S'jumba had brought Daisy to the village five years earlier, about a year after the constable himself had paid them his unforgettable visit, some disagreed with this and said they clearly remembered Daisy arriving when Loveness' father was still alive. Others said that they clearly remembered Daisy arriving when the British had just finished fighting their second war with the Germans; and still others said that they clearly remembered Daisy arriving during the Great Rains, and that she had not been pregnant when she arrived.

When Loveness said that Daisy was probably from Bechuanaland, some disagreed and said that they had heard her once say something about Nyasaland that made them think that she came from there; others said that she spoke their language so fluently that they had always felt that she was a member of their tribe; and others still said that she had not spoken their language fluently at all, and that they had always been convinced that she was from another country, a country that was much farther afield than Bechuanaland or Nyasaland... Tanganyika, perhaps. And so instead of clearing things up for the constable, the villagers kept on muddying the waters further and further.

In the end, all that could be agreed upon was that on the last night that anyone had seen Daisy, it had rained, and some villagers had heard the engine of a motor car start and the car drive off. Since the only person who had a motor car in the village was Jasper Mlangeni, the Idlazonke General Goods and Bottle Store shopkeeper, and since Jasper Mlangeni was actually in the City of Kings on the night in question, what the villagers actually agreed upon was of absolutely no use to Constable Spokes Moloi.

Had the villagers done this a few years earlier, Loveness would have thought that they were making things difficult for the constable because they remembered how his inability to keep the things he knew to himself had cost them their headman. But they had, for some years now grown accustomed to the leadership of Zwakele Mkhize's son; and so Loveness had to accept that they all said something that was really nothing to the constable because they were in complete awe of a Spokes Moloi in uniform.

Loveness herself was not immune to the beguiling magnetism of a Spokes Moloi in BSAP uniform. When she had first seen him step out of the Idlazonke General Goods and Bottle Store, she had sincerely felt that the man who had been the cause of her father taking his own life had absolutely no right to look so incredibly dashing. And what business did he have growing a moustache that only served to make his finer features more handsome? Yes, he was a man who could recite lines of literature, but for six long years, Loveness had done a commendable job of hating him with all her heart, and she definitely intended to continue doing so—even if Constable Spokes Moloi was the only man in the entire world who looked attractive in a shako helmet.

But…her wise father had said that Spokes Moloi was a brave, integrous and intelligent man, and Loveness came to see these qualities and more on constant display as he worked on the Daisy case. Since he was now always in the village, she could not very well ignore him. That was not how she had been raised.

And so sometimes when he greeted her, she stopped whatever she was doing and entered into a short conversation with him; and if he found her making her way back from Raftopoulos' caravan and wanted to walk her part of the way home, she saw nothing wrong with letting him do as he pleased; and if, whenever he found Dikeledi—who was captivated by the brass buttons on his uniform—in her presence, he chose to speak of marriage and children, what else could she (who had ascertained, as soon as he had stepped out of the Idlazonke General Goods and Bottle Store, not only that his collar could use more starch, but also that his finger could use a wedding band) do but listen to him?

And so it was quite understandable that after it took him an eternity (a full two months one week and five days, to be exact) to ask her to marry him, she felt that it would be very impolite of her, after having taken up so much of his time, not to promptly accept his offer. She could and would not toy with his affections or disappoint his hopes. That was not how she had been raised.

Now the villagers loved having Loveness in the village: in the early mornings, she loaded as many children as possible into her father's carriage and drove them to school on her way to the clinic; in the late evenings, while others listened to stories by the homestead fire, she wrote letters, under the unpredictable light of a paraffin lamp, for those who needed to communicate with relatives who now found themselves in the City of Kings and farther afield; on weekends, she, a trained midwife, helped deliver whichever of the village children had chosen to come into the world. She provided the village with these essential services without asking for anything in return. However, the villagers' gratitude could not let them overlook the fact that at twenty-five she was fast becoming an old maid, and would soon become impossible to marry off.

Loveness found that for many reasons, she could never tell them that because a man had once followed a book she held in her hands all the way from the City of Kings and then recited a line from it, she had gained a very definite idea of the kind of man she wanted to marry. The only kind. She could not tell them that she was now waiting for such a man to come into her life again, and would wait for however long it took. She chose, instead, to tell them that she simply wanted to marry a man who so loved literature that he felt it in his soul.

Upon hearing this, the villagers soon arrived at the conclusion that Loveness was not to be trusted when it came to determining her own future. They tried to reason with her, but she who was reasonable about everything else proved to be unreasonable about marriage. They believed that she read too many books, and was looking for something that she had found in them in real life—something that she thought was vastly different from anything any of them had ever felt or experienced. They lamented the fact that she had made them buy her a book, *Pride and Prejudice*, when she had passed top of her class—because it seemed to have promised her a life that was not meant to be hers.

Since all the villagers knew was the business about the literature in the soul, and since all they saw was Loveness refusing all the Krum's Place men, they had no idea that she was waiting for something that was possible; and so when Constable Spokes Moloi came back to the village, and, in a considerably short space of time, succeeded where every other man had failed, they breathed an audible sigh of relief and forever believed him to be a godsend capable of performing miracles great and small.

The night before Loveness' wedding day, her aunts had sat her down and, as was the custom of ukulaya, told her that marriage was not something that one sent a rat to beforehand, and then asked the rat what the future marriage held. Marriage was something that—for the lucky ones—started off well, and then presented issues that became predicaments which tested the bonds of marriage; and, if left unresolved, made marriage a sour thing in the mouth. Again, her aunts stressed, that was for the lucky ones. For the unlucky ones, marriage was a living hell through and through. Now her aunts wished and hoped and prayed that she would be one of the lucky ones, but even if she was one of the unlucky ones, their advice to her was the same: she would have to endure whatever came her way because men were… well… men; and marriage was all about patience and fortitude for a woman.

Loveness had barely listened to her aunts give her this not-so-sanguine advice because she was too busy admiring her immaculately white organza and chiffon wedding dress with the faux pearls along the high collar and imagining what a perfect couple she and Spokes would make as they stood at the altar.

It was true that she, like all the married women in the world who had come before her, had not been able to send a rat ahead of her; but if she had, it would have brought back only the best tidings. From the moment that she married Spokes Moloi, Loveness was convinced that she was the happiest and luckiest of women. She had waited for something, and it had arrived.

Spokes was one of those extremely rare men of whom you get the measure as soon as you meet him, and she had known as he stood looking lost in the twilight that day he had followed her from the City of Kings that she would never have to worry about another woman or a raised hand or an inability to provide.

Even when the children she had so desperately wanted when she saw him interacting with Dikeledi did not come—the children she had bought the five-piece Formica kitchen table for, the children that she and Spokes had dreamed of the eight-roomed house by the river in Krum's Place for, the children who would ensure that Spokes and Loveness Moloi carried on in many ways long after they were gone—Loveness knew herself to be the happiest and luckiest of women.

The non-arrival of these long-awaited children could have been the issue that turned into a predicament that left a sour taste in the mouth—but it was not. Even after Spokes' mother started sending young women to help Loveness take care of her five-roomed home in Mpopoma Township, Loveness knew herself to be the happiest and luckiest of women because Spokes always patiently sent the young women back to his mother, and made Loveness' life feel full enough and complete as it was.

Her husband, exceptional man that he was, deserved only the best life, and she had promised to give him that on the day she married him in 1953. But now here was Daisy making him not see things clearly. Loveness reached for her writing pad, and began a letter. It was time Spokes remembered that Daisy was more than a brutally murdered body that had been hacked to pieces and stuffed into a burlap sack. It was time he remembered that Daisy had given them the most perfect gift.

DIKELEDI

———◆———

The two letters arrived at the time that all letters arrived in the small village nestled in one of the many almost-forgotten corners of the world—early in the morning, having been delivered with the fresh bread from Downing's Bakery, in the same truck that had journeyed all the way from the City of Kings. Of all the things that Dikeledi, the postman, loved about her job—and there were many—what she loved best was the warm, oven-baked smell of the envelopes and packages that she delivered. She felt, in this way, that with each letter or present, she delivered the promise of the city. Dikeledi was not a romantic or poetic sort—far from it—but when it came to the post and its many possibilities, she allowed herself to acknowledge that some things in life could be perfect.

Only a handful of the letters that Dikeledi had delivered over the years had been addressed to the postman herself, and never in all her years as postman had she ever received two letters on the same day: so these letters heralded something new. The first letter, like all the other letters that had been addressed to Dikeledi Moyana, had been sent by the magnificent Molois—Spokes and Loveness. The second letter had not. Although she had never received a letter from this particular letter writer before, Dikeledi recognized the handwriting immediately. It belonged to her husband—the man who had abandoned her fourteen years earlier. She knew that whatever news the letter carried, it would not bode well for her; it would tip the scales of her life toward imbalance. And so she looked at her name above the address for a long time, trying to decide whether or not to open it, or let it become one of those unfortunate letters that gets lost in the mail.

In the end, she decided that since she had always been un-afraid, there was no reason to be otherwise now, and ripped open the white envelope with awfully little care, tearing the sealed seam in several places—not because she was anxious about what news her husband had sent, but because she was angry that he had sent any news at all. She removed the letter, which, she was happy to note, contained the entirety of what it wanted to say on a single sheet of paper. The letter was writ-ten on the lined paper of a school exercise-book. Knowing him, he had had children with the woman he had married in Johannesburg. The paper was folded into two equal parts, and the single fold told Dikeledi that her husband took what he had written as news that could be shared with all and sun-dry. Many folds would have meant that a secret was passing between them, and she was happy to see that he was not as-suming any such familiarity and intimacy. The letter was writ-ten with a deliberate hand that took itself so seriously that it rounded and separated each individual letter. The combined letters made for few words and an appallingly short letter, which read:

Dear Dikeledi,

I am coming home. Prepare for my return.

Your Husband,

Immanuel.

Out of seemingly nowhere, the smooth running of her life had decided to take an unfortunate turn and she would have to do much to steer it back on course again. Dikeledi was grateful for one thing, though: that he had not signed the letter "Your loving husband." At least she could still be sure she had chosen him well.

As a child, Dikeledi had known three things for certain: she did not want to be like her mother; she did not want a husband or children; she did not live in a community that would allow her to be unmarried and childless. Dikeledi had always been a very perceptive and intelligent child, but knowing these three things had made her an exceedingly shrewd child indeed, because she had had to imagine and think of ways to be free in the future.

When other girls had spent their playing hours dreaming up families and imagining future husbands, Dikeledi had prepared for her freedom. When she cooked in make-believe pots, she always cooked for one. When the boys of her youth would make clay cattle and offer them to her as a pretend bride price so that she would start playing house with them, she would take the cattle and continue cooking for one.

Dikeledi had inherited her mother's beauty, and it was because of this taken-for-granted beauty that she experienced a freedom the other girls in the village did not know they could even dream of. When she herded cattle with the boys and fought with them or scratched her knees and elbows climbing up trees or sliding down smooth hills, the boys did not mind because they could convince themselves that this was what the clay cattle had really been in exchange for—time with Dikeledi in the bush. The girls did not mind Dikeledi's time in the bush because they knew (it had been repeated often enough in their presence) that she was the prettiest girl in the village, and they were therefore happy to spend hours not being silently or verbally compared to her. The adults did not mind that Dikeledi preferred boyish pursuits because they were sure that she would, one day, as all children eventually did, leave all childhood things behind, and embrace the softness and gentleness that came with womanhood.

None of them could have known that what terrified

Dikeledi more than anything in the world was the softness and gentleness of womanhood: the softness and gentleness that reminded her so much of her mother, Daisy, who had *leaned* her softness and gentleness toward men so readily and so casually until one day she *leaned* toward a man who, in exchange, had killed her. Brutally.

Since Dikeledi was a precocious child, she knew, almost from the first, what was expected of her beauty. It helped elucidate things, of course, that the village women often would say to her, "That pretty face of yours will be sure to bring you a good husband," and some village men would reach out and try to touch her unformed breasts; and disguising the unsavoriness of their actions with laughter and a jocular tone, they would say to her, "Some very lucky man is going to be made very happy by you someday soon." Dikeledi swatted such hands away, and had, on more than one occasion, bitten a finger that had proved to be a little too determined. The owners of the hands and fingers had laughed away her rejection, appreciating the wildness in the child, and envying the man who would tame the woman that she would become.

Dikeledi had understood clearly, as clearly as she understood the pristineness of the color white, that what those men had been reaching for were the soft places of her body, and that it was her duty to herself, even as she loathed the softness and gentleness of womanhood, to safeguard those soft places against the wanton touches of men who really should have known and done better.

She realized that it was the custom for men to reach out and touch the unmarried bodies of girls and young women. Every day she witnessed a hand brushing a chest, pinching a bottom and sometimes even raising a skirt, and every day she witnessed the shy giggle that responded to the touch. She had never found a shy giggle within herself with which to respond to unwanted touch. She knew that were it not for her taken-for-granted pretty face, every swat of a man's hand would have been responded to with some denigration of her looks –the best weapon the men in the village had for putting women in their place.

But Dikeledi had known that her mother's beauty could only protect her for so long, and as soon as she could demand it, she had taken to dressing in boys' school uniforms and making sure that all those soft places that dresses, blouses and skirts made accessible to prying hands were well covered and truly protected by sensible trousers, shorts and shirts with formidable pockets over her flat chest. The only time she wore a dress was when she put on her school uniform to go to the nearby government school, which strictly forbade her from wearing the boys' uniform to school.

Dikeledi absolutely adored boys' and mens' uniforms, and had done so ever since she had seen Constable Spokes Moloi in his crisp and starched BSAP uniform with the shiny brass buttons step out of the Idlazonke General Goods and Bottle Store, to deliver the news that her mother was dead. Whatever she was going to do with her life as an adult, Dikeledi knew that it would involve wearing a uniform—a man's uniform.

For the longest time, Dikeledi's mind and body were in perfect harmony. During puberty, her body refused to blossom into soft curves of voluptuousness—her chest stayed flat and her hips narrow. Dikeledi had been happy with this turn of events; the village less so. Because of her beauty, the entire village had anticipated an easy marriage for her, and had thus relaxed. But now it began to perceive that there might be a problem where Dikeledi was concerned. There was a whisper that began to be heard throughout the village: "She may have her mother's face, but she has her father's body and ways."

When Dikeledi's body did not develop the expected soft

places, girls, long jealous of her beauty and happy to finally have something to fault in her, made fun of Dikeledi's manliness, and were surprised and then wounded when she did not respond with the shame and hurt that they expected. Boys, long intimidated by her beauty and her ability to beat them in the classroom and on the grazing fields, and happy to finally have something in their power with which to bruise her too-healthy self-esteem, made fun of Dikeledi's flatness and straightness (they would never dare to call it manliness), and were surprised and then wounded when she did not respond with the shame and hurt that they expected.

Women, now afraid that Dikeledi's alternative lifestyle would prove attractive to their own daughters and thus upset the order of things, chastised her for dressing and behaving in a most unwomanly fashion, and were surprised and then wounded when she did not respond with the shame and hurt that they expected. Men, long tired of Dikeledi's determined rejection of their advances and increasingly confused by their continued desire of her unfeminine body, decided to put an end to her waywardness, and demanded that she start behaving properly (by which they meant like a girl), and were surprised and then wounded when she did not respond with the shame and the hurt that they expected.

Dikeledi was definitely outnumbered, but she was not without resources. She wrote a letter to the two people in the world that she truly admired—the magnificent Molois—and told them of her plight. Before the village knew what had befallen it, the Molois descended upon it and proclaimed, in no uncertain terms, that Dikeledi was perfect as she was, and that she was to be left alone. To cement what they had said, the Molois gifted Dikeledi with boys' uniforms from various schools in the City of Kings. The village cowered under the collective wisdom and fury of the Molois, and it was only after they had left—weeks after, just to be completely sure—that a whisper began that as the Molois had no children of their own, they, although wise about most else, were not particularly wise about Dikeledi. They were spoiling her and unwittingly destroying whatever future happiness she might have. However, the whisper had no choice but to watch Dikeledi as she went on her merry way wearing shirts, trousers with suspenders, veldskoene and seersucker Ivy caps, her hands in her pockets as she whistled a tune merry enough for her way.

The magnificent Molois had saved Dikeledi, and she was grateful; in fact, she was more than grateful, she was happy: until her body betrayed her during her seventeenth year, when her hips flared and her chest grew two rather determined mounds. The softness that she had run away from all her life was upon her without any warning.

The village sighed a sigh of relief because at last Dikeledi would have no other choice but to be and act like a woman.

For her part, Dikeledi took to standing naked in front of the tarnished mirror in her grandmother's hut, and in the paltry light provided by a wax candle, she tried to bring herself to hate her soft places—her breasts, her belly, her thighs, her behind—but found she could not. They were a part of her and she could not hate herself, no matter how hard she tried.

She remembered how her mother Daisy had *leaned* her softness across a counter and used it to bargain for something that she wanted in exchange. She remembered the hands— black, brown, white—that had touched Daisy's soft places, and the shy giggle that they had received in return for their endeavors. She remembered how the shy giggle allowed Daisy to walk away with a packet of toffees, a few yards of fabric, an exercise book. Dikeledi remembered the rich buttery taste of those toffees, the feel of the blue-and-white dress that had been made from the fabric, the stick figures she had drawn *ad nauseam* in the exercise book, and the shaky handwriting that had written her name for the first time, the D looking like an A.

Dikeledi looked at her soft places and decided that she would never use them as her mother had used hers—to curry the favor of men. She, Dikeledi, would never *lean*. She had always been clever about her body, and she would continue being so.

When, at eighteen, Dikeledi finished her schooling, she knew that only a few options were open to her. She could leave the village and make her way to a teachers' or nurses' training institution. She could stay in the village and take some home-craft classes. After doing one of these three things, she could go to the City of Kings and make a living. She knew that whichever option she chose did not really matter because at some point in all of this, she would have to find herself a husband, have his children, and become a wife and mother. It would only be after she had had the husband and children that she would be deemed a successful woman.

Dikeledi did not want to be a teacher. She did not want to be a nurse. She did not want to be a homemaker. She did not want to bring just knowledge, wellbeing or joy to others. She wanted to bring the thing that could contain *all* these things and more—she wanted to bring the post. Dikeledi's ambition was to be a postman. She loved the idea of delivering the world to her small village nestled in one of the many almost-forgotten corners of the world.

Dikeledi had been fascinated by the post from a young age. Sometime after her mother had been killed and her distraught and heartbroken father, S'jumba, had left the country to try and start his life anew in South Africa, a letter had arrived all the way from Johannesburg. The letter had been addressed to her illiterate grandfather, who had had to walk the many miles to the school where it had been delivered, to collect it. Her wary and weary grandfather had given the letter to Dikeledi, trusting and believing that the three years of education she had under her belt would be more than sufficient to enable her to read and understand the letter. Her grandmother proudly called other members of the homestead and other villagers to hear her granddaughter read the letter. Dikeledi, who was still struggling with literacy herself, read the letter haltingly but assuredly, confidently mispronouncing most of the English words, which had not always been spelled correctly. The nine-year-old Dikeledi read to an appreciative audience that was for the most part none the wiser.

The letter said that the father-son had settled in Johannesburg (a city brighter than anything they could ever imagine), had found a job at a gold mine, and was doing relatively well. Enclosed in the envelope, along with the letter, was a money order whose amount proved how well settled the father-son was in his new land. The letter, which could have carried with it sad news, brought joy. Her grandmother ululated and her grandfather danced a jig as he balanced on his walking-stick-cum-knobkerrie. They said that their troubles—troubles that Dikeledi had not known about—were over, and that happy days were here again.

As Dikeledi held the letter in her hands, she understood its power, and decided there and then that she wanted to be a postman. Even when, during her sixteenth year, a letter, not written in the handwriting of the father-son, was received from Johannesburg and contained within it news of his death, not in a mining accident as his mother had always feared, but from a corruption that had surreptitiously entered his lungs when he had worked in a factory that made asbestos roofing shingles in the City of Kings, Dikeledi did not give up her desire to become a postman.

At eighteen, she had known that there was only one way

she could realize her dream to be a postman—she would have to marry, and marry very wisely. She would have to choose a man who would give her her freedom without his knowing that that was what he was doing. In Immanuel Moyana, she found the perfect man for her purposes. He had a roving eye, a weak resolve, and a highly suggestible mind. He loved what he saw when he looked in the mirror and believed that others would be as enamored of him as he was of himself; and so when Dikeledi, the most beautiful girl in the village, smiled at him, he was not surprised, and believed that he had been half-expecting it all along.

Even before Dikeledi hinted to Immanuel that they should get married, she had cannily put it in his head that he should go and find his fortune in the mines of Johannesburg or Kimberley. She spoke, with genuine admiration, of the many things her father had managed to achieve from such a great distance—school fees for his daughter, eye surgery for his father, a donkey-drawn Scotch-cart for the fields, a brick house, a communal well. Immanuel saw himself building a brick house that would be the envy of the entire village. He saw himself living in that house with Dikeledi and their beautiful children, and he could not wait to leave the village. His wedding night was a near-disaster because of his excitement at being both in the room with Dikeledi and on his way to South Africa. It did not help matters, of course, that Dikeledi was very reluctant to let him touch her soft places.

Soon enough, Immanuel was gone and Dikeledi found herself that rarest of things: a married woman who was free to do as she pleased. And Dikeledi definitely did as she pleased. For two years, she went through the motions of preparing a home for herself and her husband, all the while knowing full well that Immanuel would never return from the bright lights of Johannesburg, which was where he had chosen to settle. As

Dikeledi cooked for one and ate alone and contentedly in her hut, the villagers, waiting in vain for a letter and a money order, began to whisper. They had always known that Immanuel was no good, and now here he was proving it by neglecting their very own jewel. They should never have sanctioned such an obviously ill-fated union—and they would not have, but she had been so very determined, hadn't she?

Dikeledi listened to the whispers and smiled to herself in the dark recesses of her hut. She let the matter move through the village like an errant whirlwind that picked up both wanted and forgotten things. In the third year of what was now spoken of as her abandonment, Dikeledi made a plaintive plea to her community. As they could see, her husband had never, not even once, provided for her, and she had had to live on their charity and good will for the embarrassingly long time during which she had waited for Immanuel to do his duty by her. But he had not. And now she was left with no other choice but to look for work herself. She did not want to leave the village and go to the City of Kings. She had made a comfortable and lovely home for herself and her husband, and she did not want to leave it.

As everyone remembered, she had received a good education, and it would make sense for her to go for teachers' or nurses' training, but she feared too much time had passed and she would need to relearn so many things that she had already forgotten. Would it not be better, did they not all think so, if she found a job right here in the village? Perhaps... and this was just occurring to her, so they should please excuse its unformedness as a thought... but perhaps she could collect the post that was delivered to the school and bring it to the residents of the village. It was some distance to and from the school, and often the journey to collect the letters had to be done by the very old or the very young because everyone else was busy, either in the fields tilling sustenance out of the land, or in the city eking a living out of the factories. Would it not be a wonderful thing if the village had its own postman who delivered letters to each homestead?

There were murmurs of approval from the villagers before Chief Cele Mkhize said, "But the very word itself is prohibitive. Post*man*. You cannot do a man's job." There were immediate murmurs supporting the headman's sagacity. "However, it is a brilliant idea and I am surprised I never thought of it," Chief Cele Mkhize continued. "I will speak to both the postmaster and the schoolmaster and see if such a post can be created forthwith—for a man." The chief was not a man without understanding, and so he added, "All the other things you say are true, we have all seen them. To rectify your problem, I will write to Immanuel and demand that he do right by you."

The murmurs of approval after Chief Cele Mkhize's proclamation were loud, and Dikeledi knew better than to challenge him directly. So, as the headman worked to create the paid position of postman, Dikeledi wrote a letter to the magnificent Molois and told them of her situation. Before the village knew what had befallen it, the Molois descended upon it and proclaimed, in no uncertain terms, that Dikeledi was the perfect candidate for the postman job. To cement what they had said, the Molois visited the schoolmaster and gave Dikeledi a glowing reference. The village cowered under the collective wisdom and fury of the Molois, and it was only after they had left, weeks after, when, just to be completely sure, Dikeledi was already donning the uniform of a postman and delivering the post by bicycle, that a whisper began that Chief Cele Mkhize had been wrong to have someone else prosper from an idea that had been Dikeledi's brainchild.

It had taken some doing, but Dikeledi had finally realized

her dream, and become that even rarer thing, a woman who gets exactly what she wants in life. Dikeledi lived her life exactly how she wanted, and did with it exactly what she wanted. Here, in this village, in one of the many almost-forgotten corners of the world, she had managed to carve for herself an element of freedom.

With her first pay check, she bought a full-length mirror and placed it in her hut. There was nothing that delighted her more than standing naked in the temperamental light of a paraffin lamp and watching as her postman's uniform gradually covered all her soft places... places *she* would never *lean*.

And so it had been for almost twelve years, but now here was this letter addressed to her and signed, "Your Husband, Immanuel." At a rare loss as to what to do, Dikeledi carefully opened the other envelope, the one from the magnificent Molois, and was happy to find that, as always, they had a ready solution to her problem. The letter, written in Loveness' graceful hand on yellow and pink writing paper, was neatly folded into four equal squares and contained a secret about a man named Livingstone Stanley Tikiti. The letter suggested that Dikeledi come to Mpopoma because Loveness and Spokes needed her to maintain the secret.

———•———

A change had come over her, and Dikeledi deeply suspected that her metamorphosis had something to do with the magnificent Molois and the firm belief that they both had in this thing called love. They found love in each other, and in the books they read, and they seemed eager to let it beam onto the few people they allowed into their sphere. Dikeledi, who had never sought love, and, therefore, had never found it, was one such person for the Molois. They loved her with the love that they would have given the children they had always longed for, but never had. They loved her in a way that made

Dikeledi question the workings of a god who would make the Molois, who were so very deserving of a child's love and happiness, childless. Now that Dikeledi was beginning to understand the workings of love, she realized that the magnificent Molois had always found many ways to love her. At present, they were loving her by allowing her into their intimate reading circle, in which they were currently reading Zora Neale Hurston's *Their Eyes Were Watching God*.

Try though she might, Dikeledi could not help but be wary of the make-believe love that the pretend people in books felt.

"She shoots him because she loves him," Loveness said, as they both used silver cookie cutters to cut mounds of soft, cottony dough into perfectly round scones.

"No. She shoots him because he has rabies," Dikeledi said, sensibly.

Loveness laughed indulgently before saying, "And if that is not an act of love, then what is?"

Dikeledi frowned at this reasoning before asking: "What else can you do with a rabid person, besides kill him?"

"You can leave him to die a painful death... leave him to suffer through something that he cannot even comprehend," Loveness said. "The entire book is a call to love: love of oneself, love of another." Loveness stole a glance at Dikeledi before she continued, "It shows that you need to love yourself enough to wait for the right person to come along."

As Dikeledi watched Loveness contentedly grease four baking trays, she realized that it was easy for Loveness and Spokes to believe in love because they had found it in each other; but not everyone was so fortunate. While she was aware that Spokes and Loveness had waited for each other to come along, she was mistrustful of the logic of making this a universal expectation and decree; but even with all her suspicions and misgivings about love, Dikeledi had to admit that she was beginning to see something that could only be called love at play in her life.

For instance, she was certain that had she not been living with the magnificent Molois, she would not have bought the girl's uniform—the uniform, with its alternating teal, azure and white vertical stripes and a silver zipper that ran down its front, the uniform that the cashier informed her, before she paid for it, was the uniform for Eveline High School, and therefore not a proper dress at all. The cashier had told her this so as to prevent the embarrassment that would surely be visited upon Dikeledi were she, a woman of thirty-two, to be seen walking around the city in a girl's uniform.

But something about the colors, the texture, the feel, the smell of the fabric reminded Dikeledi of her mother, Daisy. It was the sort of thing she would have chosen to make a dress for her daughter. Dikeledi touched the fabric and almost wept. She found it difficult to return the uniform to the clothes' rack, and the ignominy of not having been purchased, the mortification of almost having been bought. And so she purchased it and went even one better; she looked forward to the day that she would wear it.

It just so happened that Dikeledi chose to wear the uniform on an ordinary and rather mundane Friday afternoon, which, coincidentally, was the very Friday afternoon that had long been fated to be the one that changed her life.

There was a knock on the door, and even though Dikeledi's thoughts had, only minutes before, been extremely cautious and suspicious about love, she felt absolutely no apprehension when she went to open the door because she did not know that standing on the other side of it was the man toward whom she would someday very soon find herself *leaning*.

LUKHA

———•———

In the beginning, none of her made sense. He was sure she was a woman, she certainly looked like a woman in her thirties, and yet she was wearing a school uniform. And where had she come from? She had not been here when he had come before; why was she here now? Why was she suddenly before him, seemingly so immovable with her arms crossed at the waist? Lukha decided there and then that she was an inconvenience, something standing between him and his desire to talk to Chief Inspector Spokes Moloi.

"You are wearing a school girl's uniform," Lukha said because that was the only thing he could think to say.

"And you are wearing a faded T-shirt that says, 'Build a better tomorrow,'" she said without missing a beat. He got the impression that she could have said so much more, and had had to hold back.

Lukha looked down at the wrinkled yellow T-shirt that he was wearing. It had a bright rainbow printed on it and the words 'Build a better tomorrow' written in a 1970s psychedelic font that followed the arc of the rainbow. When was the last time he had paid any attention to what he wore? He didn't even remember receiving the T-shirt in one of those bales of donated clothing that came from Scandinavian countries via the Lutheran World Federation and were distributed in the camps. When he looked up, she was looking at his hair, which is what made him dig his fingers through mountains of hair that had not welcomed a comb in many months, and scratch his scalp.

"I'm here to see Chief Inspector Spokes Moloi," he said.

She looked at him for so long a moment that he began to fear that perhaps the Chief Inspector and his wife, Mrs. Loveness Moloi, had moved away. He really needed to talk to the Chief Inspector. But what if he couldn't? Lukha was on the verge of panic when she said, "He is not here." Before he could respond to this news in any way, she asked, "What do you want with him?"

"I need to talk to him," Lukha said, his fingers still raking his hair.

She was about to respond in a way that Lukha would not have liked when another voice came from within the house.

"Who is at the door, Dikeledi?" it asked.

"A stranger," Dikeledi replied.

Dikeledi would probably have left it at that, but luckily the door was opened wider and Mrs. Loveness Moloi and a warm vanilla scent greeted him.

"Oh, it is you, Lukha," she said with a smile. "It so good to see you again. Please do come in." Her invitation and the hand she placed on his arm were even warmer than the scent of vanilla. It was all too much for Lukha.

"I'm here to report a murder," he said, refusing to be let into the house.

"A murder?" Mrs. Loveness Moloi said, her warmth neither dissipating nor diminishing.

"A murder I committed," he said.

Dikeledi sharply sucked in her breath and gave him an "I knew it" glare, but Mrs. Loveness Moloi simply said, as she guided him into the house, "The Chief Inspector will be here soon, and you can tell him all about it."

Lukha had no choice but to follow her into the inviting home.

The Chief Inspector arrived less than an hour later, and in that short time, Mrs. Loveness Moloi had fed a reluctant but ultimately grateful Lukha a bowl of oxtail stew with rice, and then offered him two warm scones slathered with butter and homemade strawberry jam and a mug of piping-hot condensed-milk tea. He had enjoyed the food even though he had had to eat with an audience—Dikeledi. She sat across from him at the five-piece Formica table with her hands bunched into fists and placed under her chin, silently daring him to make the slightest move that she did not like.

"My wife tells me that you are here to report a murder," the Chief Inspector said, sitting himself down at the table at which Lukha and Dikeledi sat.

Lukha expected Dikeledi to excuse herself from the table, but she did not, and the only thing that made her presence slightly more bearable was the fact that Mrs. Loveness Moloi joined them at the table as well, taking the last chair. He watched as she offered her hand to her husband, and he watched as the Chief Inspector took her hand in his. Lukha had never seen this before—a man and his wife holding hands at the kitchen table—and began to feel that he was on the verge of making some kind of discovery... a discovery about the importance of the simple things in life.

"So, you murdered someone?" Dikeledi said, rudely interrupting his thoughts. Why was she here? Who was she? Why did she seem to think that she mattered?

"Murdered... yes," Lukha said. "But not someone... quite a lot of people. They say that all is forgiven, they call me a hero. But all cannot be forgiven, can it? They say I fought for their freedom, but I did no such thing. I fought, not for them, but for something else entirely."

"Eh! You say quite a lot of people—how many is quite a lot

of people?" Dikeledi asked.

"I killed six people and permanently maimed two."

"During the war?"

"Yes, during the war—but before I joined the war."

"Dikeledi, let the man find his story," the Chief Inspector said. "Lukha why don't you tell me what happened? From the very beginning."

---•---

His mother had wanted a girl, but knew he was a boy because during her pregnancy she found that she really enjoyed sucking on the crusty soil that formed the outer layer of an anthill, was nauseated by the smell of fish, and was quick to lose her temper. When her labor pains began on a Sunday afternoon, she was grateful to him for being so considerate as to come on the day of rest. She called for her mother-in-law who, suspecting why she was being called, brought her sister along as well. Both women walked as fast as their age would allow them, and along the way gave instructions to the children playing tsoro at the edge of the homestead to bring boiled water and their packets of medicinal herbs from the kitchen, and to be quick about it. In the hands of the two women who had delivered most of the children in the village, he came safely into this world with both his hands resting, open-palmed, on his stomach, which was a sign that he carried within him an important task—a task given him by the other world.

His father, hoping that his third son would be a great hunter like his great-grandfather, who had been such a renowned hunter that apparently there was still a legend of him in Swaziland, made him his namesake, and to stress the point, gave him 'hunter' as his middle name so that his full name was Lukhayezi Mzingeli Hlotshwayo.

For the early part of his life, Lukha lived up to the expectation of his name with great ease. His slingshots and traps saw him bring home all manner of things he was proud of having killed: locusts, birds, rabbits. When he was not hunting, Lukha went through life herding cattle, practicing ukujaqa with other herdboys, swimming naked in rivers, climbing mopane, marula, mqokolo and mulberry trees, and eating their sun-kissed fruits while perched on tree branches. Lukha would only know that the exquisite feeling he felt during this time of his life was called happiness later in life, when there was no happiness to be found around him.

His troubles began when he was ten years old and the Native Commissioner of the district visited the village and announced that all children over seven years old, especially the boys, would have to attend a nearby school that the government had built for native education. Lukha attended the school, but when he tried to read, the letters that seemed to stay put for everyone else would not do so for him. For him, the letters moved around and jumbled up the words, thus turning them into little puzzles that he could never quite crack. He toiled at this labor unsuccessfully for two years before his parents decided to defy the government's edict, and encouraged him to stay home and do the things he loved to do—hunt wild animals and herd cattle.

It was not altogether lost on Lukha's parents that education tended to take children away from home, and that someone would someday, after they were gone, have to look after the homestead. As his parents had predicted, Lukha's brothers soon left home in triumph using words printed on things called 'certificates' to get jobs: one as a teaboy in the City of Kings, and the other as a messenger boy in a nearby mine.

At this point, Lukha had arrived at the center of things. It was time to reveal the crux of the whole story.

"The land around us was declared a National Park, and

all of a sudden we were not permitted to freely hunt in it. When I was eighteen, perhaps because I was no longer able to hunt, I became restless. For a long time, I could not find a place to put down the restlessness, and then one day I went to the bottle store and found that the shopkeeper had placed a foosball machine outside. Although it was a newly introduced thing, everyone seemed to know how to play the game, and everyone wanted to play it. It was so popular that it even got a nickname, iSlug. Boys and men would gather around the machine to take turns to play it. I looked at the machine, and I was not intimidated by the rows of miniature red and blue, stiff soccer players. It took some waiting, but I eventually tried my hand at it.

"I have never been particularly good at anything the white man has introduced, so imagine my surprise when I found that I was good at this game. I knew exactly when to strike the ball and when to block it. I even found a way to turn the handles with crowd-pleasing flourish. After two or three games, I had learnt enough about the game to be able to play it and not lose. You see, I could somehow see how it all worked... came together... and that allowed me to anticipate my opponents' moves. My brain just understood the movement of things. Much like it does when I am hunting or tracking.

"Soon after I started playing, I realized that people had taken to coming to the store just to watch me play. The shop-keeper realized this too, and started having people place bets on me. I played against many opponents and remained unde-feated. I will admit that it was nice to be watched while doing something I was good at. I liked being the center of attention. I got free beer from the bottle store, I had money in my pockets, and girls started slowing down their pace and giggling when-ever I approached. A man who had more in his life would probably have handled the situation better, but I was still a boy in many ways, and I let it all go straight to my head.

"The only thing I had to do every day was to take care of my father's twenty head of cattle, leave them to graze in some nearby pasture, stop over at the bottle store to play iSlug, and make sure that the cattle were in their kraal before sunset. No… that is not entirely true. The only thing that I had to do every day was to herd my father's twenty head of cattle and make sure they were in their kraal before sunset. After I discovered the game, I stopped herding the cattle and left them grazing in pastures unattended, hoping that they would not stray into other people's farms or become integrated with another herd. I was always diligent about making sure that the cattle were in the kraal before sunset. For a long time, my luck was good. The cattle grazed in their designated pasture and did not stray.

"On 11 November, Armistice Day, 1965, my luck ran out. Festus Malunga challenged me to a game—and man, was he ever good. We played game after game after game after game, and he came very close to beating me. We played for so long that even I wanted him to actually beat me just so that I would know that he could. Before I knew it, the usual crowd had become a throng chanting my name as I beat Festus one hard-won game after another.

"The chants of 'Lukha! Lukha! Lukha!' were deafening, but even so we all heard the screech of tires and the thunder of the rolling car somewhere along the main road that leads to the City of Kings. As soon as I heard the sound, I knew I was responsible for it. The night was pitch black. There were no stars to be seen. Where had the day gone? Where were the stars that night?

"A man does not know that he is a coward until he performs an act of cowardice. I did not know that I was a coward until, instead of going home or to the scene of the accident that evening, as many at the bottle store did, I walked in the opposite direction, until I found my way to Zambia. And once there, I was co-opted by the boys fighting in the bush.

"I was in the bush for nearly fifteen years, hiding more than fighting." Here Lukha stopped and looked at Dikeledi, who was no longer glaring at him. "Livingstone Stanley Tikiti taught me how to still the moving letters," he continued. "Once I could read, he made me a medic, which is what I did for the duration of the war. When the ceasefire was announced, I went to seek out Emil Coetzee so he could punish me… but Emil Coetzee is nowhere to be found."

Lukha noticed that Dikeledi's now unfisted hands were on the Formica table top. Her hands looked unexpectedly and remarkably lady-like—graceful, dainty, and delicate—as though they *needed* to be held.

"Yes… " the Chief Inspector encouraged Lukha to carry on with his story.

It took Lukha some time to find the thread of his story again. "After Livingstone Stanley Tikiti and I came to visit you, I found that I could not hide anymore. I had to go back home. Upon my arrival, I found that my mother, my older brother, and his entire family had just been murdered, and that my oldest brother's second wife was the prime suspect. She didn't do it, I know she didn't do it. Things like these are not the work of man, they are the punishments of the ancestors. My mother, my brother and his entire family are dead because of me, because of what happened in 1965. I tried to explain this to my family, but they only cried and touched my face as though I were a newborn child. They think it is a miracle that I am alive because they had long suspected that I was dead. I told them about my responsibility for the accident, but they would not listen, and told me what the BSAP had reported to them.

"A car carrying six members of a wedding party, bride and

groom included, came careening down the road. Another car was driving along, going the opposite direction, with its headlights bright and undimmed. The driver of the wedding party car was briefly blinded by the light. When his eyes re-accustomed themselves to the road ahead, the car's headlights fell on a dark object in the middle of the road. He brightened his headlights just in time to see that there was a cow in the road. The driver swerved off the road to make sure that he did not hit the cow when his headlights fell on two pedestrians walking on the strip on the side of the tarred main road. He tried to avoid hitting them, but could not, and sent them pirouetting through the dark night, at which point he lost control of the vehicle. The car rolled its way into an embankment and burst into flames, killing all on board.

"They told me that there was no responsibility in the case, as it had been ruled an accident. That was not the worst of it. They called me a hero, told me that I had liberated the country. But I am not a hero. I am a coward who found himself fighting a war *after* I killed six people and maimed another two. I cannot live as a hero the way they expect me to. My sister-in-law is likely to hang because the ancestors righted a sin that I had committed, and there is nothing I can do or say to save her."

There was a long silence that Dikeledi surprisingly did not interrupt. And then the Chief Inspector said, "Do you know who is handling the investigation?"

"Sergeant Dhlamini."

"Dhlamini? I know him. He is a good man, good at his job. I trained him. Let me talk to him and see what can be done."

This was not why Lukha had come here. He had come so that someone would finally hold him accountable for what he had done. Even though he was disappointed that that did not seem to be happening, he found himself saying, "Thank you,

Chief Inspector."

"You can stay with us for as long as you like. I promise we will not expect you to be anything other than what you are," the Chief Inspector said.

SPOKES

———◆———

There were two light-blue manila folders in Spokes' in tray—
one was the thin familiar folder faded with age and dog-eared
from too much handling; and the other was new and thick,
with photographs and case notes. Although he had already
solved the latter case, it was to be the last of his career, and so
he treated it with the sense of ceremony that it deserved. He
read over the case notes, made sure the "i"s were dotted and
the 't's crossed, and that his initials, S.M.M., appeared at the
bottom of each page before looking over the photographs that
were attached to the case file.

It had been a sad case, and the accompanying photographs were deceptively peaceful: an entire family whose
members—father, mother, three children and one grandmother, ranging in age from four to sixty—lay strewn on the ground
of their homestead as though they were fallen angels recently
deposited by the heavens. All the members of the family were
dead, and in their dying moments they had reached out to one
another creating a strange kind of beauty that Spokes found
difficult to reconcile with the heartbreak before him.

The tragedy that took place on the eve of independence
actually had its roots in an earlier tragedy that had taken place
in 1977.

On one of his weekend visits back to the village, Lukha's
oldest brother, then a foreman on the factory floor of the best
shoe factory in the City of Kings, had decided to be a Good
Samaritan and had given a lift to two school-leavers he found

hitchhiking on the outskirts of town. The school-leavers had informed the Good Samaritan that they were trying to make their way to a farm so that they could find work as laborers. The Good Samaritan, who was an avid small-scale subsistence farmer himself, had plenty to say on the subject, and was even kind enough to suggest the names of the most reasonable commercial farmers in his district.

The journey had been rather pleasant, and because he had made this very trip several times before, the Good Samaritan had easy passage through the first two roadblocks, greeting the policemen and soldiers he now knew by name. The problem arose when they arrived at the third roadblock, and found a newly dispatched group of young RF soldiers manning the roadblock who were eager to prove just how thoroughly they had been trained. They stopped every vehicle, inspected the contents of the boot, and interrogated its inhabitants.

It was here, at the third roadblock, that things fell apart. Upon interrogation, the two school-leavers, their knees knocking, broke down and admitted they were making their way to join the guerrillas. All of this was news to the Good Samaritan, but the something-to-prove soldiers manning the roadblock had chosen not to believe in his innocence and had forwarded his name to his employer—who then had had no choice but to overlook his twenty years of loyal service and hard work, fire him, and place his name on the national blacklist register.

Prior to the hitchhiking incident, the Good Samaritan's employment in the best shoe factory in the City of Kings had made him the well-off older brother who had, over the years, managed to secure his place as a member of the petite bourgeoisie. Having started as a teaboy, he had worked his way up until he was a foreman, which had enabled him to build a brick house on his homestead and buy a second-hand jalopy of which he was very proud; and which, coincidentally, was the very car that would prove to be his undoing.

Having pulled himself up by his bootstraps, the Good Samaritan had expected his siblings, whom life had handed the same opportunities as him, to follow his example and do likewise. However, because he was the oldest brother in the family, traditionally, much was expected of him; and, as a result, his modern and rather cavalier attitude toward the up-keep of his siblings was much discussed and frowned upon within family circles. When his siblings struggled, he was expected to sacrifice what little he had to make their lives more comfortable; and when he did not, he was said to be decidedly hard-hearted, which, of course, was not the only way to read the situation.

Unlike the family he had been born into, the family he had created—his two wives and seven children—were happy with him because while he spent his five working days in a township in the City of Kings, he spent his two days of rest with his family in the village. He not only made sure that his immediate family was well provided for; when he was home, he was a very industrious man, helping to cultivate the fields and performing whatever repairs were needed around the homestead. His immediate family loved him, but even they could not use that love to smooth over the rough patch that had come with his being placed on the blacklist.

As the immediate family's situation deteriorated, the Good Samaritan's second wife accused the younger brother—the future victim—of foul play, saying that his jealousy over his brother's success had made him go to inyanga, who had somehow devised the two hitchhikers that had ended her husband's successful career. Animosity between the two families, which were also neighbors, grew, especially after the younger brother—the future victim—who had been a messenger boy at a nearby mine for fifteen years, unexpectedly received a promotion and found himself apprenticing to become a junior clerk.

It was as though the narrative of the family could not contain within it two moderately successful sons, and so the rags of one son were said to have necessitated the riches of the other. The entire village weighed in on the matter, but not with the intention of resolving it.

When another tragedy struck, this time taking the younger brother's entire family, the village elders suspected witchcraft and—as was often the case in a case of witchcraft—they suspected that a woman, one of the wives of the Good Samaritan, was behind it all. Because she had not shed a single tear at the mass funeral, the second wife was an easily-arrived-at chief suspect. She was all but pronounced guilty by a jury of her peers long before an official investigation had been properly conducted, and a magistrate engaged to weigh in on the matter.

Although Spokes did not believe in evil, he did believe in the fallibility of humans; and so when Dhlamini handed him the case with its presumed-guilty prime suspect, he knew that, beyond simply proving innocence, he would also have to prove that witchcraft did not play a part in this tragedy—and that that would be the most difficult part of the case.

In his experience, all crimes had their roots in the universal deadly sins: lust, gluttony, greed, pride, envy, sloth and wrath. When Spokes first heard of this tragedy from Lukha, he had believed that greed or envy would be at the bottom of the matter, as this was usually the case with family, especially siblings. However, Spokes soon realized that there was something different about this case. Envy would have perhaps killed the brother. Greed would have perhaps killed the brother and his wife. But to kill *all* the members of a family, including the mother that you shared—that did not fit the profile of any of the deadly sins.

The burgeoning feud between the two brothers could not account for the decimation of an entire family. As Spokes looked at the photos of the family reaching for one another, and at the girl's small and soft hand held firmly and reassuringly in her mother's larger and calloused hand, what he saw before him was a family which was close even in death. Spokes was certain that in that closeness, one of them was communicating more than love. He followed the mother's other hand, which lay with all fingers pointing toward the kitchen—and found another entry point that opened up the case.

At the epicenter of the case was an unmarked brown bottle, which Spokes had found in the kitchen. His investigation revealed that the brown bottle had had affixed to it a label with the word 'arsenic' written in a deceptively pretty and curlicued cursive when Mrs. Bramley, wife of the mine manager, had thrown it out. The brown bottle, with its label written in the kind of handwriting that would be attractive to a nine-year-old child—a child who had only attended a few weeks of school before the war put an end to her education in 1977, a child who (at the moment her education was curtailed) had just started learning how to write, and had aspired to such a handwriting herself—was picked up by said child while she was out rummaging with other children on rubbish collection day. She had taken it back to her homestead, where she had peeled off the pretty-looking label and left the brown bottle unmarked.

The child had loved pretty and perfect things, and because the brown bottle had never been what she wanted, she, feeling generous, had taken it to the hut that was her mother's kitchen because her mother was always looking for things to put other things in. That done, she had put the pretty-looking label among her collection of pretty and perfect things—a marbled stone, a colorful butterfly wing, a piece of pink ribbon, a sea shell with the sound of the ocean contained within it—which she kept hidden and secret and for her eyes only under her bedding in the hut that she shared with her two siblings. It was in this almost-perfect hiding place that Spokes found the label and deduced its journey there.

The girl's mother, upon finding the empty brown bottle among her kitchen things, could not believe her luck, and immediately put it to use as a handy conveyance for cooking oil—the convenient brown bottle would prove so much better than lugging a gallon-sized can of Olivine oil to and from the fire. Because the bottle had looked clean, she had not bothered to wash it. Because the light in the hut was poor, she had not seen the remnants of the liquid at the bottom of the bottle before she carefully poured in the Olivine oil, determined not to waste a drop. As she had cooked the supper, she had sung to her children and shared in their laughter, and none of them sitting around the fire, happy together, had known that they would not live to see the morning sun.

It had not been an easy case to solve, but Spokes had done it; and as he had explained to the magistrate what had happened, the villagers, who were in attendance, had sat there, mouths agape with awe, too shocked and saddened to cry. The only one of the villagers to have made a sound had been the second wife of the Good Samaritan—the very woman everyone had readily labeled a witch. She had wailed in a keening voice and carried her arms on her head as she repeated the name of the little girl who had loved pretty and perfect things—Khethiwe! Khethiwe! Khethiwe! Khethiwe—the chosen one.

Spokes shook his head at the pathos of the whole affair before he selected one of the rubber stamps on his desk, pressed it onto the inkpad, and stamped the words 'Case Closed' across the light-blue folder thick with photographs and case notes, and then placed it in his out tray.

That left the thin, light-blue manila folder faded with age and dog-eared from too much handling. After a long, long time, Spokes slowly and carefully lifted it out of his in tray and gently placed it in his out tray.

SITSHENGISIWE

———— ✦ ————

On what was to be the last day of her life, Sitshengisiwe Dlodlo woke up with a knowing deep in her bones that she was just about to fulfill her life's purpose. She set off for work in her usual blue-purple oversized overalls, but somewhere along the way she saw the headlines announcing the dates for the upcoming elections—the elections that would usher in majority rule—and she decided that it was as good a day as any to start her new life. She returned home and put on her best dress—a gorgeous georgette dress that she had saved for and bought at Sales House herself. The air was filled with independence, and so she went to the National Breweries to tender her resignation. For her, there would be no more checking the quality of beer bottles as they passed through the assembly line; and, if she could help it, her husband Philemon would not be the Rutherford's garden boy for much longer.

As she waited at a bus stop on Mafeking Road, she was filled with so much anticipation of a brighter future that she removed from her handbag the magic marker that she used to tally the number of defective bottles, and wrote on the wall of the bus-stop shelter: "And now these three remain: faith, hope and love. But the great is love."

In writing this quotation on the wall, Sitshengisiwe did three things: the first and most obvious being that she made a mistake and misquoted the verse of scripture, because she could see the bus coming from up the road and had written the quotation in haste; the second being that she had defaced public property and had thus broken the law; the third—definitely the most important and also the least apparent—being that she, unlike many women in her position, had written something that would long outlive her, and that would be read by and inspire many people in the years to come.

Sitshengisiwe, having written the quotation and thus left her mark, had then boarded the bus, paid the conductor, and received her small white printed square ticket from the driver before sitting on the first two-seater at the front. For the duration of the short distance to Founders High School, which was her destination, she valiantly warded off the rather determined advances of the conductor, who chose to ignore the ring on her finger, even though she kept turning it around and around and around until it had no choice but to regain some of the sparkle it had lost a long time ago.

Sitshengisiwe knew that the conductor was only having his fun, but she also knew she was not something to be toyed and trifled with. She sat there with her back straight, her eyes looking out of the window, her lips unsmiling and pressed together, the ring all the while going around and around and around on her finger. She may have fallen far from grace, but she was still the proud daughter of Cosmos Nyathi, one of the country's richest black men, the owner of the MacKenzie group of businesses. She was also a deacon—the only female one—at the Baptist Church that she attended.

When Sitshengisiwe alighted from the bus as soon as it had reached Founder's High School, she made her way to the headmaster's office, stopping several times to ask for directions. Once there, she enrolled herself and Philemon in the adult literacy classes that her new next-door neighbor, Mrs. Bodecia Mthimkhulu, had told her about. The application and enrollment process did not take long because Sitshengisiwe had had something of an education. She was in and out of

Founder's High School in less than twenty minutes, and so the bus that came to pick her up and take her to town was the very bus that had brought her there.

After receiving her ticket, she ignored the conductor and went to sit at the long bench-seat at the back of the bus. There was a discarded copy of *The Chronicle* on the bench, and Sitshengisiwe opened it and looked for Saskia Hargrave's "Where's Emil Coetzee?" article. According to this latest report, Emil Coetzee had been cryogenically frozen by the Secret Intelligence Unit and would be unfrozen in fifty years so that he could become Prime Minister when majority rule failed. *White people never ceased to amaze,* Sitshengisiwe thought as she folded the page with the "Where's Emil Coetzee" article and put it in her handbag. Philemon worked for a man high up in the SIU, and Sitshengisiwe knew better than to put such craziness past them.

She was relieved to see that the conductor had found a more receptive audience for his advances in a group of female factory workers from Dunlop, who, exhausted from their shift, were happy to shrug off the conductor's overtures as nonsense and laugh the hardships of the day away.

Sitshengisiwe was thus left to indulge her thoughts in peace. Her thoughts inevitably went to the New Year's Day party that the Mthimkhulus—Bodecia and her husband, Silas —had thrown, and invited the entire street to attend. The food and beer had been abundant (which had made Philemon very happy), but what had caught Sitshengisiwe's eye was the way the house was furnished and decorated. There was an obvious quality embedded in the things that the Mthimkhulu's owned—in the feel of the velveteen sofas and their crocheted doily covers, in the almost weightless fragility of their drinking glasses, in the shine and shimmer of their silver, in the crinkle of the handmade Christmas decorations that hung from the ceiling—and this quality of things reminded Sitshengisiwe of her childhood and made her miss it and want it back. She wanted back the comfort and abundance of her life in one of her father's many houses as the last and therefore favorite of his thirteen children.

Perhaps it was the fact that Silas Mthimkhulu had made his wealth the same way that her father had—by owning stores that sold goods to Africans who lived in the villages and townships—or, perhaps, it was the fact that Bodecia, with her georgette navy-blue dress, Berkshire-stockinged legs, sturdy Mary-Janes with golden buckles, hot-comb-ironed straight hair, and healthy, glowing skin that looked like it was advertising something—Ambi, perhaps—reminded Sitshengisiwe of the woman she had always thought, as a child, that she would become. Whatever the reason, the result was that at the end of only a few hours in the Mthimkhulu's house, Sitshengisiwe had felt that after twenty years of marriage to Philemon, their luck, which had hitherto neither been particularly good nor bad, just theirs, was about to change.

The journey to Founders all began because Sitshengisiwe's throat, long accustomed to weak orange squash and no longer used to the strength of Mazoe Orange Crush, had tickled and caused her to cough after she took a sip from a glass Silas Mthimkhulu had placed in her hands. By the time Bodecia, the perfect attentive hostess, came to her rescue with a glass of water and a gentle pat on the back, Sitshengisiwe was hacking rather embarrassingly. Bodecia had then been kind enough to strike up a conversation, and Sitshengisiwe had found herself telling Bodecia about her life with its very comfortable beginning and not so comfortable present. Sitshengisiwe had to lay her change in fortunes at the door of something other than her husband, and so she laid it at the door of her incomplete education. Bodecia, who, quite naturally, knew of Cosmos

Nyathi and his empire, was sympathetic, and suggested that Sitshengisiwe finish her education through the adult literacy program that the new government, once elected, would certainly be putting in place.

So lost in her thoughts was Sitshengisiwe that she completely missed the bus stop at which she should have alighted, and found herself at the bus's last stop, the bus terminus at City Hall. She did not much enjoy coming into the heart of the City of Kings because, even though they were no longer in place, as a child she had been intimidated by the written and unwritten segregationist laws and policies that had policed the city. She alighted from the bus and almost tripped over a young Coloured man in RF military fatigues sleeping in the afternoon sun with his back against the wall of the public toilets, which smelled of concentrated urine and other bodily functions. Although the public toilets on the corner of Gray Street and Eighth Avenue were meant for blacks, Sitshengisiwe had never had the heart to use them. She did, however, find it in her Christian heart to feel sorry for the sleeping soldier, even though during the war he had probably not hesitated to kill people who looked like her. It helped that his long hair made him look a little like Jesus. She carefully stepped over him and was grateful that though her life had indeed sunk low, it had not sunk so low that she no longer had any dignity to hold on to.

Navigating the terminus filled with several bus stops was a nightmare, and for a time that was all Sitshengisiwe could concentrate on because there were so many white people on the pavement waiting to board buses. There were blacks, Colorueds and Indians as well, but Sitshengisiwe almost did not see them because she was so intent on not bumping into and therefore accidentally touching the white people. She did not know much about white people, but she definitely knew that they did not like to be touched by black people. Yes, there had been a ceasefire, and, yes, it looked like the country was marching toward independence and majority rule, but Sitshengisiwe was certain that none of this meant that white people were suddenly all right with being touched, albeit accidentally, by black skin. By the time she was ready to cross Fife Street at the pay-to-use toilets reserved for whites and kept clean by attendants who, at the top of every working hour, sprayed a powdery-smelling air freshener that Sitshengisiwe could detect even as she stood outside the facilities, she was exhausted from the conscious effort it took not to connect with her fellow countrymen.

As Sitshengisiwe crossed Fife Street, she decided that she would go to Lobengula Street and do some window shopping to while away the time before going to TM Hyper to buy the cheap and salty smoked salmon (which probably wasn't salmon at all) that Philemon loved so much he demanded that it be prepared on his birthday every year. She would have to be very delicate about how she presented the future she envisioned for them.

She made quick work of the remaining streets by walking off the pavement and zigzagging her way around the cars parked diagonally at coin-collecting meters. Lobengula Street was, as always, a triumph and a revelation. There was so much color, noise, movement, excitement, and just the right amount of danger, that one could not help but be infected by it all. Sitshengisiwe brushed past brown and black skins that did not mind human contact as she allowed herself to be jostled this way and that, and carried along until she was deposited into a store that called itself a bazaar, where she spent too much time gazing longingly and lovingly at pastel-colored dresses. Before she knew it, it was four o'clock, the very hour she was supposed to be at home preparing to cook the meal that Philemon would expect to eat at six o'clock sharp—exactly thirty minutes after he had arrived home from work.

Sitshengisiwe made her way out of the store and onto the street, too eager to be home to look both left and right before crossing. As she ran across Lobengula Street, a car screeched to a stop right at her feet. *Dear God, I almost died. I will have to tell Philemon that I almost died,* she thought, as she crossed the street more carefully. The person driving the car that had almost hit her rolled down her window, and, over the impatient and angry hoots of other cars, called out Sitshengisiwe's name. Sitshengisiwe made sure that she was safely on the other side of the road before she turned to see who was calling her name.

The driver of the car was Eunice Masuku, the woman who had once worked with Philemon. She had been the Rutherford's housemaid, and now here she was driving her own car, obviously having moved up in the world. Eunice Masuku gestured to Sitshengisiwe that she would park the car and that Sitshengisiwe should wait for her.

Once parked, Eunice invited Sitshengisiwe to join her in the car, which she did.

"A present from my son," Eunice said by way of greeting, as her hands proudly ran over the steering wheel of a Datsun 120Y. She said these words easily, as though it had not been almost fifteen years since last they had spoken.

"Your son? You mean the boy? He bought you this car?" Sitshengisiwe said with the sufficient amount of astonishment in her voice to satisfy Eunice. Sitshengisiwe was very suspicious of the verity of the information she was receiving, and so she was happy that her misgivings were not evident in her voice.

"Well, Dingani is a boy no longer. He is a man now. Living in America. Training to become a doctor," Eunice said with a pride that puffed out her chest until it almost interfered with the steering wheel.

This information did nothing to convince Sitshengisiwe that Eunice was telling the truth. The one and only time that she had seen Eunice's son was the day that Eunice had brought him to work. Sitshengisiwe, at the time living with Philemon in the boy's kia of the Rutherford's house, had caught a glimpse of the boy in his ill-fitting, blue paper-boy suit as he clutched his mother's gloved hand and allowed his knees to knock, and she had been convinced then that he would never amount to much. That had been the day that Eunice's fortunes had changed because she had talked to Emil Coetzee—about Lord knew what—and stopped coming to work. Eunice now informed her that after that conversation with Emil Coetzee, she had been able to train to be a nurse and to educate her son at one of the best schools for Africans in the City of Kings.

"America? A doctor?" Sitshengisiwe said, a little too late because she was still having a difficult time believing that the boy was amounting to anything much at all.

"Yes," Eunice said, with an obvious bite in her pride.

Sitshengisiwe knew then that some of her doubt had shown, and so she smiled and nodded with more eagerness.

"Married that beauty queen. You know the one. The one on the covers of all those magazines. Thandi Hadebe," Eunice said, her already puffed-out chest moving beyond the steering wheel and making its way to the windscreen.

Although Sitshengisiwe was not altogether certain which one of the many beautiful faces to grace the covers of magazines belonged to Thandi Hadebe, she said with sufficient enthusiasm, "Thandi Hadebe!"

"Yes. Thandi Hadebe," Eunice said, as her puffed-out chest pressed against the windscreen. "They called me all the way from America and said to me, 'Mom'… That is what they call me now, 'Mom'… 'Mom, you can't be forever walking here, there and everywhere. We have bought you a car. All you have to do is go and pick it up at Duly's." At this point, Eunice's chest was threatening to crack the windscreen.

Not knowing what else to say, Sitshengisiwe said, "At Duly's?"

Satisfied, Eunice nodded like a queen before she asked, "And you? Still with Philemon?" She somehow made the name Philemon sound like something she wanted to get off her skin.

"Yes," Sitshengisiwe said, rotating her wedding ring, which had once again lost its sparkle, around and around and around.

"And your children? How many are they now?"

"Four. One more came after you left the Rutherford's. All the maids that came after you were not up to your standard. Even Madam said so."

At the mention of her history as the Rutherford's maid, Eunice actually stiffened and shivered, and her puffed-out chest eased off the windscreen.

Sitshengisiwe realized that she had inadvertently scored a small victory, and so she carried on, "The children are all living with my mother and receiving a rather fine education. The first two are actually attending Convent High School. We are very proud of them."

"Oh," was all Eunice could manage as her puffed-out chest came to rest on the steering wheel.

"Yes," Sitshengisiwe said. "I am rather lucky that although my parents banished me from their lives, they found it in their hearts to accept my children."

"Oh," Eunice said again, her chest now comfortably back to its normal size. After a pause, she added, "Were you on your way to the TM Hyper? I am going there myself to do some grocery shopping."

Sitshengisiwe thought of the cheap piece of salt-cured fish that she had been thinking of buying, and knew that she could not possibly enter a store in which Eunice would put things in a trolley while she, Sitshengisiwe, carried a solitary piece of fish whose cheapness told her that it was not really salmon.

"No," Sitshengisiwe lied. "I was just making my way to the bus rank."

"Then wait for me. I should not be long. Just picking up a few things. Essentials. I will drive you home," Eunice said, magnanimously. "I take it you are still living in the Rutherford's boy's kia." She smiled benignly to ensure the right twist of the knife.

"Oh no. Not anymore. Not for quite some time. Some years now, in fact. We moved to a two-bedroom in Phelandaba," Sitshengisiwe said, sitting back-straight in the passenger seat. She conveniently forgot to mention that the house had been bought for them by the Rutherfords as thanks for Philemon's many years of service.

Eunice, her hand already on the door handle, hesitated and then let out another rather deflated, "Oh." She did not open the door, but said, instead, "If you are in a rush, perhaps it is best that you go to catch your bus. I would not want to keep you. I might take rather long in the store."

Sitshengisiwe, now wanting nothing more than for Eunice to see the two-bedroomed house, made herself more comfortable in her seat, and said, "Oh, no worries. I have all the time in the world. And I am sure that Philemon would be very happy to see you again." Her smile belied the many lies that she had just told.

As she waited for Eunice, Sitshengisiwe thought of Philemon and their many years together. They had met in 1960 when she was seventeen and he was twenty-three. She had been on her way to write her English Literature national examination. She, at seventeen, had wanted more than anything to be in love, but love had not as yet visited itself upon her. The boys of her youth, it seemed, had allowed themselves to be intimidated by both her father's wealth and her beauty, which had made her a very daunting prospect. When Philemon approached her that first day, he did not seem to find her at all intimidating; and luckily for him, he had a sweet tongue she believed readily and easily when he told her that he had been waiting for her all his life. Feeling the first pangs of love, Sitshengisiwe had gone to write her exam, but had promised him that she would see him soon after finishing it. Which she did.

They met every day after that, and because he made her feel good in ways that she was young enough to believe only he could, she prioritized her time with him above all else, and stopped going to write her exams altogether.

Things, as they say, lead from one to another, and before long her monthly visitor did not come calling. Sitshengisiwe had had enough of an education to know what this meant. She told Philemon about their predicament, and he told her that he would do right by her, which he did. He paid a visit to her father in order to make his intentions known, and that was when her father had discovered not only that his youngest and favorite child had a boyfriend, but that he was also a garden boy in the suburbs. Had she asked Philemon what he did for a living? Sitshengisiwe no longer remembered. What she knew was that he wanted to be a horticulturalist. He certainly did not dress or talk like a garden boy, and because she saw herself fitting in relatively nicely in the future that he envisioned for himself, she wholeheartedly agreed to marry him. When her father forbade the match, she carried out her one act of defiance—which, at the time, had seemed much like bravery.

Sitshengisiwe had left home with all its petite-bourgeoisie trappings and gone to live with Philemon in the Rutherford's boy's kia. Philemon had presented this as a temporary measure, as he would soon leave the employ of the Rutherford's and find more suitable and respectable work at a garden center before venturing out on his own.

That had been twenty years ago, and Philemon was still working for the Rutherfords, who continued to be grateful for his many years of service.

Sitshengisiwe had left home at seventeen with a suitcase filled with her favorite dresses and the book that she had been reading in school for literature class, *The Return of the Native*. When she became pregnant with her second child, two years later, she was still living with Philemon in the Rutherford's boy's kia, and she was still wearing the dresses that her body had long outgrown. She had stopped reading books, finding in them nothing but empty promises.

After the birth of their second child, Philemon gave her a suitcase stuffed with his madam's second-hand clothes. He was almost brought to tears by Madam's generosity, and wanted Sitshengisiwe to be as well. He never talked about the small-scale horticultural farm of his dreams anymore. He was more interested in making sure that Madam's garden won first place in the local, regional, and national home and garden shows. When Philemon received his own suitcase full of clothes from Mr. Rutherford, Sitshengisiwe understood why he had looked so good when they had first met.

When she found herself pregnant again, she told Philemon that she refused to raise three children in a one-roomed boy's kia, and that he needed to be a man and do something about it. Evidently he had understood her to mean that she wanted the Rutherfords to extend the boy's kia, which is what he asked them to do. That was when Sitshengisiwe had fully understood the measure of the man she was married to.

When Eunice left her job as the Rutherford's maid, Sitshengisiwe realized that other things were possible for her as well. So when Philemon told her, with great pride, that Madam wanted her to take over from Eunice, Sitshengisiwe lied and said that she had already secured herself a job.

Luckily, a trip to the industrial sites the next day had seen her, because of her education, gain immediate employment as an apprentice to the foreman in the bottling section of the National Breweries. Philemon, who was still looking to please Madam, had a lot to say about he being a man and she being a woman and tradition dictating that he not only be listened to, but obeyed. In response, she had told him that he had wooed Cosmos Nyathi's daughter, that he had wed Cosmos Nyathi's daughter, that she was Cosmos Nyathi's daughter still, and that she would die as Cosmos Nyathi's daughter. Philemon was silent on the subject of her employment from that day forward. Sitshengisiwe used this advantage to make Philemon promise that he would leave the Rutherfords and find a better job at the first opportunity. He had made the promise, and then never kept it.

Over the years, not wanting to feel the loss of too many things at once, Sitshengisiwe had turned to the church, allowing it to consume her and swallow up most of her disappointments.

Now as Sitshengisiwe watched Eunice totter two taxi-bags full of groceries to the car, she determined that it was time that Philemon made good his promise to her to leave the employ of the Rutherfords. And what better way to do that than to show him how far Eunice had come in the world?

As it turned out, while Eunice had been shopping, she had also been plotting revenge of sorts, because she gave Sitshengisiwe a lift for only part of the way and then seemingly out of the blue remembered that Dingani and Thandi would soon be calling her for their weekly chat with "Mom," and that she could not possibly miss the call. She was sorry to do this to Sitshengisiwe, especially at such a time, but she was sure she would understand. She parked the car at the side of the road, explained that this was where she needed to turn off in order to make her way home to Barbourfields, and then reached over and opened the door on the passenger side of the car. She sincerely hoped that they would be able to meet again soon, and was looking forward to seeing Sitshengisiwe and Philemon's home. It was really unfortunate about the timing of the call, but if Dingani and Thandi called and she was not there to receive their call, they would probably worry. Sitshengisiwe had no choice but to get out the car, and Eunice smiled at her sweetly before shutting the door and driving off.

Eunice really was something else. Leaving her at the side of the road so that she, Sitshengisiwe, could *feel* the difference in their circumstances. *Some people never change,* Sitshengisiwe thought as she chuckled. When she got home, she would tell Philemon about her encounter with Eunice... Philemon! He was probably already at home, wondering where she was, and worrying about how late his supper would be. She would appease him by telling him this story of a never-changing Eunice, and together they would laugh, and all would be forgiven and well again.

The setting sun was creating beautiful color in the western sky as Sitshengisiwe stood at the side of the road trying to orient herself. Where exactly was she? What was the direction home? She looked for a landmark to anchor herself, found it, and began her journey homeward. It would take her anywhere between thirty minutes to an hour to get home. By then there would be stars in the sky, and all the light of the world would be becoming a memory.

Sitshengisiwe had walked in this unfamiliar township long enough to have grown accustomed to seeing faces she did not know, so when a car hooted and she turned and saw someone whose face was familiar, she was momentarily taken aback. What was he doing here? He asked her the same question. She told him that a friend had dropped her off, and she was making her way home. He did not tell her what he was doing there. There was still quite some distance to go before she arrived home, he said, opening the passenger-side door and inviting her in.

Now, Sitshengisiwe certainly understood the danger of getting into the car of a man you did not know very well. Another man, and she probably would not have gotten into the car. But this man… this man she knew. Perhaps she did not know him very well, but she knew him well enough. Even so, she did not immediately get into the car, but hesitated, wondering what Philemon would think when he saw her alighting from such a car.

The man understood her hesitation, and reminded her that in order to get home she would have to go through an area of bush where all manner of things were said to happen at night. After that, Sitshengisiwe did not need any further convincing. She got into the car, fastened the seat belt, and thus ensured her safety. Once she got home, she would find a way to convince Philemon that he had nothing to worry about—that the lift had been a kind gesture and nothing more. The man smiled at her, and she smiled at him, feeling comfortable and secure. He would have her home in no time, he promised.

After a short while, the man said he knew a shortcut and turned into a section of the township that was still under construction. She believed him. She felt so safe that she did not think she had anything to fear as they drove down a dusty and dark road. She only realized she did not know the man as well as she thought she did when he stopped the car without warning, and she felt the sharp, cold steel blade of a knife at her throat.

PHILEMON

———◆———

They say one should not sleep with anger, but that just goes to show how much "they" know. When Philemon had gone to sleep the night before, he had been a tightly coiled ball that would only unfurl itself as rage once Sitshengisiwe got home. He had been sure that he would have a most restless night, but when he woke up in the morning, he felt more refreshed than ever before. This was most unfortunate, because he had wanted Sitshengisiwe to come in and find him sleeping in some twisted and tormented position that would make her feel sorry for having neglected him.

He opened his eyes slowly, yawned, scratched and stretched—and then got the sense that something was wrong. Sitshengisiwe was not sleeping beside him, which was not the unusual thing; she always woke up before he did. What was out of the ordinary was the absolute quiet of the house. Sitshengisiwe started work at the factory at 7 a.m., and bathed and fed by now, would be busy in the kitchen preparing his breakfast and heating up his bathing water. So why was the house so quiet—and eerily so?

Philemon decided to investigate. He reluctantly got out of the warm bed and put his feet on the cold, Sunbeam-polished concrete floor. He yawned, scratched and stretched, and looked at the alarm clock by his bedside table. It read 7:30 a.m. It must be wrong. He looked at the sun shining through his bedroom curtains; it was not in its usual position at this time of morning. It dawned on him then that perhaps he had overslept. But where was Sitshengisiwe? Why had she not woken him? He tip-toed across the cold floor and made his way to the kitchen.

She was not in the kitchen. In fact, the kitchen was just as he had left it the night before. On the stove top, there was the cast-iron pan he had used to fry his toasted bread. On the table, there was still one placemat. On the placemat, there was the plate on which he had eaten his toast and tinned baked beans. The meal had not been fit for a man who had spent the whole day working, but it was the best he had been able to do. He felt last night's anger return.

He understood that Sitshengisiwe wanted them to move on, or rather up, in the world, that she wanted him to break what she called his "dependence" on the Rutherfords, and what he called his "collaboration" with the Rutherfords. The kitchen itself was a reminder of and testament to that collaboration. He had received the stove, the cast-iron pan, the placemat, and the dinner plate from Madam. Most of the things in the rest of the house had also once belonged in the Rutherford's home—the sofa, the curtains, the display cabinet, some of the sheets that they used—and, yes, the very pajamas that he was wearing.

But this still did not excuse Sitshengisiwe's bad behavior. When he had come home after work and found her not in the house, he knew exactly where she was. Hadn't it been the case almost every evening since the New Year's Day party? She spent most of her time after work with Bodicea Mthimkhulu, enjoying herself and not really caring that she would only start to cook for her husband at 7 p.m., knowing full well that the last meal he had eaten had been at 1 p.m. All of a sudden, nothing mattered to Sitshengisiwe more than Bodicea, not even her duties as a wife, which she had vowed before a pastor to always uphold. Some deacon she was.

The evening before, he had waited in anger, expecting her to arrive late to cook his dinner as usual, but when 8 p.m. had struck, and there was still no sign of her, he had decided not to give her the satisfaction and had made his own dinner. If she expected him to go and fetch her from the Mthimkhulus, make some kind of scene that she would use to prove a point that he didn't know she was making, then she, as Madam liked to say, had another thing coming.

He had gone to sleep fully expecting her to return chastened at some point during the night, but now it seemed as though she had not returned. *She had, instead, chosen to spend the entire night in another man's house!* But even as he thought this thought, it did not seem possible: she was too much Cosmos Nyathi's daughter to do such a thing. Perhaps that was it? Perhaps she had simply gone back to being Cosmos Nyathi's daughter and stopped being Philemon Dlodlo's wife. Could it be that she had finally actually left him?

Philemon's entire body tensed with a fear that predated even Sitshengisiwe's unholy union with Bodicea.

It had begun with the artichokes. Madam had been determined to have artichokes—coated in breadcrumbs, deep-fried, and served with a lemon and herb butter sauce—served at her Christmas party. She had enjoyed something of the kind on a recent trip to Cape Town, and she had wanted, more than anything, to win the hearts of her guests by replicating the recipe. Suspecting that artichokes would not grow easily in the City of Kings, Madam had encouraged Philemon to plant the seeds months in advance. He did as he was told, but the artichokes had predictably struggled, even though he coaxed them almost daily. Luckily, after a few false starts, his labors bore fruit. It had been very hard work, but when he saw the vegetable peep through the soil and then grow to its protea-like full glory, he was very proud of his work. So was

Madam, who had encouraged Baas to give Philemon an even bigger bonus at the year's end.

All was well until Philemon got to work on the 27th of December. Madam had informed him that the artichokes had been a great success and had been raved about by all. She did not look as happy as he expected her to, however, and he did not understand why until she said in passing, "Emil Coetzee was not there... I am sure he would have enjoyed them. He really should not have let go of Kuki. She was always so very good at organising his social calendar for him." As far as Philemon was concerned, the only thing that made Madam not as perfect as she ought to be was her unrequited attachment to the undeserving Emil Coetzee.

Despite Madam's tempered enthusiasm, for his part, Philemon had been happy to hear that the artichokes had been a great success, and allowed himself to feel his usual pride in his work... until he opened the rubbish bin and found heaps of the stalks and outer leaves of this thing called an artichoke that he had lovingly labored over for months. Why had so much of the plant been discarded? The answer to his question came when Madam said, "I saved some for you because you did such an excellent job," as she handed him a saucer with two scooped-out artichoke hearts. This was it? This was all that was eaten of the vegetable? He took a bite and almost immediately spat it out. He did not like the taste at all. But he chewed and swallowed and smiled because Madam was there. As Madam watched him eat, it was obvious that she was very proud of what she called *their* hard work. *Philemon was so angry at the waste that even as he pretended to enjoy the artichokes,* he thought it was very little reward for *his* hard work.

The incident with the artichokes would probably have soon been forgotten had Sitshengisiwe not accepted a New Year's

Day invitation from their newly arrived neighbors, Silas and Bodecia Mthimkhulu. Although it had been Sitshengisiwe's idea to go to the party, to be fair, Philemon had been curious to see how their new neighbors lived ever since he had seen the Biddulphs moving truck deliver their belongings two weeks earlier. He had not known until that moment that a Biddulphs moving truck, which he saw almost every day in the suburbs, could venture into the townships. As he watched the Mthimkhulus' possessions being offloaded, there had seemed to Philemon to be too much... stuff... for a black family to own; and so he, quite naturally, became suspicious.

His suspicions grew when, the day after the Mthimkhulus arrived, a big-screen television set was delivered from Bradlows. The set was soon rumored not only to be fully paid for, but a color TV into the bargain. Philemon, who had long held the honor of being the only one in their neighborhood who owned a television set—a second-hand, battery-operated, black-and-white Sony Micro Television received from Madam—was very doubtful that a television with such a big screen could exist, and, that if it did exist, it could belong to a black person; and so, like Thomas, he had decided to see the television for himself.

When Philemon arrived at the Mthimkhulu's house for the New Year's Day celebrations, it was as he had hoped and feared. The furniture was plentiful, but there was too much for the size of the house; and, therefore, it looked crushed, crammed and crowded. In addition, it was gaudy and ostentatious without a hint of the real glamour and style that had seen Madam (who had natural good taste) and her home and garden featured in several magazines. Having been exposed to the genuine article almost every day of his adult life, Philemon knew that the Mthimkhulus were a cheap imitation of the real thing. Sitshengisiwe was unfortunately taken in by it all, and ooohhed and aaahhed at everything Bodecia showed her. He could not fault his wife entirely; her tastes had been shaped by the Cosmos Nyathis and Silas Mthimkhulus of the world—people who sold the second-grade goods solely intended for the African consumer.

The television set was, indeed, huge, but although technically a color TV, it could only show images in black and white because the country had not been able to upgrade its infrastructure during the war. Philemon was sufficiently appeased by the lack of color that, during the party, he joined the men congregated around the TV in order to watch Highlanders play Dynamos. Every minute or two someone would exclaim that it was like they were actually there at Barbourfields Stadium watching the soccer match, because that was how clear the picture quality was. Philemon was not sure if his fellow watchers were taking aim at him through their compliments, until someone joked about how they had had to squint when watching the games on Philemon's minuscule set. Most laughed, forgetting how grateful they had been, not so long ago, just to have a television in their vicinity.

Philemon was not amused. He had decided then that since Silas Mthimkhulu was evidently a man of great means, he would take great advantage of his hospitality. And so he had liberally helped himself to the food and alcohol on offer. It was while he was on his fourth Castle Lager that he heard his wife tell the lady of the house her riches to rags story. She told of how she, Sitshengisiwe, had been born into wealth, and how he, Philemon, had pulled her down and halted her progress and advancement in the world. She did not say this in as many words, but he heard it in the gist of what she was saying. And then she told Philemon's deepest and most closely held secret—she told Bodecia that the house and most everything in it had been given to them by the Rutherfords.

Since Philemon had long kept this a secret from his neighbors, Sitshengisiwe talking about it so casually had felt like more than merely a betrayal; it had felt like a dagger in the back—plunged in when least expected.

Philemon knew that he had let his wife down, that he had promised things in the beginning of their courtship that he had left unfulfilled during their marriage. But it was not as if he had not provided her with a good life. Yes, they might have received most of what they owned from the Rutherfords, but they had received it because of *his* hard work. They lived in one of the better townships, and owned some of the finer things—things meant for the European consumer—thanks to him. How could she not see that? How could she be so ungrateful as not to see that?

The way Sitshengisiwe carried on, it was as if she had not disappointed him in turn. Long gone was the wild, pretty young thing who had laughed at all his jokes. In her place was a sober Christian woman who wore a Baptist doek to bed and made Jesus Christ too much of her Lord and personal Savior. Philemon did not go about complaining to other men that he could not remember the last time she had allowed him to lie with her in the biblical sense, because he respected their marriage too much to air their dirty laundry in public.

Listening to his wife betray him, Philemon had decided there and then to begin 1980 with a bang. He had intended to use a large part of his bonus to buy the latest fashions for his children, but instead, he spent it on himself. Over the next few days, he drank himself into a stupor every night at MaDlodlo's Beer Garden. He bet on a horse at Ascot, Lucky Strike, and the winnings from that allowed him to continue his festivities for a few more days. He slept with one or two ladies of the night, and paid them handsomely for their services. Before he knew it, his pockets were empty and his heart was filled with regrets. He had meant to punish Sitshengisiwe through his bad behavior and neglect of her, but even though he had never acted like this before, she had seemed unfazed—as though she had always expected him to sink so low—and, definitely not feeling punished, her only response had been to tighten the Baptist doek around her head.

He began to feel that perhaps she was right, and that he had squandered not just the beginning of 1980, but most of his adult life. What had his dreams been? What had he at twenty-three years of age whispered to Sitshengisiwe when he way-laid her on her way to school and slept with her on the cold aluminium floor of a disused train car? What had made her leave the wonderful life that she had known and follow him? What dreams to come had Philemon promised her that had made her walk away from the honor and pride and privilege that came with being the daughter of Cosmos Nyathi? Cosmos Nyathi who, as he was always quick to remind people, had shaken the hands of the British Royal Family.

Philemon tried to remember what he had thought he would become, but he could not. All of his ambitions had turned to dust and been blown away by his many years of service to the Rutherfords. The fear came then, when, after the incident with the artichokes, he realized that his greatest ambition might very well have always been to grow something that would mostly be discarded, save for the heart.

He found that even he could not expect Sitshengisiwe to remain attached to a man with so little ambition, and his fear had compounded. He began to feel certain that she would soon leave him—he saw the signs of it in her friendship with the Mthimkhulus. Powerless to do anything else, he turned his fear into anger and waited.

A keening cry splintered his thoughts, and he became aware of the commotion on the street outside his home for the first time. As the sound of wailing approached, Philemon felt his entire body become so weak that he crumpled to the floor. And that was how he knew that the cry contained within it news of Sitshengisiwe.

She had finally left him.

RUTHERFORD & SPOKES

————◆————

Rutherford had been hoping for a much gentler good morning when "Tickey! Tickey!" woke him up. Agnes had not called him that in so long that he had even forgotten that it was her nickname for him.

"Tickey! Tickey!" After the night he had had, this was the last thing he needed. He tried valiantly to hold onto sleep, but heard his bedroom door open. "Tickey! How could you possibly be asleep at a time like this?" She approached his bed. "Tickey! Tickey!" If he wasn't careful, she would shake him awake. They hadn't touched each other in years. He slowly opened his eyes to find Agnes's cold-creamed face looming over his, and gave an involuntary start.

"Oh please, like you haven't woken up to much worse in some brothel," she mumbled through lips that were holding on to a Kingston cigarette for dear life.

"What is it, Agnes dear?" he said, his hangover wanting more than anything for him to keep the peace.

"Sitshengisiwe is dead. Been killed,"

What in God's name was she talking about?

"Sitshengisiwe, Philemon's wife is dead. Murdered!"

"I don't think that's how you pronounce her name."

Agnes made a frustrated sound in her throat: "Who cares how you pronounce her name? What I'd like to know is what you intend to do about it."

"About what?"

"Tickey, I swear! Philemon is downstairs. He is so beside

himself that he can't even think of gardening. My poor African violets!"

"Agnes... "

"Come and talk to him. Poor man is shaking like a leaf. He's seen the body, you see. Apparently the whole thing is very gruesome."

The impressive length of ash on Agnes' Kingston gave up the fight and fell onto Rutherford's sheets.

"Agnes!"

"Just come downstairs at once and make yourself useful." Agnes left his bedroom, not bothering to brush aside the ashes first.

She hadn't always been like this. In the beginning she had been more... malleable. Easy to shut up with a backhand across the face. That was before she had started taking self-defense classes, at his suggestion, during the war. The idea had been that she would be able to defend herself against a terr attack of any nature. No terrs had attacked their serene suburb during the war, but the last time he had raised a hand to her, he had found himself on the ground, his arm twisted behind him, her foot on his neck.

"Tickey! Tickey!"

Oh, for the good old days, Rutherford thought as he slowly got out of bed.

Rutherford had not even put his other foot on the kitchen floor when Philemon said, from where he sat at the kitchen table, "My wife, baas, she is dying."

What was it with these people and the present continuous tense, Rutherford thought, and not for the first time. "Is your wife dying, or is she already dead?" he asked.

Philemon blinked at him for a moment, and then said, "Yes, my wife, she is dying, truesgod."

"Is she dying at this very moment? Right now, as we

speak?"

Philemon looked at him, incredulous. "No, baas, I am telling you, she is dying."

"Dead. She is dead. She has already died. She is not in the process of dying."

Philemon looked very confused.

"Tickey!" Agnes said, entering the kitchen. The cold cream had been wiped off her face, but her hair was still in rollers and her terrycloth morning gown was still knotted at her waist. "A grammar lesson at a time like this! Honestly, where is your humanity?" She tsk-tsked as she sat herself down next to Philemon and put a hand over his trembling hands. "Poor man is in shock."

The truth was, Rutherford didn't know what to do. The man's wife was dead. What exactly was required of him in such a situation? Rutherford had always spoken to Philemon as a baas, and Philemon had always responded as a boy. None of their previous exchanges had anticipated having to communicate something as intimate as death.

"What say I make you a strong cup of tea with plenty plus sugar in it?" Agnes said, patting Philemon's hands as she got up from the table. How was it that she knew exactly what to say and do?

"Someone is killing my wife," Philemon said in utter disbelief.

Rutherford looked at his garden boy, trying to gauge whether or not he had loved his wife. Rutherford felt certain that if he knew this, then he would know exactly how to act and exactly what to feel. He thought back to all the times he had heard Philemon mention his wife, and it seemed to him that every time, Philemon had been complaining about his wife. Nothing new there, what husband did not complain about his wife? They were, by nature, a bloody nuisance, but unfortunately also a necessary one. Even after this rumination, Rutherford was none the wiser about how Philemon felt about Sitshengisiwe. Rutherford vaguely remembered her from the many years that she had lived in his boy's kia with Philemon. She had been rather fecund, and the only distinguishing thing he could remember about her was that he had thought she did not carry herself as she ought.

"Someone is killing my wife," Philemon repeated when Agnes placed the yellow Kango enamel cup filled with hot, sweet tea in front of him.

Tired of feeling helpless, Rutherford was relieved when he realized he knew exactly what to do.

————•————

Spokes looked at the man sitting opposite him and watched as he struggled to lift the egg-yolk yellow Kango cup. Its contents were in grave danger of spilling. Spokes nodded at the man after he had managed to take a sip of tea. "I am very sorry for your loss."

"Thank you," the man stammered, placing his Kango cup carefully on the kitchen table.

"First things first, what is your name?" Spokes asked.

The man stared at Spokes and then said, "Philemon... Philemon Dlodlo."

"Thank you, Dlodlo. And your wife's name is?"

"Sitshengisiwe Dlodlo," Philemon stammered.

Ah, Sitshengisiwe... so that was what Mrs. Rutherford had been trying to say, Spokes thought. After all these years, most whites still struggled to pronounce African names and words, but instead of seeing this as a failing on their part, they saw it as a point of pride. Mispronouncing African names and words might be a way of inoculating themselves against going native, Spokes concluded.

"She is the daughter of the late Cosmos Nyathi," Philemon

added.

Spokes nodded and wrote down this piece of information. You never knew what might prove to be relevant later on.

"You've reported that your wife is no longer with us," Spokes said

"Yes... yes," Philemon slowly said, as though he were weighing whether or not Spokes was to be trusted with the truth. "They are cutting up her stomach and placing her there in the bush. They are killing her for witchcraft," he divulged. The reality of the situation dawned on him afresh, and he cried freely and loudly.

Spokes let the man cry. He was glad that he had managed to remove Rutherford and Mrs. Rutherford from the kitchen. It had taken some doing. *She* had been particularly difficult. But her verbal abuse had been worth it, because Spokes knew that there were certain things that could never be said in front of the baas and the madam.

"They?" Spokes asked after a respectful time had passed.

"People say they saw two men... one white, the other black... in a very expensive car, in the early hours of the morning when they thought the township was sleeping. But the township is never sleeping. They removed her body from the car and dumped it in the bush," Philemon provided before allowing himself to cry long and hard again. Spokes took the opportunity to make him a fresh cup of strong, sweet black tea.

"Sir, I am thinking I am knowing who is doing this thing," Philemon said hesitantly as he received the Kango cup from Spokes. He was again weighing whether or not Spokes was to be trusted.

"I see," Spokes said, sitting himself down.

"Yes. It is Silas Mthimkhulu. Our new neighbor. He is the one doing this thing, truesgod. He is the one witchcrafting my wife."

"Witchcraft?"

"Yes, sir."

Spokes allowed Philemon to drink his tea.

"Yes, it is Silas Mthimkhulu," Philemon said again, seemingly fortified by the tea. "He is living next door and he is being a very rich man. Too rich for an African man. There is only one way that an African man is being rich like that, and it is being through witchcraft."

"We will definitely question Mr. Mthimkhulu," Spokes assured Philemon.

"He is using my wife's body for witchcraft. Why is he doing this thing? Why is he doing this thing to my wife? My wife is being a very good person. She is going to church every Sunday. *Every* Sunday. No matter what, truesgod. Every Sunday. She is even being a deacon... the only woman deacon. She is being a very good wife to me."

"I am sure she was."

"We are being very good people."

Spokes smiled at Philemon. "We will find whoever did this, I promise," he said. "In the meantime, I think it is best that you come to the station with me. Officially report the crime and make a statement."

Philemon was more than willing to go with Spokes, but Mrs. Rutherford proved difficult.

"Where on God's green earth do you think you are taking him?" she demanded, blocking Spokes' access to the police bakkie door.

"To the station. He needs to—" Spokes tried to explain.

"He needs to do no such thing. Do you know who my husband is?"

"Clement Rutherford."

"Yes, Clement Rutherford. Very high up in the SIU, I can

tell you."

"Your husband is the one who called me."

"I know, but certainly not so that you could take Philemon away. If that is what you think, then you have another thing coming."

"That may very well be—" Spokes began and was again interrupted.

"Do these look like the hands of a murderer to you?" Mrs. Rutherford asked, holding up Philemon's calloused hands. "No, they do not. Of course they do not," she responded to her own question. "These are the hands of the best gardener in the City of Kings—what am I saying, the best gardener in the damn country. Do you have any idea how many times this very garden has been featured in *Better Homes and Gardens* and *Good Housekeeping*? How many times it has taken first place at garden shows? There are too many to count on both hands, I can tell you. A man who can create something this beautiful would never kill anyone."

"No one... except you... has said anything about Mr. Dlodlo murdering anyone," Spokes said as delicately as he could.

Not liking Spokes' insinuation one bit, Mrs. Rutherford narrowed her eyes and then, without warning, screamed at the top of her lungs: "Tickey! Tickey!"

Spokes half-expected a large dog—the one that the Basopa Lo Inja sign on the gate had warned him about—to come bounding up from nowhere and bear down on him.

"Tickey! Tickey!"

A window was flung open and Rutherford's tired face stuck out of it. "Agnes, dear, let the Chief Inspector do his job."

"Tell the Chief Inspector about the artichokes, Tickey," Mrs. Rutherford ordered undeterred.

"The artichokes?"

"Yes, the artichokes. Remember, they were all the rage at our Christmas party. Tell him how well Philemon nurtured them, cultivated them, and cared for them. A man who could be so patient and gentle could not possibly kill anyone or anything. Tell him, Tickey. Tell him."

"Well, I think you just did, Agnes dear."

"Is that all you have to say, Tickey?"

Rutherford stole a glance at Spokes before saying, "I think it is best to let the Chief Inspector get on with what he came here for. I will accompany them to the station and see what can be done, if that will make you feel better."

It took a concerted effort and many instances of prying Mrs. Rutherford's fingers off Philemon in her spirited attempt to impede their progress, but Spokes and Rutherford at last succeeded in getting a very willing Philemon onto the back of the police bakkie. "She is wearing a very pretty dress," Philemon said as Spokes closed the bakkie door. "She is working at the factory, so why is she wearing a very pretty dress?"

SPOKES

———◆———

Spokes rang the doorbell. A house in the townships with a doorbell—interesting. A man cracked the door just enough so that Spokes and the two detectives with him could see his face; he looked directly at Spokes, placed as much of his body as he could behind the door and never removed his hand from the door handle. Behind him, there was a hive of activity.

"Spokes Moloi," Spokes said by way of introduction, intentionally omitting his rank. "We are with the BSAP," he added, inclining his head toward the two detectives with him.

The man smiled, rolled down his shirt-sleeves, and extended his hand. "Silas Mthimkhulu," he said, shaking hands with Spokes.

"May we come in?" Spokes asked.

"Oh... I... this is about what happened yesterday, I gather. Sad business, that. Yes, please do come in, do come in," Silas Mthimkhulu said, opening the door wider. "Sad business, that."

Spokes and the two detectives walked into the house, which seemed filled to the brim with stuff and people. Not only was there already a surfeit of furniture, but there were also pamphlets, placards and posters, and crates of Coke, Fanta, Sprite, Stoney Ginger Beer and Canada Dry. The people, mostly women, were gathered in groups working on things that all seemed to have Silas Mthimkhulu's face on them—pens, envelopes, stationery, and the aforementioned pamphlets, placards and posters. There was much chatter and laughter and lots of loud music—Lovemore Majaivana coming from a state-of-the-art stereo sound system. Silas Mthimkhulu was not a man for half measures.

Silas Mthimkhulu surveyed the room and then grinned sheepishly: "Running for election. Member of parliament."

Spokes could barely hear him over the barrage of sound. "Could we go somewhere quieter?" he asked, almost shouting above the music.

It is likely that Silas Mthimkhulu did not hear what Spokes had asked because he said, "Let us go outside, I think. It will be somewhat quieter there." He made his way out, and Spokes and the detectives followed him.

It was indeed quieter outside, but only barely so. A group of men was playing a heated and constantly challenged game of draughts, while sharing scuds of opaque beer. Spokes realized that for most of these people, it was as if Christmas and New Year's had come and never left. Their extended season of merry-making was thanks to Silas Mthimkhulu, and their gratitude toward him showed in the appreciative nods they kept sending his way.

As though reading Spokes' thoughts, Silas Mthimkhulu said, "Unabashedly currying favor, I'm afraid. I find, at this rather late stage in my life, that I am something of a political animal." As he spoke, there was an unapologetic look on his face.

All the garden chairs in the backyard were occupied by the men playing the game of draughts, and so Silas Mthimkhulu, not wanting to upset his future constituents, collected four empty crates that he found around his small backyard and arranged them under a large mango tree, heavy with overripe fruit. Spokes and the detectives sat on the overturned crates, and Silas Mthimkhulu remained standing.

"Before you make yourselves too comfortable, gentlemen, may I offer you some refreshments?" Silas Mthimkhulu said. "I am more than happy to provide you with anything that your hearts desire. Apart from what you've already seen, there are lots of lagers and spirits locked in the pantry."

"Thank you, but not while we are on duty," Spokes said.

"I see," Silas Mthimkhulu said, sitting himself down on the remaining crate.

In order to sit, Silas Mthimkhulu had to pull up his maroon trousers at the thighs as the polyester material there was stretched too tight. He was wearing a white shirt with wide lapels that was also slightly too tight. Silas Mthimkhulu's clothes fit him too snugly not because he was a man who had grown too hefty for his clothes, but because he wanted his clothes to fit him that way—tight-fitting clothes were, after all, the fashion of the day. His fashion sense also explained the wide, bell-shaped bottoms of his trouser legs, and the fact that he had not fastened the first three buttons of his shirt, leaving it open in a large V-shape that showed off his thin gold chain. The thin gold chain was meant to complement his thin-trimmed moustache and his hair, which was just an inch shy of being a full-blown afro. Spokes was certain that there were only a few years between them, and so he could not help but wonder what business Silas Mthimkhulu had dressing the way he did. Besides, it did not seem like the kind of look that would make for a very reliable politician.

As though yet again reading Spokes' thoughts, Silas Mthimkhulu said, "I know that my wardrobe leaves a lot to be desired. My wife assures me she is working on changing my image. It is just that I have been a businessman for most of my life—the Idlazonke Stores, you know. Certain image to uphold, you see. Have to be seen to be 'with it.' Some habits are just hard to break."

Spokes was not sure if that explained even the half of it.

"About yesterday," one of the detectives, said tentatively.

"Ah... yes... yesterday. Sad business, that," Silas Mthimkhulu said, shifting in his seat.

"Did you notice anything out of the ordinary—anything unusual?" the detective asked.

"Well, we only moved here two... three months ago. Still getting to know the neighbors, you understand. Um, let me see. No, nothing out of the ordinary... she liked to sing in the morning. An early riser."

"Would you mind if I talked to some of the people here?" the other detective asked. "I take it most are from the area... have known the Dlodlos longer."

"Ah, yes, of course," Silas Mthimkhulu said, attempting to stand and being hindered in his progress by the tightness of his trousers. "I can show you the ones who are neighbors."

"Thank you, but that will not be necessary," the detective said, staying him with his hand.

As Silas Mthimkhulu watched the detective leave, the remaining detective said, "You were saying about yesterday morning?"

"Yesterday morning?" Silas Mthimkhulu asked, his composure beginning to fray.

Spokes was very proud of the way the two detectives were handling the situation. Silas Mthimkhulu was a man not only accustomed to being in charge, but to having his own way. He was too comfortable under the circumstances, and needed to be shaken up a little bit. Well, he was definitely shaken up now, if only a little bit.

"Yes. Yesterday morning," the detective said.

"Let's see... yesterday morning... no, nothing out of the ordinary," Silas Mthimkhulu said.

"So she was singing as usual?"

"Singing… yes. Singing as she prepared breakfast, but not as early as she normally did. She is… was a factory worker, early shift, according to my wife. Yesterday when she sang, it was later in the day."

"Later… how much later?"

"Definitely after nine in the morning. My friend, Dr. Gustav Mabuse, came to visit then. He also heard her singing because he commented on her voice, I remember. She has… had a very beautiful voice."

"What song was she singing?" Spokes asked.

"A Jim Reeves song. *'This World Is Not My Home'*, I believe."

Spokes nodded, and the detective took that detail down.

"Houses are built much too close here," Silas Mthimkhulu was saying. "People expected me to settle in the white suburbs when we returned. But I am a man of the people. I have to be among them—be part of their heartbeat."

Well, at least Silas Mthimkhulu had not hidden the fact that he was a political animal, Spokes thought. At least in that sense, he was an honest politician.

"I take it that is all," Silas Mthimkhulu said, looking at his watch.

"We will let you know if we need to speak with you at a later date," the detective said, rising to his feet.

"I will be happy to help in whatever way I can," Silas Mthimkhulu said, standing up only after preparing his trousers for the sudden movement. He offered both men his hand for a hearty handshake, and then he hesitated.

Spokes knew that whatever Silas Mthimkhulu was about to say was something that he had intended to say from the moment he apprehended who they were and why they were there.

"Naturally, one does not want to speak ill of the dead,"

Silas Mthimkhulu began. "But, yesterday, now that I think about it, something did occur that was out of the ordinary. I am sorry that I forgot to mention it before. In the morning, Sitshengisiwe put on her work overalls and left, only to return a few hours later, once Philemon had left. She changed into a very pretty dress and then headed out again. Now, this is probably neither here nor there, but I get the distinct impression that Philemon Dlodlo is one of those men who married a village girl and brought her to the city with the intention of making her forever in awe of him. Some men like that sort of imbalance in their relationships. I do not think that she was dressed like that to go to meet with him."

"I see," Spokes said with a nod. "Sitshengisiwe Dlodlo was not a village girl," he continued. It was now his turn to stand up. "She was the daughter of Cosmos Nyathi; you know, the famous businessman."

"Cosmos Nyathi!" Silas Mthimkhulu exclaimed, his composure leaving him for the moment. "I had no idea that she was his daughter. Then why did she carry herself as though she was… a nobody?"

"Perhaps that was just her way of being humble," Spokes said, not quite able to stop himself from looking at the gold chain around Silas Mthimkhulu's neck. Was that a scratch mark right under his left ear?

Silas Mthimkhulu laughed. "As I said, my observation was neither here nor there. I would make a terrible detective."

Spokes smiled before saying, "And that was the last time you saw her?"

Silas Mthimkhulu's laughter died abruptly. "Saw her?"

"Sitshengisiwe Dlodlo—the last time you saw her, she was in her pretty dress?"

It took Silas Mthimkhulu too long a moment to say the simple "Yes" that was required. "The last time I saw her she was in her pretty dress," he added.

"Did you and your friend hear her sing before or after she put on the pretty dress?"

"Silas, is everything all right?" a woman's voice inquired.

Spokes turned to see the owner of the voice, even though he already knew who it was: Bodecia. As soon as Philemon Dlodlo had mentioned his neighbor's name, Spokes had known that he would find himself standing before her after so many years.

"Spokes? Spokes Moloi? Is that you?" Bodecia asked.

The detective next to him made a sound in his throat that Spokes ignored. Silas Mthimkhulu's body stiffened, and Spokes ignored that too. He looked at Bodecia, who was no longer shy and retiring and was now tall and commanding.

Spokes removed his fedora from his head and said softly, "Bodecia."

She smiled a smile that made the words that she said next seem like a contradiction: "Spokes Moloi. The Man Who Disappointed Me. Standing before me without a care, as though he did not break my heart many years ago."

Bodecia stretched both her arms toward him, and Spokes had no choice but to awkwardly hold both her hands in his. The detective next to him expertly swallowed a chuckle.

Bodecia had said more to him in the minute that they had become reacquainted than she had ever said to him in the entirety of their knowing each other long ago, when they were supposedly courting. Whenever he had spoken to her then, she had shyly looked at the floor or the ground, finding something to occupy her—a blade of grass, a smoothed-out stone, a piece of lint. It was apparently this shy, retiring quality that had made his mother certain that Bodecia would make him a good wife.

"How did he break your heart?" Silas Mthimkhulu asked

with a smile that was tight and forced.

"In the worst possible way. We were supposed to marry… but then we did not," Bodecia said, her eyes still looking into Spokes' eyes, her hands still holding his.

"Ah, I see," Silas Mthimkhulu said before he disengaged them as politely as he could, taking his wife by the arm and pulling her to his side. "Then I have a lot to thank you for, Chief Inspector," Silas Mthimkhulu continued. "Without you, I would not have known true happiness these past twenty-two years."

It was Bodecia's turn to smile a smile that did not quite reach her eyes.

Chief Inspector? Spokes had not told Silas Mthimkhulu his rank.

"The Chief Inspector is here enquiring about the sad business next door," Silas Mthimkhulu informed Bodecia, his arm finding its way to the small of her back.

"Poor Sitshengisiwe," Bodecia said, moving away from her husband and toward the house, making all of them follow her.

"Did you know her well?" Spokes asked, as he entered the house with Silas Mthimkhulu close behind him.

"Well enough," Bodecia said. "Talked to her during our New Year's Day party. I liked her. I think she was in need of a friend. Took to visiting some evenings before her husband returned from work. She was not happy with the turn that her life had taken, and was ready to do something about it. You have to admire a woman like that. She was Cosmos Nyathi's daughter, you know."

So Bodecia and Silas Mthimkhulu did not tell each other everything, Spokes deduced as he let Bodecia lead him and the detectives toward the front door. He realized that he could hear her clearly because most of the merriment in the house had died down. He got the distinct impression that

Bodecia had put an end to the music as soon as she arrived, and judging from the stolen looks in her direction from the other women, Spokes knew he was right. She had a powerful presence, standing there in her brown and cream kaftan dress. She was a woman worlds removed from the reticent girl he had known.

Bodecia and Silas Mthimkhulu accompanied Spokes and the detectives to their police bakkie.

"I am sure we will meet again," Bodecia said, as they stood by the car. She offered him both her hands again, and he had no choice but to take them. "Under better circumstances, I hope," she added.

Spokes had nothing to say to that, so he simply smiled at her and briefly held both her hands in his.

Silas Mthimkhulu broke off their contact by offering his hand for Spokes to shake.

"I really wish we could have been of more help," Silas Mthimkhulu said as they shook hands. "Perhaps I can get my good friend Dr. Gustav Mabuse to examine the body. He is the Chief Pathologist."

Spokes knew when a man was doing more than offering a kindness, and so he said, "Would you? The Chief Pathologist does not usually involve himself in cases like this. It would be wonderful if he could."

"It is the least that we can do," Silas Mthimkhulu said, pulling Bodecia close to him.

As the BSAP bakkie drove away, Spokes could not help but think about the odd couple that Silas Mthimkhulu and Bodecia made. She was a woman who wholly embraced the maturity that came with the middle of life and womanhood, and he was a man who was tenaciously holding on to a youth that had never been his. That was just one of the many differences between them. How did such a woman end up married to such a man? The answer came quickly to Spokes—because a man called Spokes M. Moloi had disappointed her.

He felt almost certain that he would disappoint her again. He had long wanted to meet Silas Mthimkhulu, the Idlazonke shop-owner who had sent his shopkeeper, Jasper Mlangeni, to a country up north, and had therefore taken away Spokes' chance to question his prime suspect in Daisy's case. Silas Mthimkhulu—the man he had believed was Jasper Mlangeni's accessory after the fact.

"Did you notice how she did that, sir?" one of the detectives asked, breaking into Spokes' thoughts.

"You mean the way she skillfully ushered us out of the house," Spokes said.

"Yes, sir."

"Yes, I noticed," Spokes said. He had also noticed how overly familiar she had been. Why the need for the performance?

SPOKES

———•———

As Spokes alighted from the police bakkie, he looked at the cat lying sleepily in the shade of a flame tree and at the pigeons eating the birdseed that the white man, sitting on a bench under the tree, was feeding them. The man had a shock of white hair and was wearing white overalls, black gumboots, and two-toned glasses—one lens was tinted black and the other one was clear. The man threw the birdseed closer to the cat, and the pigeons fluttered toward the seed. The cat remained blissfully uninterested.

"You don't see that every day, do you?" the white man said to Spokes.

"No, I suppose you don't," Spokes said pleasantly, before making his way toward the whitewashed building with a maroon paint strip running along its base.

"I wouldn't bother going in there as yet. I don't think you will find the man you are looking for," the man said before being seized by a coughing fit.

Spokes had no choice but to turn around. 'Are you all right?" he asked.

"It's all this smoke in the air," the man informed him. "The city is up in flames. Every furnace and incinerator in every government building is working overtime."

Spokes looked at the billowing smoke rising up from different points in the city's skyline.

"You know what we are witnessing?" the man asked. "The erasure of history," he responded to his own question, and then offered his hand for Spokes to shake.

"Chief Inspector Spokes Moloi, I presume," the man said. 'I believe I am the man you are looking for. I am Dr. Gustav Mabuse. Silas called to let me know to expect you."

Spokes sat down next to the man, "I thought—"

"Let me guess: that I would be wearing a lab coat and a stethoscope hanging like a noose around my neck? Well, maybe not a stethoscope given what it is that I actually do," Dr. Gustav Mabuse said.

"Yes… something like that."

"Well, despite appearances, I am the Chief Pathologist here," Dr. Mabuse said, throwing the last of the birdseed at the pigeons.

"And a good friend of Silas Mthimkhulu."

"A very good friend. It was not easy for me—born between the wars to German parents who chose to live in a British colony—to make friends; and then along came Silas. It was not easy for us—given the particular character of this country of ours—to remain close to one another. But we did. There is nothing that I would not do for him."

"So you've examined Sitshengisiwe Dlodlo?"

"Yes. Sad business, that. She had such a beautiful singing voice."

"You've heard her sing?" Spokes asked as though this were news to him.

"Yes, a Jim Reeves' song it was. *This World Is Not My Home,'* I believe. Very sad business, that. Such a waste," Dr. Mabuse said, looking at the smoky horizon. "I take it you would like to see her."

"Yes," Spokes said, following the Chief Pathologist into the building.

There were several bodies—mostly white—in the lab, some with sheets covering them entirely and others with sheets folded discreetly at the waist. Two other doctors, both white, wearing lab coats were busy examining a body. An assistant, black, also wearing a lab coat, was in the corner labelling vials.

Dr. Mabuse stopped and removed a sheet from over Sitshengisiwe's body. Next to it was folded a dress that was very pretty indeed. And for the longest time, that was Spokes' only coherent thought because there it was—on her chest: a Y-dissection. Without warning, there were many dots wanting to be connected all at once. The doctor was speaking, saying things that Spokes could not hear above the beating of his own heart. After a time, he managed to excuse himself and made his way out of the lab.

Dr. Mabuse found him sitting on the bench next to the cat and the pigeons.

"I'm sorry. Should have better prepared you," Dr. Mabuse said, handing him a glass of cold water. "I just assumed that you had long become inured to such things." He sat down next to Spokes.

It was a very long while before Spokes could find words again. "Thank you," he said, taking a sip of the water.

"It definitely shouldn't be a sight that anyone gets used to," Dr. Mabuse said in commiseration.

Spokes tried to get a hold of his usual composure, but could not. "Did she… did she come to you like that?" he asked.

"Like what?"

"With that dissection?"

Dr. Mabuse did not respond immediately. He removed his glasses and wiped them on his overalls. "No. I made that dissection," he said.

"And the other cuts?"

"Those she came with," Dr. Mabuse said.

"Defensive wounds?"

"Arms, palms, fingers… put up quite the fight. She definitely did not go gently into that good night," Dr. Mabuse said, looking at the smoky skyline of the city.

"Anything under her fingernails?"

"Nothing conclusive, I'm afraid," Dr. Mabuse said, still looking at the skyline. "Body found in situ, but an animal—a dog most probably—got to her before she was discovered. Licked her fingers. Contaminated evidence."

"In situ… so you think she was killed in that bush?" Spokes said.

"All indications point to that conclusion."

"And yet," Spokes was back to being himself again, "it's been reported that the body was dumped in the bush by two men…one white, the other black…driving an expensive car."

Dr. Mabuse continued looking at the smoky skyline, and said nothing.

APRIL 1980

SPOKES

———•———

By the time Spokes arrived at White City Stadium, Silas Mthimkhulu had already cast his spell over the crowd. They were in an uproar—ululating, clapping their hands, stomping their feet, shouting, "I-DLA-ZO-NKE!" or chanting his name—"Mthimkhulu! Mthimkhulu! Mthimkhulu!"—at the end of every point that he made.

Silas Mthimkhulu stood at the podium wearing for him, a somewhat subdued and obviously tailored three-piece navy-blue suit. Gone were his maroon bell-bottomed trousers and wide-lapelled shirts. He looked exactly like what he was: a middle-aged man who had long arrived in the world. He spoke into the microphone, and Spokes heard his voice come through the nearest loudspeaker.

Spokes watched as Silas Mthimkhulu smiled at the crowd as though he were a beneficent savior. Like a god, he raised a hand to silence them, and they obeyed.

"You know what they say about us in the press?" Silas Mthimkhulu said. "They say we are Marxists. That we are intent on making you socialist slaves. That we want to take away your freedoms. *They* speak of freedom now as if they know what it is. Where has this noble idea of freedom been for the past one hundred years?"

"I-DLA-ZO-NKE!" the crowd shouted.

Silas Mthimkhulu milked the moment for all that it was worth before stepping away from behind the podium and standing beside it. "Now tell me, good people," he said, turning his dapper-looking self around in a slowly rotating revolution. "Does this look like a Marxist to you?"

Laughter erupted from the crowd, and Spokes suspected that some of the laughter was uncertain because the truth was that many people did not actually know what a Marxist was— let alone what one looked like.

Satisfied with himself, Silas Mthimkhulu went to stand behind the podium again before leaning conspiratorially toward the crowd and speaking into the microphone in a softer voice: "Come now, good people. You know me."

"Mthimkhulu! Mthimkhulu! Mthimkhulu!" the crowd chanted before he could finish his sentence.

Silas Mthimkhulu obviously had things well in hand. Those who could not easily grasp English, and therefore could not understand everything he was saying, were too carried away by the spirit of equality and camaraderie imbued in his performance to care for much else.

"How many of you here shop at an Idlazonke store?"

The crowd's enthusiastic applause made Spokes' ears ring.

"I can see that we know each other very well," Silas Mthimkhulu said with a chuckle. "It is not a secret that I am a businessman. In fact, it cannot be a secret, as I am one of the most successful black businessmen in the country."

"I-DLA-ZO-NKE!" the crowd shouted.

Silas Mthimkhulu had to raise his hand to quiet them once again before he said, "So, yes, I am a capitalist. Now I know many of you here have been led to believe that a capitalist is a very bad man."

A hesitant and perhaps confused silence settled over the crowd.

"But I am a capitalist…with a heart."

Light and somewhat relieved applause greeted this statement and Silas Mthimkhulu patiently waited for it to die down before continuing: "How many of you have taken advantage of my buy-now-and-pay-later schemes at the Idlazonke Home Emporium stores over the years?" Many hands in the crowd shot up, as though Silas Mthimkhulu had all of a sudden turned teacher and the people in the crowd were his eager students. Silas Mthimkhulu leaned forward conspiratorially again and asked, "How many of you have received imbasela with your purchases at the Idlazonke General Dealers?"

The people in the crowd laughed as they clapped their hands, some even going so far as to give him the thumbs-up sign. "You see, good people, you are my people. And as much as you know me, I know you. I know that things have often been difficult for you under colonialism, and I have tried, in my own way, albeit small, to make things better for you where I can."

Heartfelt applause and ear-piercing ululations and whistles greeted this remark. "A true capitalist thinks only of profit. A capitalist with a heart thinks only of the people and of how to make their lives better. A capitalist with a heart is really a socialist."

There was something of a battle in the crowd as some chanted, "Mthimkhulu! Mthimkhulu! Mthimkhulu!" and others, "I-DLA-ZO-NKE!" It took forever for the frenzied furor to die down.

"The government we want to usher in," Silas Mthimkhulu continued when at last he could, "is one that is for the people. One that puts you, my friends, first. One that is solely interested in making *your* lives better."

The crowd went wild chanting the name of the political party to which Silas Mthimkhulu belonged.

"*They*, as well you know, have never put you first."

The crowd agreed by deriding the invisible "theys" with boos and thumbs-down signs.

"And so when we say we are for the people. That we want to put the people first. That we want to give you good education and health care for free. That we want to give you back the land that was stolen from your ancestors—" Here Silas Mthimkhulu was interrupted by a greatly impassioned uproar, and had to wait a very long time before he could continue. "They try to make our putting you first seem like a bad and ugly thing. They try to make it look like *their* exploitation of you, your children, your land and your wealth, for a century, was somehow for *your* own good. They want you to think that small steps forward under their leadership were actual giant leaps. But *you* know the truth. Some of you went to war, willing to make the ultimate sacrifice because you knew the truth. You have always known the truth. You have always seen through their lies. You have never been fools. You have always been wise."

In response, the crowd did many things at once—ululated, whistled, chanted, clapped, stomped—creating a deafening cacophony that made it very clear to all that if Silas Mthimkhulu were to run for the office of Prime Minister, many would vote for him.

Having taken the people exactly where he wanted them to go, Silas Mthimkhulu knew that he could do with them whatever he pleased.

"Now be honest with me, my good people. How many of you, when you saw posters of me around the townships asking you to vote for me as your Member of Parliament, thought to yourselves, "What does Silas Mthimkhulu the businessman know about politics?"

The crowd laughed shyly and sheepishly.

"How many of you not only thought it, but said it out loud?"

The laughter grew more comfortable.

"How many of you not only said it out loud to yourselves, but also to family and friends at home and at the beer garden?"

The comfortable laughter grew even more comfortable.

"You were right to wonder, of course. It is your right to want competent people to lead you. But I ask you out here in the open, what is government if not a business? A government is about providing goods and services to its people. In order to do that, the government has to know how to trade. In order to do that, the government has to know how best to manage its resources."

The crowd nodded at the apparent sagacity of his words.

"Who then can better understand government than a businessman?"

"Mthimkhulu! Mthimkhulu! Mthimkhulu!"

Even though the crowd was heartily chanting his name, Silas Mthimkhulu said, "I can see that some of you have doubts about my bona fides." The crowd predictably objected to this, to Silas Mthimkhulu's great satisfaction. He continued, "I know some of you have heard rumors about me helping our boys cross over into Zambia...about me providing them with much-needed shelter, clothing, food and medical supplies."

The murmurs from the crowd could have been because the people had heard such rumors, or because they had not.

"The rumors are true," Silas Mthimkhulu continued. "I did help our boys in the ways that I have mentioned, and in other ways that were available to me. Does that make me a hero?"

The murmurs grew louder, and for a moment it seemed as though that would be the only response, and then the crowd erupted with a highly appreciative: "I-DLA-ZO-NKE!"

Silas Mthimkhulu was gracious enough to say through the din, "If I am a hero, then I am one among many."

It took what seemed like forever for the "I-DLA-ZO-NKE!"

chant to die down. But no sooner had it ended, than another of "Mthimkhulu! Mthimkhulu! Mthimkhulu!" began. Silas Mthimkhulu appreciated the crowd's appreciation, as he paced to and fro on the platform, smiling and waving, managing somehow to look both humble and proud. When he eventually took his seat next to Bodecia, he looked extremely pleased with himself.

Spokes was far from satisfied with the spectacle he had just witnessed, and wondered how the crowd could be so jubilant. Were they not worried the way he was worried about how Silas Mthimkhulu managed to make everything about himself? What about the sacrifices that they—the people—had made during the war? What about their own innumerable small acts of courage and heroism? What about the futures they had been fighting for and wanted to realize? Had they not seen that his whole performance was an exercise in self-aggrandizement? Had they already forgotten how the Idlazonke stores sold goods of dubious value and questionable quality? Had they already forgiven Silas Mthimkhulu for the high interest rates that accompanied his buy-now-pay-later schemes? And what exactly had their memories done with the images of the Idlazonke collection trucks that traversed the townships daily, seizing the very goods that had been bought under these schemes?

Spokes watched as Silas Mthimkhulu turned and whispered something into Bodecia's ear. She smiled, and Spokes chose to believe that it was part of the performance.

Several other men spoke, all, like Silas Mthimkhulu, hoping to be Members of Parliament in the new government. They were a motley crew who, soon after the failure of the 1979 elections, had cobbled together a party meant to be more moderate than the two main nationalist parties that were seen as being too Marxist (which made many white people ill at ease). The party was, on the other hand, more militant than the black-led party built around Christian ideals (which made many white people feel at ease) that the 1979 elections had intended to place in power. This new party was in fact made up of men who had not risen high enough in the ranks of the major nationalist parties to have real power once independence was realized; this was, therefore, their chance at gaining such power.

Some spoke eloquently but uninspiringly, some spoke competently but drearily, some spoke articulately but had very little of substance to say. One poor fellow was near incomprehensible. They were all overwhelmed by the prospect of what potentially lay ahead—actual freedom and the responsibility it entailed. The ceasefire was only a few months old, and now the country's first elections were looming, and these men had barely had enough time to get their bearings. Seemingly on the spot, they had had to decide on whether to eschew the communist principles that had guided them thus far, and continue with the country's capitalist model; or create the socialist society that they had long fought for. Each speaker had some variation of this conflict contained in his speech, and it was quite obvious that the party line regarding the party's political future was something of a moving target.

The crowd, primed by the man of the people, Silas Mthimkhulu, was generous enough to not look too closely at such things, and to hold on to the promise of a future that was different from the one they had previously imagined for themselves. They saw messiahs in ordinary men.

———◆———

Even after Spokes showed the four formidable men guarding the entrance to the VIP Lounge his BSAP badge, they were reluctant to let him through. They did not seem to understand that his being with the police meant he had right of entry.

"It is all right," a woman's voice said. Spokes turned to see Bodecia standing behind him, beaming. "He is with me," she said.

She was dressed in stunning African attire, with an elaborate and impressively arranged scarf wrapped around her head. Perhaps it was because he had spent the past few hours watching her on stage, but she seemed larger than life.

"Mrs. Mthimkhulu," Spokes said as he removed his fedora from his head.

Bodecia was amused. She was obviously laughing at him, but at what about him, Spokes did not know. His old-fashioned ways, perhaps?

"Since when have I been Mrs. Mthimkhulu to you?"

"Since you married Silas Mthimkhulu," Spokes said wryly, offering her his arm.

Bodecia laughed outright as she casually put her hand in the crook of his arm, accepting his old-fashioned ways.

Again, Spokes marveled at how far removed she was from the quiet and painfully shy girl that she had been. The way she strode around the room evinced how comfortable she was in this place filled with politicians, cigarette smoke, and glasses and bottles of alcohol. This was her environment. These were her people. She raised a fisted hand into the air: "Viva!" she cried. "Viva!" came the response.

She spoke the language. This was her world.

Spokes tried to see her clearly through the haziness of the room, but he could not.

The atmosphere was festive, and the volume of everything—the conversation, the music, the laughter—was too loud for Spokes. He could not hear himself think. He needed to hear himself think.

Not being able to hear completely, not being able to think coherently, not being able to see Bodecia clearly: this put Spokes on edge and made him somewhat uncertain. Perhaps he should have chosen a different day to do what he had come here to do. Bodecia turned to him and smiled that genuine smile of hers, and in that instant Spokes knew that he was making a serious mistake. He was trespassing on their moment of happiness. It could all be saved for another day—tomorrow. He stopped in his tracks, and was just about to apologize and head back outside when Silas Mthimkhulu came up to them, smiling a smile that was far from genuine and not necessarily meant for Spokes, but for whoever was watching this moment unfold. The smile said: I am absolutely fine with my wife's closeness to this man. He was still giving his unctuous performance.

Silas Mthimkhulu, still seeming genial, looked at Spokes with something sharp and potentially dangerous in his eyes before he said, "I did not know that the police were allowed to publicly show their support for a political party." To demonstrate the good-naturedness of the moment, he patted Spokes on his back and then accepted an ice-cold Castle Lager that a waiter served to him on a tray..

"I am not here to show my support," Spokes said in a voice that struggled to be heard above the din.

Spokes only knew that they had both heard him because he felt Bodecia stiffen beside him, and saw the something sharp in Silas Mthimkhulu's eyes flash.

"Can we talk somewhere more private and quiet?" Spokes asked.

It was an outwardly cheerful Silas Mthimkhulu who led all three of them to the caretaker's storeroom, a small, dark and cramped room that smelled of cleaning supplies. Silas Mthimkhulu flipped the light switch, which was thankfully connected to a working lightbulb, and closed the door behind him. They squeezed in amongst the brooms, mops, feather dusters, buckets, tins of polish, and drums of disinfectant. It was obvious to Spokes from the easy way Silas Mthimkhulu had found the switch that it was not his first time in the room; and he could not help but wonder under what circumstances he had come here before. Spokes surveyed the room—all manner of things could happen in such a room, and all of them clandestinely.

By the time that Silas Mthimkhulu spoke again, he had recovered enough to ask, with the appropriate amount of concern in his voice, "Is this about our neighbors—Sitshengisiwe and Philemon? Of course, if there is anything further that you would like to ask us, we would both be happy to oblige."

"Thank you," Spokes said. "But this is not about Sitshengisiwe's case. No, this is about...well, I was listening to your speech at the rally—"

"I hope you enjoyed it," Silas Mthimkhulu interrupted.

"It certainly did move the crowd, and I was a part of that crowd," Spokes said, diplomatically, if noncommittally. "I heard you mention that you had helped some of the boys cross over into Zambia."

"Some girls...women and children too," Bodecia said. "Not just boys and men fought this war." The amusement was long gone from her face.

"Of course," Spokes said. "I didn't mean to imply—"

"Don't tell me you have come here to arrest me," Silas Mthimkhulu interrupted. "I know you BSAP boys did not take kindly to liberation war sympathizers, put us in jail every chance you got. I know we were on different sides—you chaps wanting colonization to go on forever, us chaps wanting colonization to come to a necessary end—but surely so close to independence helping freedom fighters cannot still be seen as a crime. I was just doing my part, as they say."

"Oh. I see I have not made myself clear," Spokes said,

choosing to ignore the intended sting of Silas Mthimkhulu's words. "I am not here to charge you with anything."

Silas Mthimkhulu and Bodecia both visibly relaxed.

"Far from it—I am here to ask for your help," Spokes continued.

"My help?" Silas Mthimkhulu asked, evidently taken aback.

"I suppose that this is a matter that both of you might be able to help me with. You see, there is a man who came to see me recently. He is one of the boys who crossed the Zambezi into Zambia."

"And I helped him cross over?"

"Well, no. He found his own way, from what I gather."

"So where do I come in?" Silas Mthimkhulu asked, no longer at ease.

"You see, he saw torsos and limbs floating in the Zambezi," Spokes said.

If anything had shown on Silas Mthimkhulu's face—shock, revulsion, confusion, anger, anything—Spokes would have doubted in that instant that he was on the right track, but nothing appeared on Silas Mthimkhulu's face. It chose, instead, to give nothing away and made itself an inscrutable object. And that is when Spokes knew with certainty that after all these years, he had found his man.

"Torsos? Limbs? The Zambezi? Floating?" Bodecia asked, her face the picture of perfect incomprehension.

Spokes could not help but feel relieved. "Yes," he said. "Torsos with Y-dissections carved into them."

"You say that as though it should mean something, but I cannot for the life of me understand what you are on about," Silas Mthimkhulu said testily, his inscrutable mask slipping.

"The man—" Spokes began explaining.

"The man? What man?" Silas Mthimkhulu asked, his hands

gesturing in such a way that some of his beer sploshed out of the bottle.

Bodecia put a placating hand on her husband's arm.

"The man I told you came to see me recently—" Spokes said.

"Chief Inspector Moloi," Silas Mthimkhulu interrupted. "I am sure you can appreciate that we are very busy. Since this does not seem to be a pressing matter, perhaps we can discuss it after the elections. When things have quietened down. You can come by our house. We would be happy to have you. But right now, I am sure you can appreciate that we are very busy. This is a rather stressful time," Silas Mthimkhulu said with a very tight smile.

Bodecia looked from her husband to Spokes. It was her turn to make her face illegible as she said, "Why put off till tomorrow what you can do today? In what way can we possibly help you about the limbs and torsos?"

"I just wanted to know if you had heard any stories. You lived in Zambia for quite some time, and now I discover that you were involved in helping the freedom fighters cross over—"

"How very convenient," Silas Mthimkhulu interrupted yet again. "Now that the war is over, you call them freedom fighters. Not so long ago they were terrorists, according to you. You thought they should be hanged for treason. You BSAP boys, you definitely know how to dance to the piper's tune."

Spokes saw the diversionary tactic for what it was, and carried on with his question. "As I was saying, perhaps you heard of limbs and torsos floating in the Zambezi. Perhaps there were people you helped cross over who never made it to you. That sort of thing. Anything might prove useful."

"I heard of bodies and limbs," Bodecia said tentatively. "Some could not make it across, and drowned. Some were shot as they crossed. Others were attacked by crocodiles and hippopotami. So I heard of bodies and limbs…we all did. Very painful ways to die. Never heard of torsos with Y-dissections though."

"You see, Chief Inspector, the answer was rather simple all along. If only you had come out and asked a direct question to begin with," Silas Mthimkhulu said.

"I take it then that you never heard of these torsos floating in the Zambezi either?"

"Of course not. My wife and I share everything," Silas Mthimkhulu said, reaching a hand toward Bodecia which she did not immediately take. "If I knew about the torsos, then she would too, and vice versa. I am sorry that this man saw what he saw or thinks he saw."

"I just thought this was the kind of detail that you would remember, Mr. Mthimkhulu."

"Me? Why?"

"Well…because of Daisy."

"Daisy? Who in God's name is Daisy?" Silas Mthimkhulu asked, his gesticulations making half his beer slosh out of the bottle and splosh onto the floor. He refused to look at his wife, and Spokes knew then that there had been many other women besides Bodecia.

"Daisy lived in the village next to your first Idlazonke store. Chief Cele Mkhize's village. She was murdered. Her limbs hacked at and her torso carved open with a Y-dissection."

"A Y-dissection?" Bodecia said, as she took an obvious step away from her husband, and chose not to look at him.

Silas Mthimkhulu composed himself enough to say, "Oh yes, Daisy. I remember now. Sad business, that. Very sad business. My shopkeeper, Jasper Mlangeni, was briefly a suspect, if I remember correctly. As were several other men."

"Yes. And your shopkeeper, Jasper Mlangeni, he followed

you to Zambia, from what I gather," Spokes said, laying his last trap—knowing full well that Jasper Mlangeni had left the country before Silas Mthimkhulu.

"Yes. He opened several stores for me there in the 1950s and 1960s," Silas Mthimkhulu said before he registered the full import of what Spokes had said to him: the door he had just opened, and not recognizing it for the trap that it was, he gladly walked through. "Yes, he followed us to Zambia," Silas Mthimkhulu said, hammering the final nail into the proverbial coffin.

Bodecia frowned. Spokes noticed. Silas Mthimkhulu did not.

"Would it be possible to speak to him?" Spokes asked.

"He's still in Zambia, I'm afraid," Silas Mthimkhulu said, at long last allowing himself to take a swig of what remained of the ice-cold beer that had been sweating in his hand. "Taking care of business. But he will be joining us next week. I'm sure he will be happy to talk to you when he arrives."

It was evident from the deeply furrowed brow on Bodecia's face, and the lost look in her eyes, that she was trying to put all the information she had heard together, and it was equally evident from the self-satisfied smirk on Silas Mthimkhulu's face that he believed he was no longer a suspect in Spokes' eyes, and that he probably never had been. Mission accomplished.

"Unfortunately we never got to question him fully at the time, but we've long felt that the heart of the matter lay with him," Spokes said.

"Yes, I'll have him come and talk to you as soon as he arrives," Silas Mthimkhulu said. "We want nothing more than to co-operate fully with you, Chief Inspector," he graciously added.

SILAS

———— ◆ ————

Silas looked at himself in the mirror and tried to accept the man that he saw reflected there. He could not. Gone were his John Travolta shirts and bell-bottomed trousers. Bodecia had promptly donated those to the Salvation Army after she came home with an armload of Pierre Cardin three-piece suits and business shirts that she had bought at Sanders Department Store.

"You are no longer a businessman. You are a politician now," she had declared. "You need for people to take you seriously. A few tailor-made pieces won't go amiss either."

She had been right, of course. Even about his hair, which was now of a length he could not quite get used to. He patted his head, fondly remembering the glorious near full-blown afro that had proudly stood there throughout the seventies. Bodecia had even taken away his 24-carat gold chain and the ring he had worn on his pinkie finger on special occasions. He had always known that the jewelery was a bit over the top, but he had so loved the sheer decadence of it—the fact that they were an unnecessary exclamation mark proclaiming his obvious wealth. He reached for a tie, and was just about to put it on when he decided to do something else with it.

Silas, with shirt unbuttoned at the top and holding the tie in his hand, headed over to the bed where Bodecia lay sleeping. He held the tie in both hands and his right hand coiled the fabric around his left hand. Now that he was close enough, Silas could tell from the way she was breathing that although her eyes were closed, Bodecia was not sleeping. He watched her breathe in and out. Her face did not have that peaceful look that it often had when she was in deep slumber.

He envied her that—her peace and her ability to sleep contentedly, without any worries. He was a businessman, and there was always something to worry him out of peaceful sleep. He took pride in knowing that by marrying her, he had made such sleep possible for her. She had this and more besides to be grateful to him for, and she was losing sight of that.

He would have liked to blame the Chief Inspector for this change, but he knew it predated Spokes Moloi. Bodecia had forgotten that when he had first met her, she had been a village girl doubled under the dual yoke of tradition and Christianity. The only valuable asset she had possessed then was a smattering of English she had acquired *after* her father had finished educating his male children. Now she could confidently address the Women's Assembly at political meetings and rallies—all because of him and the schooling he had encouraged her to get. He wasn't one of those men who wanted to be the only one able to read the newspaper at the kitchen table. Other women in his life could be ignorant, but his wife had to be intelligent because he needed someone who could help him run his businesses. Perhaps he had been generous and open-minded to a fault.

Tie still in hand, Silas sat down on Bodecia's side of the bed, next to her warm body. Even though their bodies were touching, she did not stir. Silas unraveled the tie and placed it clumsily around his collar. He waited patiently for her to open her eyes, which eventually she did. She looked right at him with that thing in her eyes that Chief Inspector Spokes Moloi had put there—suspicion, doubt, fear, the beginning of hatred—he could not tell which. He would know exactly how deeply whatever it was that she felt had manifested itself by how she would respond to the test that he had just set for her.

At first, it looked as though she would fail. She kept looking at him with that thing in her eyes; and then she said, stifling a yawn, "You leaving to go vote? We really should have voted together yesterday." With that, she did not quite pass the test, but at least she had made an effort with the "we."

"Voting together would have been the proper thing to do… the expected thing. Casting our votes for a country we have long fought for." She sounded more like the politician that he was pretending to be. In truth, she sounded like what she was—a woman who had taken an active part in the Women's Assembly for over fifteen years, and who had helped the nationalists' cause by tirelessly asking other countries for charitable donations and support.

"I needed to continue campaigning," Silas said.

"You are worrying needlessly, as I keep telling you. The people will vote for you. They worship you. Have genuine affection for you."

"Which, I suspect, is more than what my wife feels for me at this moment."

"What?"

"Genuine affection."

Bodecia had the decency to furrow her brow.

"You think I have not noticed that things have changed between us since Chief Inspector Spokes Moloi's last visit?"

She at least continued to look him in the eye, which gave Silas a little hope, even though that something Chief Inspector Spokes Moloi had put in her eyes was still there.

"The way you look at me has changed."

"Has it? I have not noticed any change. I think I am mainly confused. I mean, why did he question you?"

"He did not question. He insinuated. He is a clever one, that one. He knew that if he asked me a question outright, he would get an answer he did not want, and so he muddied the water; and in so doing, he planted the seeds of doubt in your mind because that is what he wanted to do all along. Don't you see? He wants to drive a wedge between us. He wants you."

"Spokes is not that type of a man," Bodecia said, trying and failing to seem nonchalant. "Everyone in all the townships of the City of Kings knows that for Spokes Moloi, there is only one woman: Loveness Moloi."

Something had crept into Bodecia's voice that Silas did not want to examine too closely. It was time to shift gears, and so he said, "You understand why I couldn't say anything to him, of course?"

Bodecia frowned, no longer thinking about the unavailability of Chief Inspector Spokes Moloi, and thinking instead about the reality of Silas Mthimkhulu, which was as it ought to be.

"You know who he suspects, don't you? Who is the one person who is connected to Daisy's body and the torsos floating in the Zambezi?" Before Bodecia could answer with the much-dreaded "You," Silas continued with "Jasper Mlangeni." He watched as her frown deepened.

"Jasper...Mlangeni?" Bodecia asked, looking extremely confused.

"He was besotted with that Daisy woman. Obsessed. Even though he knew the kind of woman that she was."

The lost look in Bodecia's eyes gave way to deeply felt pain. How long had she been in love with Jasper? How long had Jasper been in love with her? Silas had only learnt of their mutual affection a few years ago when he heard them singing a church hymn—there was an obvious closeness in the way their voices harmonized together. They had too much respect for each other and for him to ever do more than sing together, but love is love. It was Jasper who had made her forget all the things that Silas had done for her.

Bodecia recovered enough to say, "The kind of woman that she was?"

"I never met her, you understand, but from what I gathered, she was nothing more than a commonplace whore."

Bodecia flinched at the sound of the word; she was once again the green young woman that he had married.

"She was apparently friendly with half the men in the village. But Jasper was in love, and for the longest time he refused to see it… and the rest, as they say, is history. Now, I know you like Jasper very much. The two of you get along so very well. But he is the missing link, don't you see? Chief Inspector Spokes Moloi definitely sees it, and now so do I. She must have befriended one man too many and driven poor Jasper to do whatever it is that he did."

"Jasper… Mlangeni?" Bodecia asked again, incredulous.

"Yes. Now there is no denying that he was a brilliant shopkeeper and he is a superb general manager. I trust him with my business affairs, but how well do we really know him? He is a man in his fifties who has never married. You wouldn't know this, but I've seen him when we are out together. He prefers the company of ladies of the night—the Daisys of the world."

"You want me to believe that Jasper murdered a woman, dismembered her and then, for whatever reason, ripped a "Y" into her torso? Jasper, whom I have never seen so much as hurt a fly, killed a woman in cold blood?"

"What I am saying is that you can never fully and truly know anyone," Silas said, taking her hand in his.

Bodecia looked at him long and hard with an expression that he was happy to see was not the one Chief Inspector Spokes Moloi had put there. "I suppose you could be right," she eventually said.

"Jasper has been exceptionally loyal and faithful to me for over thirty years," Silas said. "All I can do is be loyal and faithful to him in turn. You understand now why I seemed rather nervous about Chief Inspector Spokes Moloi's questions."

Bodecia slowly nodded. "Yes…Yes," she said quietly, still looking at him. And then she leaned forward and did what he had wanted her to do all along. She buttoned the remaining buttons of his shirt, and looped the tie through the collar before tying it into a very accomplished full Windsor knot. And with that, she had passed the test that Silas had set for her.

Satisfied, Silas patted her lightly on her thigh. "Perhaps you should come with me," he said.

"To vote? Would love to," she said leaning back against her pillows. "But after standing in that long line yesterday, I am utterly exhausted and not up for much today."

She may have added the last words because his hand had stopped patting her thigh and had started stroking it instead, as his eyes traveled appreciatively over her body. She was a phenomenally attractive woman even in middle age, and his continued desire for her always took him by surprise. He tended to prefer his women young and, if not young, definitely impressionable; and she was no longer a young, impressionable woman, but no matter how far and wide he strayed, he always came back to her. Perhaps, like Chief Inspector Spokes Moloi, he was a man in love with his wife.

"Whatever you do, don't go to the front of the queue because you are one of the candidates. Stand in the line, join it at the back, and be one with the people. They will appreciate that sign of humility," Bodecia advised.

Just then the phone, which was on Bodecia's bed-side table, rang. *What you don't know can't hurt you,* Silas thought as he watched his wife answer it. First there was confusion.

Then there was shock. Then there was great disbelief. And finally, there was a scream. All within a matter of seconds.

Silas had to stop himself from mouthing the words along with Bodecia when she said, "Jasper has been killed... a car bomb." He arranged his face into a look of complete incredulity so that Bodecia had to say, "Jasper... is dead."

Whatever little thing had been holding her together until that moment snapped, and she became a mass of heaving sobs. Looking adequately shocked, Silas took the receiver from her hand and hung up the phone before gathering his wife into his arms. She let him comfort her, which allowed Silas to be hopeful about their future.

Later, when asked for comment by the media, Silas had a ready answer: he had obviously been the target of the car bomb. The car that Jasper Mlangeni had been killed in belonged to him. And why would anyone want to kill him? Well, because he knew something damning about the leader of a rival political party—he would not say which one; because he had long been a target of the South African government, who knew that killing him would create havoc; because he had never been a friend of the security forces who had marked him public enemy number one for all the help that he had rendered the freedom fighters right under their noses. The media could take its pick of a reason as long as it understood that Silas Mthimkhulu had been the intended target of the car bomb.

"Such a sad business, that."

DR. GUSTAV MABUSE

———— ◆ ————

Dr. Gustav Mabuse was once again feeding the pigeons when the Chief Inspector approached him outside the pathology lab. He did not look up even when the Chief Inspector got close. "I knew I would see you again," Dr. Mabuse said, as he made room for him on the bench. The Chief Inspector sat down, and the pathologist offered him the packet of birdseed. The Chief Inspector scooped a handful of seeds and broadcast them toward the pigeons. "Silas feared it would come to this. As soon as he met you, he was afraid you would make him have to sacrifice Jasper," Dr. Mabuse said. It was obvious from the way the Chief Inspector furrowed his brow that he had not been expecting a confession—at least not so soon. For a moment they silently watched the birds hop from one seed to the next.

"'That man has the instinct of a hound and the soul of a hunter,' he said to me that first day when you questioned him about his dead neighbor," Dr. Mabuse continued. "What an unlucky coincidence that was. He thought she was a nobody. Little did he know that killing her would bring him into your orbit. Needless to say, he knew who you were. Had known of you ever since you started investigating Daisy's murder. He knew you were a dog with a bone, and had always felt relieved that you had never picked up on his scent and had, instead, concentrated all your efforts on Jasper. But he could never be sure of you, and so he followed your career very, very closely over the years, as did I. I think when years passed and you did not question us about Daisy's murder, we relaxed—and then we made two mistakes. The first was that we thought you had given up trying to solve her murder. The second was that we thought we had gotten away with it. When the two of you met, he could tell that you remembered his name from the Daisy case and he panicked. He tried to steer you away by 'helping' you and sending you to me, which, was of course, his…our undoing. The only way I can make a straight line down the middle of a torso is if I first form a 'V' shape at the top. As soon as you reacted to the dissection, I knew we had been right to continue worrying about you."

The Chief Inspector did not react or respond in any visible way; he continued to watch the hopping pigeons.

"You're wondering why I'm telling you all this," Dr. Mabuse said. "No, you're realizing I'm telling you all this because there is nothing that you can do about it. Truth is, there never was. Not since the 1960s anyway, when Silas joined the SIU as an undercover operative around the time that the nationalists were beginning to agitate for independence or war. The SIU would never have let you touch him. And yet he still was afraid of you."

The Chief Inspector's head moved slightly—a sign that he had received information that he had not hitherto known.

"The torsos in the Zambezi: what were they? The work of the SIU?" the Chief Inspector asked at last. The calm in his voice surprised Dr. Mabuse.

"After everything you know about Silas and me, you still want us to have some goodness in us, I see," Dr. Mabuse said, smiling thinly. "You want us to have done things because we had to, not because we wanted to. Those torsos in the Zambezi belonged to young men and women seeking to fight for their country, willing to die for a cause. I suppose in some people's way of looking at the world, they were the good guys."

"And in yours?" the Chief Inspector asked.

"War is war. There are no good guys. There are no bad guys. There are only people after different outcomes. Generals, majors and lieutenants speak in terms of ideals, but what they really want is cannon fodder—an endless supply of people to die for another man's idea until that idea is realized. The truth is that that idea is rarely realized—at least, not in its original form. In a way, we saved those young men and women seeking to fight for their country from ever learning that they were willing to die for an empty promise—for nothing. And when I say nothing, I mean, nothing. I saw the mass graves many of them ended up in, most of them never having had the chance to fight for what they believed in—they were not even afforded that dignity... that honor. We, at least, made them die for *something*. Their internal organs allowed others in various parts of the world—people who valued their lives—to go on living. Their deaths gave the gift of life." Dr. Mabuse said all this in a voice that lacked compunction.

"You mean...you harvested their organs?" the Chief Inspector said incredulously, letting his inscrutable façade slip.

"Yes. Mostly from those who had been badly maimed and were in a lot of pain. Make of that what you will. Disabled people are treated abominably in this country, and the sale of body parts is a lucrative international business," Dr. Mabuse said plainly. "At a time when what was expected was death, we gave life."

"What you did was murder innocent people so as to profit from their deaths."

"Innocent? How very black-and-white you are, Chief Inspector. What they were doing was fighting for nothing, and what we did was give their lives a purpose—meaning. Good *or* bad, right *or* wrong: in your profession, that is how you have to think. I don't think like that. I think in terms of good and bad, right and wrong. They don't ask for complete allegiance. Something can be both good *and* bad, right *and* wrong, and that is all there is to it."

The Chief Inspector was silent for a long time before he said, "And Daisy? How do you justify killing her?"

"Daisy was a real tragedy," Dr. Mabuse said, wiping his spectacles on his overalls. "Silas did not mean to kill her. That is what he told me then, and I believe him even now. He had heard things about her. About how she was very friendly, especially with men who had money in their pockets, and so he decided to have his chance with her. Unfortunately for him, it all went wrong. He had known that his shop-keeper, Jasper, had arranged a rendezvous with Daisy, and so he purposefully sent him to the city to get supplies, and then went to the store in Jasper's place. She arrived at the store wearing a brand-new dress that Jasper had given her. Instead of Jasper, she found Silas. He made his advances. She rebuffed them. He had not been expecting to be rejected. He was, after all, the owner of the store and the wealthiest man around. Needless to say, that he did not take the rejection well, and there was an altercation and a struggle. At some point he pushed her, and she fatally struck her head on the corner of the counter top. He panicked and called me— a friend and a doctor in training. I believe it was only once I suggested we cut her open that the possibilities became clear to us—he wanted to fortify his business, I wanted to learn more about human anatomy…and so we found uses for her organs. I helped him dispose of the body; and I think that in the process we recognized something in each other. The rest, as they say, is history."

"If I had caught you then, then you would not have had much of a history," the Chief Inspector said, his voice a mixture of pain and regret.

"How could you have caught us then when you were so set on Jasper? Raftopoulos, the Greek travelling salesman, put the fear of God into us when he kept talking of the two men—one white, the other black—he had driven past on the night in question. We can only thank colonial race relations that not much was made of what Raftopoulos said. What else could we have been but baas and boy? By the time you found out that Jasper had an airtight alibi, Silas had already packed him off to Zambia where he could not put two and two together. We had covered all our tracks, but we never stopped fearing you."

"And Sitshengisiwe Dlodlo?"

"Let's just say that Silas really wanted to be a Member of Parliament."

"Wanted?"

"Well, now it turns out that he is going to be the new Emil Coetzee."

"The new Emil Coetzee?"

"Yes, the Head of the Organization of Domestic Affairs. He called me this morning with the news," Dr. Mabuse said. "He is definitely untouchable now. And if you can't touch him, you can't touch me. But even so, if you want to know the truth, I believe we are still both a little afraid of you, Chief Inspector Spokes Moloi."

SPOKES

———◆———

The smell of smoke was overwhelming as the incinerators of The Organization of Domestic Affairs burnt unwanted history. Spokes looked around the antechamber in which he was currently sitting, and trophies of impala, kudu, sable, and duiker stared blindly back at him. This was the kind of room meant to impress a man very different from who he was. He had not been put in this room during his one and only previous visit; he had been made to wait downstairs until Emil Coetzee himself came to collect him.

"The Head will see you now," a voice in a maid's uniform said before scurrying away.

Spokes stood up and opened the door that led into an office that he remembered well, with its rich and plush red, white and green décor. For a moment he felt that perhaps the voice in a maid's uniform had been in error and had directed him to enter before he had been asked for, but then he realized that Silas Mthimkhulu, in a Savile Row-type suit, was only pretending to sign the many papers before him. This was another tactic to keep Spokes, who did not know whether to approach the desk or stay put, waiting. More than that, it was meant to impress upon Spokes how much he was meant to be impressed.

"So it is true," Spokes said, approaching the desk. "You are the new Emil Coetzee."

Silas Mthimkhulu blinked at him as though only becoming aware of his presence then. *So much unnecessary perfor-*

mance, Spokes thought, as he seated himself on one of the two chairs opposite Silas Mthimkhulu.

"Please do," Silas Mthimkhulu said, gesturing toward the chair that Spokes had just occupied. "The new Emil Coetzee? Yes… yes, I suppose I am the new Emil Coetzee."

"You are the man himself," Spokes said.

"Yes, yes—I am the man himself," Silas agreed with a mirthless chuckle. "I like that: The Man Himself."

"Very… imposing," Spokes said, looking around the opulent office.

"It is rather. Although I am thinking of changing quite a lot of things."

"Is that so?" Spokes replied.

"What do you think of the name, 'The Organization of Domestic Affairs,'" Silas Mthimkhulu asked, leaning back in his chair.

"I think it is a name that does not quite represent what happens in this building," Spokes replied.

Silas Mthimkhulu's eyes narrowed and hardened slightly—this was obviously not the response he was looking for. "Too long by half," he said. "Now what do you think of, 'The Organization?'"

Spokes was waiting for more, but it was evident from the self-satisfied way Silas Mthimkhulu looked at him that that was all there was to it. "It is very short," Spokes said.

"Exactly!" Silas Mthimkhulu said, triumphantly. "Yes, there are going to be many changes made here," he continued before adding, "All made by the new Emil Coetzee: the new *and improved* Emil Coetzee. They say Coetzee always used the stairs and never took the lift. I run up the stairs two at a time!" Silas Mthimkhulu said, standing up and walking toward an impressive collection of amber and brown-colored liquids in crystal bottles. "Can I offer you something to drink?"

"No, thank you," Spokes said.

"You know, they actually gave me this post as punishment," Silas Mthimkhulu said, pouring himself a drink. "You saw how popular I was at that rally—I-DLA-ZO-NKE! Mthimkhulu! Mthimkhulu! Mthimkhulu! It made them very very afraid. Afraid that if I really wanted, I could be Prime Minister in five years. They think they have been immensely clever in assigning me to this post; they are patting themselves on the back," Silas Mthimkhulu said, sitting himself back down. "Most of them were in the bush for ten, fifteen years, so they don't know. They don't know that this very office that you and I find ourselves sitting in is the seat of power in this country." Silas Mthimkhulu took a sip of his drink and let the weight of what he had said sink in for Spokes. "You have no idea the amount of information contained within these walls, and what is information if not power? The BSAP, CID, SIU put together cannot touch The Organization." He savored another sip of his drink before adding, "Now granted Coetzee was a man of limited scope; he could not see what he had. But I—the new and improved Emil Coetzee—I am nothing if not a visionary. Look at what I have been able to do with the Idlazonke stores. Started with that first store in Chief Cele Mkhize's village, and now there are more stores—Emporiums, General Dealers, General Goods Stores, Bottle Stores—than I can count here and in Zambia, and I am looking to expand to other African countries. Why not? It's a new day, anything is possible. Especially if one is the most powerful man in the entire country. Oh, yes, they did me a huge favor placing me here. I could not have planned it better myself."

Spokes did not know if he was meant to respond to this. The trophy of a roaring lion on the floor beside him seemed to be expecting him to say something.

"Gustav told me that I should expect a visit from you," Silas Mthimkhulu said, bringing Spokes' attention back from the petrified roaring lion.

"I thought he would."

"So you finally solved Daisy's case."

Again, Spokes did not know if he was meant to respond.

"I suppose congratulations are in order," Silas Mthimkhulu said, raising his glass. "Must be a weight off your shoulders to at last know 'whodunit,' as they say."

"It is," Spokes sincerely replied.

"But ultimately very frustrating because there is nothing you can do to get your man."

"It is that as well."

"The thing that surprises me is that with all your intelligence, you don't see it, Chief Inspector."

"See what?"

"That you and I are essentially the same man."

Spokes felt a shiver run through him.

"When I started building that first store, I heard so many stories about you, I found it difficult to believe that you had only been among the villagers for one night. You were a legend. They should have hated you for what you had done, but they spoke of you with open admiration—the man who revealed that their chief had pushed his best friend into the dam," Silas Mthimkhulu said before he went to refill his glass.

Spokes waited to hear how all this was connected to them being the same man.

"How many have you pushed into the dam, Chief Inspector Spokes Moloi?" Silas Mthimkhulu asked as he sat down.

"How many what?" Spokes asked.

"How many of your own people have you pushed into the dam?"

"I have never pushed anyone into a dam."

"You are an intelligent man, Chief Inspector. You know I am speaking metaphorically. You've been with the BSAP for how many years…thirty-three?"

"Yes."

"And in all those years how many people—black Africans—have you put in prison? Some to be sentenced to death by hanging."

"Justice must be served."

"Justice!" Silas Mthimkhulu spat out. "Justice? The BSAP, like all colonial institutions, is inherently a racist organization, and you happily and obediently served in it for thirty-three years. In those years, white men who committed the same crimes as their black comrades were given lesser sentences or not convicted at all, and through all that, you continued to be happy and obedient in your service. And you want to speak to me of justice? Did you once think of your grandfather… your father… and what the white man you've blindly served for thirty-three years—no, make that forty years, since you served in the war as well—did to them? Forty years of servile servitude to the very people who put a noose not just around your grandfather's neck, but your father's as well."

Spokes realized that this was a speech Silas Mthimkhulu had been waiting to deliver for some time.

"And you come here in all your righteousness thinking you are a better man than me when at heart we are the same man," Silas Mthimkhulu scoffed. "I use body parts to fortify my businesses. I sell human organs to make me an even wealthier man. We are both men who eat our own. The only difference is that I know and accept this *truth* about myself, and don't hide behind lofty words such as justice. How was justice served by the hanging of both your grandfather and your father? The British took away your lineage, and you thanked them by pushing your own people into the dam."

Spokes got up to leave.

"This country was at war for almost twenty years, and not once did you stop pushing your people into the dam! They were dying in those killing fields in Zambia and Mozambique, deaths you don't even want to imagine. You have no idea how pathetic that war became—the senseless deaths, the empty sacrifices... I saw it all, and decided to do something about it. And you kept pushing and pushing them into the dam here at home. At least I did what I did for something tangible—money. You did what you did for something you have never seen or experienced—justice. If anyone has the right to be righteous here, I believe it is me, Chief Inspector."

Spokes made his way to the door.

"I think about my grandfather and father everyday. My grandfather worked many many years helping European men prospect for gold," Silas Mthimkhulu continued. "One day one of the men—Gustav's grandfather–struck it rich and thanked my grandfather with several nuggets of gold. My grandfather took the gold and continued helping European men prospect for gold. My father inherited the gold, but went to work at the Mabuse mine. I grew up seeing those nuggets every day without understanding what they were—without knowing that they were the way out of our abject poverty. There were days my mother made us—a family of twelve living in one shack on a mining compound—eat soil for the nutrients: that was how poor we were. It was my older brother who told me what a valuable thing we had in our possession once he himself had gone to work in the mine that the Mabuses had been forced to give to the British in 1919. The first opportunity I got, I took those nuggets and, through Gustav, sold them and used that money to build my first Idlazonke store. My father and brother continued working for the white man, while I shed my name and everything I had previously been, and became Silas Mthimkhulu. Mthimkhulu—a mighty tree. Once they saw what I had been able to do, they tried to claim what was mine as theirs—but it was not theirs, it was mine, solely mine, because I was the one who had had the vision. I was the one who had seen what was possible. Some men see what other men never will. It is just the way of the world. I have absolutely no regrets in this life."

Spokes opened the door, thinking all the while of mighty trees and small axes.

"Before you leave, Chief Inspector," Silas Mthimkhulu said. "Can you tell me how far you've gotten with the Coetzee case?"

"The Emil Coetzee case?"

"Yes. What strides have you made toward catching Golide Gumede?"

"Golide Gumede had nothing to do with whatever happened to Emil Coetzee."

"The SIU have told me as much, so I know that. You know that. But the people out there still want Golide Gumede to pay for what he did during the war. He will make the perfect peace offering, Coetzee be damned. They expect me, as the new Emil Coetzee, to do something about it, and I intend to."

"The new *and improved* Emil Coetzee," Spokes corrected.

"Yes, exactly. The Man Himself," Silas Mthimkhulu said. "And if any man can find Golide Gumede, I do believe it is you, Chief Inspector."

"You want me to push another one into the dam?"

"What is one more?"

"I'm afraid I am not the man for the job. I am retiring."

"What? Is Golide Gumede's skin too pale for you?"

"I have never seen Golide Gumede," Spokes said, his hand on the door handle. "Is his skin pale?"

Silas Mthimkhulu looked at him for a very long time;

something flashed in his eyes, and then he mirthlessly chuckled. "Very well then, Chief Inspector," he said before holding up his glass. "Here's to your retirement."

"To my retirement," Spokes said with a nod. "You know Emil Coetzee started The Organization because of Daisy... because of what happened to her." Spokes gestured grandly at the room. "So in many ways, you owe all of this to her." He put on his fedora and walked out of the office—the seat of power.

KUKI

The day Kuki was born, 18 April 1937, seemed such an unremarkable day to be born. Little did anyone know then that forty-three years later she would share her birthday with the new country that had risen out of the ashes of the old country where she had been born, and that it would be on her birthday that they would all have to usher in this thing called independence.

Since she had become a wife and a mother, Kuki had successfully managed to not have a fuss made on her birthday. "A generous slice of chocolate cake and the two men in my life is all I'll ever need,' she would say every year. She threw amazing parties for her beautiful, golden-haired boy. She did wonders for her parents, Emil's parents, and her friends. The City of Kings was still talking about Beatrice Beit-Beauford's fortieth, which had taken place three years earlier. Kuki was not averse to other people's parties; she just did not like it when she was at the center of things. But now B was determined to throw her a party. A party just for her. A birthday party at that. Such a dreaded thing.

In the past, it had helped that she shared her birthday with Emil. Whenever B started advocating for a party for Kuki, Kuki would rope Emil in, and that would deter B. But Emil was not around now to put a convenient end to B's plans.

According to Rutherford, Emil had chosen death by misadventure over independence, and the state had in turn chosen to make it seem like a terrorist—Golide Gumede—had killed

Emil. Kuki had not been given a choice; she had been told that, for the good of the country, she needed to accept things as they were, and attend a sham of a funeral—which she had done, much to B's anger and chagrin. Kuki's acquiescence had created a rift in their friendship that had been bridged by a very unlikely source—Saskia Hargrave.

When Saskia Hargrave had started entertaining the City of Kings with her "Where's Emil Coetzee" column, B, happy that the state had not gotten its way, had begun to thaw, and forgave Kuki her moment of weakness. For her part, although she thought Saskia Hargrave a harpy, Kuki appreciated the fact that she was the only one who had given her a choice in all of this—she could choose to take offense or choose to take comfort in the stories that appeared in *The Chronicle*. Kuki had not yet made up her mind as to which to choose, but she liked having a choice before her.

To make amends for her earlier intolerance, B had insisted not only on throwing Kuki a birthday party, but on calling it an Independence Day party as well. There was an abundance of Independence Day parties being thrown all over the City of Kings, mostly by the Africans. Those parties were celebrating majority rule; but Kuki's party, B emphasised, would celebrate an adult life lived beyond the shadow of Emil Coetzee—the shadow that had made Kuki understand herself as no more than a wife and a mother. And it was, of course, Kuki's shying away from the limelight for many years that B used as evidence of Emil's long shadow. But that was because B did not know that Kuki's aversion for the limelight predated her marriage to Emil by many years... because B did not know about the parties of Kuki's childhood.

Kuki had spent every one of those parties ensconced in layers of itchy lace that she pretended not to feel because she had been socialized into a ladylikeness that would not allow her to scratch herself in public. The parties, although held in her honor, had been largely adult affairs. Her parents invited their acquaintances, and if their acquaintances happened to have children, then Kuki had companions on the day; and if not, she spent her birthday alone at the children's table, while her parents entertained.

At some point, Kuki would be called to parade before the adults, who would perfunctorily say nice things about her appearance before her mother nodded at her, which was Kuki's cue to leave the room and join the other children, if there were any. Together they would politely go through the stages of her birthday—meal, presents, cake—without saying much to her or each other. They all seemed to exist as props that gave texture to an adult world, but not much else.

The only child of parents who had had her rather late in life, Kuki's world, although rarely filled with other children, was filled with so many dolls, toys, and books that they had to have their own room. Because of their busy social lives, her parents became adept at giving Kuki everything her heart desired save what it desired most—companionship—and so Kuki could not escape loneliness as a child.

Kuki understood that the things that made up the bulk of her life—the dolls, the spinning tops, the fairy tales—were supposed to make her happy, and so she pretended at happiness, even as she constantly surprised herself by wanting something else. When her parents were not busy entertaining or being entertained, and focused their attention on her, Kuki caught a glimpse of what that something was. It was not being at the center of things; but rather, the time spent happy together that she yearned for most.

She must have made a wish, because in her ninth year, what she had always wanted most became a reality in the form of the baby boy her parents brought home from the hospital. Everleigh Sedgwick. A little brother… just for her. As Kuki held him in her arms, she knew that this was what she had been waiting for all her life—the joy of togetherness. She spent her days peeping into his cot playing peek-a-boo, singing lullabies, rattling his favorite rattle, reading fairy tales, and giggling at his gummy toothless smile. Kuki was lonely and alone no longer—she at last had the desired companion.

But then one day, some months after his arrival, Kuki went to Everleigh's cot and found him blue in the face. She tried to use his favorite rattle—white with a blue tortoise on it—to wake him, but he did not wake up. Her parents came and carried him out of the house, and returned a few hours later without him. They soon after removed all traces of him from the house, loaded them into the car, and drove them away. All save for the white rattle with a blue tortoise on it, which Kuki had put in her pocket and temporarily forgotten about. Her parents returned a few hours later without the traces of her baby brother, and never spoke of him again.

Kuki thought of him always—Everleigh—the one who would have been her constant companion; the one who would have never let her feel alone. After Everleigh's daily non-return from wherever her parents had taken him, Kuki determined to be a pleasant, agreeable and cheerful child, so that his absence would not be too keenly felt. In short, she carried on being the kind of child that she had always been, except that now in the place of loneliness was a waiting… a waiting for a constant companion. She probably would have begun to think that she had imagined Everleigh were it not for the fact that she had in her possession the white rattle with a blue tortoise on it—his most favorite thing. And so she held on to Everleigh as one would a secret joy.

Birthday parties became even more difficult affairs after Everleigh came and went, as everyone seemed intent on pretending that Kuki was the only child the Sedgwicks had ever had. And as Kuki entered adolescence, the difficulties of her birthday parties took another turn. She had been a pretty enough child, but whatever beauty she had possessed had escaped by her twelfth year, leaving behind an awkward, gangly girl with pimples. Even with these devastating changes, the birthday parade of Kuki in itchy lace still took place, with the guests finding fewer and fewer pleasant things to say in their generous hearts.

Happily for Kuki, her adolescence also brought with it Beatrice Beit-Beauford. On their first day at Eveline High School, Matron Pulvey had singled both girls out for having dirt under their fingernails, and while the other girls had gone to breakfast, she had ordered Kuki and Beatrice Beit-Beauford to remain behind for ten minutes so that they could feel mortified at their lack of cleanliness. The truth was, there was not much dirt under the girls' fingernails, but Matron Pulvey made it a point at the beginning of every year to single out the two girls who came from the most prominent families. This was her diplomatic way of bringing those girls down a peg or two, and creating some equality with the rest of the students. Kuki could not have possibly known any of this as she scrutinized her nails. Never having defied authority, she had done exactly as she was instructed, shivering with embarrassment under her straw hat, her face shamed into the color of beetroot.

However, Beatrice Beit-Beauford seemed to have other ways of being. She looked at her fingernails and left whatever dirt she found intact before she took Kuki's hands in hers and examined her fingernails. "I don't know, I think it gives us character. Dirt under the fingernails means we have been up to something… something unexpected… something perhaps even a little shameful—our hands have not been idle. I like that about us. What does Stinkerbockers know, anyway?"

Kuki laughed at the nickname Stinkerbockers. It was a genuine laugh, perhaps the first that she had shared with one of her peers. The laughter was definitely her first transgression, and she reveled in it. Beatrice Beit-Beauford smiled at her, her eyes sparkling with delicious mischief, and with that smile transformed into B: B, Kuki's first and lasting friend. B, her constant companion.

There had been other cherished companions after that, namely Emil Coetzee, who was anything but constant, but who did an exceptionally good job of looking devastatingly handsome in a tuxedo that she had chosen for him, and saying all the right things whenever they went out to parties and events. He could charm when he wanted to, that one, and he did it all in a halting, self-deprecating manner that made you love him all the more.

And then of course there had been her most cherished and precious of all companions...her beautiful, golden-haired boy: her very own Everleigh. Emil had wanted to name him Frederick, but she had insisted on Everleigh. When he was a baby, she had even given him his namesake's white rattle with a blue tortoise on it as something of a talisman, and he had survived childhood... had grown up happy and healthy. And then the war had come. But that was still too painful to think about.

Feeling very fortunate to have two very handsome men in her life, Kuki had been a faithful wife and a devoted mother. She loved her husband and her son with ease. She understood that her marriage was far from perfect, but what marriage ever was? She had known of Emil and his... exploits long before she married him. Yes, perhaps she had once hoped that in having married her, his roving eye would cease to wander, but when it had carried on unbridled, she could not really blame him for something she had always known was in his nature, now could she?

Early in their marriage, she had reasoned that while he was brave and strong, he also had a weakness, and that his affairs were not a means to be cruel, but rather a force of habit. She hardly gave a thought to his philandering, preferring instead to think about what it was like to be held in his arms at night… the tenderness of it… the gentle cradle… the unexpected softness of touch. Especially on those birthday nights after they had shared a slice of chocolate cake, and Emil held her carefully… delicately… like she was a fragile, precious and rare thing.

Now Kuki was sitting in front of a mirror, putting on her face for the party. The party just for her. As she applied her lipstick, she caught herself humming a tune: 'Wake Up Little Susie.' There was the sound of a car approaching; B was driving up the driveway. Kuki froze as she recalled hearing Everleigh, her beautiful, golden-haired boy, say to his father, before going off to war: "You know what she does? What she has always done since I can remember? She waits to hear your car in the driveway, and then starts to sing. And do you know why she does this? She does this so that you, who have never tried to make her happy, will think that she is happy." Kuki heard B slam the car door shut and make her way to the front door. So she was still pretending at happiness. When had she become so like Pavlov's dog?

Kuki sat in front of the mirror and watched as her beautiful, golden-haired boy's words changed her narrative of a happy-ish and not altogether loveless marriage. Over the years, there had been B's observations about her marriage, but those had been easy to counter because B's thinking was always so very different from the norm. Kuki could not, however, shrug off the realities presented by the words of her beautiful, golden-haired boy. Could it be that for all those years, she had imagined herself comfortable and happy enough in something that should have left her feeling otherwise? Had she become so practiced at pretending at happiness that she had fooled even herself? When others shone a light on aspects of her marriage that had, until then been in the dark, Kuki could not help but wonder if she had created the darkness herself so as not to see that the environment she believed she thrived in was not particularly good for her.

Perhaps she, who had been infatuated with Emil long before she met him, had forgiven him too much. He had not been overtly or intentionally cruel, but that did not mean that he had not been cruel nonetheless. He had said words that had cut deep, and she had been the one to heal their wounds. There had been the hand raised against her because Emil was afraid of what the beautiful, golden-haired boy was. It had been a fight, something rare between them, and she had felt grateful both because he had not struck her, and because he had never forgiven himself for raising his hand; but perhaps she should have felt more over his having thought of striking her in the first place. Yes, he had held her tenderly in the night… but those had been the nights when he was at home. There had been periods when the nights away from home far outnumbered the nights at home: what had she told herself on those nights when there was no tenderness, no gentle cradle to be found?

In the end, she had left Emil not because she had stopped loving him, but because she had felt that they were partners in crime—the crime that had led to her precious, beautiful, golden-haired boy, her very own Everleigh, being taken from them the way he had. But had Everleigh not stepped on that landmine, would she still be pretending at happiness as Mrs. Coetzee?

This was too pathetic a picture, and Kuki began to feel that she was using it to protect herself from something even more frightening... something she had long not wanted to come to the light.

And then she remembered the anger that had visited itself upon her in 1975 at the Stockley's party, when she had opened the door to their sun room and found the two of them—Emil and his best friend's widow, Marion Hartley—together, alone... not coupling. In retrospect, she would have preferred it if they had been, because there would have been the shock of it, and then the acceptance of that shock. But they had not been coupling. Emil was sitting on the window ledge and Marion was standing close to him, within arm's reach. They were not touching... not yet. Marion, her hands palm-flat on the glass, was facing the garden, when she turned toward Emil, who was looking up at her. They did not speak. They did not need to. They simply looked at each other and looked at each other and looked at each other, until Emil reached out his hand, his eyes never leaving Marion's, and touched the hem of her peach-colored dress. Emil's hand on her dress must have had some seismic force, some pull... because Marion's body started to move toward his. Still, they did not speak, merely looked at each other. Kuki anticipated what would come next, but it did not happen. They did not kiss. Instead, Marion ran her fingers through Emil's hair, and Emil gathered her in his arms... that tenderness... that gentle cradle... that unexpected softness of touch: for someone else.

For all the twenty years of her married life up to that day, Kuki had thought that her husband, Emil Coetzee, regardless of whatever he did with other women, did not love them. She had believed that what had happened to him at the Selous School for Boys had left him too broken to love anything. She had taken a sad kind of refuge in that belief. But as she had watched him hold Marion Hartley, she had discovered and known another truth.

As Kuki walked away from the Stockley's sun room, many responses had presented themselves to her, and out of all of them, she had chosen anger because she liked its multitude of dangerous, pointy edges, and she liked how, if need be, she could use it both as a weapon and as a shield.

Now, sitting in front of the mirror on her forty-third birthday, Kuki realized that instead of pointing that anger toward Emil, she had used it solely as a weapon against herself, and that she had, for the longest time, held on to the mirage of happiness because what she really was, what she had long become, was a festering and always weeping wound.

B stuck her head through the doorway. "I come successful in my quest,' she exclaimed. She held up a Gordon's plastic bag. "The cocoa powder has been purchased. It is Independence Day and all businesses are closed, but I suppose I am not Beatrice Beit-Beauford for nothing. I'm off to make your chocolate cake myself," she declared, and left the room.

Kuki looked at her reflection in the mirror. Her face was made up. Her body was dressed up. Ready for the party. The party just for her. Her Independence Day party. She looked good—very good—for forty-three. *How had that happened?* she wondered as she contemplated going to help B with the baking of the chocolate cake. She started to stand, and then stopped. Today was her birthday: her day. She did not have to do anything else but be happy in it. She practiced a smile in front of the mirror, and tears immediately welled up in her eyes. Kuki clapped her hands: "That's it! No more pretending at happiness, Kicks," she said. "Any happiness you feel from today onwards will be the genuine article."

———•———

The party that was just for her was, of course, filled with

people Kuki did not quite know. They were members of B's set, intentionally so. "All the people you know are mothers and housewives," B had said, explaining her reasoning. "You need to know and experience other ways of being a woman." *What other ways of being a woman were there?* Kuki had wondered.

Instead of experiencing these other ways of being a woman, all Kuki had done so far was sit on a settee alone in a corner, and, slightly amused by the manufactured antics of the multiracial gathering around her, diligently make her way through a packet of Everests. Although the times were changing and things were shifting around and between them, the guests seemed intent on being happy and on looking forward to the future. To Kuki, it all seemed a little too much like a performance to be real, but what did she know?

"Would you mind terribly?" a voice asked, before its owner sat himself down beside Kuki without waiting for her response.

"No, not at all," Kuki said, shifting so as to make the man even more comfortable.

Earlier, she had noticed him as soon as he entered the room. He was, like her, a gangly type, somewhat out of place. Now he kept running his fingers through his chestnut hair, and she kept trying not to look at his immaculately manicured moustache because she knew that looking at it would make her look at his mouth, and she did not want to look at his mouth. She looked into his eyes, which were a heart-warming hazel color that made her blush and look away.

"Are you comfortable?" Kuki asked, shifting again, this time trying to create as much distance as she could between them. She was too aware of his presence—his closeness.

"No. I have not come for table. I have come for tea." He held up his tea cup and smiled a naughty boy's grin.

Kuki surprised herself by laughing heartily. The laughter kept on coming until there were tears rolling down her face. It was an old joke, and not a particularly good one, but to her, in that moment, it was the funniest thing that she had ever heard.

He looked at her with laughter welling in his eyes.

"If I had known that that was all it would take, I would have sat down next to you a lot sooner," he said. "But I have been standing in that corner for over an hour, agonizing over what I would say to you."

His sincerity immediately sobered Kuki.

He offered her his hand: "Todd Carmichael."

"Kuki Coetzee," she said, shaking his hand and marvelling at how warm it was. "It is a pleasure to make your acquaintance."

"The pleasure is all mine, I'm sure," he said.

They were still holding hands when Kuki found herself telling him about the beautiful, golden-haired boy that she had lost two years earlier, and the ex-husband that she had lost even though he had never really been hers. Todd also shared with her the wife, the son, the daughter, the maid, the gardener and the dog which he had lost during an ambush when he was in Geneva trying to negotiate a ceasefire.

Kuki looked at her hand in his, and because they had already shared so much, found the courage to say, "I prefer a birthday that is a much quieter affair. A generous slice of chocolate cake is all I need. A generous slice of chocolate cake and... and... someone to hold me. Since my beautiful, golden-haired boy passed, what I have wanted more than anything is for someone to just hold me... to comfort me. I know this is an odd request, but I was wondering if you could hold me...just... hold me."

Todd Carmichael gave her hand a squeeze. "And here I have been looking for someone to cleave unto me," he said.

Hours later, as Kuki looked at the remnants of a slice of chocolate cake in a saucer on the night stand—her back pressed against Todd's chest, feeling his heart beat—she reveled in being held so securely, as if she was something he wanted to never let go. Her eyes left the remnants of the chocolate cake and rested on a white rattle with a blue tortoise on it before she drifted off.

Cleave: what an interesting word... a unique word... a word with two contradictory meanings. A word that held on and let go in the same breath.

Cleave: that was exactly what she, Kuki Coetzee, née Sedgwick, would do in this, her year of independence.

THE RED ASTER

Marion Hartley stood in her garage with a choice before her. She could get into the red Pulsar and drive off, not altogether certain that it would have a successful journey, or she could get into her red Aster—old-fashioned, but very dependable— and arrive at her true destination. She did not trust this new breed of cars mass-produced for convenience. Definitely not built to last. Not built like her Aster, in which she could drive off as one last hoorah. What she would give to be able to drive around in all that luxury, comfort and... substance again.

She looked at the Aster shining as though brand-new. She was oh so very tempted, but it had long been declared a collectors' item and insured as such: a bona fide antique car. A keen buyer had, for years now, been offering her a fortune for it, but she would never part with it, not for anything, not for the world. She had been standing beside the Aster when she had first seen him—a man in a cowboy hat and boots in the middle of the City of Kings—a man she had not known she was looking for until she found him.

Even then he had been broken and in need of repair. She had not known in that moment that she would one day love him more than she loved herself. Then, she had only known that he was an extremely attractive man who seemed so beautifully and tragically out of time and place—a visitor from a distant world. A world that he, a peregrine, had perhaps returned to after his long sojourn amongst them.

It was, perchance, foolhardy to go in search of such a man,

but that was exactly what Marion Hartley intended to do as she got into her red Aster and blissfully journeyed into the unknown that was her future.

———•———

After Chief Inspector Spokes Moloi had told Philemon what had happened to Sitshengisiwe, and what, unfortunately, could not happen to Silas Mthimkhulu, Philemon had been waiting for a sign. The sign would let him know that he had done the right thing. As soon as he saw the red Aster driving past the Rutherford's house, he knew it was the sign he had been waiting for.

There had been a red Aster that had frequently visited the Hartley Farm years ago, and on its journeys to and from the farm, it had passed the village in which Philemon lived. It was in this village that Philemon's grandmother had taught him about medicinal herbs and plants and roots—which ones could heal and which could kill. It was the liquid residue of one of these roots that Philemon had put in Silas Mthimkhulu's tea when he had come to visit…

To think that Silas Mthimkhulu had actually accepted the invitation to tea, entered the home of the woman he had so callously killed, and consumed, without suspicion, the tea that had been offered him. Philemon knew that Silas Mthimkhulu did all this because he was so amply fortified, he felt invincible. It had helped that Philemon had drunk the tea himself, which had allayed whatever fears and misgivings Silas Mthimkhulu might have had. Philemon was rather proud of the fact that he had successfully deceived him. There was no way that Silas Mthimkhulu could have known that the root's liquid residue was not in the tea, but in the tea cup. There was no way that Silas Mthimkhulu could have known that wherever he went now, something was slowly but surely eating away at him, hollowing him out, not resting until it would eventually leave him as nothing but an empty shell.

It would take the doctors many years to understand what was happening to Silas Mthimkhulu, and when they ultimately did, it would be too late, and it would not matter anyway because there would be no remedy for the excruciatingly unbearable pain that he would be experiencing. Philemon himself would probably be dead by then, but he would die happy in the knowledge that he had avenged Sitshengisiwe's death. All of that was in the future. Now, as Philemon trimmed Madam's bougainvillea hedge and watched the red Aster drive by, he was more than grateful for the sign that he had done the right thing.

————◆————

She had come to visit them so often that Gemma and Johan Coetzee had taken to calling her "Our Girl." She more than occasionally did their grocery shopping, collected their dry-cleaning, and drove them to their doctors' visits, which, at their time of life, were many. She did not strike them as a particularly giving person, and so they cherished her attention all the more. To make new friends so late in life was definitely something to rejoice in. They loved best that she listened to all the stories they had to tell about Our Boy and the good old days, and never seemed to tire of them. They had long ceased to read *The Chronicle* so they did not know of her "Where's Emil Coetzee?" series, but chances are it would not have made a difference because they recognized in her something that they recognized in themselves—a need of each other.

Besides, Our Girl had completely won them over when she gave them a poem about Our Boy that she had written:

Emil Coetzee: A Jumble of Small Things
Five azure-blue notes
A folded letter
A brown Stetson

A beige bakkie
An echoed ache
These things remain.

They did not understand the meaning of the poem, but fully appreciated its sentiment.

It was Our Boy's birthday, and Our Girl was coming to spend the day with them. The cake had already been baked and decorated. Gemma had just removed the shepherd's pie from the oven, and Johan was setting the table, when Gemma heard an old but familiar sound. She looked out of the window and sure enough, there it was: a red Aster at the intersection of Selborne Avenue and Borrow Street—the very spot where she and Johan had met. She called him to the window, and together they watched the car turn left on Borrow Street.

"I do believe there was such a car on the day we met," Johan said, as he gave her hand a tender squeeze.

"I believe so too," Gemma said, smiling at the story already waiting to be told to Our Girl.

————•————

Clement Rutherford was genuinely surprised to find that all his personal belongings fit into a medium-sized box that he could comfortably carry out of his office. So many years of service, and this was all that he had to take with him. He was aware, as he packed the box, that all eyes were on him—*all eyes*—but when he left the office, no one would look at him directly. The men he had commanded for years either swiveled away from him, or busied themselves with long-neglected paper work. It definitely was not the kind of send-off he felt he deserved. He wondered at their refusal to acknowledge what was happening, and decided that they were cowards all.

With a carton of HB pencils precariously balanced on top of the medium-sized box, Rutherford struggled to push the lift button. He was already safely in the lift when he saw Joseth enter the glass enclosure that he had just vacated, carrying a medium-sized box of his own. As the doors were closing, he had enough time to see Joseth remove a carton of HB pencils from his box and place it on his desk.

Rutherford's new office with the floor-to-ceiling windows that looked out over the City of Kings was the kind of office a man worked hard to one day occupy. It was the kind of office that exuded its importance with expensive furniture and carpeting, and the gradual suffusion of light throughout the day. Before Rutherford even had time to put the medium-sized box on the desk, a teaboy—his personal teaboy—entered his office and asked what he would like for tea. No more eating at the high table in the canteen for him. No more soggy, yet very delicious, egg-and-bacon sandwiches for ten o'clock tea for him. No more strictly two Highlanders or Shrewsbury biscuits for four o'clock tea for him. Now he could have tea whenever he asked for it. Now his lunches would be the creation of a professional chef, and eaten in the executive dining hall with the rest of the top brass.

Rutherford could see how he was supposed to be happy with his promotion, but he was not. He placed the medium-sized box between a stack of letterhead stationery and an ink-pad and rubber stamp set. From now on, that would be all that was required of him—his signature and stamp. Sure enough, when he opened the top drawer of his desk, there was an impressive array of fountain pens and an antique-looking wooden ink blotter. He looked at his luxurious surroundings and decided it was the kindest way to be put out to pasture. The trappings were awe-inspiring enough, but he was not fooled, just as none of the men downstairs were fooled; he knew that he was no longer a man with any real power.

Even from his office on the seventh floor, Rutherford could hear the commotion on the streets below, and he went to stand by one of his many windows in order to witness it. Independence Day. People dancing in the street as if they did not know what tomorrow held. He wanted to pity them for their optimism and short-sightedness, but found that he did not have the power to do so. They were so like ants from way up here, but were not ants at all…far from it. They had always seemed to him to be more like cockroaches, and they had definitely proved to be just as resilient. The sun had at long last set, and Prince Charles had already arrived in the country to confirm this fact and collect the Union Jack. And they were dancing in the street. It all came down to dancing with these people.

Needing something else to do, Rutherford looked at his watch. The direct flight to Heathrow would be taking off from Johannesburg any moment now, carrying with it Mrs. Tom Fortenoy and her children. Chief Inspector Spokes Moloi had been wrong about her. She had wanted more than to know what had happened to her husband, and she had wanted more than to find comfort in that knowledge. She had wanted the life that the Fortenoys would have had if they had never left England, and she had made sure that the price for her silence would make such a life possible. The best thing that Tom Fortenoy had probably ever done for his family was walk down Selborne Avenue during the early hours of New Year's Day. Rutherford took a sharpened HB pencil out of his breast pocket and twirled it between his fingers. Some people got what they wanted, and he got an office on the seventh floor. He bit into the pencil. At least he could take some pleasure in the fact that Chief Inspector Spokes Moloi had not been right about *everything*.

As Rutherford looked at the ongoing melee down below, something truly beautiful caught his eye—an antique car bleeding its way through the crowd on Eighth Avenue.

Watching it, he felt an emotion that was akin to hope. Things could still go wrong.

———◆———

The car was such an unexpected and exquisite red that Vida de Villiers could not help but stop his journey toward the Downing's Bakery alleyway to watch it travel up Eighth Avenue. He was so absorbed in its splendor that it took him some time to realize that something was wrong. A group of people had just turned the corner on Main Street. Unlike the other people dancing and singing in the street, this group was toyi-toying and chanting war songs. Guerrillas… the people he had gone to the war to fight. The former guerrillas seemed intent on growing in number, and kept on collecting and co-opting—sometimes by force—vendors, beggars and passers-by into their ranks.

All Vida wanted was to make his way to that alleyway next to Downing's Bakery where he had successfully hidden from the woman with the clickety-clacking shoes, and the scent of a woman's cheap perfume or a cheap woman's perfume. He had liked the smell of warm baking bread that was contained in the alleyway, and wanted to return to it.

Luckily for him, the former guerrillas toyi-toyied past him without accosting him in any way. Apparently, they saw in him something that he did not see in himself.

Vida resumed his journey, but was not able to venture far before a sound became too loud for him to ignore. A group of former guerrillas had surrounded a small white car, and were now rocking it back and forth as they beat on it. After the treatment he had received at the hands of both the BSAP and the SIU when he reported the dead man's body on Selborne Avenue on New Year's Day, Vida had vowed never again to involve himself in anything he saw happening in the lives of others. But then he saw the driver—an ancient white lady looking as though she had already seen her death. Vida tried to ignore her panicked and stricken expression, but he could not. She was after all someone's loving mother... someone's doting grandmother.

Vida was surprised at how easily he made his way through the former guerrillas surrounding the car. They actually parted to make way for him, and let him tap on the ancient white lady's window. 'Please roll down your window,' he said, at a loss as to what was appropriate to say and do in the situation. He repeated the request a few times before she slowly and very partially opened her window.

"You can go away, Jesus," she said. "I don't believe in you."

Jesus? What was she talking about? Obviously she had been more frightened and shocked than he thought. "I'm sorry, Madam. Are you all right?" Vida asked.

"Yes, yes, quite all right. Got a little fright, that's all, but I am fine now, thank you. You can go away, Jesus."

"She called him Jesus!" one of the former guerrillas said with a laugh. The other former guerrillas who were looking on laughed as well.

"We didn't mean to scare the old white lady, Jesus," one of the former guerrillas said. "We just wanted her to join in the festivities. We wanted her to know that Independence is for us all."

"Independence is for us all!" another former guerrilla shouted. His words became a chant that carried them all away. "Independence is for us all!"

"My name is Vida," Vida said. "I need to make sure you're all right to drive on."

"My name is Rosa... Rosa Adair," she said.

"I think maybe I had better drive you home," Vida said, smiling at Rosa Adair.

As Vida drove down Eighth Avenue, the former guerrillas started chanting, "Jesus! Jesus! Jesus!" The sound followed Vida and Rosa Adair for quite some distance.

———•———

Saskia Hargrave had been watching the Independence Day revellers for some time and followed them at a safe distance as they traveled up Eighth Avenue. When they began chanting, "Jesus! Jesus! Jesus!" she, for reasons she could not quite fathom, decided to join them. She let the throng, on its way to Grey Street, carry her down Eighth Avenue. When she got to Grey Street, she would dislodge herself from the crowd and resume her journey to Flat 2A at the Prince's Mansions.

The revellers seemed happy to have her in their midst. She understood why. She was the white woman who authenticated their right to happiness. She was the one who made it possible and necessary for most of them to chant, "Independence is for us all!" Saskia soon found that one could not be part of something so joyous without being affected by it, and so she joined in the chant as well. "Independence is for us all!"

By the time the throng arrived at City Hall, Saskia was feeling something very close to satisfaction itself. With the crowd of revellers cheering her on, she found herself climbing up a flagpole. Her initial thought had been to shock the onlookers by removing her T-shirt and waving it. However, when she got to the top of the flagpole, she surprised herself and the onlookers by removing the Union Jack instead. After a stunned silence that lasted long enough for Saskia to feel almost afraid of what she had done, the crowd erupted with applause and good cheer. Situated high above them, Saskia was for a brief moment their heroine. She relished the moment for all it was worth, and basked in its glory.

As she looked down at the City of Kings and its inhabitants, Saskia thought that perhaps this thing called independence would not be an altogether lamentable thing—that perhaps the Great Stuffer of Things was at that very moment emptying all of them out and leaving them as bags full of promise and potential, bags that could—from this moment on—choose what kind of miscellany they wanted to hold.

From her vantage point, Saskia saw a magnificent red vehicle circle the roundabout surrounding Cecil John Rhodes' s statue before continuing along Main Street, and she allowed herself to share in its unbounded feeling of freedom.

———•———

As Marion Hartley drove down Main Street, she remembered how, during their first encounter, Emil had taken her hand in his and instead of shaking it, had held it as he searched for words to say and failed to find them, thus making her aware of the sheer depth of feeling between them. One moment they were strangers, and the next they found themselves in something so honest, undeniable, and profound as to be overwhelming. And to think that when she had first felt it, Marion had not recognized it for what it was—that she had mistaken it for simple physical attraction.

The feeling had not been as fooled as she had been. It had followed her everywhere. It had made her write seemingly innocuous letters she never posted. It had occasionally woken her up in the middle of the night with a start. It had stayed with her so long that it became an old and familiar friend. It had been very patient with her, and did not let her go until she had called it by its truest name.

That old and familiar feeling was the reason why she had journeyed so far, and why she was now turning the red Aster onto a small untarred road that led to a farmstead. Once at her destination, Marion parked the car next to a verdant lawn bordered by all manner of colorful flowers. There was a woman sitting in the middle of it all on a wrought-iron bench.

She waited for Marion to turn off the car's engine before she put aside the plate of pastries resting on her lap and turned the Mills & Boon she had been reading face-down.

"You don't see those every day," the woman said, as she motioned toward the car.

"And more's the pity," Marion said as she alighted.

"Don't make them like they used to," the woman said.

"No, they don't," Marion said as she walked tentatively toward the woman. She stopped where the flowers began. "Mrs. Alcott?"

"Mrs. Louisa Alcott," the woman corrected.

"Mrs. Louisa Alcott," Marion said. "My name is Marion Hartley. I am here because I read about your Emil Coetzee sightings."

Mrs. Louisa Alcott's demeanor changed slightly. "You one of those who don't believe me?" she asked.

"No, no… I am not one of those," Marion said. "In fact, I was wondering if I could join you."

"Join me?"

"For a sighting. It's his birthday today," Marion said.

Mrs. Louisa Alcott looked at her for some time, and then made room for her on the bench. "Please feel free," she said.

Marion sat on the bench, and when Mrs. Louisa Alcott offered her a koeksister, she graciously accepted it.

"Radio says it's Independence Day today," Mrs. Louisa Alcott said.

"It is that and more," Marion said. "So much more."

SPOKES

———•———

Spokes had expected the gold watch and the car that they had wanted to give him when he became Chief Inspector, and which he had requested they give him upon retirement. He had expected the lovely Loveness to look radiant as she sat next to him on the dais set up on the lawn of the Western Commonage, one of her beautiful brown hands held in his. What he had not expected was to have Dikeledi and Lukha— *leaning* toward each other—sitting among the invited guests and looking up at him with such great pride, but they were a wonderful and unexpected thing.

He had been to enough of these send-offs to know that there were three speeches—one from the Deputy Commissioner, another from Chief Superintendent Griffiths, and the last from the retiree himself—after which the BSAP band struck up "Kum-A-Kye" on the bandstand, and then the gathering went to the canteen for tea and cake before dispersing. The entire thing rarely took more than two hours, and so that was what he had prepared for—but none of it was going according to plan.

It began with the speeches. First, the Commissioner gave a short speech about the history Spokes had made in becoming Chief Inspector. Second, the Deputy Commissioner gave a surprisingly lengthy and detailed speech that seemed to take great pains to elaborate on what the Commissioner had said. Third, Chief Superintendent Griffiths gave a predictably lengthy speech that started off by using fishing as a metaphor for police work before launching into what Spokes had accomplished in his thirty-three years of service: the deserved rise through the ranks, the criminals brought to justice, the unmatched number of cases solved, the dedicated maintenance of law and order. "In a country whose politics has been forever shifting, Spokes Moloi has been unwavering in his dogged pursuit of justice. He has ruffled some feathers. Got under thin skin. Some of us on this dais have butted heads with him as we tried to make him do the more expedient thing—but there was never any dissuading him from doing what is absolutely right. I, for one, will miss having the fedora-wearing and bicycle-riding Chief Inspector—" here Chief Superintendent Griffiths took a moment to clear the frog that had found its way into his throat before continuing, "—the fedora-wearing and bicycle-riding Chief Inspector whose middle name is... not... Magnanimous... amongst us here at the Western Commonage."

After the applause and laughter that followed the Chief Superintendent's speech died down, Spokes prepared to stand, but the lovely Loveness stayed him with her hand, and that was when he noticed that the Sub Inspector was rising to give a speech of his own. He was followed by the Sergeant Major, who was in turn followed by the Senior Sergeant, who was in turn followed by the other Senior Sergeant, who was in turn followed by a group of junior officers Spokes had worked with on various cases, and who took turns to thank him for all the things he had taught them over the years, and vowed to carry on his example. By this time, the still radiant and smiling lovely Loveness was crying. Her tears turned to tears of laughter when a group of young constables read out a litany of words beginning with the letter "M" in the hopes of landing on the Chief Inspector's middle name.

By the time Spokes stood at the podium, four hours had

passed. He told the crowd the story of a young man who had returned home from the war with only a singular inheritance to his name—a grandfather and father both hanged by the neck until they were dead and silenced forever. The young man could have worn this inheritance with shame and anger, but he did not want to. He felt that there was a lesson in these deaths that he needed to learn. It was only when he, quite by chance, solved his first case that he understood what that lesson was: the dead need not be silent forever; past wrongs need not go unpunished; the truth need not remain always hidden. Justice had to prevail. It was the purpose of the BSAP and the CID to ensure this, and he was very proud to have served in their ranks for all these years. He had been humbled by what he had learned from each and every one of them, and he urged them to continue their good fight against the forever silence.

Spokes did not think the speech warranted the standing ovation it received before the BSAP band, to his surprise, struck up "The Regiment Continues," and the officers and invited guests made a procession to the canteen where more than tea and cake awaited them. The ladies of the Women's Institute chapter to which the lovely Loveness belonged had prepared a veritable banquet, much to the officers' delight.

It was only when they left the canteen two hours later that Spokes found the courage to look at his leather wristwatch. The 33rd Annual City of Kings' Township Ballroom-Dancing Competition would commence in exactly forty-five minutes at City Hall. They had no time to lose. As the lovely Loveness, Dikeledi and Lukha made their way out of the building, Spokes stopped by the Desk Sergeant's desk to sign over the various keys still in his possession.

"Is it Magnificent?" the Desk Sergeant asked as Spokes signed his full name for the first time on the necessary forms.

"Not even close," Spokes said, shaking the sergeant's hand.

It was as Spokes was opening the station door that the Desk Sergeant exclaimed: "Mercy! It is Mercy!"

Spokes smiled as he put on his fedora and shut the door of the Western Commonage Police Station firmly behind him.

———◆———

Apparently a man can put on an entire tuxedo suit in less than ten minutes, Spokes learned as he left the changing rooms and went to join the other ballroom contestants eagerly or anxiously waiting for the competition to begin. A dazzling Loveness joined him a few minutes later, and Spokes was yet again truly amazed that such exquisite beauty was his to behold. As the contestants' numbers were being pinned, the Sigaukes came all the way from their place in the front to settle behind the Molois. Spokes was not even aware of their presence because the lovely Loveness was smiling up at him. The double doors to the hall opened as the Master of Ceremonies said, "Ladies and gentlemen, welcome to the Thirty-Third Annual City of Kings' Township Ballroom-Dancing Competition." Le Grand Kallé et l'African Jazz's "Independance Cha-Cha" began to play, and when Loveness placed her beautiful brown hand in his, all Spokes knew in that moment was this…

Man leads with right.

EPILOGUE

———— • ————

A place changes its character many times within its lifetime, and with each metamorphosis it asks those within it to
change along with it. This is a choice; although those who
hold power never treat it as such. A person can choose to let
go and follow the tide of change, and a person can choose to
hold on to herself or himself. Spokes' grandfather and father
had both chosen to hold on to themselves; and as a result,
had both been hanged by the neck until they were dead.

Now, the year was 1983 and at sixty, Spokes found the
character of his country changing yet again. The euphoria
and optimism of independence had settled, and in their place
something darker was beginning to take shape. As it had been
during the war years, something was feared, but this time it
did not go by the name "terrorist," "guerrilla" or "freedom-
fighter;" it went by the name "dissident," and it was deemed
to exist in certain parts of the country.

The most notorious dissident, according to The Man
Himself and The Organization, was one Golide Gumede.
Golide Gumede was still at large after his alleged murder of
Emil Coetzee, and his reign of terror was purportedly spreading throughout the country. There was a large reward—$10
,000—for anyone who helped The Organization apprehend
Golide Gumede. Where there was reward, there was often
punishment when The Organization was involved, and so
anyone caught harboring, aiding or abetting Golide Gumede
would be sentenced to death by hanging. Spokes had long

found that history repeated itself in highly unimaginative ways.

Spokes and the lovely Loveness had been happily retired in peaceful Krum's Place for three years now, but, although their lives were filled with the gentle pursuits of fishing, baking, reading books that they borrowed from the mobile library—their latest title being Dambudzo Marechera's *House of Hunger*—or working their way through Heinemann's African Writer's Series, a gift from Dikeledi and Lukha—they had hardly known a moment's peace.

First, there had been the return of Immanuel when Dikeledi was expecting Lukha's first child. Disentangling that union had proved so very knotty that Chief Cele Mkhize had sought Spokes' advice at every turn. The villagers seemed to be of one mind: since Dikeledi and Lukha had met in Spokes' home, he was partly responsible, and had to help put things to rights. Besides, what else did he have to do now that he was retired? they mused. Not finding a satisfactory answer, they requested his presence at almost every case that came before the head-man. Whatever *his* intentions were, *they* could and would not let him let his brilliant mind go to waste. Then Dikeledi and Lukha's baby, Daisy, failed to thrive, and the lovely Loveness decided that it would be best if they all came to live in Krum's Place so that she could keep an ever-watchful eye on the baby. Therefore, the Molois found themselves helping with the baby's feedings, nappy changes, and rockings to sleep. It must have been while the Molois were doing these things that Dikeledi and Lukha found the time to make another baby.

Upon discovering that Dikeledi was pregnant again, the villagers had demanded that Lukha not only pay damages a second time, but also do the right thing by Dikeledi and marry her. Lukha proposed to Dikeledi, was promptly accepted, and it was left up to the Molois to put together the wedding. The wedding had apparently been too extraordinary, because now every couple which got married in the village wanted at least part of the ceremony to take place at the Moloi's homestead in Krum's Place; and so a lot of their weekends were taken up by that. *Sometimes—but only sometimes—*Spokes thought that Krum's Place was perhaps a little too close to Chief Cele Mkhize's village.

At present, a small-fisted hand tugged at one of the cuffs of Spokes' trouser legs, and he looked down to see a toddler looking up at him with an expectant smile. He bent down to pick up Daisy, and reconciled himself to the fact that while he and the lovely Loveness had not known many moments of peace since coming to Krum's Place, they had experienced a newfound happiness. Spokes tickled her belly and, as he listened to her unrestrained giggles, life was quite simply a very beautiful thing.

The car was packed and ready to go. As Spokes handed Daisy over to the lovely Loveness, he could smell the scones, meat pies and samosas that she had prepared for the journey. He kissed her dimpled cheek, very happy that while many things changed, some things remained the same.

"Happy anniversary," he said as he got into the car.

"Happy anniversary," she said as she made Daisy wave goodbye to him.

Lukha and a very pregnant Dikeledi, in her postman's uniform, double-and triple-checked that everything with the car was in order before Spokes and Lukha drove off.

On their journey, Spokes and Lukha came across six roadblocks manned by soldiers armed to the teeth and policemen shrouded in riot gear and carrying batons. Although there had been many changes made post-independence in both the army and police force, there were officers at each of the roadblocks who knew Spokes and affectionately referred to him as Chief Inspector. When they perfunctorily asked where he and

Lukha were headed, he replied that they were off to do some fishing on the Beauford Farm and Estate, and Lukha added that his wife was very pregnant and wanted to eat nothing but fish, and not just any fish—fish she had had once that had been caught at the Beauford Farm and Estate—and so here they were. Most officers were very understanding about the particularly strange appetites of pregnant wives, and granted them easy passage. When a soldier who was suspicious of two men travelling all the way to the Beauford Farm and Estate just to fish asked them to open the boot, all he found were fishing rods, tackle, and a bucket of worms wriggling in damp soil.

Their passage through the roadblocks was a lot smoother than even Spokes had anticipated. It was a good thing that he knew, from his many years of dealing with criminals, that the best way to lie was to have the lie consist mostly of the truth—Dikeledi was indeed pregnant, and had an appetite only for fish... fish caught by Spokes in the river in Krum's Place. It certainly did not hurt that most of the officers he came across remembered him as a brave, integrous and intelligent superior—a man who never broke the law.

Even with the time it took them, after the last roadblock, to move the rods, tackle and buckets from the boot to the back seat, Spokes and Lukha arrived at the Beauford Farm and Estate an hour before they had planned. Spokes brought the car to a stop opposite a gorgeous field of green and gold as far as the eye could see—sunflowers.

It was only once the car was parked that Spokes allowed himself to release the anxiety that he had felt, but could not show, throughout the drive. He did something that he had not done since his days as a soldier in the African Rifles; he borrowed a Madison cigarette from Lukha, lit it, took a drag, rolled down his window, and blew smoke rings out of the window. When he made it back to Krum's Place, he would blow smoke rings at Daisy, and, knowing her, she would try to catch them before they disappeared. Spokes found himself smiling at this imagined future.

"Saskia Hargrave writes this week that Emil Coetzee has been sighted in Angola fighting as a mercenary in their war," Lukha said as he read *The Chronicle*. "Look, she even provides a photograph," he chuckled as he showed the picture to Spokes.

Spokes looked at the grainy image of a man who could have been anyone because of the photograph's poor quality. "I understand why she does it," Spokes said. "But people need to let that man go."

"So he is definitely dead?" Lukha asked as he folded up the paper.

"Emil Coetzee walked into the bush and did not walk out of it. That is the end of his story," Spokes said.

Lukha helped himself to a scone, and then a meat pie, and then a samosa.

"Do you feel as though we are being watched?" Spokes said, allowing himself to be a little more at ease. A place without curiosity was something to be highly suspicious of.

"Yes," Lukha said as he opened the car door and got out. He walked to the edge of the sunflower field and casually made as though to relieve himself as he surveyed their surroundings. "Two children in the field. No one else," he said as he washed his hands with water from a bottle before getting back into the car.

Lukha was reaching for another scone when they heard three gentle taps coming from behind the backseat. They waited as the boot of the car opened and Golide Gumede slowly and painfully climbed out. Spokes and Lukha also got out the car, their eyes forever vigilant. Once satisfied that there was no one around but the two children in the sunflower field, they allowed themselves to feel happy and hopeful.

It had taken three years of The Organization—who let it be known that they had eyes and ears everywhere—making it increasingly difficult to accomplish this feat; and they had succeeded. They—Spokes, the lovely Loveness, Dikeledi and Lukha—had all been repeatedly followed over the past three years; the home in Mpopoma had been ransacked soon after they left; the home in Krum's Place had been thoroughly searched by The Organization and soldiers in red berets twice, and there had been one very close call. It was only very recently that The Man Himself seemed to have decided that perhaps his suspicions were wrong.

Now, the three men cheerfully shook hands and grabbed each others' upper arms in heartfelt congratulation. It was a time for celebration. Their elation of necessity had to be short-lived because Spokes and Lukha had to make their way back to Krum's Place while the sun was still in the sky—before the mandatory curfew for the region took effect.

"Try not to miss Loveness' cooking too much," Spokes said as he started the car.

"All I can promise you is that I will not miss living in your ceiling," Golide Gumede said with an abundant smile. He saluted. Spokes and Lukha returned his salute—soldiers all.

Spokes drove some distance and then stopped the car so that Lukha could take the bucket out the car, remove the layer of worms in dirt, open the tightly sealed packet of fish caught in Krum's Place, pour water over them and then put the bucket, rods and tackle in the boot. As Lukha did this, Spokes got out of the car to stretch his legs before the long journey home.

He could not help but smile to himself with satisfaction.

A promise had been made, and that promise had been kept.

If The Man Himself and The Organization came to know of what he had done, and hanged him by the neck until he was dead, so be it. He had long known that bravery, integrity and intelligence were costly possessions. And, knowing this, he had long ago chosen to hold onto himself, as his father and grandfather had done before him.

With eyes for beauty to see, Spokes looked at the road he had just traveled, and witnessed something truly wondrous— a flash of color and light dashed out of the sunflower field and Golide Gumede caught it before throwing it in the air. Even from this distance, Spokes could hear a daughter's joyous laughter welcome her father home.

It was a beginning. Beautiful and golden.

ACKNOWLEDGEMENTS

The novel that you hold in your hands began many years ago as a story my grandmother, Kearabiloe Ndlovu (née Mokoena) told me. A brilliantly gifted storyteller, my grandmother epitomized the very best of the oral tradition—she was a dramatist, novelist, poet, actress, singer all rolled into one. Any story that was fortunate enough to find its way onto her tongue was brought to colorful life. One such story was of a policeman who instantly fell in love with a woman journeying to her ancestral village. He followed her and proved his worthiness for her hand by solving a long-unresolved mystery. My grandmother told me many stories during our long knowing of each other, but when she passed away in April 2014, it was the story about the enamored policeman that I found myself trying to write and thus Spokes Moloi was born.

The line between what was fact and what was fiction was extremely blurred in my grandmother's storytelling and she liked it that way. Therefore, when it came to writing the character of Spokes, I decided to give this fictional character the characteristics of someone I had known and loved well, my grandfather, Sibabi Charles Ndlovu—a man who was integrity personified. My grandfather, in his roles as reverend, husband, father, grandfather, was a great listener, counselor, confidant and peacemaker. He had a keen understanding of human psychology and a heart brave enough to truly love and be loved. I have many great memories of my grandfather because in my mind he was the greatest of men – a superhero without a cape always making the world better and safer. My grandfather's character made the character of Spokes Moloi possible.

My grandparents gifted me many, many things—I now count *The Quality of Mercy* in their number. The most important gift they gave me was a mother, Nokuthula Sarah Ndhlovu, whose unconditional love and support made possible the impossible dreams I dreamt. Mom, thank you stereki for everything.

Somewhere out there there are gods that love books and ensure that they find the perfect visionaries on their way to completion. Those gods have smiled upon me once again and placed my work in the excellent hands of Jenefer Shute, Catriona Ross and Fourie Botha at Penguin Random House South Africa and Jessica Powers, Ashawnta Jackson, and SarahBelle Selig at Catalyst Press. Thank you all for your invaluable insights and guidance. *The Quality of Mercy* also has the added fortune and privilege of having been edited by the brilliant Helen Moffett. Helen, thank you so much for championing the novel from the first and for making the editorial process a wonderful, collaborative and enriching experience. Karen Vermeulen, many thanks for putting together a wonderful cover that captures the essence of the story. I don't know how you do it, but I am very glad that you do. Frieda le Roux, as always, thank you for all that you do.

I wrote the first draft of this novel as a Morland Scholar in 2019. I thank Miles Morland and his foundation for giving African writers the opportunity and means to focus on a writing project. To the foundation's manager, Mathilda Leigh, thank you for never commenting on the quality of the 10,000 words I sent you every month. Giles Foden, thank you so much for not only making sense of the extremely rough first drafts of the story, but for also seeing its potential and providing great encouragement. I also thank you for putting me in touch with Bryony Rheam who also endured an early draft of the novel and gave her feedback. Thank you Bryony.

Many thanks to Bongani Ngqulunga and his generosity in offering me two residential stays at the Johannesburg Institute for Advanced Study—the first in 2020 as a writing fellow, the second in 2021 as a writer-in-residence. My time at JIAS allowed me to polish the manuscript. Layla Brown, NoViolet Bulawayo, Amber Day, Pier Paolo Frassinelli, Michele Kekana, Fazil Moradi, Nthabiseng Motsemme, Francis Musoni, Charl-Pierre Naudé, Mphuthumi Ntabeni, Lebohang Pheko, Nisha Rayaroth, Olivia Rutazibwa, Amaha Senu, Malebo Sephodi, Carien Smith, Zukiswa Wanner – thank you all for the conviviality. Malume, Seaka Sibanda, thank you for feeding us, counseling us and ensuring that all was well at JIAS. Emelia Kamena, Vanessa Kennedy, Maria Matla, Johanna Menyoko, Sivuyile Momoza and Reshmi Singh, thank you for all your hard work in ensuring the smooth running of the institute.

I owe a long-overdue debt of gratitude to the staff at the Bulawayo branch of the National Archives of Zimbabwe. Sindiso Bhebhe (Principal Archivist), Trevor Gumbo (Librarian), Emma Ndlovu (Administration Officer), Acquiline Bunure (Secretary), Zanele Sibanda (Receptionist) and Tafara Hove (Intern), thank you all for your tireless assistance over the years. No query has ever been too big or too small, too vague or too specific for you to help with, which is every researcher's dream.

And lastly, I will end it the way my grandmother began it—by telling a story. There once was a man who rode a bicycle up the dusty road on which I lived. He wore a hat and his trouser legs were pegged. He was one of many such men—returning home from a hard day's work—seemingly unremarkable. He smiled at me, took off his hat in greeting and then continued riding towards the sunset. I thank him for that lasting memory.

Kearabiloe Ndlovu (née Mokoena)
and Sibabi Charles Ndlovu

Siphiwe Gloria Ndlovu

Praise for Book One
THE THEORY OF FLIGHT

———————•———————

"*The Theory of Flight* is a prodigious, time-stopping concerto that decisively places Siphiwe Gloria Ndlovu on the global stage. A writer to watch."
  —NOVIOLET BULAWAYO,
    author of *We Need New Names*

"Ndlovu's deeply moving and complex novel is astonishing for the amount of hope it evokes despite the darkness that's so pervasive in Genie's world, where she creates her own reality in order to survive. This transcendent and powerful testament to the indomitable human spirit is not to be missed."
  —*PUBLISHERS WEEKLY*
    (starred review)

"A dazzling novel of delicate and astonishing magic. *The Theory of Flight* is a joyful tapestry of characters shaped but never deformed by the tensions of the times they traverse, narrated in prose of devastatingly beautiful simplicity."
  —TSITSI DANGAREMBGA,
    Windham-Campbell Prize author of
    Nervous Conditions and *This Mournable Body*

"There is an ethereal enchantment that the prose brings to the tumultuous history of this unnamed country."
  —THE MILLIONS

"An unnamed country in the southern part of Africa springs to

life in this delicate work of magical realism. [...] *The Theory of Flight* is unlike anything you've read before."
—BUSTLE

"This epic novel weaves magical realism and myth in the life story of Imogen "Genie" Zula Nyoni (who is HIV positive) and her South African family history, including wars, poverty, colonization, love and race."
—*POZ MAGAZINE*

"Here is a story of the most beautiful liberation struggle, a quest to inhabit the wilds of the imagination. Ndlovu peels back the shroud of despair that haunts Zimbabwe forty years after independence, to look with rare empathy at the inner lives of characters we would more likely pity or fear than love. Told with a potent blend of historical detail, magical realism and the matter-of-factness of those who live close to death, this reverse Icarus fable dares imagine that no matter how humble, any person of courage, conviction and radical tolerance can soar into true freedom."
—TSITSI JAJI,
author of *Mother Tongues*

"*The Theory of Flight* is a beautifully told narrative, memorable and innovative, and a skillfully structured novel. [...] The fact that this is a work of nearly ten years in the making manifests in its maturity of vision and execution, despite this being Ndlovu's first novel."
— *LITNET*

"When we want to base our shared reality with each other on facts, we also must allow, acknowledge, and cherish the existence of magic. *The Theory of Flight* is full of magic, a magic willing to be observed by eyes that can see the beauty in knowledge, facts and far beyond."
— *FULL STOP MAGAZINE*

"When I reached the final pages of Siphiwe Gloria Ndlovu's *The Theory of Flight*, I recognized that I had read something truly rare: an intelligent novel with a big heart."
— *THE RUPTURE*

"This is not a tale about morality or the vagaries of war, although these are real issues in the novel. It is, rather, a clever reimagination of childhood, family, community and power in a postcolonial Africa, with a generous dose of magic. Genie is a charming character, and witnessing her coming of age is an intimate experience. *The Theory of Flight* comprises a complex plot, and there are plenty of personalities who are not easily forgotten. Ndlovu manages to keep the reader reined in throughout this rolling tale, taking on heavy issues such as war, patriarchy, corruption and disease without weighing the spirit down. A triumphant story told in a magical way."
— KARABO KGOLENG,
Litnet

"[*The Theory of Flight*] strikes what feels like an impossible balance—splitting its attention between how history defines lives and how lives, nonetheless, exceed such historical definition... it exemplifies the most textured work emerging from the region."
—JEANNE-MARIE JACKSON, Public Books

"Incandescent and wryly largehearted, *The Theory of Flight* is a tale of epic scope. Ndlovu's unique and beautifully composed debut confirms her right away as that rare phenomenon: a born storyteller with a poet's ear. Beguiling, brilliant and brave."
— MASANDE NTSHANGA,
author of *Triangulum*

"An epic novel written with such wit and ingenuity. I was unable to put this book down, in awe of Ndlovu and her stunning virtuoso, the ways she brings these unforgettable characters into a magical world with such delightful prose. Beautiful and utterly

sublime. My novel of the year."
—NOVUYO TSHUMA,
author of *House of Stone*

"With the lightest of touches, a cast of unforgettable characters, and moments of surreal beauty, *The Theory of Flight* sketches decades of history in this unnamed Southern African nation. It does not dwell on what has been lost in its war, but on the daily triumphs of its people, the necessity of art, and the power of its visionaries to take flight."
—*TROPICS MAGAZINE*

"*The Theory of Flight* may be Siphiwe Gloria Ndlovu's first novel, but it's written with the kind of excellence and detail one would expect of an author with decades of experience. Enchanting... you feel as if you're part of the very fabric this interconnected story is woven on. The book is a delightful, heartrending, thrilling and heartbreaking read that will leave the reader sad that they couldn't be a part of Genie's short yet impactful life."
—PAM MAGWAZA,
Drum Magazine

"This is an extraordinary novel, painted in luminous gold, silver and blue with the finest of brushes. A mystery shrouds Genie's life and death which is revealed slowly and deftly with the author's characteristic delicacy of touch and fine taste in metaphor. A rare achievement, exquisite in its language and insight. I am enriched."
—JENNIFER DE KLERK,
Artlink

"Ndlovu is a gifted storyteller, skillfully interweaving the real and the magical, beauty and devastation, historical and personal perspectives, simplicity and complexity. She has a vivid imagination and the tale shimmers with magic... A marvelous and unusual flight of fancy. When Genie dies, and flies away

on huge silver wings, she will take a little piece of your heart with her."
    —KATE SIDLEY,
    Sunday Times

Praise for Book Two
THE HISTORY OF MAN

"60 Notable Books of 2022"
    —*OPEN COUNTRY MAGAZINE*

"The Best Books to Read in January"
    —BUZZFEED

"63 Anticipated African Books of 2022"
    —*BRITTLE PAPER*

"[*The History of Man*] braids the social and the personal. Her style is deceptively simple as she describes the great mysteries of how we come to be who we are. Through the figure of Emil, a white man on the wrong side of Zimbabwean liberation history, she paints a fine-grained portrait of lost forms of Rhodesian city life."
    —JEANNE-MARIE JACKSON,
    The New York Times

"With rhythmic prose and sly humor, *The History of Man* tells the story of one man's inevitable failure to live up to his potential."
    —*FOREWORD REVIEW*

"Siphiwe Ndlovu's unique voice, unclassifiable, takes us to a time and space which is all time, all space; where we find ourselves, never bullied or cajoled, but caressed, beguiled— so subtle is her point of view—from laughing out loudly to breathing in quietly; from condemning settlers as perpetrators, to considering that they too, may be victims of history. For Emil Coetzee is no stereotype."
— JOHN EPPEL

"In her prize-winning debut novel *The Theory of Flight,* Siphiwe Gloria Ndlovu surprised and delighted readers and critics with her ingenious excavation of the post-colonial moment in an unnamed Zimbabwe-esque Southern African country. In *The History of Man,* her second novel, she turns her attention back in time to the colonial era, in the same country. While quite different in tone, more linear and less obviously touched by folklore and magic, it shares its predecessor's intriguingly slippery relationship with history, and its author's skilful execution."
—*SUNDAY TIMES* (South Africa)

"*The History of Man* extracts the history and beating heart of an unnamed African country, seen through the eyes of one man, Emil Coetzee, a white male in his fifties, on the eve of his country's ceasefire. Emil reflects on his life, from boyhood to adulthood, and Ndlovu reveals it with empathy, generosity, and unflinching truth."
—*THE RUMPUS*

"Ndlovu takes on the challenge of exploring what has turned Emil Coetzee, a white civil servant in an unnamed African country (but clearly Zimbabwe), product of a beloved childhood in the savanna, into a middle-aged man with blood on his hands during its war for independence, and she does this with remarkable grace. If Doris Lessing and Jane Austen had a book baby together this might be it [...] Ndlovu has that same extraordinary talent as Austen for skewering society without dogmatism and

that's no small talent. I couldn't put it down."
— ANNE KORKEAKIVI,
   author of *An Unexpected Guest and Shining Sea*

"Siphiwe Gloria Ndlovu is both a chronicler and a conjurer whose soaring imagination creates a Zimbabwean past made of anguish and hope, of glory and despair: the story of the generations born at the crossroads of a country's history."
— 2022 Windham Campbell Prize committee

"Ndlovu impresses with a fresh and astute perspective on colonialism, race, and family that focuses on white South African-born civil servant Emil Coetzee, who appeared in the author's debut, *The Theory of Flight*. [...] Ndlovu deserves credit for her brilliant and meticulous characterization. This leaves readers with much to think about."
— *PUBLISHERS WEEKLY*

"From the author of *The Theory of Flight*, this book is a remarkably insightful and sensitive 'excursion into the interiority of the coloniser'—at once a psychological exploration and a searing political examination, but at its core intensely human and filled with empathy and pathos."
— *JET CLUB* (South Africa)

"Siphiwe Gloria Ndlovu's *The History of Man* allows the reader to feel and sympathize with an unlikeable protagonist, which, in itself, is a feat in storytelling. *The History of Man* is not just a history of man but a history of a country and colonialism as told by an unapologetic and sensitive writer who loves the place they write about."
— ZUKISWA WANNER,
   author of *London Cape Town Joburg*

"Ndlovu's perceptive portrayal of her central character at once highlights both the complexities and subtleties of the colonial endeavor. Her strength is enabling her readers to feel both anger and sympathy for him, for he is a real character and certainly no stereotype. Ndlovu looks beyond the limits of race, revealing the sadness, the vulnerability, the sheer joy of being human."

— BRYONY RHEAM,
　　author of *This September Sun*

"The ego and paradox of the well-meaning colonizer, and the ways they naively deny the fallacies and violence of colonization, are at the heart of Ndlovu's exuberant tale. In Emil Coetzee, Ndlovu paints a nuanced portrait of a man whose ambition and desires blind him to truths he refuses to reckon with. This sentient history is one a reader won't soon forget."

—ANJALI ENJETI,
　　author of *The Parted Earth*

"[A] superb piece of writing, and a troubling and thought-provoking book."

— *The Witness* (South Africa)

"A transfixing story of the corrosive stains of racism and colonialism."

—FINANCIAL MAIL

Printed in the USA
CPSIA information can be obtained
at www.ICGtesting.com
JSHW021658170923
48498JS00002B/2

9 781946 395863